The Way Home

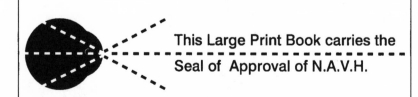

This Large Print Book carries the
Seal of Approval of N.A.V.H.

The Way Home

Megan Chance

Thorndike Press • Thorndike, Maine

Published in 1998 by arrangement with HarperCollins Publishers, Inc.

Thorndike Large Print ® Basic Series.

The tree indicium is a trademark of Thorndike Press.

The text of this Large Print edition is unabridged.
Other aspects of the book may vary from the original edition.

Set in 16 pt. Plantin by Juanita Macdonald.

Printed in the United States on permanent paper.

Library of Congress Cataloging in Publication Data

Chance, Megan.
    The way home / Megan Chance.
        p.   cm.
    ISBN 0-7862-1448-1 (lg. print : hc : alk. paper)
    1. Large type books.   I. Title.
    [PS3553.H2663W39   1998]
    813'.54—dc21   98-13540

For Maggie,
so you always know how very much I love you.

Now I face home again,
   very pleased and joyous;
(But where is what I started for, so long ago?
And why is it yet unfound?)

                — *Walt Whitman,*
     "Facing West from California's Shores"

1

1876, Richmond, Texas

She had been watching him for a long time. She knew that he took his meals at the Red Rock Saloon before he crossed the street to gamble at the Bluebonnet. She knew he took a dime bath every evening, and that he liked to walk down the street afterwards, smoking a cigar, with the warm spring air breaking sweat on his freshly washed face. She knew he liked fancy waistcoats, but the rest of his clothes were somber and unadorned.

She had met him once, a week ago. She'd been walking out of Olsen's General Store, her mouth full of crackers, and he and Peter Griggs nearly ran into her. He'd tipped his hat to her, and Peter had introduced him. His voice was rough and crackly, and when he said her name it sounded like striking matches. *"Eliza Beaudry. Pleased to meet you, Eliza Beaudry."*

She hadn't said much to him in return — her mouth was full — but she'd smiled and he smiled back, and then he and Peter walked on. She thought he'd seemed taken

7

with her. Well, he'd winked at her, anyway, and she was desperate enough to hope that meant something.

Eliza sighed and leaned her head back against the rough, weathered wall of the shack that was home. The dirt was cool and damp where she sat, the hum of insects and her father's low and tuneless whistle seemed to ring in her ears, a constant music. She imagined she heard words in it: *Get out, get out, get out of this damned town.*

Yes, she was desperate all right. It seemed she'd spent the last ten years of her life waiting for a man like Cole Wallace to saunter through Richmond — at least since she was thirteen, when her parents had given up their failing farm to sharecrop these straggling acres of cotton. She could no longer count the nights she had lain on her thin, narrow mattress, listening to her parents' quiet fumblings across the room, wishing for someone to take her away.

Cole Wallace. Eliza closed her eyes and pictured his face. He was handsome, with his dark hair and hazel eyes, but what she liked most about him was the way he always seemed to be laughing at some hidden joke. She never saw him that he didn't make her smile. People liked him, too, even though he was a professional gambler who didn't plan to stay. She'd heard the talk that his father was rich, and maybe that was where Cole Wallace had learned his manners, because he was the most polite man she'd ever met — at least he was polite to her, which was more than she could say about most of the men in this town.

All in all, he was the closest thing to rescue Eliza had ever seen.

Her mother's rocking chair creaked; Eliza heard the whoosh of Mama's breath as she rose, the soft thump of her footsteps. The door was open to let in the moist and cooling air of evening, and so Eliza counted the footsteps and knew the moment her mother was standing at the door, looking out into the growing darkness.

"Lizzie, honey, come on inside." Mama's voice was low and quiet as a lullaby. "The skeeters'll eat you alive out there."

Eliza slapped lazily at one that hovered around her face. "They ain't bad yet."

Daddy broke his whistling long enough to say, "Come inside, Lizzie. You been gone all night. Your mama and I want to have a word with you."

She didn't want to go inside. She didn't want to answer their questions. The night air was soft, and the dark, reedy scent of the Brazos caught on every breath, and she wanted to sit out here until the night came on full, looking at the moon and dreaming of Cole Wallace. She wanted to imagine him coming for her across the cotton fields, smiling down at her with an arched brow and saying, *"Eliza Beaudry, come away with me and be my wife —"*

"Lizzie, come on in."

Eliza sighed. "All right, Daddy." She got to her feet, brushing off her dress, and went to the door. Her mother stood back to let her in, and then she shut the door, closing out the night. Eliza was swallowed up by dim lamplight. The cabin was hazy with smoke from the smudge her mother had lit to keep away the mosquitoes. It burned her eyes.

Her father bent over the table, whittling. He barely looked up when she came in. "You wore your best dress into town tonight," he said.

Eliza flushed at the scold in his words. "Yeah," she said neutrally.

"Why is that?"

She shrugged and looked at Mama, who carefully looked away. "I just felt like it is all," she said.

Daddy glanced up. "You whorin', Eliza Mae?"

Eliza flinched. "I ain't."

"Then where'd this come from?" Daddy

reached under the table and pulled out her pretty blue hat with the stuffed bird on it. He slammed it on the table so hard the bird bobbed like it was alive.

"Will Ames gave that to me last week."

"Now why would that no-good Ames be givin' you presents?"

"I-I went to supper with him."

"And?"

Eliza turned to her mother. "Mama —"

"You talk to your daddy about this, Eliza," Mama said, and then she eased back into the corner, hiding so far into the shadows that all Eliza could see was the shine of her mother's dark Indian eyes.

"What else, Eliza?" her father asked. "What else did you give Will Ames?"

Eliza swallowed. Daddy was still hunched over his whittling stick, but he stared at her like he could see into her soul.

"What else, girl?"

"Nothing." Eliza's chest felt tight. She forced out the words. "It was just supper."

"Supper." Her father spat the word; his disgust filled the space between them. He reached under the table again, then slapped down a string of pretty gold beads. "What about these?"

She'd hidden those beads in a slit in her mattress. She'd never worn them, not even once, but she'd saved them and hoped that one day she'd have something to wear them with, a place to wear them to.

"I bought those myself," she said quietly.

"With what?"

"They were only a few pennies."

"Christ, girl! Where the hell did you get a few pennies? Or did Will Ames give you those too?"

"No. I —" Eliza took a deep breath. "Peter Griggs gave them to me."

"Peter." Daddy's lips tightened. He put aside his whittling stick and his knife, and got to his feet. Before she could stop him, he leaned over and jerked up her skirt, revealing her red silk petticoat. His gaze met hers. "Where'd this come from?"

Her stomach clenched so hard she thought she would be sick. "Daddy —"

He grabbed her chin between his fingers, forcing her to look at him. "I'm goin' to ask you again, Eliza Mae, and I want you to tell me the truth this time. Are you whorin'?"

He squeezed her chin so hard it brought tears to her eyes. Eliza tried to shake her head, but he was holding her too tightly. "No," she whispered. "I just . . . I just kissed them, that's all. Just a kiss."

Her father dropped her chin so quickly she staggered back. He looked at her mother.

"You hear that, Margaret? Just a kiss." He turned again to Eliza. "Kisses bought with presents, you know what that leads to, girl? You keep on this way and soon you'll be liftin' your skirts for those boys, too —"

"Jack, please." Mama stepped out of the shadows, shaking her head. "There's no call for that —"

"No call for it?" Daddy grabbed the beads and threw them against the wall. The thin string broke, the beads scattered across the dirt floor. "You see what those are worth, girl? They're worth nothin'. They're just Comanche candy. But I guess that's why you like 'em, eh? I guess it's that Indian blood in you. You're just like 'em, trading whatever you can for some . . . trinket."

Her mother flinched. The sickness rose in Eliza's throat so she could barely speak. "It ain't like that."

"No?" Her father sat heavily on the bench. He picked up her hat in his hands and flicked the bird with his finger. "Suppose you tell me what it's like, then."

"It was just kisses —"

He motioned wearily to her dress. "You think that's all it is, eh? Just kisses? Look at you, girl. That ain't no respectable dress. Your bosoms are almost fallin' out. You think they don't see that? You think they

13

don't kiss you because they think they'll get to touch those?"

Eliza's skin burned. She was hot, and the smoke from the smudge made it hard to breathe. She knew the men looked at her breasts, and she knew they wanted to touch her. Sometimes she even bent over and watched their eyes follow. And she pressed close and laughed and flirted because she knew they would buy her presents if she did. But her father made it sound so dirty. . . .

"I ain't a whore, Daddy," she said evenly. "But I won't stay stuck here in this town. I won't spend my life working in the cotton fields."

"And you think *this*" — he held up the hat — "will get you out of Richmond?"

"I think it's just a hat," she said. She looked at her mother, standing against the stove, her dark head bowed. "But someday someone's going to want to give me more than that. Someday, I'm going to find a man who'll take me where I want to go."

Daddy sighed heavily. "You got to understand who you are, Lizzie. You got to understand your place. Some things just ain't meant to be. There ain't a man alive who won't tell you lies just to get you in his bed —"

"Jack!"

"Well, it's true, and it's time she knows it." Her father looked back at Eliza. "I know you, Lizzie. I know you got big dreams. But if you think some big city boy is goin' to come and sweep you off your feet — well, I'm afraid you're goin' to be disappointed. The best you can hope for is to marry your own kind, but even that won't happen if you keep on sellin' Will Ames kisses."

But Eliza didn't think of Will Ames, or Peter Griggs, or any of the others she'd traded kisses with. She looked at her father sitting there on the bench, looking tired and old, and then she looked at her half-Comanche mother, who'd never had any choices at all. And she thought, *Cole Wallace,* until it became a rhythm in her mind, until all she heard was *Cole Wallace, Cole Wallace, Cole Wallace,* and the desperation was so tight in her head she felt it pulsing at her temples, straining behind her eyes.

She looked at her father and said, "You'll see, Daddy. You'll see."

He sighed again, and picked up his wood. He began to work it in quiet, even strokes. She heard the scrape of the knife against the wood, and the soft creak of her mother's footsteps, the hushed give of the moss-filled mattress as Mama sat down, and all Eliza could see was the darkness in the little shanty, the roughness of its windowless walls. She stared blindly at the hat on the table, at the little bird, and the smoke from the smudge wavered around it, until it seemed the bird was bobbing before her eyes, trying to fly away.

She saw her father glance up at her mother through the dimness, and then he licked his lips and looked back at Eliza as if measuring what he was going to say.

"There's another reason I wanted to talk to you tonight," Daddy said slowly. It seemed like a long time before he continued. "You know, Lizzie, you're twenty years old now. You ain't a young girl no more. Why, you're nearly an old maid."

"That never bothered you before," Eliza murmured.

"Eh? Well, no. No. But that was before I knew you were sellin' kisses." Daddy pursed his lips. "Jem Atkins called on me today. He thinks you're mighty pretty, Lizzie."

"How would Jem know that?" Eliza asked tightly. "He hardly ever even looks at me."

"Well, maybe he's a gentleman," her father shot back. "Maybe he's got better manners than to stare at what you're sellin' to the rest of the world."

Eliza crossed her arms over her chest.

"He wants to marry you, Lizzie," Mama said quietly.

It felt as if something exploded in Eliza's head. She stared at her mother. "He wants . . . to *marry* me?"

"He's a good man," Daddy said. "He'll make you a good husband."

"Daddy — he's a dirt farmer."

"So am I," her father said slowly. "That not good enough for you?"

"No! I mean —" Eliza looked desperately at her mother. "Please . . . you didn't . . . you didn't tell him yes?"

"What was I supposed to tell him, eh?" Daddy jerked his head at the hat. "Seems to me it's about time I do get you married off, before you ruin yourself."

"But, Daddy. Not Jem Atkins." The image of the man flashed into Eliza's head. Tall and thin, his face and his fingernails crusted with dirt. She knew the shack he lived in. It was about fifteen miles down the road, and it was tinier even than this place. Tiny and dark. Poor. It would be just like this life, and she would get pregnant and they would get poorer, and there would be no end to it. . . .

Eliza shook her head. "Not Jem Atkins."

Her mother's dark eyes were faintly condemning. "It's time you settled down, honey," she said. "Jem'll be here tomorrow to talk to you. He said he'd court you right —"

"I don't want to be courted."

Her father stood, bending beneath the low ceiling, and in the smoke and the dim light his anger seemed to fill the room. "You'll do what I say on this, Eliza, do you hear me? Jem Atkins is goin' to be your husband, and that's all there is to it. I've had enough of your runnin' around. This'll settle you up good."

"But, Daddy —"

"I ain't changin' my mind," he said firmly. "This is as it should be."

Eliza tried. "But it ain't what I want."

"I've let you run wild till now," Daddy said. "But no more. You're spoiled, girl, and it's time you learned what it means to be an adult. Jem Atkins is just the man to teach you."

Eliza stared helplessly at her father. She looked to her mother, but Mama just lowered her head and glanced away, and desperation welled up so hard in Eliza she couldn't speak. She thought of Jem Atkins and his clammy hands, and his fingers stained with Richmond soil. Jem was never leaving Richmond, and if she married him, neither would she.

She thought of Cole Wallace. *"Come away*

with me, Eliza, and be my wife. . . ."

She forced herself to take a breath. "All right, Daddy," she said slowly. "I'll let Jem court me, if that's what you want."

Daddy nodded with satisfaction. He sat down. "I knew you'd see the sense in it."

"But I won't be forced into marrying him until I'm ready."

Her father looked up at her in surprise. Then he shrugged. "I suppose there's no harm in spendin' a couple weeks gettin' to know him."

"Exactly," Eliza said.

"That's a good girl, Lizzie." Daddy picked up his knife again, slapped at a mosquito. "Now why don't you go wash up for bed? It's late."

Eliza nodded. She went to the door, slipping out into the cool night air, shutting it behind her. But she didn't go to the rain barrel at the side of the house. Instead, she looked up at the sky, at the bright spring moon. She had bought herself a few weeks. It wasn't much time.

She stared at the road beyond, bending away into darkness, into town, and Eliza thought of Cole Wallace bent over a table, gambling in the Bluebonnet. No, there wasn't much time at all. She gave a quick look back to the shanty, dark and shadowed

19

against the sky, and then she ran from the house, through the cotton fields to the road, the swish of her red silk petticoat filling her ears.

Cole Wallace leaned back in his chair and lit a cigar. He puffed on it until it took, and then he swirled the heavy smoke in his mouth and blew it out again, obscuring for a moment the badly painted odalisque on the wall behind Will Ames's head.

Will blinked and waved his hand before his face. "Your turn, Wallace," he said irritably. He worked the cards in his hand, rubbing his fingers over the backs. "You callin' or what?"

"Well, I don't know," Cole drawled. He made a show of reaching into his vest and pulling out his watch. He flipped it open with one hand. It was eleven-thirty. He stuffed the watch back into his pocket and took a coin from the pile in front of him. He threw it into the ante. "I'll call, I guess. And raise you" — he threw in another — "five dollars."

Beside him, Billy Richards threw down his cards. "I'm done," he said. "Down and out."

Sterling Holder stroked his mustache and threw in a coin. "I'm in."

"Pair of jacks," Will said with a smile, turning over his cards.

Cole grinned back at him. "Pair of threes," he said, laying down the pair. And then, when Will's smile grew, "And a pair of tens."

"Christ." Will's smile died. He slumped in his chair. "You got the devil's own luck, Wallace."

"That's true enough." Sterling threw down his cards in defeat and glanced ruefully down at his rapidly dwindling pile. He motioned to a passing barmaid. "Sally, bring me another whiskey! Hell — bring me two."

Cole laughed and gathered up his winnings. He'd been doing well in Richmond, better than he'd expected. His luck had turned for the better finally, and he hoped it held, because in every coin he saw a pair of deep brown eyes and a soft, quiet smile, and for once he had the feeling that Jenny Spears was getting closer and closer. A few more games; a few more dollars in the Dallas bank, and —

"Well, lookee there." Will's words came out on a long, low whistle. "If that ain't Eliza Beaudry."

Cole followed Will's gaze. The name sounded familiar, and when he saw her, he remembered why. Eliza Beaudry stood at the door, her pretty face flushed, her blond hair hanging loose around her face. Her breasts swelled above the neckline of her low-cut dress. Ah yes, he remembered meeting Eliza. She'd had on the same dress, and he'd murmured his hellos and found himself wondering if her breasts would fall out if she bent over. The picture made him smile as much now as it had a week ago. He turned back to his winnings.

"Don't she look good enough to eat," Billy said.

"Tastes like honey — or at least her kisses do," Will said. "I got me a mind to see if I can't squeeze one o' them sweet Texas melons tonight." He started to rise. Cole glanced up just as Eliza Beaudry saw them. She waved and immediately started over.

"Whooee." Billy chuckled. "Looks like she's got you on the menu, too, Willie-boy."

"If you boys are real nice, I might be persuaded to share," Will said.

Cole smiled with the rest of them. He gathered up the cards, shuffling them idly while he watched Miss Eliza Beaudry work her way to their table.

"Hey there, Will." Eliza was interestingly breathless as she pushed to their table. She smiled a greeting at Billy and Sterling, and then her smile widened when she looked at Cole, her voice softened. "Mr. Wallace."

Cole glanced down at the cards, trying to keep from laughing at Will's sudden frown.

She stepped closer, so close Cole felt the rough cotton of her skirt against his knuckles, heard the swish of — it sounded like satin but certainly Eliza Beaudry couldn't afford anything so fine. He put down the cards and sat back in his chair and looked up at her, taking the cigar from his mouth.

"It's a little late for you to be out, isn't it, Miss Beaudry?"

She flushed a little, and smiled again. It was a smile that involved her whole face; it pointed her chin and accented her cheekbones. Her teeth were crooked — or no, it was something different. Her front teeth were a bit pushed back, her eyeteeth overlapped slightly. It was vaguely charming, the kind of thing that could make a man wonder what it would feel like to run his tongue over those teeth. Eliza Beaudry was sex wrapped up in a too-tight package. Cole didn't wonder that Will and Billy were practically quivering at the sight of her.

"My daddy sent me to pick somethin' up for him," she said softly, looking right at him. "And now I guess I'm going to have to walk home in the dark by myself."

"Well, I —" Will started.

Deliberately, Eliza Beaudry turned her back to him.

She'd set her sights on Cole, that was clear

enough. And Cole was bored with poker and ready for a little distraction. Teasing sweet Eliza might be amusing. Teasing Will and Billy certainly was. Cole smiled and rubbed his chin. "Well now, we'd hate to have you do that, wouldn't we, boys?"

Billy leaned forward eagerly. "I'd be happy to —"

Cole held up a hand to stop him. "Don't trouble yourself, Billy," he said. "I believe I'm done here for the evening, Miss Beaudry. I'd be pleased to see you home."

She widened her eyes at him. If possible, her smile grew bigger. "Well, thank you, Mr. Wallace. That's mighty kind of you."

Will threw him a dagger look, and Billy sighed and sat back in his chair. Sterling chuckled and grabbed the cards. "See if you can't round us up a fourth on the way out, will you, Wallace?"

"I'll do what I can." Cole gathered up his winnings, shoving the money into his pocket, stubbing out his cigar. He offered his arm to Eliza, and she eased so close to him he could smell the scent of marsh water and dirt on her skin. He wondered if it would be possible to walk out of here without tripping over her skirts.

"Later, boys." He tipped his hat to them, and Eliza nodded, and together they moved to the door. Just before they went out, Cole threw the man at the door a dollar and told him to find a fourth for his table, and then he and Eliza went out into the cool and quiet night.

Her hand tightened on his arm, and she looked up at him, her hair falling back from her face, her eyes bright. "You expectin' to be in Richmond long, Mr. Wallace?"

"A few days," he said. The air felt good; the river smell was soothing after the smoke of the saloon. Cole lifted his face into it, shoved back his hat.

"And then where?"

Her voice was pretty, light and accented. He liked the way she rounded her words. "Who knows?" he said. "I just go where the games take me."

"So what they say is true? You make your living at the tables?"

He laughed at the interest in her voice. Miss Eliza Beaudry was as transparent as glass. "Yeah, I guess that's the truth of it."

She sighed; he watched her breasts rise and fall with her breath. She looked up at him again with those wide, innocent eyes. "Do you s'pose you'll ever want to settle down?"

He'd lost track of how often women had asked him that question; Cole had grown used to answering it. "I don't guess I'm the settling kind, Miss Beaudry."

He waited for the light in her eyes to die, the way it always did. There wasn't a woman alive who didn't believe she could settle down a wandering man, and Cole was sure Eliza Beaudry was just the same. But her eyes didn't dim. Instead, she sparkled and smiled — that big smile he found he liked — and it was so surprising Cole found himself grinning back.

"Well, I guess I know just how you feel," she said. "Why settle down when the world is full of interesting places?"

He had come to Richmond for one thing, and that was to make money. But now Cole looked down into Eliza's eyes and found himself thinking of other things, of her easy smile and that too-tight dress.

He looked away, up at the starry night. "I don't know about that. All towns are pretty much the same."

Eliza pulled him closer, close enough that his boots swished through her skirts, and pressed her breast against his arm. "Is that so?" she asked on a sigh. "I would've thought anyplace was more interesting than here."

There was a wistfulness in her voice that startled him — so much so that he looked down into her face, into her small, sad smile.

He'd barely caught it before it was gone, disappearing into her grin, into a hushed laugh, and Cole looked away again, down at his boots. He saw the edge of her petticoat; in the light from a nearby saloon, it looked like red lace. Red lace falling over his boots, half-hidden by the threadbare cotton of her skirt.

Red lace.

Cole looked back into Eliza Beaudry's face. She was looking up at the sky, and her eyes were bright, and she was laughing as she talked. Some nonsense about the stars. And in spite of his own warnings, he could not keep from wondering about her. Wondering where a poor girl had got a red silk petticoat, wondering about her smile and the feel of her teeth beneath his tongue. He laughed silently at himself. She was just a pretty flirt, like a hundred others he'd met. She was just a nobody looking for something better.

He couldn't deny there was something about her that intrigued him. Maybe it was the petticoat, or maybe it was the wistfulness behind her smile. In any case, he was strangely attracted to her.

The feeling disconcerted him, and so he didn't look at her as she talked, kept his eyes from lingering on breasts that seemed impossibly white in the pale moonlight, and he told himself again that he didn't need a woman. Not with Jenny waiting in Dallas.

He told himself that all the way to the road that led out of town and into the darkness. He told himself that as Eliza assured him she could make it the rest of the way by herself. He stood there and watched her race away into the darkness until he could no longer see the faded cotton of her dress.

But still he had to work to think of Jenny as he made his way back to his hotel.

2

Cole saw her again the next morning. He was talking to Will Ames in front of the Feed and Seed. She was in the little alleyway between Olsen's and the Painted Lady, clinging to the shadows of the general store. Cole pretended not to see her at first. He went on talking to Will about the weather and how the cotton was doing, though he didn't give a damn about either. From the corner of his eye, he saw Eliza moving forward, pressing against the wall as if she wanted to stay hidden but couldn't resist the lure of their conversation. He told himself to ignore her, but she intrigued him enough that he couldn't concentrate on what Will was saying.

". . . weren't much of a market last year," Will drawled. "They say it —"

Cole couldn't stand it. He turned toward her. "Miss Beaudry!" he called.

Her head jerked up in surprise; she stiffened warily. He smiled at her and beckoned. "Miss Beaudry, come on over here a minute."

Will looked in her direction. His face darkened. "She lurkin' again?"

Cole ignored him. He watched Eliza step from shadow into sunlight. She was wearing a hat, he saw. A blue one with a stuffed bird on it. It was gaudy and too bright, and it made her look faintly ridiculous — that old, threadbare dress from last night and the shiny new hat. She was still hesitant; she came toward them slowly, and with every step he saw the hint of red lace around her ankles, the jiggling of her breasts above the low neckline.

"Hey there, Mr. Wallace," she said when she came closer. She smiled, shyly, uncertainly. She nodded to Will. "Hey, Will."

"Eliza." Will nodded shortly. He was looking unabashedly at her chest. "You're in town early this mornin'."

"I . . . uh . . . I had to get something for Daddy."

"You been his errand boy a lot lately." Will slanted a glance at Cole, then looked back to her. "I guess you prob'ly don't mind, eh?"

Eliza met Will's gaze, even though a flush moved over her pale skin. "I don't mind," she said, and then she smiled at Cole. "Not lately, anyway."

There was no way Cole could mistake her

30

meaning. He reached into his pocket for a cigar. "Well," he said slowly. "You looking for an escort home this morning, Miss Beaudry?"

She shook her head. "No," she said. "But . . . my, something smells good, don't you think?"

For the first time, he noticed the smell of coffee on the air.

"Just the Red Rock," Will said dourly. "Smells like that every day."

"Oh," she said. She laughed a little and looked right at Cole. "Well, it sure smells good. It makes a body hungry."

Cole nearly laughed at her audacity. He tucked the cigar back into his coat without even putting it in his mouth. "I was just on my way to breakfast, Miss Beaudry. Would you care to join me?"

He was surprised the moment he said the words, but when she gave him that big, wide smile, he was strangely glad he'd asked her.

"I'd like that," she said, tucking her hand into his arm, pressing as close as she had last night.

Cole glanced at Will. "You want to join us, Ames?"

He felt the way she stiffened against him, and Will, who was watching her, frowned and shook his head. "I got work to do," he

31

said. "And I don't suppose your daddy'll look too kindly on you missing yours, either, Liza."

"I'll thank you to mind your own business, Will," she said sweetly.

Will scowled at her for a minute. Then he tapped his hat at Cole and walked off. Eliza's fingers tightened on Cole's arm.

"How 'bout that breakfast?" she said brightly.

He didn't spend much time agonizing on where to take her. A lady wouldn't eat breakfast at the Red Rock, but Eliza wasn't a lady, so it didn't matter. When he took her into the saloon, the waitress, Sally, raised a brow, but she didn't say anything when he took Eliza to his usual table by the window. He held out her chair for her and she sat down, spreading her skirts like a society matron, settling herself primly. On Eliza, the gesture was faintly ridiculous. The bird on her hat bobbled as if it were trying to eat the bright purple peony perched beside it.

"I've never eaten here," she said. "You'll have to tell me what to order."

He motioned to Sally, who sashayed over, coffee in hand. She set down a cup in front of Cole and poured it, and then she hesitated.

"Coffee?" she asked.

Eliza smiled brightly up at her. "Please."

Sally looked back at him. "The usual, Cole?"

"Two." And then, to Eliza's questioning look, he said, "Steak. It's the only edible thing here."

Sally walked away. Cole took a sip of coffee. It was hot and black and tasted of tar, and it was the sole reason he came to the Red Rock Saloon every day. Their food wasn't as good as half the other saloons in town, but the coffee he loved — it was so bitter, it raised the hairs on his tongue. It reminded him of White Horse, and his father's coffee, and getting up every morning before the sun to tend the animals.

He wondered if Aaron was still making the coffee that strong now that Pa was —

Eliza choked. "My, that's strong coffee."

The image of his father's farm faded away. Cole smiled at her. "Drink it up," he said. "It's good for you. It'll make you strong."

"Is that so?" Her eyes sparkled. She tried another sip. This time she only cleared her throat. "Why now, I guess you're right. I already feel strong."

He laughed. It was absurd that she was sitting across from him in this saloon, with her too-tight-to-breathe dress and that . . . that *hat*. He remembered last night, remembered his admonition to himself to stay far away from her. He tried to think of Jenny.

But just then Eliza laughed at the way some farmer's horse was bucking and stalling down the road, and he forgot Jenny. By the time Sally brought their steaks, he was wrapped up in fantasizing about Eliza. About lifting that hat off her head and lowering that dress —

Sally set the food before them, and Eliza took up her fork and knife and sawed away at it. The meat was tough. Her whole upper body tightened with the effort to cut it. Finally, she took a bite and chewed. And chewed.

He laughed. "So tell me, Miss Beaudry," he said. "How do you spend your days here in Richmond?"

He liked to watch her talk. He liked the faraway look in her eyes and the way she forgot herself when she spoke.

"You don't want to talk about Richmond," she said, frowning a little in distaste. She sighed, resting her elbows on the table, leaning forward. "I always wanted to travel. I never been anywhere, you know. Except when I was a little girl. We had a farm in Waller County."

"What happened to it?"

"Lots of things. It was mostly dust then.

I guess it's mostly dust now." She took up her fork, played with the meat on her plate. "Daddy said there were outlaws, too, and Indians, but I never saw any. I think it was just an excuse. Anyway, we pulled up and came here. Been here ever since."

"There're worse places than here."

"Maybe." She looked up at him, gave him a crooked smile. "But I'll bet those places aren't boring — at least not at first. You been everywhere, I guess you prob'ly seen a lot of things. You prob'ly even seen outlaws."

"One or two," Cole said.

Her eyes widened. "Really? Tell me."

"There's not much to tell."

"Oh."

She looked disappointed, and he thought briefly of making something up to please her, but it was too much effort, and all he really wanted was to figure out a way to raise that red silk petticoat above her thighs and kiss her breathless. He was amazed at the thought. Slowly, he brought his mind back to what she was saying.

". . . Daddy always says they're just ordinary men, that the war treated them bad and that's why they turned to crime. But I think he was afraid of them anyway." She turned to look at him, gave him a soft, flirtatious smile that made him grin in response. "I'll bet you've never been so afraid that you'd run away like that."

He laughed shortly. "Hell, yes, I've been that afraid."

"You ever been robbed?"

He shook his head. "No."

"Me neither. But they don't come around here much. Daddy says they're mostly out west."

The way she said it, *Out West,* as if it were capitalized, as if it were a spot on the map like Abilene, or Oklahoma. Someplace easily identifiable. *"Ah, here we are at last, Out West."* Cole wanted to laugh at her ignorance. Instead, he only said mildly, "Not so far from here. There's no point in being an outlaw if there's no one to rob."

"You say that like you know."

He shrugged.

"How do you know?"

She looked at him so intently he felt uncomfortable beneath the force of her stare. Her strangely dark brows slanted to the frown lines between her eyes, the delicate bones of her face seemed finely etched beneath her skin.

The hunger started deep inside him. Cole shoved his coffee aside, reached for his money pouch. "Let's go," he said brusquely, throwing a couple of coins on the table.

She didn't even blink. "All right." She got up. The little bird on her hat bobbed with the movement, and he thought again how strange she looked. Such a study in contrasts. When he came around the side of the table, she reached for his arm and clung to him. His whole body tightened; Cole had to swallow and close his eyes to keep from pulling her back into the shadows of some building, taking her against a wall.

He glanced down the street as they stepped outside. His hotel wasn't far. A few more steps, and they could be in a quiet room. The whole afternoon was ahead of them —

She pulled away suddenly. It surprised him so much he stared down at her. She was looking at the sky, at the bright sun, and there was panic in her face. She gave him a weak smile. Her hands twisted nervously in her skirt. "I . . . I got to go. Thank you for breakfast."

She left him then. She turned away from him so quickly there was no time for protest, and her skirt kicked up and red lace danced over her boots. She clutched her hat and hurried down the road. He watched her until she disappeared into the shadows between Olsen's and the Painted Lady.

He wanted a smoke. Badly. Cole took a

cigar from his pocket and bit off the end. The breeze came up just as he tried to light it, but he finally got it lit, and he puffed on it and walked slowly down the street, letting his desire melt into frustration. The afternoon stretched empty before him now, and he told himself it was just as well. Eliza Beaudry was a pretty girl, but she should be married and locked up somewhere, before she could do damage to some poor unsuspecting stranger.

Cole clamped his teeth on his cigar. He looked back at the alleyway where she'd disappeared. It was dark and shadowed. He wondered about the dread he'd seen on her face. He wondered where home was for Eliza Beaudry, which of those little sharecropping farms along the road belonged to her family, and then he realized he didn't really want to know.

Cole turned away and headed toward the livery to check on his horse. It was almost time to leave this little town. He was starting to know these people far too well.

Eliza hurried down the road, nearly falling over her own feet. The sun was bright and hot, beating down on her head, wilting the wildflowers by the side of the road, bringing up their heavy fragrance. She hadn't meant to stay away so long. She'd meant to be back in time to work with her parents in the cotton. All she'd wanted was to see Cole again this morning, to watch his routine and think of how he'd talked to her last night, the way he'd smiled. She wanted to hold those images close to her heart, to think of them over and over again in her head — her own private song to make work go faster.

But then he'd called to her, and it was like a dream come true, and she'd forgotten all about her parents and the trouble she'd be in if she didn't help in the fields.

Eliza rushed around the bend in the road. Her father's fields spread just beyond; she saw the silhouette of their shanty shimmering in the sun, saw the bent figure of her mother and the tall, lean shadow of her father beyond. Her chest tightened with dread. Daddy would skin her the moment he saw her. She didn't even have a good excuse. She couldn't tell them about Cole, not yet. It was too soon to drag him into things. But if things kept going the way they had this morning . . .

In the fields, her mother straightened and put her hand to her eyes, and then she turned and motioned to Daddy. Eliza swallowed and steeled herself. The wrath of God was about to come crashing down on her.

There was nothing to do but take it. Eliza drew closer, to the edge of the fields, and waited while her father made his way over. He pushed his hat back on his head and squinted at her.

"Where you been, girl?"

"In town," Eliza said. She waited for him to start yelling.

But he only jerked his head toward the cabin. "We'll talk about this later. Right now, you'd best get on up to the house."

Eliza frowned. "Why?"

"You forget what I told you last night, about Jem callin'?"

"You mean he's here?"

"He's been waitin' an hour. He's a busy man, Eliza Mae. You'd best go over and apologize to him." Daddy frowned. "And you better hope to hell he still feels like talkin' to you."

Eliza looked at the shack. She saw Jem then, skinny Jem Atkins, sitting on a stool outside the door, his reddish hair sticking all out around his head. Her stomach lurched, but Eliza nodded at her father and walked to the cabin. Jem got awkwardly to his feet when she approached. He was a young man, but he looked old. His long face was lined from hard work, his fair skin blotched with sunburn. He was so tall he had a habitual bend in his back; his shoulders slumped forward.

"There you are, Lizzie," he said. He grinned. His teeth were crooked and stained with tobacco. "Where you been? I expected to find you workin' with your folks."

"I was in town," she said. She tried to smile back at him. "Visiting friends."

"Well, you'd best do your visitin' now, 'cause when we're married you'll be workin' like a good wife."

Eliza looked away, over cotton fields that stretched almost to the horizon. "I don't recall agreeing to marry you yet."

"I don't see anyone else poundin' down your door."

"Maybe they don't think I'm ready to settle down."

"That could be," Jem agreed good-naturedly. "But it seems to me if you don't settle down quick, you might not get any more offers."

Eliza looked back sharply. "What d'you mean?"

Jem shrugged. His bony shoulders seemed to fold clear up to his ears with the motion. "I'm only sayin' that if you keep on this way —"

"What way?"

He gave her a knowing look. "Come on,

Lizzie. I seen you with those boys in town. All that playin' and flirtin'. There ain't many men here'll even think twice about marryin' you."

Eliza regarded him stonily. "I guess that makes you my savior, then."

He sighed. "All I'm sayin' is that you got a reputation."

"And I can count myself lucky that you want to marry me."

"I don't want to boast, but I'd guess that's the way of it." Jem scratched his neck. "Things'll change once we're hitched, though. No more of this runnin' around town at all hours. You'll be my wife, and I got my good name to consider."

"Well," Eliza said, "I'd hate to ruin your good name."

Jem leaned back against the wall. "I think you'll find me a fair man, Lizzie, which is more than I can say for most of the farmers around here. After all, I don't hold your blood against you."

Eliza looked away again, back toward the horizon. She crossed her arms over her chest, tightening her fingers on her forearms until it hurt. She saw her mother, bending over the cotton, her black hair gleaming in the sunlight.

"— I'm willin' to take the chance, but

there ain't many men around here who'd marry an Injun."

Despite herself, Eliza felt the heat of shame. It seemed to take everything from her — her anger, her dread. She swallowed. "I know that," she said quietly.

"I'm a fair man," Jem said again.

"You keep saying that."

"I'll work hard to keep temptation from you, Lizzie. You can't help that savage blood, and I know that. But maybe, with enough prayin', God will see fit to help us triumph over it."

He took her hand. His skin was rough and callused, his fingers so thin and worked they felt like bones against hers. "I'll be a good husband, Lizzie. And if you let me guide you in all things, I think you'll turn out to be a good wife."

Eliza couldn't keep the sarcasm from her voice. "You sure you want to take that chance?"

"Well, a man's got to take some risks in life to get what he wants." Jem held her hand tight and looked right into her face with his squinty eyes. "And I reckon I want you."

She laughed humorlessly and drew back her hand. It took everything she had to keep from wiping it on her skirt. "You want me, Jem? Or maybe it's just kisses you want. You know you don't have to marry me for that."

"I want *you*," Jem said firmly. "I need a wife. Your daddy tells me you know how to cook, and you can sew. I figure that'll serve me well enough." He glanced away, and his mouth tightened. "And I ain't heard any man say you've . . . well, that is to say you're still . . . untouched."

Eliza lifted her brows. "Untouched?"

"I heard it's only kisses you been givin' away." He looked at her sharply. "You tell me now, Lizzie, that's the truth of it, ain't it?"

Eliza had told her father the same thing just last night, but coming from Jem it made her feel . . . dirty. She hated the feeling. And she hated him for making her feel it. "I guess you'll just have to trust what you heard," she said.

Jem took a deep breath. "You think about this, Lizzie," he said. "There ain't many men willin' to take on your fast ways and that Comanche blood. I don't see no one knockin' down your door to offer for you. Not a respectable offer, anyway. But I am. I'm askin' you to be my wife, and I don't do that lightly."

He looked toward his fields, reached into his pocket and took out a bag of chew. He opened the bag and reached for a plug of tobacco, biting off a hunk and storing it between his teeth and his cheek before he nodded to her. "I got to get back to work now, but you think on what I said. I'll be back tomorrow, and we can start the courtin' right."

She watched him walk away, and it seemed the world narrowed down to just him, to just a thin and stooped man stumbling over the muddy furrows, his thinning hair glowing in the sun. She saw how it would be. He was a sharecropper, just like her father, and she would be a sharecropper's wife, and Richmond would close around her, keeping her in her place, and her children would be born and some of them might have her mother's hair and those dark Comanche eyes, and it would go on and on. They would never respect her here in Richmond, and if she married Jem, she would never escape it. Her children would never escape it.

She felt the sun beating down on her head and the close east Texas air, growing more and more humid with every passing day.

She would not live through another year in Richmond. She would not marry Jem Atkins and be grateful to him for the rest of her life because he'd dared to take on her "fast ways and Comanche blood."

She would not do it.

Eliza glanced at her mother and father toiling in the fields, and then she looked down at her toes, where the red lace of her petticoat peeked beneath the too-short hem of her gown. She remembered how Cole Wallace had studied it. She remembered how he'd looked up at her with sudden interest in his eyes.

She knew that look. She'd seen it in a dozen other eyes, and she knew that Cole Wallace could be made to want her. And if he wanted her enough, he would take her with him when he left. She had told Daddy that she wasn't a whore, and she wasn't. But her choices were narrowing. On one side was Jem, who wouldn't marry her if she wasn't a virgin, and on the other was Cole, who wanted her and was leaving this town. If it took more than kisses to get out of Richmond . . . well, she would do whatever it took.

Eliza looked out at the road stretching to town, and she thought of how it would be when she was riding down it, following it to wherever it led. Someplace far away.

3

When he woke the next morning, he knew he'd dreamed of Eliza. She was the first thing he thought of when he opened his eyes, and he had the feel of her about him, the soft touch of her skin beneath his fingers, the smell of her skin. He got out of bed and washed and dressed, then walked slow and easy down the warped stairs of his hotel and into the bright spring sunshine. He blinked and pulled his hat down low over his eyes, watching the people pass as he walked to the Red Rock for breakfast. It wasn't until he realized he was watching for Eliza that he looked away from the street and hurried his step.

The bartender at the Red Rock greeted him with a smile. Cole took his usual table by the front window. Before long, Sally came by with a cup of hot coffee.

"Mornin', Cole," she said. "No guests today?"

Cole took the coffee from her. "No guests," he said.

She arched her brow at him, cocked her hip. "Well, you can do better than Liza Beaudry, you know."

"Can I?"

She grinned. "You know you can."

He smiled into her eyes, but when she smiled back he thought of Eliza's crooked-toothed smile.

"I'll get your breakfast," Sally said. She walked away, hips swinging.

His dream came back to him then. He'd been walking with Eliza by the river, and she'd smiled at him and he had kissed her. She'd undone her dress and lowered it until her breasts were bare, until she wore nothing but a red silk petticoat. Then she had knelt in a bed of bluebonnets, and the perfume of the flowers had been so strong it made him dizzy.

He'd awakened then, with the smell of the flowers still in his nose and her smile imprinted on his brain. Cole took a deep sip of the hot coffee, nearly burning his tongue. He tried to remember the last time he'd had a woman. There was that little whore in Houston over three months ago, but since then, nothing. He'd stopped in Dallas soon after that, and the sight of Jenny had made him suddenly want more from life than cheap sex.

But that was three months ago, and the way he wanted Eliza had nothing to do with his feelings for Jenny.

"Here's your breakfast, Cole." Sally leaned over him; he caught the whiff of strong perfume and sweat as she set the steak before him. She rested her hand on his shoulder. "You enjoy that, now."

He raised a brow at her and looked pointedly at the meat. It looked as dry and chewy as ever. "How old was this cow, Sally?"

She laughed, waving her hand at him as she walked away. Cole tucked into the meat, but after one bite it seemed to settle uncomfortably in his gut. The fried potatoes were no better. He pushed the plate away and took another sip of coffee, staring out the window at the people passing by. He nodded to a pair of ladies — Mrs. Nevins and her daughter — and a man he'd gambled with two nights ago whose name he couldn't remember. He saw Will Ames come out of the Painted Lady across the street, his hat off and his hair wet from bathing. Wagons lumbered down the dusty street, the farmers slumped over the reins, their eyes shadowed by their drawn-low hats. One by one, Cole watched the businesses open: the general store and the Feed and Seed, the milliner's. He saw a woman come around the corner of the Painted Lady and head toward Olsen's. The sun shone on her bare head as she settled herself on the steps of the stoop, drawing her knees up to her chest. The edging of her petticoats showed over her boots. It was red lace, and her hair was blond. It glowed golden in the sunlight.

Eliza.

Cole set aside his coffee. He thought of his dream last night, of Eliza kneeling naked in a bed of bluebonnets, her hair falling over her shoulders.

Damn, it had been a long time since he'd had a woman. Cole pushed back his chair. He fumbled in his pocket, left two bits on the table to pay for his meal, and gulped the last of his coffee. He told himself he was being a fool, but still he went out the door of the Red Rock and stood there on the street, looking at her. She raised her head, and he knew the moment she caught sight of him, saw her smile, her tentative wave.

"Mr. Wallace!" she called. "How nice to see you."

He dodged a wagon and crossed the street. She rose from the stairs and the red lace of her petticoat disappeared. She wore a different dress today — it was older, a many-patched gray, with a demure neckline. But it was still too tight, and it clung to her like a second skin.

"Good morning, Miss Beaudry," he said, tipping his hat. "What brings you into town today?"

"Well . . ." She tilted her eyes at him as if deciding whether or not to tell him a secret. "It was too pretty a day to stay home."

"Playing hooky?"

She grinned. "You know," she said, bending close, lowering her voice, "It's cool in the bottomlands."

"Is it? I haven't been there yet."

"I . . . I could show you," she offered.

"I'd be delighted if you would."

Her smile was bright and quick. He liked the wideness of her mouth, the way those slightly crooked teeth made her look innocent and seductive at the same time.

Cole nodded toward the saloon. "What do you say I grab a bottle and some dinner? We could make a day of it."

She looked surprised. "Why, that'd be . . . I'd like that."

"Good." Cole offered his arm. When she took it, he led her back across the street to the Red Rock. She waited outside while he asked Sally for a bottle of whiskey and whatever food she could scrape together.

Cole eased out the door with some bread

51

and steak and a bottle. Eliza hurried toward him as if she'd expected he might disappear inside the Red Rock.

"I thought maybe you'd changed your mind," she said breathlessly.

"Now why would I do that," he asked, "when I've got such a pretty lady waiting for me?"

She flushed — she was so damned easy to please. It made him laugh, and when he did, she laughed with him, even though he knew she had no idea what had amused him. Her laughter was light and simple; it had a way of wrapping itself around him, of creating intimacy, and Cole took her hand and set it into the crook of his arm. She leaned into him; he smelled again the marshwater scent of her hair, the warm tang of her skin. She was going to be good when he finally got her into bed, he knew, and the anticipation of it tightened his whole body; it took everything he had to rent the wagon and help her into it without easing his hands over her breasts or kissing her there in the street.

She seemed oblivious to his tension. She bounced beside him in the wagon, talking about how warm it was and how much it had rained these last weeks. It was so rare this spring to see a sunny day, had he noticed? The wildflowers were beautiful this year, perhaps it was due to all the rain — wasn't it something to remark upon?

He answered her as best he could, but he couldn't recall afterward what he told her. She sat close to him on the seat, so close her arm brushed his and he felt the heat of her through his coat.

When they got to a grove of live oaks near a small oxbow lake, he helped her down from the wagon. The moment her feet touched the ground she grabbed the bag of food and headed for the bank. She looked over her shoulder at him, waving for him to follow, and Cole found himself stumbling along behind her like some mooning boy. She plopped herself in the dappled shade of an oak and set the bag beside her, and then she unfastened her boots. She wasn't wearing stockings, and Cole watched, transfixed, at the play of sunlight and shade on the bones of her ankle. She scooted to the edge and braced her hands behind her, and the next thing he knew she was dangling her feet in the water, splashing playfully and tilting her head so her hair fell down her back, catching the light.

"Oh, take your boots off," she said. "The water feels good."

He thought of what else would feel good.

"Come on, Mr. Wallace," she urged. "Sit down."

He walked over and squatted beside her. "Suppose you call me Cole, Eliza."

She grinned. "All right then, Cole. Take off your coat and stay awhile. You look ready to run clear to Dallas."

He took off his coat and laid it beside him on the grass. There was a breeze coming off the lake; it eased through the thin linen of his shirt. Eliza paddled her feet in the water. The sun glanced off the splashes, off the wet arch of her foot, like golden little fishes jumping.

The oak was twined with wild grapevine that dangled close to her hair — it caught a strand and held it, and the strands shimmered out like spider's web in the light, fragile, too tentative to be real. Then she moved her head slightly and the web was broken. She looked over her shoulder at him, and her glance was quizzical and faintly amused.

"You worried about alligators?" she asked. "I never saw any here." She nodded to the distance, to a grove of trees shadowed by Spanish moss. "Now that over there, that's marsh. It leads right down to the Gulf. That's where you'll find 'em."

"I've never seen one," he said.

"No?" The smile again. "I don't guess

you've spent much time in this part of the world, then."

"Not much." He edged closer.

"Sometimes you can hear them. At night mostly. They roar." She shivered and looked back out at the water. "You know when you hear it that something's going to die." She took a deep breath and glanced back at him. Again she patted the ground beside her. She caught her lip between her teeth, widened her eyes. Her dark brows winged above them. "You want to kiss me, Cole?"

She was a born coquette. There was just the right flirtatiousness in the question — not too forward, not too shy. It was the kind of tone that sank right to the center of a man's gut and made his heart beat faster. Cole knew without even touching her that her kisses would be sweet. Like honey, he remembered Will saying. The kind that led to sweeter things.

Cole grinned and glanced away, to where her foot played in the water. She'd pulled up her skirt and her petticoat, and her calves were bare and white.

"You can kiss me, you know," Eliza said. "I'll let you, if you want to."

"I don't know, Eliza," he teased. "I think I'd rather just take you by surprise."

She blinked, and then she laughed. "All

right," she said. "Surprise me."

He liked her laughter as much as he liked her smile. She laughed like she meant it; there was nothing ladylike about it at all, nothing forced. She wasn't innocent, but there was an unaffectedness to her, a naturalness that made him think she would be equally unaffected once he had her undressed and in bed. He wondered how long it would take to get her there, and then realized that he wanted to dangle it out in front of him like a prize; he wanted the foreplay of laughter, the long slow build to consummation.

Cole grabbed the bag of food. He pulled out the whiskey and twisted off the cork, taking a long, slow swig of it before he handed it to Eliza. She met his eyes and drank from it slowly, holding his gaze, and then she let it go with a gasp. Her eyes watered. She wiped at her mouth with the back of her hand.

"My, that's . . . powerful," she said.

He sat down beside her. "That's pure Kentucky whiskey, my dear." He took the bottle back and drank again, and then he held it out to her. "More?"

She laughed breathlessly, but when she reached for the bottle, he held it just out of her reach. She gave him a puzzled look, and he watched realization dawn in her pale eyes when he pressed the bottle to her lips and tilted it. He tipped it a bit too much; she choked and the whiskey coursed over her chin, wetting her dress. But she only laughed when he pulled it away, wiping ineffectually at her bodice.

"You're not so good at that," she teased him.

"Well, I've never done it before," he said. He pulled out his handkerchief and wiped at her face. His thumb brushed her cheek. Her skin was warm and soft, and just that touch mesmerized him. Then, before she had time to react, he lifted her chin and bent to kiss her.

He heard the catch of her breath, but at the touch of his lips she leaned into him, and her mouth opened under his without any prompting. She tasted like whiskey; he smelled the faint scent of dirt beneath the sweetness of her skin. She knew how to kiss; he'd never kissed a woman so good at it. She curled her tongue around his and pulled him deep inside.

There was no pretense to her, not the subtle tightening of censure, nothing to hold him back. This was just like his dream. Cole pressed into her, and in that moment he abandoned the idea of light, playful kisses, of teasing foreplay.

He ran his hand through her soft, fine hair, smoothed it back from her temples, trailed his fingers down her back to her waist. She was sweetly curved; he brought his hand up slowly, from her waist to her breast, and she pressed against him so hard he had to move back a little to touch her. She moaned a little when he cupped her breast through her dress, and the sound made him drunk and hard.

She had her hands in his hair, and she was teasing his mouth, and he was too impatient for finesse. He reached around and fumbled with the fastenings of her dress. He wished she was wearing the low-cut gown he'd seen last night, because then he would have just plunged his hand into her neckline, and the hooks on this were small and hidden beneath a seam. Still, he managed to get one un-hooked, and then another and another. She squirmed beneath his fumbling; her breathing was harsh and impatient. Cole pulled the dress over her shoulders, drew it down. She wore no chemise underneath, no corset, nothing to cover herself.

He backed away to look and she crossed her arms over her chest in reflex. She looked dazed and a little shy, and the expression made him smile. He took her hands and eased them down, exposing her breasts. High, full, perfect breasts. The sunlight fell through the leaves, dappling her skin, and he closed his eyes against how beautiful she was. He reached for her, cupping her breasts, filling his palms with their heaviness. She sighed and leaned into him, and then he was kissing her again, exploring those crooked teeth with his tongue.

It was all he could think about: the taste of her, the feel of her. He laid her back on the grass and pushed her skirt down, undid the tapes of her red silk petticoat. She didn't protest when he eased it over her hips, over her well-shaped legs; she merely lifted to help him, wrapped her arms around his neck to bring him close. She was completely naked beneath him, and he undid his trousers and his underwear so hastily he felt buttons pop. When he parted her legs with his knee she opened for him and pulled him down on top of her.

She was everything he'd thought she would be. She moaned into his mouth and clutched him. She lifted her hips against his, and there was such artlessness in the movement that it nearly brought him to climax then, but he eased away from her for a moment, struggled for breath. She reached for him, arched to meet his mouth when he teased her breasts with his tongue. She was wild beneath him, and he wanted her so badly there was hardly any foreplay before he thrust into her.

He heard her little cry as she froze and tried to push him away. Her knees came up around him, her nails dug into his shoulder. "Oh," she said, her whisper harsh and pained. "Oh, no —"

He tried to slow down, but he was too far gone, he couldn't hold back, and he pressed her to the ground and rocked against her until he came.

The force of it was so powerful it took his breath and his strength. He collapsed on top of her, burying his face in her shoulder, in her hair. He turned to her cheek, felt something wet on his lips, something salty. Tears.

Damn.

Cole rolled off her, looked into her face. "You've never done this before."

She smiled a little wistfully, shook her head. "No."

He opened his mouth to say, *Why didn't you tell me,* but it was a stupid question, and the fact was that he'd known already. Deep inside, he'd known she was a flirt, but not a whore. It wasn't important anyway. What was important was the question he was afraid to ask: *Why me?*

Because he was afraid, he didn't ask it. He didn't want to hear her answer. He wanted to believe it was just sex, and they had both wanted it, and his only obligation was to make sure she enjoyed it.

He leaned over and kissed her, and he knew by the way she sighed and nestled into him that she wasn't angry. The little twinge of guilt disappeared when he felt her hip nudge into him, when she ran her finger down his chest. He forgot everything except the feel of her body beneath his.

He made love to her twice more before the afternoon turned.

When the sun began to set and the shadows grew long, he pulled away from her, finally sated. He grabbed his trousers and looked up at the sky. He had an hour, maybe more, before the gambling started in earnest at the Bluebonnet. It was time to get back.

She stretched and reached for him, smiling lazily. "Come on back, Cole," she said. "It's early yet."

He tossed her the dress, the petticoat. "We've got to go," he said. He pulled on his trousers and walked to the edge of the lake, sliding down the shallow bank. The water was so cold it made his toes curl, but he scooped it up and splashed it over his face until the languidness of lovemaking faded and he felt alert again.

When he turned back to her, her dress was on but unfastened, falling open over her shoulders. She looked swollen and blowzy, with her hair tangled and falling into her face, her dress wrinkled and grass-stained. Cole felt a stab of distaste. He wondered now what it was he'd seen in her. She was the kind of woman he'd seen in a hundred other towns, poor and desperate. Nothing special. The urge to leave pressed in on him. He stepped up the bank.

"Could you help me?" she asked. She made a little motion of helplessness. "The hooks —"

His coat was abandoned on the bank. He picked it up and shrugged into it, reaching into his pocket for a cigar. He clenched one between his teeth, and then he went to her, fumbling with the damn tiny hooks until she was all done up. Then he stepped away, lighting his cigar. He'd taken two puffs on it before he realized she was looking at him with a soft, infatuated expression.

She reached for him; her fingers tightened on his arm. "D'you have to go back so soon?" she asked quietly. "Maybe we could go to supper?"

Cole sighed. "Not tonight, Eliza," he said,

working to keep from sounding as impatient as he felt. "I've got work to do."

"Oh yes. Work." She smiled at him.

Cole patted her hand perfunctorily, and she released him. She followed him to the wagon and he helped her onto it and seated himself. She was quiet on the way back, and that was how he liked it. It gave him time to think about whether Billy Richards would be in the Bluebonnet tonight, and how best to beat him. The man had money to spare, but he didn't part with it easily. He was a decent player and clever enough to spot a bluff. It always took some work to draw him in —

"Cole?"

He'd almost forgotten she was there. "Hmmm?"

"Is . . . is something wrong?"

He frowned at her, irritated by the interruption. "What?"

She put her hand on his arm. "You're awfully quiet."

He wished she would stop touching him. The livery was just ahead, and he could hardly wait to set her down and get away from her. But there was a pleading in her question, and it was more trouble than it was worth to hurt her, so he said, "Just thinking."

63

He saw the Painted Lady ahead, and the sign that advertised baths for ten cents. Damn, he wished he had time for a bath, but he'd be lucky if he could fit supper in. He pulled the horses to a stop outside the livery and jumped down, going to her side to help her. When she was on the ground, he made to step away, but her hands tightened on his arms, stopping him, and that infatuation was there again in her eyes.

"What do you think about supper?" she asked. "I know not tonight, but do you think —"

"Sure," he said. "Sure." He looked away and waited for her to release him. "I'll let you know."

She smiled happily and let go of him. "Should I come by, or —"

"I'll find you," he said. He gave her a distracted kiss. "See you later, all right?"

"All right." She turned away from him then, but she only took a few steps before she twisted and gave him a little wave. He waved back, and then he handed the reins to the stableboy and watched her walk away, her hips swaying beneath her dress, her hair bouncing.

He sighed and puffed on his cigar, tasting the smoke, blowing it out in a slow, steady stream. She'd been good today; he'd rarely had better. But he turned away before she disappeared, and he wasn't even halfway to the Bluebonnet before he forgot all about her.

4

Eliza walked home leisurely, swinging her skirts, humming a tuneless melody. The sunset was gold and red and perfect, and she took great deep breaths of the bluebonnets perfuming the side of the road just to pull the smell inside her.

She felt beautiful. Sore and sleepy and too beautiful to be alive. She played the afternoon over and over in her head, from the moment she'd seen him in town that morning until his last, lingering smile. She closed her eyes and thought of how he'd touched her, how he'd run his fingers through her hair and loved her.

It was different than she'd thought it would be. Better. After that first pain, she'd been swept up in feeling; she blushed now at the memory of the things she'd done. She was pretty sure she was in love with him. She felt shivery and happy just thinking about him. She wanted to be with him more than anything. Thank God he'd come to Richmond. It was almost as if he'd come just for her, just to rescue her from Jem, from her future. Jem was no threat now, and she was *in love.*

Eliza tried the words out in her head. She was in love with Cole. He was in love with her. They were *in love.* She wondered how long it would be before he came to declare himself. Not long, she hoped. She didn't know how she could go through another hour without him.

She was so happy that even the sight of the dilapidated shanty couldn't dampen her mood. Eliza saw her father coming in from the fields, a hoe slung over his shoulder. He stopped when he saw her, and straightened, waiting. Eliza's heart jumped, but she reminded herself that it was only a few more days, and that took away her dread. She only had to bear it until Cole could find a chance to talk to her father.

"Where you been?" Daddy's voice was flat. She saw the anger in his eyes, the clenching of his hand on the hoe.

"In town," she said. She tensed, waiting for him to yell, but he only looked at her. His gaze was so hard she had to look down at her feet. She wondered if he knew, if he could tell what she'd done just by looking at her. She felt so different, it had to be obvious.

But Daddy only sighed and said, "You'd best be havin' your good times closer to home, girl. You're a promised woman now."

Eliza had to bite her lip to keep from answering him. Cole would tell him. She would wait for Cole.

She nodded tightly. "I know it."

His eyes narrowed, but he only jerked his head at the shanty. "Go on in and help your mama with supper."

Eliza closed her eyes in relief when he turned and walked away. He hadn't been that angry, not as much as she'd thought. She watched him go, half expecting him to turn around again, to scream at her. But he didn't, and finally she went inside the dark house.

Mama was already inside, pouring cornbread batter into a pan. She looked up when Eliza came in and wiped her hands on her patched skirt. "We could've used your help today, Lizzie," she said quietly.

Eliza flushed with guilt. Daddy could yell a blue streak, but nothing he said ever made her feel as low as Mama's simple words. She tried to cover her discomfort by grabbing a piece of leftover cornbread. Crumbs scattered over the hard-packed dirt floor. She pushed at them with her toe. Cole loved her, she reminded herself. All she had to do was wait for him. "I was busy," she said.

"Were you now?" Mama raised a heavy, dark brow. "Doin' what?"

Eliza turned her back to her mother and leaned against the doorjamb, looking out into the fading sun. "I was on a picnic."

"Not with Jem Atkins, I know," Mama said. "He came over to ask himself to supper tomorrow."

"And I suppose you told him that would be just fine."

"You are promised to him, Lizzie."

"I ain't agreed to that yet."

Mama sighed. The sound settled around Eliza like a heavy shroud. "Oh, Eliza."

Eliza heard her mother's movement, the clanking of pans, the heavy thud as Mama set aside the lid to the salt pork barrel. She thought she should turn around, help her mother, pretend Mama hadn't sighed, that Eliza hadn't heard a wealth of disappointment in the sound. But she couldn't move, couldn't tear her eyes away from the setting sun, or her father's heavy shadow as he gathered his tools.

She was leaving here. None of this mattered. Cole was coming for her. Eliza put her fingers to her mouth, wet them with her tongue, pressed them against her lips and closed her eyes, pretending it was Cole's lips she felt and not her own fingers, pretending she was kissing him again. But it wasn't right, somehow, and she couldn't remember what his kiss had felt like — how silly, that it had been less than an hour ago, and she couldn't remember —

Mama sighed again. "You know why I married your daddy."

It seemed such a strange thing to say, so unconnected, that Eliza turned from the door with a frown. "What?"

Mama looked right at her. "You know why. I was expectin' you. Your daddy and I had to get married."

"So?"

"It started just the same," Mama said. "I sneaked out to meet him. At first, it was only kisses. A picnic. Then it was . . . somethin' more."

Her mother's meaning dawned on Eliza slowly. "It ain't going to happen to me," she said tightly.

"Not if it's only kisses. Is that what you're tellin' me, Lizzie?" Mama asked quietly. "That it was only kisses today?"

Eliza didn't say anything. She turned her face from her mother's dark gaze, those too-knowing eyes.

"You were with a man today, Eliza,"

Mama said. "And you're promised to Jem Atkins. What is it you think you're doin'?"

Eliza jerked from the door. She sat on the bench and glared at her mother. "I'm not staying in this town, Mama. Not for another year, not another second if I can help it. I'm not going to spend my life watching people look down on me because —"

"Your mama's half-Comanche." Mama finished.

Eliza didn't look away. "And my daddy's a sharecropper," she said.

Mama nodded slowly. Her Indian eyes looked suddenly old. "Well, you can't help the family you're born to."

"I'm going where it doesn't matter," Eliza said, and though she tried to temper the anger in her voice, it was still so strong she saw her mama wince. "I'm going to a place where no one knows who I am. Where ladies smile at me in the street and ask me to tea."

"Oh, Lizzie —"

Eliza looked away. Her shame was like a fist in her gut, but it had been there so long it was easy to ignore. "I'm sorry, Mama," she said stubbornly. "But that's the way it is."

"And there's some man you think is goin' to take you away from all this?" Mama asked.

"You really think he'll marry you when you're givin' him your body for free?"

It sounded so ugly the way Mama said it, and it wasn't that way at all, not the way Cole had kissed her, the way he touched her. There was nothing ugly about that.

"Well, maybe he will." Mama sat on the bench. It shook unsteadily beneath her weight. "And maybe he won't. Maybe he'll get you with child and leave you. Have you thought of that, Lizzie? Have you thought of what you'll do then?"

Eliza met her eyes. "It ain't going to happen that way."

Mama laughed shortly, quietly. "Oh, Lizzie —"

"It *ain't* going to happen that way."

"You think so." Mama sat back. She sighed, and then she rose. "I'm not goin' to tell this to your daddy," she said. "At least not yet. But you listen to me, Lizzie, and you listen good. When you tempt fate, sometimes you get burned. If there's one thing I do know, it's that."

"I'll keep that in mind," Eliza said.

"I hope you do." Mama went back to the stove. "For your sake, I hope you do."

Eliza spent the next day waiting for him to come for her. She worked in the fields alongside her mother and waited. The sun was hot and glaring; Eliza had to shade her eyes with her hand just to see the road. And she looked up at it a lot — every time she heard a wagon or a horse. She dug and weeded and sweated, but her mind wasn't on the cotton plants pushing through the dirt. She daydreamed about how it would be, how he would ride down that road and stop at the edge of the fields. How he would call her father over. They would talk for a moment, and then Daddy would turn to her and say, *"Eliza, come here,"* and she would be free. She would run into Cole's arms, look into his shining eyes. Together, they would ride away.

But he didn't come. By that night, when she crawled beneath the threadbare covers on her pallet in the corner, she yearned for him so badly she couldn't sleep. She missed him so much, surely he felt the same? Surely he was tossing and turning on his lumpy hotel mattress, wanting her?

She closed her eyes and pictured him lying in his bed, bare-chested, staring at the ceiling. She pictured him dreaming about her, thinking about their picnic, thinking about her. She willed him to miss her.

When dawn came, she was still imagining it. But what had seemed possible in the dark quiet of night seemed like a dream in the morning. Eliza got up before her parents and stepped outside, watching the sun come up fully. She sat on the ground beside the shanty and leaned her head back against the rough walls. The sparrows chased each other, a bunch of crows fought over a dead snake in the road. A few red wildflowers struggled against the bare dirt of the yard near the side of the house.

Eliza watched the world wake up and tried to tell herself everything was all right. Cole was just busy; he'd come for her when he could. He'd said he would find her, she should trust him. But by the time Daddy came out the door and stumbled around to wash his face in the rain barrel, Eliza felt sick. Mama's words came back to her. *"You really think he'll marry you when you're givin' him your body for free?"*

She looked down at her hand, at her chipped and dirty fingernails, at the rough skin of her knuckles and the stain of soil, and the sickness inside her grew, a certainty that she couldn't just push away. He was not coming for her. Not now, not ever. He didn't love her. He had used her, and now she didn't matter to him at all.

Daddy came around the corner of the house, shaking water from his face. His blond hair stood on end, wet and glistening in the sun.

"What're you doin', Lizzie?" he asked, his pale eyes narrowing. "Ain't no time to rest today. We got work to do."

Eliza nodded to him. She braced her bare feet against the dirt and pushed herself against the wall. "I know, Daddy."

"Come on then." He walked around her, disappeared into the house. "Come and eat."

She heard her mother moving around inside, the clank of pans, the hiss of frying salt pork, and Eliza's whole life spread out before her: breakfast and work, dinner and work, supper and sleep, only to get up in the morning and work again. She thought of growing old in the hot and humid Richmond sun, waiting for Cole to come get her, waiting for him to call.

Eliza grabbed her boots from the door and shoved them on, barely pausing long enough to tie them up. If she hurried, she might catch Cole just before he went to the Red Rock. Maybe he'd take her to breakfast. Maybe they could go on another picnic. Maybe . . .

She splashed her face in the rain barrel, raked her fingers through her loose hair. Then Eliza ran. She didn't stop running until she was to town and the weathered wood buildings were shimmering before her. Eliza ducked between the Painted Lady and Olsen's General Store, hurrying down the shadowed alleyway, catching her sleeve on the splintered boards. At the edge of the Olsen's porch there was a bunch of wildflowers growing, and she picked them and held them tight, thinking she would give them to Cole.

She rushed across the street to the hotel, holding the flowers against her chest so they wouldn't break. She glanced up at the window to his room. The shades were drawn; but it was still early. Maybe he was still asleep.

She hurried inside. She was nearly across the lobby to the stairs when Ben called to her from the front desk.

"Slow down there, Eliza," he said. "What's your hurry?"

Eliza barely paused. "Mornin', Ben."

"Who're the flowers for?"

"No one."

"No one?" Ben laughed. "I don't reckon Old Man Anderson is too interested in flowers, and it's only him and a dirty cowboy upstairs today."

She slowed and turned. "Ain't Cole staying here?"

"Cole?"

Eliza nodded. "Cole Wallace."

Ben frowned. "Well, he's gone, Eliza. He left last night."

Eliza stared at him in disbelief. "But, he . . . that can't be true. You sure you know who I mean, Ben? Cole Wallace?"

"I know who you mean, Eliza," Ben said.

"But he can't be gone," she said. "He can't."

Ben sighed and shook his head. "I'm sorry. He paid up his bill last night and rode out."

Eliza was so shaken she didn't even notice the tears in her eyes until Ben began to blur before her. "This ain't a joke?"

"No joke." Ben's voice was soft and slightly chiding. "He's no good, darlin'. He's nothin' but a gambler. You knew that."

Eliza nodded dumbly. She swiped a hand over her eyes, wiping away her tears, but it only blinded her more, and the tears didn't stop coming.

She turned away from Ben, hurried back across the lobby, ashamed to be crying in front of him, ashamed that he'd seen her there at all. Her legs felt like they wouldn't hold her, but still she managed to make it to the porch, and then to the street. The sun was blinding now, and Richmond was harsh and ugly and sad. He was gone. He hadn't even bothered to say good-bye.

Eliza looked blindly down. She was still clutching the flowers, holding them so hard they'd wilted in her hands. She thought of the last time she'd seen him. The way he'd looked away from her, the carelessness of his words. *"I'll find you."*

He'd never meant to look for her. He'd known he was leaving then, and he hadn't told her.

She didn't know whether to cry with pain or with rage, or who to hate more: Cole for leaving or herself for believing he might take her with him.

"Hey, Liza!"

The voice came from behind her. Quickly, Eliza wiped her eyes and turned. It was Will Ames. The sight of him made her feel tight and empty. "Hey, Will," she said.

He came up beside her, slinging his arm over her shoulder, pulling her close into his side. He'd never done such a thing before, but Eliza was too miserable to care. Maybe he knew Cole was gone. Maybe he wanted to comfort her. She felt like being comforted.

"Early for you to be in town, eh?"

"Yeah," she said. She looked down at her feet. "I guess."

"Lookin' for some company?"

She shrugged.

His hand tightened on her shoulder.

"Well, I was thinkin', now that Cole's gone . . ."

Her heart jumped at the sound of Cole's name. Eliza glanced up at Will. "Did you see him go?"

"No." He shook his head. "Played with him last night, though. He wasn't thinkin', or somethin'. He was losin' left and right. I never saw him play so bad. Billy says he was playin' like that the night before, too."

Eliza looked back down at her feet. "Oh. Maybe that's it, then."

"That's what I figured," Will said. He jerked her closer. "So, like I was sayin'. Now that Cole's gone, I was thinkin' maybe you'd like a little company."

Eliza smiled wanly. "That's nice of you, Will, but I'm not feeling much like company right now."

"Maybe tonight, then." His eyes shone as he looked down at her. "Or tomorrow. You name the time."

"I'll see." Eliza tried to pull away, but Will held her tight. "You know Daddy doesn't like you much, Will. I'm not sure he'll —"

"Come on, Eliza. Your daddy won't even know. You escaped him quick enough for Cole."

It dawned on her slowly what he was saying. They were only words at first, and she was too unhappy to really hear them. But now she did. Now she realized he was holding her too close, and his hand was caressing her waist, close to her breast. She saw the leer in his eyes.

In that moment, the realization of what she'd done hit her. She'd never bothered to hide her intentions toward Cole from anyone. She'd walked with him alone in the moonlight and gone to breakfast with him. She'd ridden off with him to the lake. The whole town had to know she'd been with Cole Wallace. The whole town knew. No wonder Will was holding her so close. He must think . . . They all must think —

She pushed Will away so hard he stumbled back. "Don't touch me," she said, and she heard a hysterical edge in her voice that she couldn't hold back. "Don't you touch me."

Will reached for her. "Liza —"

"I ain't a whore," she said. She shook her head, stepped away from him. "Not yours, not anyone's. Do you hear me?" He stepped toward her. Eliza held up her hand. "D' you hear me?"

He stopped and frowned. "Yeah, sure," he said. "Whatever you say." He glanced around. "Look, no one has to see, if that's what you're worried about. If you come at night —"

She ran down the street away from him. Her skirt caught in her legs, tripping her up. She heard his footsteps behind her, catching up to her.

"Eliza, wait. Hey, slow down." Will came up even with her. He lowered his voice. "I didn't mean to get you so riled up, all right? I'm sorry. *Slow down.*"

Eliza glanced over at him.

"I'm sorry," he said again. "All right?"

She slowed, but she didn't stop. "All right."

Will smiled and stepped closer. "Listen, I wasn't thinkin'," he said in a low voice. "I guess you didn't understand. Whatever Cole was givin' you, I'll double it —"

She felt light-headed, numb clear to her bones. Will kept talking, but she didn't hear the words. She forced herself to take a deep breath, forced herself to swallow. And then she gave Will Ames the coldest smile she could muster. "You want to know what Cole paid me?" she asked. "Is that what you want to know?"

Will licked his lips. "Yeah," he said. "Tell me."

Eliza thrust the flowers into his face. Her hands were shaking. "He gave me nothing," she said, and then she laughed meanly. She let the flowers fall, and he grabbed at them like he thought they were important.

"Nothing, Will," she said again. "Double that."

She spun away from him, and then she began to run. She ran and ran, past town, down the road to home, where cotton fields stretched long and bleak before her.

5

Jem was at the shanty the next day. When Eliza woke up and stumbled out to the rain barrel to wash her face, he was there, standing in the yard, staring at the rising sun. Waiting for her.

Eliza stared blearily at him. He nodded to the rain barrel. "I reckon I'll wait," he said.

She stared at him a moment longer. His face was tight, his thin lips all drawn up, and in the light of his gaze she felt ugly. Her eyes felt swollen from crying, and the way he looked at her she knew her face was blotchy and her hair was tangled. Eliza didn't say anything to him. She went to the rain barrel, skimming the surface scum of flies and dead mosquitoes, cupping water in her hands. She took her time washing up, not wanting to talk to Jem — or anyone else — but not caring enough to avoid it. Nothing meant a damn now that Cole was gone.

Eliza wiped her face on her sleeve and dried her hands in her skirt. Jem hadn't moved from where he stood, and his expression hadn't changed. In fact, it seemed worse now. He stood there, twisting one ankle while he stared at her, pulling his cheeks in until his face was so angled and hollow he looked like a corpse. Like Old Man Willoughby last fall, lying in his coffin all shrunken and carved out. They said he'd starved to death, and Eliza had believed it; he'd always stared at her like he was starving — that same hungry way Jem was staring at her now.

She walked around to face him. "What d'you want, Jem?"

Daddy stuck his head out the open door. "Hey, Jem. Thought that was you standin' out there. Want some biscuits or somethin'?"

Jem shook his head. "No, thanks, Jack. I just come to talk to Eliza a minute."

"All right, then." Daddy nodded. He frowned at Eliza. "You be a good girl, now, Lizzie."

Jem cleared his throat when her father disappeared back inside. He jerked his head to the fields. "Come on out there. What I got to say to you I'd rather not insult your pa with."

Eliza raised a brow at him, but she didn't protest. She followed him out into the fields until he stopped and stood poking his toe into the dirt.

He was quiet for so long Eliza grew impatient. "Spit it out, Jem. The day's wasting."

He nodded and pursed his lips. "I was in town last night, Liza."

He was looking at her as if his words should mean something to her. Eliza looked back at him. "And?"

"I heard some talk that's got me mighty disturbed. Mighty disturbed."

It didn't surprise her. She'd known what Jem came to talk to her about the moment she saw him this morning.

"I was talkin' to Billy Richards."

Billy Richards. Not Will Ames. So the whole town knew. She was common gossip.

She didn't want to think about what that meant, and so she concentrated on Jem's face, on her unexpected relief. She wished he would just say the words and go away. Just say, *I don't think I can marry you, Eliza,* so she could think about the fact that she wouldn't be married to him, wouldn't be living in his shack, raising his children, and not about what the townspeople would think of her now, what she would be.

Jem went on doggedly. "He says you . . . you and some gambler . . ." He looked at her expectantly. "Well, I guess you know what I mean."

She eyed him steadily. "I guess I do."

"Is it a lie?"

She shook her head. "No."

His brows came together like he was concentrating hard. "Let me see if I got this right, then. You tellin' me you was with him?"

"Yeah."

His throat worked as he stumbled over the words. "I . . . You mean you —"

"What d'you want me to tell you, Jem?" There was a meanness inside of her that Eliza couldn't shake, a bitterness that made her give Jem a cool, long look, that made her be cruel. "He kissed me. He took off my clothes. I laid with him. That enough for you? Or d'you want me to recount the whole thing?"

She felt bad the moment she said it. Jem turned ashen, his whole body went stiff. He looked at the ground, at the trees in the distance, at anything but her "You were promised to me, Eliza," he said softly, and the wealth of disappointment and reproof in his voice made her flinch. "You was goin' to be my wife."

Eliza shook her head. "We wouldn't suit, Jem."

It was like he didn't hear her. "I can't marry you now." He looked up at her then, and the disappointment was gone; there was only anger and pain. "I ain't the only one who feels that way. No one'll have you now, Eliza. I should've listened to what they said about you. I guess they're right. You're just a whore."

Anger surged through her body into her hand before she could think about it, and she hit him with all her strength. Jem jerked back She'd hit him so hard the imprint of her fingers was red against his cheek.

His hand went to his face. "Damn you —"

"Go to hell, Jem." She struggled to control the shaking in her voice, but her hands were shaking too, her whole body trembling. She twisted on her heel, meaning to stomp away from him, to run away, when he grabbed her arm and wrenched her back. He stuck his face in hers, so close his pointy chin nearly stabbed her.

"I wanted to spare your pa this," he ground out. "But you've gone and done it, Eliza. I was goin' to lie to save him —"

"Don't lie," she spat. "Tell him the damn truth if you want." She yanked away from him, rubbing her arm where he'd grabbed it, and then she stumbled over the furrows, past the shanty, out to the road, but when she got there she realized there was no place to go, no place to run. Cole was gone, and the whole town knew what she'd done with him. It was bad enough now, the way the Richmond ladies avoided her, the way they turned their heads when she approached. The men already leered at her; what would it be like now?

She knew what it would be like. It would be like yesterday morning and Will. Eliza worked to swallow her tears, but they welled up in her throat and pressed behind her eyes until her whole head ached with them. She looked over her shoulder to see Jem walking slowly to the shanty, and she knew what he would do when he got there.

She wondered how long she could stay away from home. Maybe there was a place she could go, a place to hide. But she didn't have any money — she wasn't even wearing shoes — and she wouldn't be able to escape her father's anger, no matter how long she stayed away. Better to face it now, to get it over with.

Jem was at the door. Eliza saw her father meet him there, wiping his hands on his pants, inviting Jem in. She saw Jem say something and Daddy stiffen, and then he was looking to where she stood.

Eliza steadied herself. She squeezed her eyes shut to banish her tears, and was surprised to find they were gone already. She walked across the road, back to the shanty.

When she got there, the house was quiet. Eliza stepped inside. In the dimness, she saw Daddy sitting there, staring into his coffee while Jem rubbed his fingers nervously across his cheek. Mama had disappeared into the corner.

Disappointment lingered in the air like smoke from a mosquito smudge. Daddy looked up at her, his expression deader than she'd ever seen it.

"Eliza Mae," he said heavily. "Is it true what Jem says?"

"If what he told you was about Cole Wallace and me," Eliza said quietly, "then it's true."

He nodded. His blunt fingers gripped his cup. "What is it you were thinkin', girl?"

"That he'd marry me," she replied honestly. "That he'd take me away from here."

"You hated what I'd planned for you that much?"

Eliza met Jem's gaze. She nodded. "Yes."

Jem flinched and looked away. Daddy sighed. He seemed boneless, like his whole body was sagging into the table, into his coffee. She couldn't breathe for the weight of his disappointment.

"Daddy —"

He shook his head, cutting her off. "You

go on outside, Eliza," he said. "Get to work. I don't want to see your face just now."

She stepped toward him. "Daddy —"

Mama emerged from the shadows. She jerked her head, a tiny movement. "Go on out, Lizzie," she said quietly.

The softness of the command brought Eliza up short. She looked up at her mother. Mama's eyes were burning; the anger in them surprised Eliza as much as her father's quiet.

She swallowed and straightened, backing away. "All right," she said. "All right." She turned and left them there in the single dark room, trading their disappointment and anger for the bright sunshine, and a sadness that seemed to sink into her very bones.

It was a hot day. She felt the heat on her back, blasting through her dress, felt the sweat gathering where the brim of her hat pressed against her forehead, trickling between her breasts. It was too hot for spring, and with a start Eliza realized it was nearly June already.

She sat back on her heels, wiping at her face with the back of a dirty hand. Summer. She'd sworn she wouldn't live another one in Richmond, but here she was, and she had no plans to be anywhere else. It had been two months since Cole left, and she was still here, working these damn cotton fields and looking up at the sun and wishing — praying — she were somewhere else.

Eliza bent back down to the plants, attacking one so viciously the effort left her a little faint. She took a deep breath and glanced to where her mother was, a few yards away. Mama worked at the same pace whether it was a cool spring day or the hottest summer one. Eliza wondered what her mother thought about, what things went through her mind as she stared down at that cotton. Mama barely ever even lifted her eyes.

Eliza sighed and looked back down. The plants swayed for a moment; a wave of nausea passed through her so quickly she thought maybe she'd imagined it. It felt as if the sun were draining the life from her; the heat, the work . . . she was just so tired.

"Eliza!" Daddy's voice floated across the fields.

Eliza twisted, shading her eyes with her hand as she watched him come toward her. It was so surprising that he was talking to her she didn't even feel dread. Daddy had barely spoken to her since Jem took back his marriage proposal.

She got to her feet. When he was within talking distance, he reached into his pocket and took out a coin. "I need you to go on into town and pick me up some twine," he said, handing it to her.

Cold sweat rose on her skin. *Town.* Eliza's mouth went dry. "You sure you need it?" she asked. "Today?"

He frowned. "Don't sass me, girl. Hurry now."

"Daddy —" The coin felt hot and heavy in her hand. "Maybe I won't find the right kind —"

Daddy's brows came down over his eyes, his gaze darkened. "Just some sisal twine, Eliza. Paul Adams'll show you what's what."

"I don't —"

"You get your ass into town, Eliza Mae," he said, and his voice was cold and heavy. "And come right back. I don't got time for your lollygaggin'."

He turned and started back across the fields. Eliza glanced at her mother, who was watching with dark and quiet eyes, and she saw the pity come into Mama's face before Mama looked down again.

Eliza clutched the coin. She looked to the road — the road that had been her path to freedom just weeks before — and a chill made her shiver in the hot sun. She felt truly sick now. The thought of going into town, of seeing the looks . . . she didn't want to do it. Not today, not ever again.

She'd gone into town once since the morning Cole left, and she never wanted to go back. She'd seen the men whispering about her, saw their hungry eyes, and she'd been halfway to the Feed and Seed when Peter Griggs came walking up with two men she'd never seen before. Cousins, he'd said. From Dallas. They talked nice enough, but Eliza had seen the sharpness of their eyes, and she'd been afraid as they walked her to the Feed and Seed.

She'd been desperate to get away, but she smiled and tried not to look afraid. When she finally got to the store, she'd called out to Mr. Adams and acted stupid and asked for him to please show her where the birdseed was, because there was a crane that kept coming round and she thought if she fed it, it might stay.

Mr. Adams had laughed and told her cranes ate fish, and she was lucky it came by at all, given that dirt-yard they lived on, and that had made the others laugh too. They left her then, but she'd cut out the back just to be sure and hurried home. She hadn't been to town since. She was scared to go back.

"Go on, Lizzie," Mama said. "Before your daddy gets mad."

Eliza looked at her mother. "Mama, I don't think I can."

Mama's lips pursed. "You made your bed, now you got to sleep in it."

Eliza winced. She looked away. There was a numbness working its way through her body, tightening around her heart.

She clutched the coin and started walking back through the fields, out to the road. She was sweating and sick by the time she got there, it was so hot. She took her hat off and fanned herself with it, but the air was humid and heavy and hard to breathe, and Eliza stopped, trying to take a breath, swallowing the nausea forcing its way up her throat.

She told herself to relax. It was just a quick trip into town. She'd stay behind the buildings until she got to the Feed and Seed, and then she'd slip between the Brass Key Saloon and the druggist's. If she raced across the street, maybe no one would see her. She would go as fast as she could. . . .

Eliza stopped, pressing her hand into her stomach as a wave of light-headedness hit her. The nausea came on so strong she fell to her knees, vomiting her breakfast into the cotton.

When it was over, she sat back, taking great deep gulps of air, wiping her hand across her face. Her eyes were watering. She looked to the rain barrel; it looked impossibly far away. "What the hell're you doin', girl?" Daddy yelled out at her. "Stop sittin' around, and get on into town, you hear me?"

Eliza stumbled to her feet. She felt better now, a little stronger, but she was so hot and light-headed. So damn hot . . .

She took two steps and crumbled. She felt her head hit the ground, and then there was nothing.

When she opened her eyes again, she was in the shanty, lying on her own pallet. It was dark, and the darkness and the cool humidity of the house felt good against her eyes. There was a sound beside her; she looked to see her mother wringing out a cloth.

"Feelin' better?" Mama asked.

Eliza nodded.

"Good." Mama smoothed back Eliza's hair. The cloth was cool and wet. It made Eliza want to close her eyes and sleep.

"I'm sorry," she murmured. "I was just so hot. Must've been heatstroke."

"Mmmm." Mama kept stroking. "When'd you last have your monthlies, Lizzie?"

Eliza tried to shrug, but it was too much effort. "Ummm, I don't know. Maybe . . . a while ago."

95

"Before you met that gambler?"

Eliza squeezed her eyes shut, tried to remember. She nodded. "Think so."

Mama dipped the cloth into a pan of water and wrung it out again. She pressed it to Eliza's face. Eliza couldn't remember the last time her mother had done this. When she was little, maybe, and she had a fever —

"Eliza." Mama's voice was gentle. "You ain't sick."

Eliza opened her eyes. Beyond the gentleness was a light rebuke, a scold. She felt the sudden, sharp ache of tears, and Eliza struggled to her elbows, pushing away her mother's hand.

"I s'pose it was the sun —"

"I think you're with child."

The words were like a blow, so surprising, so hard. Eliza fell back, staring at her mother. She'd been hearing things. Surely Mama hadn't said —

"You're expectin', Lizzie."

"You're joking, ain't you?"

Mama shook her head slowly, a slight smile on her face. "No, I ain't jokin'. How you been feelin'? Tired? Kind of sore? You been sick a lot?"

"I never threw up before today."

"Still, you felt sick."

"It's been hot. The sun —"

"The sun doesn't have anythin' to do with this."

Eliza tried to swallow, but her throat was so tight it just caught there. "I can't be," she said. "I can't be."

"Can't you?" Mama put the cloth into the bowl of water and sat back. "You tellin' me that you lied, that Jem lied? You tellin' me you didn't lay with that gamblin' man?"

Eliza stared at her mother, feeling like any move might break her, that the slightest nod would snap her in two. "No," she said finally, slowly. "It wasn't a lie."

"You had your monthly flow since then?"

"No."

"You're goin' to have a baby, Lizzie." Mama sighed. "I'd guess, prob'ly around January, if you carry to term."

Shivers rose on Eliza's skin. She felt cold to the bone. "Oh my God," she said. "Oh, God."

She was pregnant. She was going to have a baby. She looked into her mother's eyes, and Mama's words came back to her, *"Maybe he'll get you with child and leave you. Have you thought of that, Lizzie? Have you thought of what you'll do then?"*

Eliza brought her knees up to her chest, locked her arms around them and buried her face in the crook of her elbow. "Oh, Mama," she said. "What am I going to do? What am I going to do?"

Mama sighed again. Eliza heard her mother's bones creak as Mama got to her feet, the slosh of water and the clunk of the tin bowl when Mama set it on the table.

"I don't know what you're goin' to do, Lizzie," she said, and the heaviness of her words took Eliza's breath, stopped her heart.

"But, Mama . . ."

Eliza trailed off at the sound of footsteps outside the shanty door. She heard the scrape of her father's boots, and then he was bending through the doorway, his pale gaze stabbing through the darkness, landing on her. He stopped just inside, slumping beneath the low ceiling, so quiet all Eliza could feel was his anger.

"Daddy," she said.

He just looked at her. Then he glanced at Mama. Eliza saw her mother's quick, quiet nod, and Daddy's face tightened. He lifted his rifle from the hooks beside the door, that old Henry repeater some soldier had sold him eight years ago. He grabbed the pouch of cartridges and tucked them into his belt, and then he turned back to face her again. His face was as grave as she had ever seen it.

"What was his name, again, Eliza?" he asked slowly. "Tell me his name."

6

Mid-June, Bremond, Texas

Cole waved to the barmaid for another bottle of whiskey before he fanned his cards in his palm. A decent hand, not the best, but still enough to work with. He glanced at his fellow players, watching them with a nonchalance he'd perfected over the years. He saw the old man, Harry, squint, and knew his hand was bad. Leroy Perkins rubbed the side of his cheek — a decent hand — and that fuzzy-haired Pole was as stone-faced as usual. He wouldn't give anything away until the stakes started going up.

Cole sighed and puffed on his cigar. When the barmaid brought the whiskey he poured some all around. Bremond, Texas, had been good to him the few days he'd been here. The townspeople had money to spend, as he'd expected, and there were plenty of men willing to risk it in a friendly game of poker. It had been a good idea to follow the tracks of the Houston and Texas Central. Cole had decided to keep to the rails until he reached

Dallas, and he was glad he had. The towns along the route had proved to be rich and well worth his time. With any luck, by the time he reached Dallas, he'd have enough stored in his money belt to impress a certain brown-eyed lady.

"You're smilin' there like you've won already," Leroy grumbled. He pushed two cards toward Cole. "Give me two."

"Two it is." Cole drew two cards from the deck. "Anyone else?"

The others traded in their cards, and Cole sat back and puffed on his cigar. He watched the pile of money grow in the center of the table, wildcat banknotes and pesos, a promissory note. He looked down at his cards, rearranged them in his hand, watched the others. There went the Pole, tapping his finger on the table, a steady beat. He was bluffing. Harry was still squinting. Only Leroy looked like he had anything at all.

Cole threw in another banknote. "I'll raise five," he said.

Harry threw in his cards. "Can't do it."

The Pole pursed his lips and exhaled slowly. "I'm out."

Leroy raised his eyes to meet Cole's gaze. Deliberately, he picked up a note and dropped it into the pile. "Let's see what you got, fancy man."

Cole spread his cards. "Twos and jacks high."

Leroy grinned. "Three ladies, my friend."

Cole watched Leroy scrape up the money. It was a bad loss; the worst he'd had today. He hoped his luck wasn't turning. He'd planned to stay in Bremond at least another day. He took his cigar from his mouth and picked up his whiskey, downing the shot. His own pile was still high; he supposed he could afford one or two big losses. But not more than that. Another play like that one and he'd be gone, on his way to his room above that hell of a saloon down the street.

He passed the cards to Leroy and waited for him to shuffle and deal. The music in the saloon seemed to grow louder — some amateur playing "Oh, Susannah!" on the tin-keyed piano. He winced at a sharp burst of laughter from a nearby table and poured another drink.

"Any of you boys know Cole Wallace?"

The voice came from behind him, gravelly and low. The Pole and Harry looked up with interest; Leroy kept shuffling.

Cole took a long puff on his cigar. He didn't bother to turn around. No doubt one of those losers from the other night, though he didn't recognize the voice. "Who wants to know?"

"Jack Beaudry. Sound familiar?"

It did, vaguely. Jack. Had there been a Jack last night? Or the night before? Hell, he couldn't remember. It must have been —

Beaudry.

He remembered her then. Blond hair and blue eyes with dark brows. Breasts to fill a man's hands and bug out his eyes. *Eliza Beaudry.*

Slowly, very slowly, he turned in his chair. Jack Beaudry was so tall Cole had to crane his neck to see him. Beaudry was loose-limbed and slump-shouldered, and though his face was lined and old, his hair was as blond as the noonday sun, his blue eyes sharp. He held an old Henry rifle at his side like an extension of his arm, and his knuckles were white where he gripped it.

"I'm Cole Wallace," Cole said.

"I'd like to say pleased to meet you," Jack said. "But if it wasn't for my girl, I'd just as soon see you dead."

Cole felt the boys at the table go still except for Leroy's shuffling. The *shoosh, brrr* of the cards filled his ears. Cole nodded, but his heart was racing and his fingers were numb as he ground out his cigar. He drained his glass, and then he got to his feet and turned to the others.

"Looks like Mr. Beaudry here has something to discuss with me," he said, gathering up his money. "If you don't mind . . ."

"Come on back later if you want," Harry said.

Cole nodded. He shoved his money in his bag. "Let's go outside," he said.

Jack Beaudry barely changed his expression. He followed Cole through the bar. Cole shifted his shoulders, trying to ease the itching in the middle of his back that came at the thought of that old rifle.

The feeling didn't ease once they got outside. The hot humidity knocked him back, stealing the air from his lungs. There was a cold spot in the pit of his stomach that only got worse when he turned to face Jack Beaudry and realized how much Eliza looked like her father.

Cole took a deep breath and opened his mouth to say something to the man who had come all the way from Richmond to find him.

"She's pregnant," Jack said bluntly.

Cole froze. "What does that have to do with me?"

"You're the father."

"How do you know?"

Jack Beaudry's fist cracked against his jaw so quick and hard Cole stumbled back, falling hard onto the street. Pain filled his whole head; his ears rang. For a moment he saw only blackness, but then his vision cleared and he was staring up at Jack Beaudry, who towered over him, a big, dark shadow blocking the late afternoon sun.

"You want to say that again?"

Cole struggled to his elbows. His jaw felt loosened from its socket; he rubbed it carefully and shook his head. "No, sir," he said.

"You meanin' to tell me you ain't the child's father?"

Cole sat up. He felt sick. His jaw throbbed. He thought of Eliza Beaudry tightening against him that day by the river, her soft hush of protest. He thought of lying, but Jack Beaudry's fist was still clenched, and Cole felt a dim sort of honor about protecting Eliza's reputation, such as it was. She'd been a virgin that day; he supposed he owed it to her to be honest about it. "I'm not telling you that," he said.

Jack nodded with what looked like satisfaction. He leaned the rifle against the porch pillar and extended his hand. "Come on, then."

Cole hesitated for a moment, but Jack didn't take back his hand. Finally, Cole grasped it, and the man hauled him to his feet. When Cole was standing again, Jack picked up the gun.

Beaudry started to walk away. He'd only taken a few steps when he turned around and motioned to Cole, who hadn't moved. "Let's get goin'," Jack said. "It's a long ride."

Dread washed through Cole. He stared at Jack Beaudry, feeling frozen in place. "Get going?" he asked in a low voice. "Where?"

"Back to Richmond," Beaudry said tersely. "I got a preacher waitin'."

Cole fumbled for a cigar with nerveless fingers. He grabbed one, dropped it, bent to pick it up. It rolled away. His hands shook when he finally managed to hold onto it; it took all his concentration to light it. When he finally did, the smoke choked him. His throat was so tight he could barely breathe, much less smoke. Jack Beaudry just stood there watching him, and under his sharp, pale gaze, Cole gave up. He dropped the cigar to the street, ground it out with his boot.

He licked his lips. "I can't marry her," he said. He couldn't put power in the words; they were so quiet they sounded like a whisper. He thought of Jenny, of beautiful, brown-eyed Jenny. "I'm . . . betrothed to someone else."

"Well, then, you'd better unbetroth yourself," Jack said, fingering his gun. "Because my Eliza needs a husband, and it looks like you're it."

Cole stared beyond Jack Beaudry to the road that stretched into the horizon. He wondered how fast he could run, how far he could get, and then before he could finish the thought, he saw how the sun was setting, the creeping shadows closing in before him, cutting him off. His vision narrowed to the man standing in front of him, rifle held at the ready.

Cole fumbled with his money pouch. "How much?" he asked.

Beaudry frowned. "What?"

Cole's mouth was almost too dry to form the words. "How much money do you want?" He held out the bag and met Jack's gaze. "I'll give you whatever you want. Take it back to her. Tell her I'll help support the baby. Whatever she wants."

"She wants marriage."

"That's the only thing I can't give her."

Jack advanced. His face darkened. He waved the rifle. "You're comin' with me. You're marryin' my girl."

"There's close to a hundred dollars in here," Cole insisted. "There'll be more if she wants it."

Jack was only inches away. His eyes narrowed to slits. Anger jumped in a little vein beside his temple. "You're comin' with me, Cole Wallace," Beaudry said. "If I have to hog-tie you to get you there."

Cole felt the blood in his face drain away. He knew Beaudry meant every word. But Eliza was not what he wanted. She was just a trashy poor girl setting a trap, and he'd fallen into it — hell, he'd hurled himself into it. He'd known better. He'd *known*.

What the hell would he do with Eliza Beaudry? Stick her on a farm somewhere, become a farmer like his father? Like Aaron. *Aaron. Of course.*

Hope trickled in, barely there, but hope nonetheless. Aaron would help him — he always did. Cole looked up at Jack Beaudry and thought fast. "All right," he said. "All right, I'll go see Eliza. I'll do whatever she wants. But first, I have to do something."

Jack shook his head. "No somethin's —"

"You haven't got a choice in this," Cole said. "I've got to take care of . . . things. Then I'll come down to Richmond. I swear it."

Jack frowned suspiciously. "You already ran off once."

"That was before I knew she was . . ." Cole couldn't bring himself to say it. "Look, I give you my word. Give me two weeks, that's all. Two weeks, and I'll come see Eliza.

Then we can decide what it is she wants."

Jack eyed him steadily, then he shook his head. "How do I know you won't disappear?"

Cole reached into his vest pocket and drew out his card. It was simple and unadorned, and all that was on it was his name. He turned it over and pulled out his pocket watch, uncapping a short pencil from the fob. "This is where my father's farm is," he said, scrawling the direction on the card. "You lose me, you find them. Believe me, my father will make sure you're satisfied." He capped the pencil and handed Jack the card.

Jack held it between his fingers like it was a dead rat. "I don't know what the hell this says."

"It says 'Thomas Wallace. Wallace Ranch. White Horse, Texas,' " Cole said impatiently. "That's my father. You get close to Fort Griffin or Fort Belknap, and they'll point you the way."

"Look, I don't know what you take me for —"

"I take you for an intelligent man," Cole said smoothly. He saw the indecision in Jack's face, and for the first time since Beaudry had walked into the saloon and asked for him, Cole felt his confidence return. "I'm like any man, Mr. Beaudry. I can't just up and get married without telling my family. Surely you understand that, being the gentleman you are." He opened the money pouch and took out ten dollars. "You give this to Eliza, and you tell her I'll see her in two weeks."

"Two weeks." Jack Beaudry sighed, and then he nodded. He reached for the money, tucking it in his pocket, and then his face darkened again. "But if you ain't on my farm in two weeks, Wallace —"

"I will be," Cole assured him.

"If you ain't . . ." Beaudry lifted the rifle. He trained it on Cole, shifted the sights, put it aside. "You'll wish you was dead when I'm through with you. I promise you that."

He turned; Cole watched him walk down the street. He watched until Jack Beaudry mounted a horse and rode out of Bremond.

Cole's relief was fleeting; the moment Beaudry disappeared, Cole's desperation returned. He had two weeks. Two weeks to get to White Horse. Two weeks for Aaron to get him out of this mess.

White Horse, Texas

Aaron Wallace stepped to the edge of the porch and shaded his eyes to look up at the sky. It was clear and blue, not a cloud for

109

miles, and the morning sun was already re-lentlessly hot. He sighed and shook back his hair, squinting as he looked out into the corn. Carlos and Miguel were already there; he saw the sun glancing off their hats. He should go join them. There was more than enough work for three.

But it had been a hard morning, and he was already tired. Aaron glanced over his shoulder, up to the corner window half shaded by a giant fig tree. The old cripple was in fine form today. It was amazing that a man who couldn't speak could shake up the house this much. Miguel had been so upset he'd burned breakfast — not that he didn't usually, but today's grits had been even more scorched and pasty, the corn-bread so dry it had taken nearly a pot of coffee apiece to wash it down.

It wore Aaron out just thinking about it, and so he didn't think about it. He looked away from the house and out toward the creek, to the ancient post oak shading it. The light glittered on its leaves, shimmery, silvering before it fell away to sparkle on the water. There was a crow sitting in the top branches, and the sun played on its blackness, painted a feather. The beauty of it stole his breath, and just like that, he forgot the cornfields and the Mexicans out working in them. He forgot his father.

He was reaching in his pocket for paper and pencil even as he strode to the post oak. The crow flew away with a raucous caw that startled him because he'd already forgotten about the bird. He settled himself against the trunk of the tree and pulled up the wooden box he always kept there.

The paper in his pocket was folded, the creases tearing from the many times he'd taken it out. It was already covered with his cramped writing, words and sentences played out, jumbled and careted, tiny words and tinier additions. Aaron smoothed it against the lid of the box, took his short and broken pencil between his fingers. The creek faded before him. He saw nothing but the paper, felt nothing but the rough, tactile sense of it beneath his hand, heard only the scratching of his pencil — and even those things faded in the excitement of the words.

The poem fell into place before his eyes, the phrases he'd been working on for days settled into him, meaningful at last, pointing their direction. *No, here, and . . . here. Ah yes, the word was better over there, wasn't it?* The rhythms broke in his head, the syllables fell apart and joined together again. The vision formed, beautiful and perfect. He couldn't write fast enough to get it down —

"Hello, Aaron."

The voice burst in on him. The vision shattered. He was left holding his pencil and staring down at the paper, unsure where the sentence had been leading him, not even remembering the next word. He looked up, blinking against a sun that was now high overhead, blinking into a shadow. He felt fogged, as if he'd suddenly come out of a deep sleep.

Aaron closed his eyes for a second, opened them again, and saw the man standing before him.

It took a moment for it to register. It was his brother standing there. A man he hadn't seen in three years. A stranger.

"Cole." Aaron pushed aside the box, folded the paper and stuffed it into his pocket along with the pencil. Then he got to his feet. His hair fell into his face and he pushed it back and offered his hand to his brother.

Cole shook it. He grinned. "You need a haircut."

A haircut. It took a minute for Aaron to understand. He frowned. He glanced toward the fields and saw that Carlos and Miguel were heading in. He looked back up at the sky. "You're just in time for dinner," he said.

112

Cole laughed shortly and shook his head. "Damn, you amaze me, man. You act like I only went into town for an hour or so. You don't even seem surprised to see me."

Aaron took a deep breath. The only thing that surprised him was how unsurprised he was to see his brother, though he supposed he should have felt some sense of . . . impending doom this morning, some forewarning. He hadn't; the day had started like any other day, except for Pa's temper tantrum.

That should have been warning enough.

"I guess nothing surprises me anymore," he said wryly.

Cole raised a brow. "Really?"

Carlos and Miguel had stopped at the edge of what passed for a yard. Carlos had his foot up on the tumbling split-rail fence, leaning forward to see, and Miguel had a hand against the pocket where he kept his gun.

"New boys?" Cole asked. He shoved his hands in his pocket. "Well, it's good to see they're so vigilant about protecting my baby brother. God knows you need it. You'd better introduce me before they start using my liver as target practice."

He began to stride away, but Aaron didn't move, and Cole had only taken a few steps when he turned back again, a half smile on his face. "You want them to shoot me?"

Aaron waved his hand, and Carlos and Miguel both relaxed.

"How much d'you need, Cole?" Aaron asked quietly.

Cole took a deep breath and looked toward the house. "How's Pa?"

"All right."

"Good. Good."

"Cole —"

"What do you say we talk over dinner?" Cole said. "I'm starving."

He started to the house. Aaron watched him go, feeling awkward and at a disadvantage when he saw how smoothly his brother strode to the door, how self-assured Cole seemed as he went inside, as if he'd been gone three days instead of three years. He looked good too, not like someone who needed money. Cole's hair was fashionably cut, his clothes expensive and well-kept. Aaron ran his hand through his too-long hair, looked down at his scuffed boots, the patches on his pants, and the promise of the day faded before him, the weariness he'd felt this morning came back.

Miguel had already gone to the house, and Carlos followed Cole. Now the farmhand stood on the porch, waiting, his body tense. Aaron sighed and trudged through the yard.

"*Amigo,*" Carlos said. "You do not look

114

so good. If it is this man, I can —"

"He's my brother, Carlos," Aaron said.

Carlos's mouth snapped shut. His heavy mustache twitched. But he didn't say anything else, and he stood back to let Aaron go into the house.

The first thing Aaron noticed was the scorched smell. Then he saw the smoke pouring from the kitchen. He rushed inside, instinctively stepping between piles of books and papers. Cole turned to him from the table, looking cool and unruffled.

"Looks like you need a new cook, brother," he said.

A curse echoed from the kitchen, followed by half a dozen indecipherable words. Aaron felt Carlos push past him. Carlos stuck his head through the kitchen doorway and came back out again, sitting gingerly in his chair.

"It is nothing," he said. "Tamales, like his mother used to make. He makes them cook all day, and now the water has" — he frowned, gesturing with his hands — "gone away."

From upstairs came the sound of banging, sharp, heavy raps on the floor. *Bang, bang, bang,* followed by a hoarse, garbled yell.

Aaron sighed. He glanced to the stairs. "Carlos —"

"Not me." Carlos shook his head emphatically. "I was there today already."

More cursing came from the kitchen. The banging on the floor grew harder and faster.

Cole looked at the ceiling. "Let me guess," he said. "The old man. Welcoming me home, no doubt."

"Why don't you go on up, then?" Aaron suggested. "I'm sure he'd like to see you."

Cole laughed. "Not on a bet, brother. Not without a shield." He leaned back in his chair, drawing out a cigar and putting it between his teeth. "Give him my love."

Resentment nearly choked Aaron. He stared at his brother, playing with that damned cigar, relaxed and amused, and thought of all the times he'd gone up those stairs to that *bang, bang, bang.* Something crashed against the floor, breaking and scattering, and just as he had every time before, Aaron looked toward the open door, toward the post oak by the creek, and thought about walking away, leaving it all behind, leaving this for someone else to clean up.

But he didn't. Just as he always did, Aaron went up the stairs. His father's room was at the front of the house, beneath the deeply slanted roof. Pa was yelling now, that sickening, croaking sound. Aaron stopped outside the door, calming himself, and then pushed it open and stood back, waiting for

116

the hit. It came: a water pitcher cracked against the doorjamb and shattered on the floor, joining its matching basin. He eased his head around the corner.

"You done?" he asked.

Pa glared at him — as much as he could with half of his face sagging and immobile. He lifted his left arm, banging a twisted cane fashioned from an oak branch once more on the floor, dislodging a pile of books before he leaned it against the wall. He fumbled for the slate lying across his knees, for the piece of chalk tied to it.

The scraping of the chalk was loud in the sudden silence. Aaron ducked into the room, opening the door wider, catching shards of pottery in its sweep. His bootsteps crunched.

The sun beat on this side of the house all morning, and as a result the room was sweltering. Aaron broke into a sweat just walking inside.

Pa held up the chalkboard. "IT STINKS."

"Miguel burned the tamales."

Pa erased the board so furiously it looked ready to shake loose of his clumsy hold. Aaron waited. He looked out the large dormer window, beneath the half-pulled blind. The sun played on the creek beyond; that lone crow was sitting in the oak again.

Pa rapped the side of the chalkboard.

Aaron looked over at him.

"IT STANK FOR TWO HOURS. I RANG."

Aaron looked for the bell on the bedstand. It wasn't there. He saw it angled against the wall where his father had thrown it. The sight filled him with a dim sense of satisfaction; for a moment he thought about just leaving it there, letting Pa be frustrated for the rest of the day. Then he went over and picked it up, setting it on the bedstand, within his father's reach.

"Sorry," he said shortly. "I didn't hear you."

Pa started writing. His shaggy gray hair fell into his face as his arm jerked across the board.

Aaron glanced away. "Cole's here."

The scratching on the chalkboard stopped. Aaron didn't turn from the window. He already knew what he'd see on his father's face, and the thought of it started a slow burn inside him.

The chalk squeaked again. Aaron heard his father's labored breathing; it was so loud the walls of the room seemed to bend and sway with it. *In and out, in and out.* The frayed blind shivered, and the yarn-covered pull-ring moved like a pendulum back and forth. It took him a minute to realize it wasn't in rhythm with his father at all, but moving to his own breathing.

Clap, clap, clap.

Aaron turned. Pa was slapping his good hand hard against the chalkboard. The old man's face was red. Aaron read the board.

"ABOUT TIME. FARM'S GOING TO HELL."

The farm was doing better than ever, and Pa knew it. The spring rains hadn't come this year; that was the only problem. Aaron knew this game, too, but still his father's criticism stung.

"Cole doesn't know anything about farming," he said.

"COLE'S A MAN." *Man* was underlined twice.

Aaron took a deep breath. "I'll bring him up."

He left quickly, before his father could protest, hurrying down the short hall, down the narrow flight of stairs. The others looked up as he reached the bottom. Coffee was on the table and Miguel was serving up blackened tamales and explaining to Cole that if he just took off the cornhusk, there was no burn beneath, and the scorched taste was not so bad. . . .

Cole pushed back his plate. "No, thanks, *amigo,*" he said. He looked at Aaron, a question in his eyes.

"He wants to see you."

Cole sighed. He took a sip of coffee and stood. "I can see he hasn't lost that temper of his."

"Oh, he loses it all the time," Aaron said dryly. He stepped back to let Cole pass him, and to his surprise Cole stopped.

"Come with me," he said. Then, when Aaron stared at him, Cole looked away as if he were embarrassed by the request. "He's not killing the fatted calf for me, you know. It'll be better if you're there."

7

Aaron stared at his brother. The one thing Cole had never been was afraid of Pa. Aaron had always envied him that, the way Cole never backed down, the way he shoved in and gave as good as he got. But this — this was not the brother Aaron knew.

He had no time to question it further. Cole took a deep breath and started up the stairs. "Come on," he said, "into the lion's den." He turned and waited until Aaron sighed and followed him, and then he climbed quickly. At the door to Pa's room, Cole straightened.

"Hey there, old man," he said. Broken pottery crunched beneath his boots as he stepped inside. "I hear you're as mean as ever."

Aaron saw Pa's eyes light up — even the rheumy one — though his expression was just as cantankerous as always. Aaron came forward, but Pa threw him a dismissive look, and waved him away, and the old, familiar pain over his father's favoritism hit Aaron like a blow. He caught his breath and stepped back. It had been a long time since he'd felt it, long enough that he'd thought the hurt was gone. But it was just as strong as ever; it took all his effort to swallow it and step to the window. He crossed his arms over his chest and leaned back against the sill, waiting.

"I'M NOT DEAD YET," read the chalkboard. "YOU'RE TOO DAMN EARLY FOR MY MONEY."

Cole threw Aaron a see-what-I-mean? look.

"I guess God's not listening to my prayers, then," Cole said.

One side of Pa's mouth turned down. Even though Aaron was used to it, the lopsidedness of his father's face never failed to disconcert him. It didn't seem to faze Cole; not even a flicker of surprise registered in his eyes.

Pa rubbed off the chalkboard with the sleeve of his dressing gown — a sleeve already white with chalk dust. His left hand shook as he wrote, he pressed down so hard it sounded as if he were etching words into the slate.

"WHAT DO YOU WANT?"

Cole sighed. "So much for the welcoming party."

Pa directed his gaze at Aaron, and Aaron didn't miss the order in his father's expression. For a moment he wanted to ignore him, to let Pa suffer for that earlier dismissal. But his father's glare grew more intense, and Cole was frowning, and in the end, habit won out. In the three years since Pa's stroke, Aaron had spoken for his father more often than he could tell. He knew the words, he even knew the right tone to take.

"You in trouble, Cole?"

Cole looked over at him and smiled thinly. "You the local ventriloquist, baby brother?"

Aaron didn't bother to answer.

Cole took off his hat and laid it aside, and then he tugged at his collar. "Damn, it's hot in here."

"Pa doesn't like the window open."

"I see." Cole reached into his pocket and drew out a cigar.

Aaron stepped forward. "You can't smoke in —"

Pa waved his hand wildly. He nodded at Cole, who frowned and looked from Pa to Aaron and back again.

"What's that mean? It's all right?"

Pa nodded.

Aaron sat back on the sill, feeling humiliatingly chastened. Cole had barely been back an hour and already Aaron was feeling like the ineffectual baby brother — unimportant, vaguely ridiculous. In three years, he hadn't felt like that. Not since the last time his brother had come riding home.

The air pressed in around him, close and hot, and he had the sudden urge to rush out, to leave Cole to deal with Pa on his own. But he didn't. Cole had come home because he wanted help — it was the only reason they ever heard from him — and Aaron knew Cole would turn to him, just as he always did. And though he did not want to know what Cole wanted, Aaron couldn't walk away — the habit was too strong, his father's voice too loud. *"You owe him. You'll always owe him. . . ."*

Cole put the cigar in his mouth, but he didn't light it. He shrugged off his coat to reveal a blinding white shirt and a silver vest. "Well," he said, and then, "well," again. He chewed on the end of his cigar, and then he turned away from Pa, looked at Aaron. "I guess it's really you I'm here to see."

Aaron's gut tightened, though he'd expected it. "Me?"

"Yeah. I —" Cole laughed self-consciously. "I'm in a little trouble."

"Trouble," Aaron repeated. He glanced at Pa, who was watching avidly, his heavy brow furrowed with concentration. "Trouble from the law?"

Cole looked startled. He shook his head. "No. Hell, no. Not with the law."

It wasn't much of a relief. At least a man could buy off the law.

Cole laughed. It was slightly embarrassed, a bit ironic. "It's about a girl."

At first Aaron wasn't sure he'd heard correctly. *A girl.* It was the last thing he'd expected. Cole in trouble with a girl. It was inconceivable; when it came to women, Cole could handle anything. It startled Aaron, confused him, and along with that surprise came a vague satisfaction, a sense of *finally —*

Pa slapped his hand down on the blankets, a muffled *thump.* Aaron ignored him. "What about a girl?"

Cole eased his finger behind his collar. There was a sheepish smile on his face when he looked over at their father. "Well, I . . . I got a girl pregnant."

Pa made a sound, a garbled growl. He grinned — or at least half his face did. He grabbed the chalkboard and wrote.

"IT'S ABOUT TIME."

Aaron rose quickly. "Well, Pa, there's the grandchild you've been waiting for." He couldn't keep the bitterness from his tone.

It was all he could do to look at his brother, to say a single word. "Congratulations."

Pa rapped on the side of the chalkboard. "WHEN'S THE WEDDING?"

Cole stepped in front of Aaron, blocking the door. "There's something else," he said.

Pa rapped the chalkboard again.

Aaron heard something in his brother's voice that made him stop. He met Cole's eyes. "Something else?"

Rap, rap.

"I can't marry her."

There was a pause, a heavy silence like thunderheads gathering. Then the chalkboard came flying. Instinctively, Aaron ducked. He heard Cole's curse just before the board crashed against the wall, cracking the slate so it scattered from the frame in two jagged pieces.

"What the hell do you think you're doing?" Cole jerked around to their father, rubbing his shoulder. "What the hell's wrong with you?"

Aaron took a deep breath. He picked up the frame. It was split along one side. He took the two large pieces of slate. "That's the last one until Miguel can get to town."

"Christ." Cole spun away from the bed. "What the hell's wrong with him?"

Aaron looked past his brother to Pa. "He has a penchant for throwing things. Don't you, old man?" He stepped to the bed, handed his father one of the pieces of slate and a broken nubbin of chalk. Then he turned to Cole. "My guess is that he wants to see a wedding."

Cole took a deep breath. There was resignation in the sound, but no regret. "Well, I can't do it."

Pa banged his bad hand on the bed, a clumsy, odd motion. He made a harsh, primitive sound that seemed to come from deep inside his lungs before he turned the jagged piece of slate to them. His writing was cramped on the smaller surface, harder to read. "YOU MARRY HER AND BRING HER TO ME."

Cole winced. "Look, Pa —"

Pa made that sound again. He dropped the slate and gestured wildly at Aaron. It was useless, Aaron knew already, but he did as his father asked, and said, "He wants a grandson. To carry on our 'proud heritage.' "

Cole sighed. "It's like this. There's this other girl. I'm in love with her."

The notion of Cole in love startled Aaron so much he laughed. "You? In love?"

"Well, it's true. I've been saving money. I

have about two thousand dollars in a Dallas bank —"

"*Two thousand?*"

Pa growled from the bed.

"She comes from a rich family. I didn't think I had a chance of getting her father's approval without some money of my own."

"I see," Aaron said, though he didn't at all. Cole had Pa's money to back him, and the Wallace name. He didn't need money of his own.

"I love her. I'm going to ask her to marry me."

"And this other girl? The one who's —"

"Eliza. Eliza Beaudry." Cole looked up at the ceiling, and there was something in the motion Aaron recognized, something he'd never seen in Cole before. Something like . . . like shame.

It was so odd that it made Aaron nervous. He'd never known Cole to feel shame. Not ever. Not even when Pa accused them both of letting their mother and brother die —

"I was in Richmond," Cole said. "The gaming was good, so I stayed awhile. She was . . . there."

Aaron glanced at his father. Pa's heavy gray brows were drawn low over his eyes, his crooked face was disapproving.

"She wasn't the kind of woman I usually

like," Cole went on. He took a deep breath. "She's a nobody, the daughter of a sharecropper down there."

It was all Aaron needed to picture her. *The daughter of a sharecropper.* The words brought her completely into focus. Poor, pretty, uneducated. Cole was right — she wasn't his kind. She wasn't this family's kind.

Aaron looked at Pa. He was writing on the chalkboard.

"THE CHILD IS YOURS?"

Cole nodded. "She was a virgin."

"YOU MARRY HER."

Cole looked at Aaron a little desperately. "There's this other girl . . . Jenny —"

"YOU MARRY HER AND BRING HER HERE."

"Pa, listen to me. You want grandchildren, I'll give them to you. But with Jenny —"

Pa's face was red. "MARRY THAT GIRL OR YOU'RE DISINHERITED."

Cole stared at him. "I don't give a damn about your money, old man. Go ahead. Disinherit me. I don't deserve it anyway."

Pa was shaking. There was spittle on his lips. "YOU OBEY ME. I WANT MY GRANDSON."

"You can't always have what you want."

Pa wrote furiously. "I WILL DISOWN YOU."

The anger in his words — even written as they were — made Aaron wince. But Cole only laughed.

"Old man, threaten all you want, you can't make me do shit. You want to browbeat someone, try Aaron."

Aaron went stone cold. He sat there, not quite believing he'd heard the words, not believing his brother had turned on him until he felt Pa's sudden, quick focus like the deadly bead of a rattler. Aaron's mouth went dry; he felt desperation and fear so cold and sharp it took words and motion.

"Christ, I'm sorry, Aaron," Cole stepped in quickly, but the damage was already done. "I didn't mean to . . . I didn't . . . Damn, brother, I need your help. You've got to help me. I've offered her money, or at least, I offered it to her pa. He won't take it. I've got no other choice. I know I have no right to ask you this. God knows I haven't been fair, leaving you with . . . with all this. . . ."

Pa growled. He pointed at Aaron, his finger jabbed the air. Aaron's dread swelled inside him. He watched helplessly as Pa wiped off the chalkboard, scribbled again.

"I WANT MY GRANDSON HERE."

Aaron looked at his father and forced himself to speak. "I don't understand you," he said, though that was a lie. He was afraid he did understand. He was afraid he knew just what the old man was saying, and Aaron didn't want to hear the words.

Pa jabbed his finger again, so hard Aaron imagined he felt the sharp, hard blow of it against his breastbone.

It was Cole, finally, who said the words Aaron dreaded hearing, who interpreted their father. "He's saying *you* should marry her, Aaron."

Pa nodded.

Aaron sank again to the windowsill, pressing his back against the window, catching the shade. He heard it tear at the roller, and the sound seemed to echo through his head, that quiet rip.

"You can't be serious," Aaron whispered, though he knew Cole had come home to ask this of him, that everything in the past hour had merely been leading up to it.

"I think it's a good idea," Cole said. He looked at Pa. Aaron heard his father's grunt of agreement.

He stared at his brother. "I don't want a wife." His voice broke, but the words were as true as he could make them. He didn't want a wife. He didn't want the responsibility. A wife meant stability. A wife meant he was stuck on this farm forever. A wife . . . His future ground to a halt in front of him;

he felt a terror so all-encompassing he could barely breathe.

"I know it seems like a huge favor," Cole said. "But I need your help, Aaron. You've . . . you've got to help me. Please."

Pa growled and lifted the broken chalkboard. "YOU *DO* IT."

"You could use a woman here," Cole cajoled. Come on, Aaron. Haven't you thought about it? Having someone to cook and clean? Hearing a soft voice once in a while? Someone waiting for you in be—"

"Shut up." Aaron glared at his brother.

Cole stepped back. He held up his hands, palms out. "All right, all right."

"I don't want a wife."

"Why the hell not? You have to get married some day."

"Not now."

He felt Cole's thoughtful look, and it made Aaron more uncomfortable than ever.

"I think I see." Cole's voice took on an edge that made Aaron feel faintly sick. Cole bent close, until his face was even with Aaron's, and his voice was quiet, needling. "Tell me something, baby brother. When was the last time you were in town, hmmm?"

Aaron jerked up to meet his brother's gaze, and fear came hard and fast, growing inside him.

"Seen any pretty women there?" Cole goaded. "Any one you'd care to take riding? Hmmm? How long has it been since you took a woman out behind that big oak tree and stole a —"

Aaron lurched to his feet, jerking away, pushing past his brother.

"Don't tell me you don't want it, Aaron."

Pa growled from the bed.

"You don't know what the hell you're talking about," Aaron spat. His hands were shaking.

"So tell me I'm wrong," Cole said. "Tell me you've taken out one of those little girls in town. Delilah Evans was always a pretty thing. I thought once —"

Pa growled again.

They both turned.

"HE DOESN'T GO INTO TOWN."

The words on the slate were bold and condemning. Aaron felt their judgment clear into his soul.

Cole faced Aaron triumphantly. "That's what I thought."

The room was closing in around him. Aaron worked to keep his voice even. "I don't want a wife."

"Look, Aaron, I'm doing you a favor," Cole coaxed. "You marry Eliza, and you've got a wife without even trying. You don't even have to court her."

Aaron turned to the window. The torn blind was crooked now, obscuring part of the glass, but still he could see the creek and the oak. The sight of them didn't calm him. He was smothering; he wanted to throw open the window and stick his head outside, to take deep, calming breaths of the sweltering air. But instead he pressed his hands against the glass and wished he could slam his fist into it.

"She's blond." Cole was speaking quietly behind him, his voice smooth and lilting. "She's got blue eyes and these . . . these eyebrows that look too dark for her hair. She's got this pretty, drawling voice that'll make you forget everything. Even your pretty poems."

The words sank inside Aaron, a rhythm that curled around his vitals and pulled him with them. *Blue eyes . . . Pretty voice . . . You'll forget everything. . . .* Aaron pressed his fingers harder against the glass, willing it to break beneath his force. He swallowed and tried to see into the oak.

"You need a wife, Aaron," Cole whispered.

No, he didn't. He wanted to keep on the way he was, he wanted to work every day and wait for his father to die so he could leave this place, so he could walk away from these burning cornfields and see a world he'd only dreamt about. He wanted to find other words and feel passions that didn't come from the land. He didn't want a wife keeping him here. He didn't want children keeping him here.

But into those resolves crept something else, something made from Cole's words, some little pain. Aaron thought of White Horse, and the way the people turned away from him, the curious looks of the girls in their pretty dresses. He thought of the way those dresses clung to them, to their breasts and hips. He thought of the soft, smooth line of throats and the bobbling curls of hair dangling by an ear, the fragrance of lilac and rose, jonquil and orange water. There were times — a long time ago, when he still went into town — when he'd bent close just to smell, when he'd closed his eyes and breathed deep and burned.

Ah, the smells . . .

He felt his will slipping away. Desperately, he clung to it. "I don't want a wife," he whispered.

"Of course not," Cole said soothingly. "Of course you don't."

Aaron dug his fingers into the glass. He felt the hot sun burning his fingertips. He saw the world stretching before him, out to the horizon, places he had never seen. Places he would never see because the glass held him prisoner. Because he could not open the window, and he would not break it.

He felt Cole behind him, felt his breath, his presence, pushing, pushing, and Aaron closed his eyes and tried to ignore his brother. It took all his will to state his refusal, every ounce of his strength. "I won't do it," he whispered hoarsely. "Not this time."

His words fell on stunned silence; except for Cole's harsh indrawn breath, there was no sound. Then he felt his brother lean close, heard the panic again in his voice.

"Aaron —"

Pa pounded the bed. Aaron felt Cole's movement, felt the turn, the pause, and then he heard him walking away and knew that Pa had motioned for him to go. The thought sent panic racing through him, he had a sudden, momentary urge to chase after his brother, to grab him, to say, *"Don't leave me alone with him,"* but he just stood there, and then it was too late. He heard Cole retreating down the hallway, heard him stop. He had the sudden image of Cole sitting at the top of the stairs, waiting, listening, and the thought made him cold.

But not as cold as the sound of his father's

grunt, the pounding on the bed. Slowly, Aaron opened his eyes. He took a deep breath. He turned around.

"I'm not doing it," he said quietly. "You can't change my mind."

Pa frowned, beetling his brows. Then he held up the chalkboard. "YOU DO IT, OR YOU'RE NO SON OF MINE."

The words clanged in Aaron's ears so loudly it was as if he heard his father's voice saying them, an echo of long ago, the same litany he'd heard since he was five years old. *"What kind of man are you? Your brother almost died and where the hell were you? Cowering under the damn bed like a baby. You owe him now, you hear me? You hear me, boy? Brothers take care of each other. You remember that, or you're no damn son of mine."*

Aaron felt the walls pressing in around him, the trap snapping shut. Desperately, he held it off. "Cole can take care of himself this time. I'm tired —"

Pa jabbed his finger at Aaron, and then he pointed to the open door. Aaron knew what the old man meant; he heard the words — words he'd heard too many damn times before. *"You owe him. You take care of him."*

"I've done it as well as I can, old man," Aaron said bitterly. "It's been twenty-three years, isn't the debt paid?"

Pa shook his head. His eyes were burning. He picked up the board and scrawled on it. "YOU OWE HIM. YOU'LL ALWAYS OWE HIM."

The message shook Aaron. *You'll always owe him.* Deep into his bones, he felt the fear of it, the crush of obligation. And, just as his father had intended, the words brought back the memory of the night his mother and brother died. It had been twenty-three years ago now, yet Aaron still remembered what the sky had looked like, how the air had felt.

He pushed the image away. He clenched his jaw and stared back into his father's condemning gaze. "He's his own man, now, Pa," he said. "So am I."

Pa's snort was an odd, jerky sound. He swiped his sleeve across the chalkboard, and Aaron's nerves stretched taut at the squeak of chalk on slate. He knew what the words would be almost before Pa held up the board. "YOU'RE NO MAN."

Aaron would have given anything not to have the words jar him. He would have given his life to not feel the slow burn of humiliation, to not hear the tiny, niggling voice telling him his father was right. He was no man. He couldn't even court a woman. He hadn't even tried to save his brother. . . .

It was that, finally, that brought the memory flooding back so strongly he couldn't stop it. It came just as it always did, heavy with sorrow and a guilt so strong it was a bad taste in his mouth. He'd only been five. Cole had been seven and Eli nearly thirteen. Pa had gone into White Horse to get some supplies, and it took him a long time to get back. Long enough so that the night had come on, and the spring moon had shone bright and fall in the sky.

Aaron remembered that night like a dream in his head. He remembered his mother's fear, and the way she'd pulled in the thong latch of the door and laid the rifle by her rocking chair. When he and Cole went to bed, she was still there, rocking, waiting. Her fear made it hard to sleep; Aaron had still been awake, listening to Cole's even breathing, when the Indians came.

They had raped his mother before they lanced her to the ground. Two warriors had fought over who should take Eli, and so they killed him. Aaron knew these things not because he'd seen them, but because that was what he'd been told. What he had seen were Comanche shadows bursting into the loft bedroom. He'd been awake, and he supposed that was what saved him, because at the sight of the first shadow, Aaron had rolled under his bed. He'd watched them take Cole. He'd watched one of the warriors put his knife to the back of Cole's head, saw the blood flow as they began to scalp him. Then he'd heard the guns, and the Indians ran off. Their father had come at last.

It took them a day to get Aaron out from under the bed. Finally, they'd had to drag him out. He'd been so frozen with fear and guilt he hadn't spoken for three weeks. Later, after the fear and sorrow had gone, after the anger, only the guilt remained.

He hadn't tried to save Cole, but he could have lived with that. He could have forgotten it. Except that Pa made sure he didn't forget it. From that day until the time Cole left the farm for good, Aaron had heard his father's message so often it was blazoned in his brain. *"Your brother almost died and where the hell were you? . . . Brothers take care of each other. You remember that, or you're no damn son of mine."*

Aaron swallowed. The memory didn't fade when he looked at Pa, when he saw the ferocity on the old man's face. Pa pointed again. To Aaron, to the door. *"You take care of him."* Then he jabbed his bony finger into his breastbone so hard Aaron heard the pound of it. *Thud, thud, thud.*

Aaron felt himself slipping. In the pound of his father's finger were the words that

140

hammered away at his will, at what meager self-worth he'd managed to retain over the years. *"Be a man, boy. Do this and make me proud of you."* In the force of that message, his dreams seemed very small. Unimportant, unreal. Things that wouldn't come true. Pa could linger on for thirty years, and by then Aaron would be nearly sixty, an old man himself. A man who'd never had anything.

He knew that could happen. He'd known it for years, though he tried not to think about it, didn't want to face it. It was easier to think that the day he walked out of here was the day his life started. He didn't want to think about being here forever. He'd been living day to day, waiting, putting his life on hold. He'd deliberately done nothing to make his life here more pleasant, had not given himself a single reason to want to stay.

But now the horizon Aaron had yearned for seemed so damn far away. It wavered before him in the heat, just a dream growing hazier by the minute, a dream fading in the possibility of his father's pride.

He told himself he didn't want it. The old man was bitter and angry; his pride was worth nothing. Over the years, Aaron had tried to win his father's approval, but those efforts had beaten him down, that approval was always just beyond his reach. Even if he did this, even if he married this woman, it wouldn't be good enough for Pa. There would always be something else Aaron wasn't doing right, some way he wasn't measuring up to Cole — or to the mythical Eli.

But the truth was, Aaron hungered for the old man's approval. The longing for it was a tight little knot that churned and tangled, a reason to keep trying. He wanted, just once, to see his father smile at him, to know he was doing the right thing. He wanted it, and he told himself it was dangerous. It would make him do something he didn't want to do, it would ruin his life.

"Old man," he whispered. "Don't ask me to do this."

But Pa didn't change his expression. He didn't ease his glare, and this time when he held up the chalkboard Aaron tried not to look at it. He didn't want to see the words. Still, he found himself lowering his eyes, focusing on the loud, square letters, reading the shaky chalk lines. "AFRAID OF A WOMAN?"

Aaron met Pa's gaze. He saw the mockery on his father's face, the smug challenge, and Aaron felt a chill so deep he could barely breathe for the cold of it. He could not admit the truth, not to his father, barely to himself, even if it saved him. And because he couldn't admit it, he felt himself break, felt the snap of his spine like a dry and brittle cornstalk.

Pa smiled crookedly, and the triumphant expression on his face hurt so much Aaron couldn't look at him. For a moment he thought about saying something, denying his father the win. But there was nothing he could say, and Pa knew it.

Aaron went to the window. He heard the old man pick up the bell on his nightstand and ring it; the high, tinny clang hurt Aaron's head. He waited for Cole's footsteps, for the moment that would bring him back into this room, that would seal Aaron's future for good.

And he felt nothing about it. Not sadness, not regret. Only resignation. Cole was his brother. He owed him. And this would make his father proud. This would make him a man.

8

Cole stood at the doorway, feeling the tension, afraid to go in until he realized his father would never have called him back unless he had the answer he wanted. Aaron had acquiesced.

But Aaron didn't turn from the window, and for a moment his stance was so distant Cole thought he'd got it wrong, that Pa hadn't convinced his brother. Except for Pa's uneven, wretched breathing, the room was quiet, and every second that passed tightened in Cole's chest, every moment only showed him just how much he wanted Aaron to say yes.

Aaron sighed. Then he turned, and Cole was struck by his brother's ragged expression. Aaron's face looked hollowed out, his cheekbones higher, his jaw more pronounced. But it was his eyes that startled Cole the most. He remembered when there had been humor in those dark brown eyes, but now they were sad, and Cole felt uncomfortably — strangely — like he was stealing a part of his brother's soul.

But that was ludicrous, wasn't it? Hell, in a way, he was even doing Aaron a favor. Giving him a wife. Giving him that sweet little, smooth-hipped Eliza. Aaron wouldn't even have to find a wife for himself — not that he would even try.

Cole couldn't stand another moment of waiting. "Well?" he asked.

Aaron's gaze settled on Cole for just a moment, and then he looked away, over to Pa. Pa stared back at him, so hard and intently that Cole felt excluded. Then Pa started writing again, with that clumsy, jerky motion that seemed to involve his whole body — how the hell did a man get used to that? One side of his mouth ticked as he worked; the other side was strangely, disconcertingly still.

He held up the jagged piece of slate. "SOONER THE BETTER."

Cole slid a glance to his brother. For a moment, Cole felt a stab of guilt. But it was gone the moment he thought of Jenny. The moment he saw her face before him and heard Aaron say in a quiet, quiet voice: "Yeah. All right. I'll do it."

Pa broke into a weird, lopsided smile and banged his stiff, gnarled hand on the bed. Cole slapped his brother's back.

"You won't regret this," he said.

Aaron stepped away and looked at their father. "Since it's settled, I've got things to do."

"By all means." Cole opened his arms and motioned to the door. "We'll celebrate to-night. Any of that old whiskey still around?"

Aaron gave him a strange, expressionless look. He didn't answer, and Cole felt his brother pass like a chill as he moved to the door.

"Aaron —" Cole started, but Aaron didn't stop, and Cole heard his footsteps across the floor, down the stairs.

Pa grunted; Cole turned to his father. Without Aaron in the room the old man's presence was as dark and cold as a blue norther, and now that Cole had what he wanted, he didn't want to spend another minute here. From the corner of his eye, he saw Aaron out the window, striding across the straggly, burned-off grass that passed for a yard to that twisted tree shading the creek.

Pa was holding up the board. "HE IS A GOOD SON."

Cole snorted. "And I'm just a no-good bounder. Yeah, I know." He reached into his pocket for the cigar he'd abandoned, and then he paused and held it up. "Oh, that's right. Mind if I smoke?" He didn't wait for an answer before he struck a match on the door frame and lit the cigar still in his mouth. He took a couple of puffs and exhaled, away from his father, but enough smoke to cloud the room.

Pa coughed. "TRYING TO KILL ME?"

"I don't have to. You'll be dead soon enough anyway." Cole went to the window. He could no longer see his brother, except for a foot angled out from the trunk of the tree, but he knew what Aaron was doing, what Aaron always did. He'd be bent over some paper, scribbling away as he'd been when Cole first rode up this morning. Wasting his mind and his pretty face trying to make words rhyme. Cole had never been able to understand why a man would spend his time writing poetry if he wasn't going to use it to impress some young lady. But Aaron had never had time for young ladies. He never had time for anything but words. *Lucky for me,* Cole supposed. He took another puff on his cigar.

From the bed, Pa coughed again. Cole turned.

"AARON RESPECTS ME."

Cole sighed. "I suppose I should thank you for convincing him to do this."

He heard the fury of writing. When Pa turned the board, it was covered with his cramped scrawl. "YOU WOULD DENY ME MY GRANDSON. I WILL NOT STAND FOR IT."

"Well, you don't have to," Cole said. "Aaron's going to do the right thing, like he always does." He heard the sarcasm in his own voice and he almost laughed. It was absurd, how easily his father brought back his resentment toward his brother. Nothing more than a few words — hell, not even spoken words. Words formed in chalk. Aaron had just done him the biggest favor a man could ask, and instead of feeling grateful, Cole felt . . . hostile.

He blew smoke at the old man, feeling a bitter satisfaction when Pa choked and glared back at him through the smoke. "Tomorrow I'll get the hell off this farm, so you don't have to worry that I'm plotting to get my inheritance early —"

The old man made that horrible, grunting sound deep in his chest. He scrawled on the board. "YOUR CHILD GETS IT. NOT YOU."

"Good," Cole said sharply. "Then I guess I won't worry about making any more dutiful-son visits."

Scratch, scratch, scratch. "THANK GOD."

Cole struggled to keep his temper. He ground out the cigar on the floor, leaving it

148

there to stink up the room. "I'm leaving in the morning," he repeated as calmly as he could. "I'll bring her back here and she and Aaron can get married in town. Get the preacher ready."

Pa shook his head. Gray hair fell into his face, catching on his heavy brows. "NO CHURCH. JUDGE."

"All right then. A judge. He can meet us here."

Pa jabbed his chest with his finger.

Cole frowned. "I don't understand you, old man."

Pa picked up the shard of slate. He wrote and turned it. "NO JUDGE BUT ME."

"You? Jesus." Cole shook his head. "You're retired, Pa —"

"I WILL DO IT."

"You can't even talk. What're you going to do, write a ceremony?"

Pa glared at him — as crippled as he was, that look was just as effective now as it had been when Cole was a boy. He held up the board.

"I WILL. MAKE SURE SHE AGREES."

Cole smiled thinly. "She'll say yes. I'll just tell her what a catch Aaron is."

Pa stared at him until Cole started to feel uncomfortable. Then Pa bent and wrote. He held up the board, and the words were like little stabs, white and bold against the slate, hurtful in their starkness, unmellowed by tone. "HE IS TWICE THE MAN YOU ARE."

Cole's throat tightened. He looked away, to the window. He could no longer see Aaron at all. "So you've said, Pa," he said slowly. "So you've said."

Cole sat on the porch, feeling the heat against his face, sweating in the shade. Aaron did not budge from that tree, and all Cole saw of him was a movement here and again, the glare of sunlight on paper, a boot, a lifted elbow. In the fields, the two Mexicans worked. Every now and then one of them stared at the sky, but it was as cloudless and blue as ever, hot for June. Some things never changed.

When the sun began to ease, the one farmhand, Miguel, came in from the fields. He glanced at Cole as he stepped across the porch and tipped his hat. Before long, Cole smelled chili cooking. After a while, Carlos came in, washing at the cistern. Cole heard the rattle of a snake, and Carlos's curse, and then a thud and the snake was quiet. Carlos came around the corner of the porch holding it, a headless, limp body. It was a big snake, and Carlos laid it out on the porch, stretching it across the boards at Cole's feet. Then the farmhand stood on the steps and called out, "*La cena, Señor* Aaron!"

Carlos waited a moment, and then he called it again. Soon, Cole heard a distracted, "All right," from the creek. Carlos nodded and went inside the house.

Cole waited. He saw the flutter of paper at the old tree, and then Aaron came around the side of it and was coming across the yard. As he came closer, Cole heard him murmuring, low, half-formed words. "Shivering . . . shake . . . moving — ah, no, no, no. Trembling —"

Aaron nearly tripped on the stairs. He looked up in surprise, blinking, shaking his head, and then he squinted at Cole, and his expression became carefully neutral before he glanced away at the snake.

"Yours?" Aaron asked.

Cole shook his head. "Carlos's."

"Oh." Aaron ran his hand through his hair. "For his boots, I guess. Supper's ready."

He went into the house. Cole waited a moment, and then he took a deep breath and followed his brother inside. Aaron and Carlos were already seated at the table, and Miguel was serving up chili from a steaming pot.

Aaron barely looked up from his bowl when Cole sat down. There was a bottle of tequila on the table, and Cole poured a shot and nudged his brother. When Aaron looked up, Cole lifted the bottle in silent question.

Aaron nodded shortly. Cole poured his brother a shot and grabbed a spoon. Even though he was starving, it was hard to eat under the stares of the Mexicans. They kept glancing at Aaron as if they were waiting for him to suddenly explode.

The farmhands ate quickly. Carlos rose first, and with a mumbled *"Buenos noches,"* was gone. Before long, Miguel joined him.

Finally, Aaron pushed his bowl back and cupped his hand around the tequila he'd barely touched. He stared straight ahead, stiff and faraway.

Cole took a sip of tequila and looked at his brother. "Who is it they're afraid of?" he asked. "You or me?"

Aaron looked at him as if he'd forgotten he was there. "What?"

"Miguel. Carlos. They've been watching the two of us all through dinner. They couldn't wait to get the hell out of here."

"Oh." Aaron looked down at his glass. "You, I guess."

Cole nodded. He thought Aaron was wrong — it had been him the farmhands were staring at — but then again, Cole couldn't imagine a reason for anyone to be afraid of Aaron. Hell, he never even lost his temper. Not the way Pa did, or Cole himself, for that matter. He nudged Aaron's drink. "Go ahead," he said. "You look like you could use it."

Aaron looked surprised again, but he downed the shot in one gulp, and he didn't protest when Cole poured him another.

There should have been a hundred topics between them, a thousand things to say. But Cole had been gone for three years, and he'd been home rarely before that. He hadn't spent more than a few days total on this farm since he was sixteen. He and Aaron had not been close for a long time. The silence grew between them, clumsy and loud.

Finally, Cole cleared his throat. "Pa seems . . . better."

Aaron threw him a look. "He's getting worse."

"Oh."

Aaron downed the tequila and poured again. "I guess he would seem better to you — compared to the last time you were home."

"Well, yeah. He was comatose then."

Aaron put his elbows on the table and leaned forward, staring at the doorway to the kitchen. "It's been three years, and he still can't talk. He hasn't been out of that bed for a year."

"How long does the doctor say Pa's got? A few months?"

Aaron turned to him slowly, and Cole saw resentment again in his brother's eyes, a burning anger. "Maybe that. Or maybe he'll just linger for twenty years. No one knows."

Twenty years. Cole let his breath out in a long, slow whistle. He drank his tequila and glanced at the stairs. He thought of Aaron going up them, day after day, for twenty years. Cole felt a sudden urge to change the subject.

"Had any Indian trouble lately?"

Aaron threw him an inexplicable look. "They dragged them all to the reservation, Cole. Don't you read the papers?"

There was no answer for that; it had been a stupid question. The conversation lulled and sank. Aaron sat there drinking and silent. Cole had the feeling he would sit there like that all night. But Cole couldn't stand it. Not the silence, not the tension.

He took a deep breath. There was no point in avoiding the topic any longer; it was all he could think about, and he was sure it was on Aaron's mind. "I'm leaving in the morning," Cole said. "It should take me a couple days to get to Richmond, another week or so to get back. I figure we'll be here in two, maybe three, weeks."

Aaron laughed shortly, humorlessly, and took another gulp of tequila. "Do me a favor — drag it out to three."

Cole felt a stab of guilt. "I owe you, brother," he said. "I — Look, thank you for this. I mean it."

"Don't mention it."

"I think, in the end, you'll be happy you did it." Cole picked up his glass, motioned around the front room. "If nothing else, you'll get a housekeeper. Damn, look at this. Where the hell do you sit? There're books and papers everywhere."

Aaron glanced at the room. "I like it this way."

"No wonder you never have company."

"Yeah," Aaron said wryly. "They keep away in droves because there's too much dust in my parlor."

Cole smiled. "Maybe a wife will help."

Aaron poured another shot of tequila. He gulped it down, poured another. "A wife," he said. He dragged the word out as if measuring its consonants on his tongue. "I don't think a wife will help anything, Cole. Do you?"

There was a tone in his brother's voice that

made Cole think of a long time ago, when he was about ten, and Aaron was eight. They'd been out in the back, shooting at empty whiskey bottles on the split-rail fence. The rifle was too heavy for Aaron, and every time he fired the balls splintered the fence, blew up dirt, shook a tree. He never once hit the bottle. When his turn was over, he'd handed the gun back to Cole. *"I'll never be able to save you from Indians, will I, Cole?"*

Will I, Cole?

The chili felt heavy in Cole's stomach. The scar on the back of his scalp — the scar he liked to forget — tingled. He looked down into his tequila, shook the glass so the clear liquor jiggled and sent its fumes into his nose.

"Eliza." Aaron held his glass to his lips, took a sip. "That's her name?"

"A pretty name for a pretty girl," Cole said. He tried to think of what to tell his brother about Eliza. There wasn't much — he barely knew her — so he made it up. The heat of the tequila made his words come liquid and smooth. "She's like you," he said. "She likes poetry."

Aaron turned to him in surprise. "She likes poetry?"

"Sure," Cole said. He remembered the hat she'd worn to breakfast. "She likes pretty

156

things, too. Her family doesn't have much money, but she has . . . taste." Not good taste, but there was no point in telling Aaron that. "She grew up on a farm — near here, I think. She knows the land." He remembered Will Ames and the other boys in the Bluebonnet. "Everyone likes her."

"Everyone?" Aaron lifted a brow. "She sounds like a paragon."

"She is."

"Then why don't *you* marry her?"

Cole picked up the bottle, splashed more into both glasses. "Because I'm already spoken for."

"Your Dallas lady."

"I'm in love with a pair of deep brown eyes." Cole held up his glass. "Here's to marriage, brother." He downed the shot and leaned close, slinging his arm around his brother's neck, pulling Aaron close so he could whisper in his ear. "You won't regret this, Aaron. I promise you, you won't regret it. Eliza's" — he lifted the tequila — "Eliza's easy, you know? She's like this tequila, smooth going down. You don't have anything to worry about."

Aaron looked at him. "Don't I?"

That sadness again, that *"I'll never be able to save you,"* voice. "You're saving my life here, Aaron," Cole said, and in that moment he meant it more than anything he'd ever said. "I'll do whatever I can to make it up to you."

Aaron nodded. He sighed, and then he reached for the tequila. "Then let's get drunk," he said. "So you hurt like a son of a bitch when you leave."

9

But the next day it wasn't Cole who hurt when he left, it was Aaron. Aaron leaned against the porch pillar, watching his brother ride away, his head aching from too much tequila, the burn of dehydration stinging his eyes. He watched Cole ride until he was nothing but a black spot against the wavering hills, dancing against the browning grass.

Three weeks. Three weeks until Cole came riding back with a wife-to-be in tow. The time seemed too short. Like a dying man, Aaron thought of all the things he'd ever wanted to do, the places he'd wanted to see.

But then the time telescoped down, and he felt as if he was looking into the future and watching Cole ride toward him. He imagined that black speck growing bigger and bigger, growing into two people, growing into his wife. Three weeks wasn't enough time to do anything, even if he could just leave, and suddenly Aaron wished he'd told Cole to hurry instead. He could do too much thinking in three weeks' time; too much dread could fill the days.

He glanced down at the porch, at the rattlesnake skin tacked to the rail. Carlos had thrown the carcass into the yard for the pigs, and it looked like Aaron felt. He and Cole had sat up playing cards and drinking until Pa banged on the floor around one in the morning. Aaron couldn't remember the last time he'd had so much to drink, and he also couldn't remember what he and Cole had talked about — except that Cole had done most of the talking as he'd fleeced Aaron of twenty-five dollars. Aaron had known when his brother arrived that he'd be regretting it the next day, and sure enough here he was, regretting it and wishing Cole had stayed the hell in Richmond, or Dallas, or wherever it was that he'd come from.

Aaron wanted to forget the whole visit. These last years he'd grown accustomed to waiting for his life to begin. He spent his days growing corn and worrying about the weather, his evenings with his hands dry and white from rubbing alcohol as his fingers worked his father's hairy, bony calves. He lived for those moments under the post oak, those quiet hours after Pa had gone to sleep, when he could read far into the night. He waited, and coloring every day, every moment, was the knowledge that eventually the old cripple would die, and he would be free.

Now even that was gone. Cole had even taken his hope from him. Even that. Aaron watched until his brother's shadow finally disappeared on the horizon, no longer a speck, no longer anything but heat waves shimmering across the hills, and turned back to the creek, to the shallow gurgle of water. In three weeks, Cole would be back with Eliza Beaudry, a woman growing heavy with his child. In three weeks, he would put her hand in Aaron's, and Aaron would marry her. He would take a wife and he would fight his fear and care for her and raise the child as his own. He would give up the freedom he'd spent his life waiting for.

It didn't matter, Aaron supposed, because in spite of what Pa said about owing Cole forever, Aaron knew the truth. This would be the last thing he ever did for his brother.

Time was slipping away, so Cole didn't stop except to sleep on the way to Richmond. He rode quickly, though he didn't want to. He wanted to go slowly, to take his time, to put off his meeting with Jack Beaudry. Cole had ridden away from his father's farm feeling confident and relieved, but every step closer to Eliza's father made him more tense. He'd persuaded Aaron to marry her, now it was time to persuade Eliza and her father.

It wasn't as if they had any choice; Cole was offering nothing better — certainly not himself. He felt a little guilty when he thought of how she would look at him, how disappointed she would be, but he consoled himself when he thought of the kind of girl Eliza was. She had wanted something better than Richmond. She would probably jump at the chance to marry the son of a rich farmer — even if he wasn't the father of her child.

He kept telling himself that as he rode toward Richmond, but by the time he reached it, his confidence had lost some of its luster. The smell of town brought the image of her back to him; she was more real than she'd been since he left — how long ago? More than three months. He smelled the marsh and the too-ripe smell of flowers. The scents of fish and rotting mud pressed on the already heavy air. It made him remember that day by the lake, the way she'd lay back on the grass, crushing flowers beneath her, the marsh-sweet perfume of her skin. Her smile filled his head.

He felt guilty again. Cole tried to push the feeling away, but it was too hot to work at it, so humid he was sweating through his coat. He didn't bother to get a room at the hotel — all he would do was lie there and dread seeing her and her father again. It would be better to go there first, to get her answer and be done with it. Afterward, he would go over to the Bluebonnet. Maybe by then he'd be relaxed enough to play a few hands.

The road out of town was narrow and rutted. The few wildflowers bordering it were wilted, their perfume overblown and heavy. The farms started almost the moment he left Richmond, tiny, sharecropper acres, each decorated with their own falling-down shanty. He couldn't remember which was Eliza's father's; maybe he'd never known. He paused at one when he saw a passel of tow-headed children running about, their clothes ragged, their feet bare. But when one of the boys stomped to urinate against the side of the shack, Cole rode on, disgusted. He didn't remember Eliza talking about brothers or sisters anyway.

He was a couple of miles from town when he spotted a tall, thin man in the fields beyond the road, his blond head bare in the sun. Cole recognized him even at a distance — he supposed it would be a long time before he forgot Jack Beaudry.

Cole reached for a cigar, bit it off, lit it. He took two long, slow puffs before he saw

Beaudry rise and turn to face him. It wasn't until the man waved an acknowledgment that Cole nudged his horse into the yard. He dismounted slowly and waited for Eliza's father to come to him.

Beaudry was red-faced and sweating, his shirt streaked with dirt, sticking to his chest. His face was expressionless as he came over; he nodded curtly at Cole and then went to a barrel at the side of the house. Cole heard the splash of water, and when Beaudry came back again, he was wiping his face on a ratty towel.

"Wallace," he said. "I didn't 'spect to see you before Tuesday."

"My guess is that you didn't expect to see me at all."

Jack Beaudry regarded him stonily. "Yeah. That too."

"Well, I'm here." Cole looked around. "Where's Eliza?"

"She and her mama are in the house," Beaudry said. When Cole started to the shack, Beaudry stepped in front of him, stopping him, blocking the sun. "You gonna do right by my girl, Wallace?"

Cole forced himself to meet Beaudry's eyes, even though his heart was pounding. "I have an offer to make," he said. "I think you'll be satisfied."

Beaudry frowned, but he stepped aside and led Cole across the dirt yard to the door of the shanty. "Lizzie," he said, speaking into the darkness. "There's someone to see you."

He stepped inside, and Cole followed, blinking to accustom his eyes to the dim light. The room was tiny, barely big enough for the makeshift furniture it held, and it smelled dank and close, of cornbread, beans, and sweat. He wondered how the hell three people lived here, and the thought made him vaguely sick. He tossed his cigar out into the yard and turned to face them.

He saw Eliza first. She was sitting at the table, and she rose at the sight of him. Even in the darkness, he could see the light in her eyes. Behind her, in the corner of the room, was a woman. He assumed it was Eliza's mother, but she sat so far back into the shadows it was hard to see her face.

"Hey, Cole," Eliza said. She was smiling when she came forward. She was wearing the same dress she'd had on the last time he'd seen her. His gaze traveled down her body, looking for a telltale bulge, something. But she looked just the same, except that — if possible — her breasts seemed larger.

She looked like she was waiting for him to do something. Kiss her, take her hand, something. Cole didn't move. He looked at

165

her and wondered how the hell he'd got himself into this mess. Her hair was dull and straight, her face pretty but nothing more. He couldn't remember what about her had charmed him.

She tucked a loose strand of hair behind her ear, and the motion was delicate — the only subtle thing about her. Cole's guilt came back; he thought of taking her back to White Horse, putting her hand in Aaron's, bringing her into his family. Eliza Beaudry, a Wallace. The thought was hard to take.

They were all waiting. Cole struggled for something to say. "Your pa tells me you're . . . expecting."

She looked disappointed. She nodded shortly. "Yeah," she said.

"You're sure?"

Jack Beaudry stepped forward. "You son of a —"

"Daddy," she said. She held up her hand, and her father stayed back. She looked at Cole. "I'm sure. It's yours too, in case you were going to ask me that next."

"I didn't doubt it."

She smiled then, a pretty, full-mouthed smile, and it struck a chord of recognition in him.

"Let's talk about this offer of yours," Beaudry said. He sat down at the table, and motioned for Eliza to sit as well. "Sit down, Wallace. Let's get this over with. I got work to do."

Cole nodded. He went to the table, and then looked pointedly at the still-silent woman in the corner. "Your wife, Mr. Beaudry?"

Beaudry's face tightened; Cole heard Eliza's soft indrawn breath. The woman in the corner rose. "I'm Margaret Beaudry, Mr. Wallace," she said quietly.

"Pleased to meet you, Mrs. Beaudry." Cole held out his hand, and she came forward, into the light cast from the front door.

She was skinny and she was wearing men's boots. And she was an Indian. A goddamn Comanche. Cole's gut clenched, he couldn't breathe. She took his hand, and he couldn't feel her touch; his fingers were numb. When she stepped back again he had to resist the urge to wipe his hand on his trousers.

He looked at Eliza. She wouldn't meet his eyes. Jack Beaudry was staring at him so intently Cole felt flayed by his gaze.

"You thinkin' of changin' your mind, Wallace?" he asked softly.

Cole felt cold clear into his bones. Christ, the baby Eliza was carrying would have Comanche blood. Comanche blood mixed with Wallace blood. Aaron would kill him — and if he didn't, Pa sure as hell would.

He turned deliberately away from Margaret Beaudry. "You didn't tell me, Jack," he said slowly.

Jack Beaudry raised his brow. He looked at the rifle hanging above the doorway. "You backin' out on me, Wallace?"

Cole looked at Eliza. Blond, blue-eyed Eliza. There wasn't the look of an Indian anywhere about her. Not a single thing to give her away. He felt cheated somehow, cheated and lied to. If he'd known she was a Comanche —

He cut himself off before he could finish the thought, because he couldn't say what he would have done if he'd known. He didn't remember why Eliza had charmed him, but he remembered being charmed. He remembered dreaming about her. He would have screwed her even if he'd known her mother was an Indian, because marriage had not been a possibility then. Marrying her had never entered his mind.

He had to remind himself that he didn't have to pay the price for this. He wasn't marrying her, Aaron was. After Cole took her to the farm, he could walk away and forget about this. Hell, there was no reason even to tell Aaron or Pa about her Indian blood. By the time the baby was born, Cole would be long gone. If it was a blond, blue-eyed child . . . well, there wouldn't be anything to worry about. If not . . .

If not, there would just be one more reason not to come home.

He turned away from Margaret Beaudry. He heard her nearly soundless retreat, and then she was in the shadows again, watching, listening. He tried to ignore her. Cole sat at the table, across from Eliza, across from her father. He put his elbows on the surface and leaned over it.

"I'm sure you've heard the rumors," he said. "My father has money."

Eliza jerked up to meet his gaze. Her smile was gone, her expression wary. "I don't want your money," she said.

"We ain't takin' it, Lizzie," her father said. He looked at Cole. "I already gave you my answer on that, Wallace."

"That's not my offer," Cole said.

"There's only one offer that'll satisfy me," Beaudry said. "You're marryin' my girl, and that's that."

Cole took a deep breath. "I'm not marrying her."

Eliza flinched as if he'd struck her.

Beaudry rose. "If I have to carry you there myself —"

"I don't love her." Cole ignored Beaudry.

169

He reached across the table, took Eliza's hand. "I'm sorry, Eliza, but it's true. I'm sure you feel the same."

She shook her head. "No, I don't. I love you."

"How can you? We barely know each other."

She gave him a puzzled look.

Cole sighed. He released her hand and sat back. "My father has a farm near White Horse. He's very sick. I doubt he'll last much longer. When he dies, the farm will go to my younger brother, Aaron."

"What's that got to do with anythin'?" Beaudry demanded.

Cole kept his gaze pinned on Eliza's. "My brother wants a wife," he said quickly, then hurried on to convince her. "Think about it, Eliza. I'm a gambler. I haven't stayed in a town longer than three weeks since I was sixteen."

"But you ain't ever had a wife before."

"It won't change," he told her. "I may just stay farther away. Eliza, I wouldn't know how to be a husband, much less a good one."

"We would go with you," she said. Her arm crossed her belly as if she were protecting it. "You wouldn't even know we were there —"

"A baby?" he asked. "I wouldn't know a *baby* was there?"

"I would keep him quiet." Her eyes shone; she looked on the verge of tears. "I would."

"It wouldn't work, Eliza," he said softly. He took her hand again, rubbed his thumb over the calluses marking her palm. "I'm not that kind of man. I wouldn't be able to make you happy. I wouldn't be a good father. Aaron would be far better."

In the silence that fell after his words, he saw the understanding come into her eyes. She looked at him in dazed surprise. "You want me to marry . . . your brother?"

"I could march you to the preacher right now," Jack said. "You'd say yes quick enough with a rifle in your back."

"Probably I would," Cole agreed. "But is that what you want for your daughter, Jack? A man who travels from town to town, who makes his living gambling? In a year, maybe less, she'd be right back here on your doorstep, baby in hand. Is that what you want?"

Beaudry paused.

"I ain't ever coming back here," Eliza said quietly.

"Shush, Lizzie."

Cole started at the sound of the voice behind him. He'd forgotten about Eliza's mother, and he wanted her to stay forgotten.

171

He didn't like the twinge of guilt that went through him when he remembered her.

"This brother of yours," Beaudry was saying. "What kind of man is he?"

"He's a farmer," Cole said. "He's a good man."

"Drinker?"

Cole remembered his last night there, the tequila, the cards. He remembered Aaron falling asleep over his hand. "He's not a drinker," he said.

"Is he a churchgoin' man?"

"There's no church in White Horse. Not yet."

"Is he a ladies' man? Or God-fearin'?"

Cole nearly laughed. Aaron, a ladies' man. Cole wasn't even sure his brother would be able to keep himself together when he saw Eliza. Cole remembered the last time he'd seen Aaron with a woman. The man had stammered so much Delilah Evans believed those rumors about him.

Cole met Beaudry's gaze. "Given the choice," he said dryly, "I'd say he was religious."

Jack pursed his lips, stroked his chin. He stared at Cole so long, Cole had the notion that the man saw clear inside him, that he could read his mind. But Cole didn't tear his gaze away. He hadn't spent his life win-

ning at poker for nothing. He met Jack
Beaudry look for look.

"You say this brother of yours wants to
marry Lizzie?" Jack asked finally.

"That's what I'm saying," Cole said.

Beaudry looked at his daughter. Eliza sat
there, still and quiet, but Cole saw her denial
in the stiffness of her shoulders, the stubborn
set to that wide, full mouth.

Cole got to his feet so quickly that Beaudry
looked up in surprise. Cole held out his hand
to Eliza. "Come on." Then, to Jack, he said,
"Eliza and I need to talk about this, and I
guess you and your wife do, too. We'll be
outside."

Jack frowned. "Don't go far."

Eliza put her hand in Cole's and got to
her feet. She didn't look at him as he led her
outside, into air that felt cool and fragrant
after the dark smokiness of the shanty. Cole
saw his cigar in the yard, still smoldering,
and he ground it out with his boot and
thought about lighting another.

She was quiet until they got just beyond
the house, to the edge of the cotton fields.
Then she dropped his hand and crossed her
arms over her chest. The motion tightened
the material across her breasts, and Cole
thought again that she didn't look pregnant.

"You think it would be bad, marrying

me?" she asked quietly.

Cole sighed. "I'd make a bad husband, Eliza," he said. "I'd just be traveling all the time —"

"That would be all right." She turned to him, her words coming out in a gush. "I always wanted to travel, you know. Remember, I told you —"

"You wouldn't be traveling with me," he said softly. "Think about it, Eliza. You'd have a baby to worry about. I'd set you up in a house — probably right here in Richmond, so you'd be close to your parents. I'd come and visit you now and then, but that's it."

She looked at him. "You mean that?"

"Yeah." He sighed. "I'm making you a decent offer, you know. My brother's a good man. You'll have money. The farm is a big one. It would be a good life for you."

"What if I just said no?" she asked. "What if I said I'd only marry you?"

"Then you'd be alone," he said bluntly. "Because I'd ride out of here and you'd never see me again."

She winced and looked down at the ground.

Cole forced himself to be patient. "Aaron will make you a fine husband. He's . . . well, he's a good man."

"You said that," she said. She looked away from him, out to the fields. "You keep saying it. So I guess he must be. But . . ." She stared at him, those dark brows ferocious over her eyes, her face hard. "Why's he want to marry me? I'm having *your* baby. Can't he get a wife of his own?"

"He's . . . too busy," Cole lied. "He's a farmer. And he's . . . well, he's shy."

"He's shy?"

"He's a poet," Cole said, as if it explained everything.

She stared at him as if he'd lost his mind. "A poet?"

"He writes poetry."

Eliza turned away, squinting into the sun. He saw the way her fingers tightened on her arms, so tight the tips turned white, and it reminded him of something — Aaron, at the house, pressing his hands against the window.

"I don't know much about poetry," she said quietly.

"You can learn," he said. "He doesn't talk about it anyway, but if he does, so what? It's just a bunch of words that rhyme."

"Like what?" She still didn't look at him.

"Like, oh . . ." Cole wracked his brain. Finally, he came up with something, a grade-school recitation. " 'By the shore of Gitche

175

Gumee, / By the shining Big-Sea-Water, / Lived a . . .' Oh hell, that's all I can remember."

She turned to him quizzically. "That didn't rhyme."

"Well, I guess not all of them do," he said impatiently. "I don't really know. You'd have to ask Aaron."

She pressed her lips together. "You didn't answer me."

"I don't know enough poetry —"

"Not that," she said. "Why does he want to marry me? I'm nobody, you know." She laughed quietly, bitterly. "My daddy's a sharecropper. Does he know that?"

There was a melancholy in her words that made him sad until he reminded himself of what she was doing to him, how she had trapped him. "He knows all about you," Cole said.

"Does he?"

"He wants to marry you, Eliza. I can't tell you why. I just know he does."

She nodded and looked back out at the fields. She was quiet for so long he thought she was done talking, but then she said, "You met Mama."

It was something he didn't want to think about. He sure as hell didn't want to talk about it.

"Yeah," he said. "I met her. Now —"

"She's half-Comanche."

"So I see —"

"You didn't know that, did you?"

He sighed. "No. I didn't know it."

"If you knew it," she pressed, "would you have come back? Would you be telling me to marry your brother?"

The answer was no. If he'd known about Eliza's mother, he would have kept riding and hoped that Jack Beaudry never found him. But that didn't matter now. Everything was already taken care of. If Eliza kept her mouth shut about her Comanche mother, everything would be just fine.

But he didn't tell her that, because he knew she'd use it against him. Instead, he leaned over and brushed her jaw with his finger, and smelled her marshwater perfume and the deep, rusty fragrance of dirt.

"I would have come back." He whispered the lie. "And Aaron would still want to marry you."

She tilted her head to see him, and in that moment he knew he'd won. He'd given the right answer. It was all he could do to keep from dancing across the yard.

"I guess I got no choice."

"No," he said honestly.

She nodded shortly. "All right, then," she

said, and he heard the resignation in her voice, the weight of defeat.

He took her arm and led her back to the house, walking slowly and quietly to match her bittersweet mood, though he was singing and laughing in his head.

10

When Cole rode away that afternoon, Eliza's heart went with him. He had promised to come back the next morning. Together they would leave for his father's farm — and her new husband. She told herself over and over again that she was doing this for the sake of the baby, even though it still seemed like a dream that she was pregnant — a bad dream. She was sick every late afternoon and she was so tired sometimes she could barely move. There were days when her breasts were so sore it hurt to put her dress on. Other than those things, Eliza had to remind herself that she was going to have *Cole's baby*.

She thought of it that way, like a shout in her head. She'd been counting the days for Cole's return, and in that time she'd built dreams that wiped out every other bad memory she had of him. She remembered the day he'd loved her by the lake. She remembered his smile, and in the clutch of those memories, she forgot how angry she was at him, how hurt. When he'd come riding up today, she had wanted to run into his arms and hold onto him so tightly he couldn't get loose again.

Well, things hadn't worked out exactly right. But even when she married his brother, Cole would still be in her life. Nothing could change the fact that it was his baby she was carrying — even if he didn't love her just yet.

"Stop your daydreamin', girl." Daddy's voice was low, but Eliza was so deep inside her thoughts it still startled her. "You'd best start packin'. Don't give him a chance to go without you."

She turned from the doorway. "He ain't going without me."

Daddy harrumphed. He got up from the table, his joints creaking, and went past her, stepping outside. "Go on and talk to your Mama," he said. "She's goin' to miss you when you're gone."

Eliza looked around for her mother. Mama was standing by the stove, wiping her hands on her apron. At Daddy's words, she sighed and shook her head.

"There're some things I need to tell you, Lizzie," she said.

Eliza turned back to the door. She watched her father walk away, into the cotton fields. "I already know all about how babies get born, Mama."

"Don't sass me." There was no force behind the words. Mama was suddenly there, behind her. Eliza jumped at her touch. When she was a little girl, she'd never understood how her mother moved so soundlessly. Even wearing Daddy's clumsy old boots, it seemed Mama walked on air.

"What're you going to tell me, Mama?" Eliza looked over her shoulder. "More warnings? You were wrong the last time. I told you I'd be leaving this town, and here I am, on my way."

"Oh, Lizzie, you got a lot to learn." Mama moved away. She leaned against the wall on the other side of the doorway, staring into the darkness while Eliza looked into the light. "You think just because you're goin' to a different town, things'll change."

"They won't know who I am there."

"Oh, they'll know." Mama sighed. "You think it's only place that makes a lady?"

Eliza frowned. "Don't try to spoil it for me, Mama. I'll be married to a rich man. I think they'll treat me good enough."

"They'll be countin' on their fingers when you give birth to that baby," Mama said. "And people aren't as acceptin' of strangers as you like to think."

Eliza crossed her arms over her chest and

twisted to face her mother. "My husband lives in that town. He ain't a stranger."

"He will be to you," Mama pointed out. "Lizzie, Lizzie, I don't want to tangle with you tonight. I just want to tell you. There are good men, and then there are . . . men. You don't know anythin' about this new husband of yours."

"He's Cole's brother. That's all I need to know."

"No, it ain't." Mama leaned forward, her dark eyes burning. "You listen to me, Eliza Mae. You're marryin' a man who knows you ain't carryin' his child. He knows you had . . . relations with his brother. If you think that won't make him crazy, you got another think comin'."

"He said he'd marry me anyhow."

"You ain't his wife yet. When you are, it'll be different. You treat him right. No pinin' away for his brother. When you marry this man, you be *his* wife."

The emotion in her mother's voice made Eliza hesitate. She looked away to where Daddy was walking in the fields, and tightened her hands on her arms until the press of her fingers hurt. "I'm marryin' him," she said. "That's all I'm promising."

Mama was quiet. Then she pushed away from the wall. "You ain't goin' to listen to nobody," she said. "So you go on and do what you want, just like you always do. But don't think you can come runnin' home when you're done makin' a hell for yourself there." She walked into the shadows of the house.

"You can't help who you love," Eliza said. She said it quietly, words for herself only, but she heard her mother stop, heard her turn.

"Oh, yes you can, Lizzie," she said. "You surely can."

Eliza didn't say anything. She waited, but then she heard the clang of pans and she knew her mother was finished. Yeah, Mama would miss her all right. About as much as she would miss Mama. The hurry to leave came over Eliza so strongly it was all she could do to keep from running out the door, straight to the road. She couldn't wait to put this behind her, to ride away from her mother's quiet scolds and her Indian-eyed glances. How nice it would be to not have to come home to these straggling cotton fields, to work that never seemed to end. Eliza closed her eyes to breathe it in. Tomorrow morning seemed too long to wait.

She turned back inside, ignoring her mother as she went to pack her things. There wasn't much: some underwear, her other dress, her hat. She had no hidden treasures — only the beads her father had broken weeks ago.

Carefully, Eliza laid her things in her father's old knapsack. She left the hat out; she would wear it tomorrow. Eliza took it in her hands, shook it a little so the bird bobbed. When she got to White Horse, maybe she could buy something to match it. A dress maybe, or a shawl. She rubbed the grosgrain ribbon circling the crown, and thought of silks and velvets. Except for her petticoat, she'd never worn such things, and she wondered if they made a woman feel different, if they would wrap her up in magic the way the hat did.

"You ready to go, Lizzie?"

Daddy came into the cabin, rubbing his hands. Eliza laid the hat aside and closed the knapsack. She hadn't even come close to filling it up. The bag sagged and bent when she lifted it and put it beside her pallet.

"I'm ready," she said.

"Then come on over. We'll have a last supper together."

There was sadness in her father's words, but it was a sadness Eliza didn't feel. All she felt was joy, a funny, quivery giddiness that made her heart race. A last supper together. Finally. It seemed she'd prayed for such a thing for a long, long time.

She went over to the table and sat down across from Daddy. Mama set the cornbread on and then she joined them. Daddy ladled stew onto a plate and handed it to Eliza with a sigh.

"You two get your talkin' done?" he asked.

Eliza glanced at her mother. "Yeah."

"Good." He nodded. "That's good." He cleared his throat. "Lizzie . . . I just . . . well, I want you to be happy."

"I know that, Daddy."

"I been thinkin', and I . . . I think we might've been hasty, tellin' you to marry this man you ain't never seen —"

"The way I see it, Daddy, I don't got much choice."

"You could stay here. I don't mean to push you away."

Eliza's food caught in her throat. She stared up at her father. "I can't stay here," she managed.

"You could, if you think you'd be happier."

"No." Eliza forced herself to swallow. "I promised Cole I'd go. That's what I'm going to do."

Daddy hesitated, then he nodded and looked down into his plate. "I know, I know. You just . . . if things get bad, girl, you know you can come here. Your mama and I'll take care of you and the baby. That's all I'm tryin' to say."

It would be a nightmare to come back. She couldn't think of a single thing that would make her want to. But Eliza nodded and glanced at her mother, who wouldn't look at her. "I'll keep that in mind, Daddy."

"Good," he said. "Good."

The rest of the supper passed in silence, and they spent the evening like they always did, not talking, Daddy whittling away on a stick and Mama sewing in the corner. Eliza sat on her pallet, back against the wall, knees drawn up, and daydreamed until her nightly nausea became so bad she had to lay down.

It seemed she didn't sleep at all, but she must have, because when dawn came, it woke her up. Her excitement made her too anxious to stay in bed. She got up and washed at the rain barrel, and then she settled herself on the ground outside the door to wait.

"Come on and eat," Daddy said, leaning out the door.

She wasn't hungry. She couldn't imagine trying to keep food down, but Eliza knew her father wanted her company, and so she went inside and played with a piece of corn-bread while her parents ate.

"Wonder what time he'll be here?" she asked. "He said morning."

"It's prob'ly too early for him, Lizzie," Mama said. "He's a gamblin' man."

And it was true; the morning was half-gone before Cole finally showed up. Eliza saw him just as he rounded the bend in the road. He was leading another horse, and he was moving slowly. She couldn't keep her feet still; she ran out to meet him.

He looked sleepy and a little sick, but he smiled when he approached. "Morning, Miss Eliza Beaudry," he said. "You ready to head out?"

"I'm ready," she said eagerly. She grabbed his horse's reins as he dismounted. "Let's go."

"In a minute, in a minute." He laughed a little, but when his feet touched the ground he stumbled and put his hand to his head. "A little too much whiskey last night, I'm afraid," he said. "Where's the water?"

She pointed to the rain barrel. He walked over and stuck his whole head in. When he brought it out again, water streamed over his shoulders, down his back. He shook and water went splaying out from his short, dark hair, casting rainbows.

"Let's go," Eliza said.

He raised a brow. "I think I should talk

to your pa first, don't you?"

He walked around the corner of the house. Eliza sighed and dropped the reins. She hurried after him. "My bag's right by the door —"

"Morning, Mr. Beaudry," Cole said as Daddy came walking out. "I'm here again, just as I promised."

Daddy looked grim. He nodded and reached inside the door for Eliza's bag. "She's ready to go."

Mama leaned out. She motioned to Eliza, and when Eliza went over, Mama pulled her close and stroked her hair like she was a baby. "You take care of yourself, Lizzie," she whispered. "You hear me? You remember what I said."

Eliza nodded against her shoulder. "I will," she said, though she was too impatient to think of what her mother was talking about. She pulled away, and Daddy gathered her up, pressing her so hard against him she had to bury her face in his neck.

He let her go abruptly and turned to Cole. "You see she's happy, Wallace," he said. "Or I'll know the reason why."

"I'll do my best." Cole reached for her bag. He walked to the horses and slung it behind the saddle of the second one, securing it with a few loops and tugs. He turned back to her father. "You know where we are," he said.

"Yeah."

"I'm sure Eliza will let you know if she needs anything."

"I will," Eliza promised in a rush. She waved to her mother, kissed her father's cheek, and went to the horse. Cole had her hand and was helping her to mount when she remembered.

"My hat!" She stepped down again and ran back to the house. It was there, just inside the door. She shoved it on her head and went back to where Cole was waiting. "My hat," she explained.

It seemed he winced, but he could have just been squinting into the sun. "Can't forget that," he said. Then he sighed and helped her up. He mounted his own horse, and then they were off.

Her parents were standing in front of the shanty, and Daddy had his arm around Mama, which was startling enough that Eliza paused. But then they were almost to the road, and she waved and turned her back to them, her heart singing, her whole body leaning forward in the saddle. She was leaving — her dreams were coming true. If she had her way, she'd never set her eyes on Richmond again.

★ ★ ★

He stopped early not because he wanted to, but because Eliza was lagging. He wanted to ride straight through to White Horse, despite Aaron's plea for more time. Still, everything conspired against him: his own pounding headache, Eliza's inexperience riding. She looked tired and worn out, and he looked at her skirt hiking up over her legs and the red lace of her petticoat trailing out and those torn black stockings, and had the thought — once, briefly — that she might miscarry on the journey, and his problems would be over. But he didn't like the lack of compassion in the thought, he didn't like the kind of man it made him, so he buried it. Besides, his problems *were* over. Aaron was marrying her. All Cole had to do was get her to White Horse.

He felt again that pure, overwhelming rush of relief. It made him grin, made him charitable and charming even through his headache. He looked back at Eliza. "You ready to stop for the night?"

She gave him a weary smile. "I surely think so," she said. "I guess I ain't used to riding."

"No need to do it much in Richmond, I'd guess," he said. "But that'll change some where you're going."

Eliza came up close beside him. "You do a lot of riding on the farm? It's that big then?"

"Oh, it's plenty big." Cole squinted into the sun and spread his arms. "Cornfields stretch as far as you can see."

"That must be something to look at," she said, and then she lapsed into silence as if she were thinking about it. Or maybe she was just too tired to talk.

He chose a grove of bois d'arc a short distance from the river. He rarely camped himself; there were too many towns along the way, and he didn't like sleeping in the open. But on this journey he'd deliberately stayed away from towns. He knew too many people in these parts, and the last thing he wanted was for one of his acquaintances to see him with Eliza. He saw the disappointment in her face when he led her into the grove and dismounted.

"We're staying here?" she asked.

"I thought we'd camp tonight," he said, hobbling his horse. "We can get an early start in the morning."

"Oh. Well, I thought —"

She stopped abruptly. When he turned to see why, he saw her sliding off her horse, doubling over. He heard the sounds of her retching.

He hurried over to her, taking her shoulders, holding her steady while she vomited.

When she was done, she took several long, slow breaths, wiped her face with the back of her hand and looked up at him with a weak smile.

"I'm all right," she said, but her voice was shaking, and he had the feeling that if he let go of her she would fall. She straightened. Her hand went to her hideous hat. "I'm all right."

"Maybe you should lie down."

"No, I'll be fine," she assured him. "It's just . . . it'll be gone now for a while."

He realized then what it was. Morning sickness, though it was evening now. Once again, the reality of her pregnancy hit him. He let go of her and stepped away, feeling a little sick himself. "Let's get some food into you."

She shuddered and pressed her hand into her stomach. "Oh no. Just some . . . some coffee. And maybe some water."

He handed her his canteen, along with a handkerchief, and then he turned away and set up camp. He'd bought a couple of blankets for her bedroll in Richmond, and he laid these out a short distance from his own. He started a fire and put on some water to boil for coffee, and then he reached into his saddlebags for a can of beans and some dried beef.

She was sitting beneath a tree, her knees

drawn up, her hat on the grass beside her. She'd cleaned her face with his handkerchief and the water, though there were still streaks of trail dust at her jaw, by her ears.

He held up the beans and she shook her head.

"Beef, then?" he asked.

Her forehead wrinkled in thought, and then she nodded and reached for it. "I think that'll stay down."

When the coffee was ready, he took her a cup. She padded her hands with her skirt and took the metal cup between them. She sipped it carefully and smiled up at him.

"You still look drunk, Cole," she said. "Why don't you sit down and rest awhile?"

He wasn't drunk, not anymore. But he was damned tired. He'd stayed up too late last night, celebrating his freedom, and now the whiskey was staying with him like a dead smell on a body, and he wished he hadn't had that second bottle — or that he'd brought it with him today. Cole took his own coffee and sat down.

"My daddy used to have a cure for drunkenness," she said. "You want to hear it?"

He shrugged.

"Soda powder with lemon syrup and water."

"Sounds tasty."

"Daddy says it helps."

"Well, since I don't have soda powder or lemon syrup, it looks like I'll have to live without it."

She leaned forward. "I could put a cold compress on your head."

The offer was tempting, though he knew it shouldn't be. He should be staying the hell away from her. He got up to do it, to move away. But just then the setting sun slanted across their campsite, across Eliza. Just then, she lifted her face into it. Her hair fell back over her shoulders, and suddenly he felt a kick way down deep in his gut, an ache that tightened his whole body.

And he remembered. He remembered what he'd seen in her.

Cole closed his eyes and reminded himself of who she was, a trashy swampwater nobody, a girl who was no better than she had to be. He reminded himself that he hated the thought of marrying her into his family. He hated the thought that she was going to bear his child. He told himself it added insult to injury to lust for her too.

"You all right, Cole?" she asked.

"Yeah," he managed. "I'm okay."

"Come on over here," she said. She patted her lap. "Why don't you lie down? I'll be your pillow. You look like you could use one."

"I'm okay."

"Come on." She smiled. "I know you got a headache."

When she said it, that ache at his temples felt suddenly worse. It was pounding behind his eyes now, hard and relentless, and her lap was open and waiting for him, and she wanted him there. She wanted to mother him, and though he told himself it wasn't a good idea, told himself to refuse her, he found himself walking over to her. Found himself sitting beside her, lying down, resting his head in her lap. She was warm and soft, and he closed his eyes. Just for a moment. It would only be a moment. Then he'd feel better. It couldn't hurt, surely, not these few minutes. . . .

She smoothed her hand over his forehead. He felt the roughness of her hands, but her touch was gentle, and she knew how to soothe him, she knew the right rhythm, the soft, quiet stroking. He gave himself over to it, felt his body relaxing, the headache easing, the sinking lull of peace.

He was nearly asleep when she said, "My mama used to do this for me whenever I was feeling poorly. I always thought it was so nice."

"Hmmm," he said.

"Your mama do it for you?"

Cole sighed. He kept his eyes closed.

"Don't remember. She died when I was seven."

"Oh." There was a quiet that made him open his eyes and look up at her. She was staring down at him, her hair falling forward into her face, her expression as sad as her voice had been. "I'm real sorry for you, Cole. I thought . . . I thought she was still around. You ain't told me much about your family, so I guess I'll just make mistakes now and then. I hope I don't pain you too much."

Cole sighed. She was right; he hadn't told her anything about his family, and he supposed that had been deliberate. There were things she was better off not knowing until she got there and was married, until it was too late to back out. Still, it was better if she knew something — enough so she wasn't making up visions in her head. Just enough so she wasn't disappointed when she saw the truth of it. "What d'you want to know, Eliza?"

Her eyes brightened. "You sure?"

"Yeah. Ask away."

"Well, I . . . tell me about the farm."

"The farm." He hesitated. It had been so long since he really spent time there that he wasn't sure what to tell her. "Aaron would know all this better, but . . . let's see . . . it's about a section, I think, though I remember

196

Pa bought more a while back."

"Is it pretty?"

"Yeah. It's pretty. There's a creek running through it. Hubbards Creek."

She slowed her stroking. "What about your daddy? Did he get himself a new wife when your mama died?"

"No." Cole thought about his father in bed, sinking into the mattress, bones pressing against skin, his half-paralyzed arm bent at a weird angle.

"There ain't any other women there?"

"Just you."

She nodded and sighed. "I'll be the only one," she said in a dreamy voice. She patted her flat stomach. "Unless it's a girl."

A girl. His headache came slamming back. He saw that loopy, dreamy look on her face, felt her hand on his brow, and for a moment it was as if he were standing away from his body, watching this scene, watching how tenderly she stroked his head, how she looked down at him, how she patted her stomach the way a woman did when she was carrying the baby of a man she loved. He jackknifed up, so hard and fast his head spun and she made a sound of surprise.

"What is it, Cole?" she asked.

He went to the fire and grabbed for the coffeepot settled in the coals. Her face filled his mind, the look in her eyes, and he wished he hadn't laid his head in her lap — damn, what a stupid thing to do.

"Nothing," he managed. "Nothing." He turned back to her and smiled until the fear on her face eased, faded, and she smiled back.

"All right then," she said, leaning forward, clasping her knees in her arms. "Tell me more. I want to know all about White Horse. I want to know all about your life."

His life. Not Aaron's. She hadn't asked a single question about his brother since they'd left Richmond, and Cole knew that was trouble. She should be wondering about Aaron. He was going to be her husband. She should want to know every damned thing about him.

And in his heart Cole knew he should tell her. He should talk about Aaron until she was so full up of knowing about him that it was like she was marrying an old friend. But it wasn't easy to think of things to tell her about his brother — what the hell would he say? She would be finding out herself soon enough, and it wasn't Cole's job to make her fall in love with his brother. That was up to Aaron. All Cole wanted was for the rest of this damned journey to be done with. He wanted to ride away, to forget about her.

Until that happened, he wanted everything to be easy.

So he sat down and smiled through his headache and sipped his coffee until the pounding in his temples eased. And then he set about charming her until she was smiling and laughing, and he knew she would go the rest of the way without troubling him.

11

It was late afternoon, and it was so hot they'd given up work for the day. Aaron sat on the porch, as far away from the sun as he could get. Carlos was on the steps, drinking one of Miguel's vile concoctions.

"This one is good," he said with a nod. He held the cup out to Aaron. "You should try this, *señor*."

Aaron shook his head, gave a mock shudder. "No thanks."

"It is already making me stronger. I feel it."

Aaron leaned his head back against the window. "Good. You can probably do the work of three men, then. Tomorrow, the fields are yours."

"Ah." Carlos groaned loudly. "Perhaps I make too much of it."

Aaron grinned. "Perhaps."

He closed his eyes. The day was sweltering around him, hot even for late July. It would be a dry year — just thinking about it made his head hurt. Already the creek was slowing down, drying up. It would be nothing but sand in a few weeks if the weather didn't change.

It was just one more thing to worry about, and he was tired of worrying. He was tired of lying in bed at night tossing and turning, thinking too much, fretting. He hadn't written a word of poetry since Cole's visit; every time Aaron sat down with a piece of paper, the words fell short, fluttered away like moths in darkness. He was too cluttered up to find them.

It had been two weeks since Cole left. Two weeks and two days. Any hour now he would come riding up that road, and every single minute until then filled Aaron with such dread that he almost wished Cole would show up just so he could stop waiting for him.

Aaron heard footsteps on the porch. He opened his eyes to see Miguel come out the front door, shading his eyes with one hand. He had a cup in the other.

"*Señor* Aaron," he said, holding it out. "*Esta muy caliente.* You must drink this."

Aaron eyed it warily. "What's in it this time? Rat poison?"

Miguel looked offended. "It is only some ginger and water. And sugar. *Señora* Tate, she says it is a 'switchel.' She gives me *la receta.*

It will not harm you. She says it is good for the" — he motioned with his hands — "the sun."

Aaron sighed and reached for the cup. "All right. I'll try it. Just remember, if I die, you get to take Pa his supper tonight."

On the steps, Carlos shuddered. "I would run away first."

"Take my body with you, then," Aaron said. He took a small sip of Miguel's drink, expecting a sour taste, or bitterness. Miguel hadn't got a recipe right since he'd first arrived here two years ago. But there was a pleasant sweetness to the switchel, a spiciness that tasted good going down his dry throat. Aaron took another sip, a bigger one this time, and nodded. "Not bad, Miguel," he said. "I'm —"

"Who is that?" Carlos frowned and got to his feet. He leaned forward to see beyond the porch. "Someone comes."

A chill went through Aaron. Slowly, he leaned forward. Two long shadows were moving down the road. Two horses. Two people. He'd been wrong to think he would be relieved. He wasn't relieved at all. He wanted to run — he would have run if they hadn't been close enough to see him go. The switchel he'd just drunk churned so violently in his stomach he was afraid it would come up again.

"It is *su hermano*," Carlos said, looking puzzled. "He has a lady with him."

"My wife," Aaron managed. His voice came out in a croak of sound.

Carlos turned toward him in surprise. Miguel swallowed.

"Forgive me, *señor*," Miguel said. "I did not hear —"

"She's going to be my wife," Aaron said again, more strongly this time, as much for himself as for the two Mexicans staring at him in stunned amazement.

He saw them then, clearly. They were just on the other side of the creek. He saw Cole glance up and wave, and then Aaron saw her — Eliza — look up. She was wearing a bright blue hat with something on it, and a gray dress. He couldn't see her face.

Aaron took a deep breath. He stepped down the porch, feeling the silent scrutiny of the farmhands. His feet felt leaden as he made his way across the yard. He waited there while Cole and Eliza crossed the creek. Then, too soon, they were in front of him, and Cole was smiling and dismounting and helping Eliza from her horse.

"I told you I'd be back," Cole said — as if Aaron had doubted it for a moment. Eliza found her feet and Cole stepped back with a flourish. "Aaron, this is Eliza Beaudry.

Eliza, my brother Aaron."

He just stared at her, tongue-tied. Cole had been right; she was one of the prettiest women Aaron had ever seen. She was full bosomed and full-hipped, and her eyes were blue and almond-shaped, her brows dark. She was looking at him as if she couldn't decide whether to smile or not, and then, suddenly, she did. She gave him a wide-mouthed smile that was so charming and sincere that Aaron nearly fell back from the strength of it. He understood what it was Cole had seen in her. The thought brought another, more jarring one. She had been his brother's lover.

She held out her hand. "Pleased to meet you, Aaron."

He stared down at her hand.

"Normally, you take it, little brother," Cole said impatiently. He stepped forward, grabbing Aaron's hand, putting Eliza's in it.

Aaron felt the flush of humiliation wash over his face. He swallowed, forced himself to speak. "E-Eliza," he said, and then winced at his inability even to muster a greeting.

Her smile faltered. She looked uncertain. She pulled her hand from his. He felt its lack, the sudden nothingness, the absence of rough calluses, of gentle bones.

"I guess . . . well, Cole told me a lot about you."

He wasn't sure what it was, whether it was her mention of his brother's name, or the withdrawal of her hand, but whatever it was broke the spell keeping him mute and stupid.

"You look t-tired," he said.

She flinched. Cole laughed. "You're a born romantic, Aaron. Christ, telling a woman she looks tired, especially one that's ridden clear from Richmond to marry you."

It took Aaron a moment to realize that he'd insulted her. His face went hot; he started to sweat. "I'm sorry," he said, turning to her. "I'm not . . . used to —"

"It's all right," she said, though her smile was gone. "I guess I don't look so good."

"Why don't you get us both a drink?" Cole jerked his head toward the porch. "Can one of your guards there take care of the horses?"

Aaron glanced back at Miguel and Carlos. They were flanking the stairs, looking wary. Aaron motioned to Carlos. "The horses . . ." he managed.

Carlos nodded shortly and came down the steps. He stiffened and looked straight ahead as he walked past Cole.

"Catch a bad smell there, Carlos?" Cole asked. He looked amused as he grabbed the saddlebags off the horses and turned to

Aaron. "Your boys don't seem to like me."

Aaron heard him with only part of his brain. The other part was still staring at Eliza. Staring at her pointed chin and her delicate face, and the fine down along her jaw. He longed to touch her again, was afraid to touch her. His yearning tightened his whole body. She fidgeted and looked down at the ground.

"Aaron," Cole said loudly. "Are you going to get those drinks?"

Aaron started. He'd forgotten already. He mumbled an apology and started toward the house. He heard her say something to Cole, and heard his brother's soft murmur, but Aaron was too far away to hear the words.

He went up the porch, to the door. Miguel stepped in front of him.

"I will get it, *señor*," he said. He threw a narrow-eyed glance at Cole. "You are not the servant."

Aaron stepped back, momentarily confused by Miguel's statement, by his clear dislike of Cole. Then Aaron realized that he'd been running to do his brother's bidding, just like always. He'd stepped into habit in front of the woman who was going to be his wife. Cole was a master of subtle humiliation, and Aaron felt it again, the slow rush of blood into his face, the embarrassment that made him afraid to turn around again and face them.

He stood there while Miguel went into the house. Aaron closed his eyes, took a deep breath, forcing his heart to slow, his mind to clear. He could do this. He could talk to her. Eliza Beaudry knew nothing about him. She wouldn't know the stories, the rumors. There was no reason for him to be so ill at ease.

He filled his head with reassurances and turned around. She was coming to the porch, and when she saw him she stopped. Right in the middle of the yard. Cole came up behind her, carrying the saddlebags and an old, sagging knapsack.

Cole walked up to him. "This is hers," he said, throwing Aaron the bag.

Aaron wasn't expecting the toss, and he barely caught the knapsack. It was so limp it was hard to get a good hold on it. He ended up clutching it to his chest like a baby with a beloved toy.

Miguel came out of the house carrying a bent tray with some cups and a pitcher on it. He looked around for a moment, as if he expected there to be a table somewhere on the porch, and then he just set the tray on the floor near the edge of the steps. "Here is your drinks," he said. He looked at Aaron and lowered his voice, speaking just to him. "The old man, he is awake."

Aaron winced. Of course Pa would wake up now. The old cripple had a sixth sense about things like this. He'd probably known his favorite son was coming when he woke up this morning.

Aaron glanced at his brother. "Pa's awake," he said.

Cole shrugged his saddlebags onto the ground beside the porch. "Why don't you show Eliza to her room, then? You can stop in on the way by." He leaned forward, grabbing one of the cups from the tray, twisting around to hand it to Eliza, who was standing so close to him he nearly bumped into her when he turned. She took it with a soft smile and clutched the cup in her hands like she hadn't seen water for a week.

Cole patted her arm. "Aaron'll show you your room." He smiled at Aaron. "Well, go on, little brother."

Aaron's mouth went suddenly dry. She was looking at him, and though her smile didn't go away, he saw the wariness in her eyes. She'd edged even closer to Cole. She didn't want to go anywhere with Aaron, that was clear, and Aaron didn't want to take her, not yet. Because the only room for her was the one she would share with him, and Cole had to know that. Just as he knew that Pa would hear them on the stairs, and Aaron would have no choice but to take her in there to meet the old man. They weren't even married yet. One look at Pa, and she was likely to run screaming from the house.

"Maybe later," Aaron said slowly.

"I'm sure Eliza wants to freshen up," Cole said. "Don't you, darlin'?"

She jerked a little bit, and looked surprised, and then a smile spread over her face like the sun on a fine spring morning. Cole touched her arm again. "Go on with Aaron," he said. "He'll introduce you to Pa."

She nodded and put her cup on the edge of the porch. "All right," she said, though it looked as if she would rather do anything than go with him.

There was no choice then. Aaron threw a glance at his brother, and Cole looked back at him with such wide-eyed innocence it would have been amusing if Aaron hadn't been the target. Aaron shifted the bag to his side and went up the steps. He heard her behind him, the softer tread of her boots, the hush of her breath. He felt her stare on his back, and it made his whole body tight, imagining what she saw when she looked at him, how he must suffer in comparison to Cole. He led the way through the front room, to the stairs opposite the kitchen.

"It's big," she said.

He turned to look at her. She was staring at the open room, the windows that stretched almost floor to ceiling along the front.

He had no idea what to say to her, so he just nodded. When she didn't say anything else, he started up the stairs, juggling the knapsack to allow for the narrowness of the passage. He was halfway up when Pa started ringing that damn bell.

Her footsteps halted. "What's that?"

"Pa," he said. He raised his voice, directed it to the open door at the end of the hall. "We'll be there in a minute, old man."

He turned the opposite direction when he reached the top of the stairs. He passed the middle room — the one that belonged to Cole whenever he deigned to set foot on Wallace property — and went straight to his room at the far end of the hall from Pa's. He paused at the closed door, and his heart started pounding so hard he felt the pump of blood in his ears. The doorknob slipped in his hand. He thought about taking her to see Pa first, but when he turned to do that she was standing there, blocking the narrow hall, watching him with an expectancy that fairly stole his breath.

Aaron pushed open the door with his knee and immediately got a faceful of sweltering air, despite the fact that he'd left the window open. While Pa's room faced the east, Aaron's faced west, and the late afternoon sun blasted through the small room like a furnace. He stood back, against the open door, giving her room to enter.

She stepped past him, into the room. She stopped just inside, just beyond him, and he saw her gaze shift from the unmade bed in the corner to the piles of books towering beside it, the papers littered across the frayed red-and-white wedding-ring quilt his grandmother had made. There was dust on the floor and red dirt caking the boots abandoned under the window. The curtains hanging there were pulled back with a rag from one of his old shirts — he'd long ago lost whatever that pretty thing was that held the curtains — and there was a jagged tear slicing through the half-lowered blind.

He saw all those things and immediately felt exposed. This room was his, had been his for years. Everything in it told something about him. He was too busy with Pa and the farm to make his bed. The papers were a poem he'd been working on three weeks ago — they were usually spread on the floor, but they'd been in his way this morning when

211

he was looking for his blue shirt. His work-boots were colored from the cornfields, and the tear in the blind had come when he'd lost his temper at his father a year ago.

It smothered him, how much she would know about him just by looking, and he felt the sudden urge to jerk her out again, to close the door. He didn't want to share this room with her. He didn't want her to know his secrets. He didn't want her in his bed . . . Christ, in his bed.

Fear and longing hit him so hard he closed his eyes to control it. When he opened them again, she was looking at him.

"This is your room," she said.

He managed a nod. He saw her swallow.

"I guess it's mine too, then."

He didn't say anything. He pressed against the door and looked over her to the window, to that tear in the blind.

"When're we getting married?" There was a rounding to her words, a faint and lilting accent, a low-country burr. It shivered through him, slow and easy, and he felt a stirring in his body, a thickness that brought a lump to his throat.

He cleared his throat. "There's . . . uh . . . no j-judge in White Horse. No . . . preacher either. They ride the circuit."

She threw him a look he couldn't interpret.

"I see," she said. She looked back at the bed. She took a deep breath, and then she shifted her gaze to him. "You're not . . . this ain't a joke, is it? We *are* getting married?"

Her words startled him. For the first time, he looked at her, really looked at her, and saw something like fear in her eyes, and realized that he hadn't bothered to think about what this marriage might mean for her. He hadn't wondered if she loved his brother or what she felt about marrying him. He hadn't thought about whether she was afraid.

Now, he stared into her wary face and he couldn't help knowing what she must have thought when he showed her this room, this bed, when he told her there was only a circuit preacher. She didn't know him, and Cole had already sold her out. There was no reason for her to believe that Aaron would keep his word. She was at their mercy, really. It was an uncomfortable thought.

She had been nothing but a vision before that moment. Just a faceless fear, a pretty prison. But with her question, she'd turned into a real person, and he knew she needed his help, and that he would help her. She was simply a woman who had been ill-treated, a woman who had done nothing more but make the mistake of falling for his brother's considerable charm.

He felt a wave of dislike for Cole so strong Aaron had to turn away from her, and it was that, finally, that eased that lump in his throat. "We're . . . really going to get married," he said. "No joke."

"Well then, I guess I should thank you," she said slowly.

He looked at her with a frown. "For what?"

"For marrying me."

She was serious. There was nothing in her expression or in her words that made him think she blamed his brother for not doing his duty, or that she hated Cole for abandoning her. Aaron wondered why. He wondered what she was thinking, if she'd cared for his brother, if Cole was so easily replaced. But Aaron didn't ask. He didn't want to know. He wouldn't be able to measure up to Cole anyway, so it was better not to think of himself as a replacement. It was better not to raise her expectations at all.

He let her bag fall to the ground with a thud. "You better meet Pa," he said.

She nodded and straightened her hat even though there was no mirror to look into. At the motion, the little stuffed bird buried its beak in the peony, and he thought it was strangely pretty, both her delicate fix and the lifelike bobbing of the bird. He swallowed and turned away from her, leading her down the hall, unsure which he dreaded more, introducing her to his father or being alone with her.

Pa was quiet as they approached his door, which was so completely out of character Aaron wondered for a moment if his father was still alive. He stopped just beside the door and edged around, waiting for a well-aimed crash. Pa was sitting in bed, the chalkboard in his lap, looking for all the world like a demure invalid.

Pa lifted one brow when he saw Aaron, a question, and Aaron stepped farther into the room and motioned for Eliza to follow him. She came inside eagerly — it was obvious Cole had told her nothing about their father — and stopped short when she saw him. She frowned for a moment in confusion, and glanced at Aaron. Pa was watching them carefully; beneath his scrutiny, Aaron forced a confidence he didn't quite feel.

"Pa," he said, "this is . . . Eliza. Eliza, this is my father, Thomas Wallace."

She smiled, though she still looked surprised, and went toward Pa. "Mr. Wallace," she said in that pretty, low-country accent. "Nice to meet you." She offered her hand, and then dropped it uncertainly.

But, to Aaron's surprise, Pa reached out with his good hand and grabbed hers. He smiled that odd, lopsided smile, and when she grinned back at him, he kissed her hand and let her go. He motioned to Aaron.

"He had a stroke a few years ago," Aaron said. "He can't speak."

"Oh." She looked immediately sorry. "How awful."

Pa wrote on the chalkboard and held it up to her. "I'M GLAD YOU'RE HERE," it said.

She stared at that chalkboard as if she were burning its words into her mind. Her forehead wrinkled, her brows winged together. She threw a quick glance at Aaron, as if she wanted him to say something, and then she sighed and smiled again.

"Oh. Well." She touched the hat again, nervously, and then she threw Aaron an inexplicable look and stepped back until she was beside him. She touched his arm; the contact made him jump.

Pa wrote and turned the chalkboard around. "GET THE BIBLE."

She was still so damn close Aaron couldn't think. It took him a minute to really understand his father's words, and then his heartbeat sped again; he heard its thumping in his ears.

"Now?" he asked.

Pa nodded.

"But —"

Pa rapped on the side of the board for emphasis.

"What is it?" Eliza asked. "What's he saying?"

Aaron didn't take his eyes from his father as he answered her. "P-pa used to be a . . . judge. He's . . . he's going to . . . marry us."

"Oh." She didn't even blink. "I thought you said there was just the preacher."

The room felt too hot. Aaron put his hand on the edge of his father's desk to steady himself. He'd wanted a day, maybe two — long enough to get to know her, to not feel so damned . . . clumsy around her. He wanted Cole gone, so he didn't have to look in his brother's face and wonder how Cole kissed her, how he made love to her. . . .

It was all Aaron could do to keep his expression even when Pa stared at him. When Pa pointed to the shelf on the desk.

Desperately, Aaron looked at Eliza. "We can . . . wait — if you want," he said. "This might be t-too fast . . ."

"I guess we might as well go ahead," she said.

He caught his breath; his insides seemed

to squeeze together. Pa motioned again to the shelf, and there was the challenge now in his eyes, the same challenge that had forced Aaron to accede to this three weeks ago. *BE A MAN,* it said, and Aaron turned away, willing his fingers not to tremble as he grabbed the old family Bible from the desk. The gilt words stamped into the beaten leather cover shone even through the dust, and it felt heavy and serious, important. Things done in the name of this book were not easily undone. Names written inside were never scratched out, never erased. A man went into this book when he was born and was mentioned again when he married, and even when he died his name stayed there, fading but real, a record of presence that could not be undone. *You were here,* the book said. *You left this behind.*

Now, Aaron held it in his hand and knew this was his last chance to back out. His last chance to say no. Once their names were written inside, it would be over.

He glanced up at Pa. The old man was watching him, his gaze stark and careful, and Aaron heard the words again, *AFRAID OF A WOMAN?* and he looked at Eliza, who was standing there, quiet and patient, looking vaguely confused. When she caught his gaze, she smiled nervously.

"You thinking on changing your mind?" she asked.

Aaron's gaze shifted to his father. He shook his head. "No," he said. He walked over, handing the Bible to Pa, stepping back.

Pa put the book in his lap and with his good hand opened it to the family registry. Then he thumped his bad one onto it, holding its place, and looked up at Aaron expectantly.

Aaron got the pen and ink. He put it down on the bedside table, uncorked the ink, dipped the pen. Each movement had a permanence about it, each one brought him closer and closer. He was close, but he could still say no. He could still back out. Until the pen touched that page . . .

It became a game, a pick-up-sticks of nerve. Could he do this and still be free? Could he move the pen here, dip it, pass it to his father, and not be married? Not make the move to send the sticks falling . . .

Pa took the pen. It dripped ink on the blanket, but Pa moved his hand closer to the page, closer. It was an inch away, and then a hairsbreadth, and then —

He stopped. His fingers shook on the pen, and then, his mouth curved into a mean-edged smile. He looked up at Aaron and handed him the pen, and the light in his eyes dared Aaron. *You can't do it,* that look said. *Show me you're a man.*

Aaron's game with himself dissolved; it was suddenly deadly serious. But he didn't pause. Pausing would have meant weakness, and so he turned the book toward him, bent over the elaborate family tree. He saw his mother's name and his father's, the record of their births penned in his mother's rounded and elaborate hand: *Eli Thomas Wallace, May 9, 1841; Cole Spencer Wallace, September 15, 1846;* and there, his own: *Aaron John Wallace, March 1, 1848.*

Aaron put the pen to the page. He wrote his name as carefully as he could, and then he looked up at her and held out the pen. "Your name," he said.

She stepped away. "You write it," she said. "Eliza Mae Beaudry."

There was a rhyme in it that appealed to him; he let it spin through his head for a moment before he nodded and wrote her name beside his, and then he put the date, July 24, 1876.

He dipped the pen again and handed it to his father, holding the book steady while Pa scrawled his name, almost illegible, shaking and jerky. *Thms. J. Wallace.*

It was done. Aaron closed his eyes, took a

deep breath. It was over. They hadn't even needed words.

"It's done, then?" Eliza asked. "Is it done already?"

He heard Pa close the book, and Aaron opened his eyes to see the old man smiling like he'd just created Adam. Pa reached out his hand to Eliza, who stood back, watching them both with a puzzled look on her face. When Eliza took it, Pa brought her forward, jerked his head at Aaron.

Aaron knew what his father wanted, and so he did it. He offered his hand, and Pa put hers in it just like Cole had done outside. Handing her over, entrusting her to him. The pressure of that touch made Aaron think of everything this wedding hadn't been. He thought of how Cole would have done it, how easily his brother would put her at ease, how he would have reached for her and whispered an endearment before he kissed her. Aaron looked at their hands, clasped across Pa's white counterpane, and suddenly realized he was married to her. He was married to her. She was his wife.

He dropped her hand so suddenly she looked at him in surprise. He saw her uncertainty the moment before she gave him a tentative smile. "So . . . we're married?"

Married. The word sounded so damn final.

He nodded, but his throat was too tight to speak. He heard Pa's scratching on the chalkboard.

"YOU'RE A WALLACE NOW."

Eliza came around the bed, until she was beside Aaron. "You all right?" she asked.

Pa frowned and motioned to him, waving him out. The old man wanted to be alone with her, and Aaron was happy to let him. He backed to the door.

"He wants to talk to you alone," he said.

Eliza started after him. "Alone?"

He stopped her with a gesture. The air was so close he couldn't breathe. "I'll . . . I'll be b-back," he said, and then he was out, leaving her and the old man behind, hurrying down the hall to his room. He nearly knocked down the door getting through it, and he threw himself on the bed, among his papers, hearing the crinkle of them beneath him, feeling a book slant into his hip.

He closed his eyes, forgetting her, forgetting the Bible, letting the familiarity of his room wash over him, the comforting sameness. He buried his nose in his quilt, taking deep breaths of it until his heart slowed and his stomach didn't feel so clutched up and uneasy. Then he rolled over, sat up. Relief was so clean-edged and sharp he felt giddy with it. This was his room. His room. Nothing had changed, not anything he couldn't handle. So what if she was his wife? He would manage. He always managed.

But then he saw her bag on his floor, beside his boots, and he broke out into a cold sweat. He barely made it to the window before he heaved his dinner to the ground two stories below.

12

She was scared. She'd turned scared the moment Cole told her they were two miles from the farm, and, even though he'd smiled and told her it would be all right, her heart hadn't stopped pounding since. Now, sitting in this room, alone with this odd, crippled man who made her feel more welcome than anyone else had, she was uneasy. She already liked Cole's father better than his brother — her husband now . . . oh, what a strange thought — but she wished Mr. Wallace could talk. She didn't know how long she could pretend to read those words he scrawled on that chalkboard, and she was afraid to admit she didn't understand them. It would be embarrassing, humiliating, and she wanted so badly for him to like her, to approve of her. She had nothing else but this family now. If he didn't think she was worthy to marry into it, why . . . he might kick her out. He might even undo the marriage.

It made her so nervous to think about it that her mouth went dry. She folded her hands in her lap and gave him her prettiest smile.

He held up the chalkboard. The words were just a bunch of meaningless white lines. She stared at them hard, willing herself to understand, but the words only wavered before her, and in the end all she got were watery eyes.

She broadened her smile. "I'm real nervous, Mr. Wallace," she confided. "I'm sorry, I ain't at my best."

He laughed a little. The sound was odd, but it warmed her deep into her stomach. When he waved away her protests, she felt better. She relaxed, leaned back against the hard slats of the chair. When he picked up the chalkboard to write again, she spoke quickly to forestall him.

"You got a beautiful farm here," she said earnestly. "I saw the corn when me and Cole came riding in. I never saw such fields. Why, they must reach all the way up to the sky."

He sat back against the pillows, letting the chalkboard rest on his knees. He tilted his head a little, and his eyes were bright; Eliza saw he liked her, and it made her bold.

"And this house . . . Those windows downstairs just light up the whole place."

He smiled. It was sort of a strange expression, but Eliza thought she could get used to it. He reached out his hand, motioned for her to come closer, and she pulled her chair up beside the bed. He took her hand in his big, callused one, clasping her fingers. His skin was warm and dry.

Eliza looked down, at his old fingers, at the pale skin dotted with freckles and age spots. "Mr. Wallace," she said honestly, "I know I'm only here because I'm having Cole's baby. I know that's the only reason your son married me. But I . . . I want you to know I'll do my best for this family. I'll try to make you all happy."

Mr. Wallace squeezed her hand, and then he turned it over so it was palm up in his. Eliza resisted the urge to close it again, to hide the calluses marking her fingers, the ball of her thumb. But Mr. Wallace only rubbed his thumb over hers, raised the eyebrow on the good side of his face in question.

Eliza felt herself flushing. "My daddy . . . he's a farmer too. I'm . . . I'm a good worker, Mr. Wallace. You won't have cause to think I'm lazy."

The old man laughed; it was a clenching rumble deep in his chest that came out in a short burst, a *ha!* of sound. He squeezed her hand and then released her and picked up the chalkboard. Eliza's throat tightened. She waited while he wrote something and held it up, and she felt the cold heat of sheer panic as she looked at the symbols on the board.

She swallowed hard and glanced away. "I can cook some, too. And I . . . well . . . I'll be a good wife, Mr. Wallace. You don't have to worry."

His brows came together in confusion; Eliza winced. Whatever it was he'd written down, she hadn't answered it right. She waited for him to do something, to look displeased, to order her out, but he only erased the board with his sleeve and wrote something else. Something shorter this time.

Her fear came back again, a cold spot in her heart. Eliza didn't even look at the board. She leaned over, touched his hand, forced a smile. "I can take care of you, too, Mr. Wallace. You think you'd like that?"

She felt his dark eyes boring into hers, but there was no anger in them, nothing but a puzzlement that cleared almost the moment she said the words. He patted her hand and made a sound deep in his throat, and the smile she gave him was real this time.

Eliza got up, eased him forward, fluffed his pillows. She heard him sigh when he leaned back again.

"There now, Mr. Wallace," she said. "I think we're going to be good friends."

"You'd be the only one."

She jumped at the voice, jerked around to see Cole standing in the doorway, leaning against the jamb, dangling a lit cigar. He straightened and came fully into the room. "Well, what do you think, old man?" he asked. "You like my little Eliza?"

There was something mean in his voice, something that made her shiver even though he'd called her his "little Eliza."

Mr. Wallace grumbled. He picked up the chalkboard and wrote. When he held it to Cole, Cole laughed.

"Well, what d'you know," he said. "I guess there's a first time for everything."

"A first time?" Eliza asked.

Cole lifted his brow at her. The motion made him look — for a split second — exactly like his father. "You're the first thing I've ever done that pleased him," he said. "Isn't that right, old man?"

Cole's father made a sound deep in his throat.

Cole looked away. "Where's my wayward brother?"

"He left," Eliza said. "I don't think he was feeling good."

"I imagine not."

"After your daddy married us, he —"

"Already?" Cole looked at his father in

surprise. "Fast work." He reached into his vest pocket and pulled out a folded piece of heavy paper. "Thought you might need a marriage license to make it legal."

He took the paper to the nightstand and spread it out, pushing aside the Bible to lay it flat. He picked up the pen and dipped it in the ink and handed it to his father.

"A marriage license?" Eliza asked. "When'd you get that?"

"In Richmond," Cole said. "It's been burning a hole in my pocket."

Mr. Wallace took the pen and scrawled his name shakily across the bottom. When he was done, he handed the pen back to Cole and sat back against the pillows with a smile.

"Well, that's done," Cole said. He was grinning as he puffed on his cigar. "Looks like you're Mrs. Aaron Wallace, Eliza."

There was a satisfaction in his voice, a tone that stabbed painfully into her heart. For a moment, she wished so hard that the name was different it made her sick. How much happier she would be if it were Mrs. *Cole* Wallace. She looked at him, standing there, handsome and self-assured, and thought of the man she'd married instead. The man who had turned pale the moment his father had closed the Bible, who had seemed unable to escape the room — and her — fast enough.

She managed a weak smile. "Yeah," she said. "Looks like it."

"Well, then, I'll be on my way." Cole took the license and folded it, and then he stuffed it into the Bible and stepped away from his father's bed. "Hate to wear out my welcome."

She felt a pure rush of panic. "You ain't going so soon?"

He nodded. "Time to be moving on."

"But you can't! We just got here —"

"I guess it's probably better that way." Cole threw a glance at his father. "Isn't it, old man?"

Mr. Wallace held up the chalkboard, and Cole laughed bitterly. "See what I mean?" he said to Eliza.

She didn't see at all, and she didn't know what Mr. Wallace had written on that slate, but she couldn't imagine it was hurtful.

Cole was heading for the bedroom door. "*Adios,* Pa," he said, and then he looked over his shoulder at Eliza. "Have a good life, Eliza. I expect you'll be happy enough." He went out the door.

She heard his footsteps in the hallway, and her panic grew so she could hardly breathe. She threw a glance at Mr. Wallace, and then looked at the empty door. She heard Cole moving to the stairs.

"I . . . I have to go," she said. "I'll be back." She rushed to the door, nearly tripping over her skirt as she hurried after Cole. She caught him when he was halfway down the stairs.

"Cole," she said breathlessly. "Wait. Please."

He turned to look at her.

"You can't mean to leave me yet," she pleaded. "Not yet."

He frowned. "Come on, Eliza. You don't need me here. What'd you think, that I'd just hang around once you married Aaron?"

That was exactly what she'd thought. She'd spent the whole journey dreaming about it, thinking of Cole's head resting in her lap and his little kindnesses and his smiles. Thinking of living on this farm and being lady of the house and loving him . . .

"You can't leave me," she said desperately. "I need you."

He laughed. "What the hell for?"

"To . . . to show me around. I don't know anything."

"Aaron can show you around." He turned away, started back down the stairs. "I've got to go. I want to get to White Horse before the sun sets."

"No, please." Eliza grabbed at his sleeve. "Just let me talk to you a minute, Cole.

231

Please. Just a minute."

He paused, chewed on the end of his cigar. Then he sighed heavily. "All right," he said. "Just for a minute."

Eliza followed him down the steps, through the big main room and outside. Cole leaned against the post hard enough that his weight shook the porch roof. He didn't seem to notice. He puffed on his cigar and gazed out at the cornfields stretching beyond the yard, and though he looked relaxed, his back was stiff; there was a tension in his body that Eliza recognized. He wanted to leave; she had only minutes with him.

"I don't want you to go," she said. "I . . . I ain't a coward, Cole, but I would . . . I would rest easier if you helped me out for a bit. Just until I know my way around."

He turned a little to look at her, raised his brow. "You're a married woman, Eliza," he said. "You're my brother's wife."

His meaning hit her hard. The last hour had seemed like a dream, the names written in the Bible, on the marriage license, not hers, not really. But Cole's words held a harshness that made her realize she hadn't fully understood until now that she was *married*. She was his brother's wife.

"You all right?" Cole asked, though he didn't move.

She nodded slowly. She looked out over the yard, to the fields. It was hers now, too. She belonged here. The enormity of what she'd just done exhausted her.

"This is what you wanted, Eliza," Cole was saying, and his tone was smooth and soothing, his voice low. "Anything you need, Pa'll make sure you get. You'll have money, you have a nice house. All you have to do is tolerate Aaron — nothing an enterprising girl like yourself can't handle. Seems like a good deal to me."

She thought of Aaron, of the way he'd blushed and stammered, his long, awkward silences, the way he stared. She thought of how he'd nearly run out of his father's room, how his hand had shook when he signed their names to the Bible.

"What's wrong with him?" she asked hollowly.

"Wrong?" Cole looked away. "Nothing's wrong with him, really."

She looked at him steadily. "There's something you ain't telling me, Cole."

"Look," Cole said, though he still didn't look at her. "He's a poet, that's all. Poets are strange."

Since she'd never met a poet before, she couldn't dispute that, but it didn't seem quite right, and it didn't answer her question. "You said before that he wanted to marry me. Is that true?"

"He said he'd marry you."

"But did he *want* to?"

"You're making too much of it, Eliza. He said he'd marry you, and that's the only thing that matters."

"Not to me," Eliza insisted, though she couldn't have said why it mattered so suddenly, why she cared, except that Cole was leaving and she was on her own, and it was important that she know where she stood with the people in this house. With her strange husband.

Cole took a deep breath. He took out his cigar and threw it on the ground, stepped down to grind it out on the dried and yellow grass. Then he turned fully to her. "Aaron's never been very good with women," he said quietly. "He's shy, I guess."

Eliza frowned. "Is that all?"

"Yeah." Cole nodded. "That's all."

It didn't seem like much.

"He can be strange," Cole went on, "until you get to know him. He'll spend hours on his poems, he'll forget to come into dinner or go to bed. He's not used to being around people, he kind of keeps to himself. He needs a wife to help him out."

Eliza watched Cole's face carefully, watching for a lie, but his expression was open and honest-looking. "Well, that ain't much," she said carefully. "I guess I can get used to it."

"You'll be fine, Eliza," he said. "A few days, and you'll forget all about me."

"I won't," she said. "Maybe I'll just sit on the porch and stare into the hills and wait for you to come back. Maybe I'll just pine away for you forever."

His face tightened. She saw a shadow move over his features like a cloud over the sun. "Eliza," he said finally. "I probably won't be back."

Eliza's chest tightened. She felt sick to her stomach. "What d'you mean?"

"I don't see my family much," he said.

"You mean you don't ever come home," she said slowly.

He nodded.

"You won't even see your own baby being born."

He didn't look at her. "It won't be my baby. It'll be Aaron's."

"It'll always be your baby."

"No, it won't." He turned to her, and his eyes were dark, his voice was slow and heavy. "You need to understand this, Eliza. I didn't lie to you when I said I didn't love you. The baby will be my brother's. You're his wife. Don't count on me for anything."

She stared at him. She'd known he didn't love her; he'd told her that before. But somehow, over the last days, she'd forgotten it. He'd been so nice to her. He'd smiled. He'd laughed. He'd let her comfort him. . . .

The thing her mother had told her not to forget came back into her head; she remembered it now. *"When you marry this man, you be his wife."* Now Eliza understood what that meant.

He stepped back again, and turned away from her, and she knew when he went to the edge of the porch, down the stairs, that it was good-bye. And though tears pricked her eyes, she didn't call him back. She was a married woman now. She was his brother's wife.

The house was so big that Eliza felt lost in it. She moved quietly through the open front room, but every footstep echoed to the rafters of the unfinished ceiling, and the ragged settee and chairs were so piled with books and papers she was afraid to sit down. The house felt empty, even though she knew Mr. Wallace was upstairs. The two Mexicans who had been here when she arrived were working in the fields, and she had no idea where Aaron was. It made her nervous, walking through the house, not knowing when she might run into him, so it was a long time before she left the living room, with its tall, uncurtained windows overlooking the yard and the welcoming bay window at one end.

The room was shaped like a big L, with the stairs at the back and a table and chairs opposite, near a doorway that led into the kitchen. She stepped inside cautiously, but the kitchen was empty except for the cook-stove in the corner, a big, square stove the likes of which she'd never seen before. Iron pots and pans hung from hooks in the ceiling, and there was a work table at the far end, near an open door that looked onto a dirt yard scattered with short and browning weeds, and a couple of outbuildings. The late afternoon sun slanted inside, bringing with it a hot and heavy breeze and flies that gathered on what looked like a ham resting on the table.

It was a man's house in every way. There were no fancy touches — the most feminine thing in the whole house was that bay window — and Eliza felt out of place. Even the shanty in Richmond had flour-sack curtains on the windows and a braided rug on the hard dirt floor. And it had been as clean as her mother could make it.

The thought that it would be up to her to make this house a home seemed overwhelming suddenly; so much so that she sagged against the wall, staring at that ham, at the flies covering it, and her daily nausea came thickly up her throat until she found herself slipping down, sitting on the floor with her knees up to her chest, waiting it out, unable to move from this hot and sweaty kitchen that smelled sickeningly of corn and chilies.

She was still there when one of the Mexicans came in through the back door. He waved a hand distractedly over the ham, scattering the flies, and then he caught sight of her and stopped, his hand suspended in air.

"*Señora,*" he said, "you are all right?"

Eliza nodded weakly.

He frowned. "I will get *Señor* Aaron —"

"No." Her head jerked up. "No. I'm fine." She put her hands on the floor and levered herself up until she was standing. The nausea hadn't faded; she grabbed hold of the sideboard to support herself.

"You should sit down," the Mexican said. He came toward her, and when he offered his hand, Eliza took it gratefully. He led her through the kitchen door, to the table just outside, and pulled out a chair with his foot. Eliza sank into it. He left her then, but in minutes he was back, a mug in his hand.

"You drink this," he said.

She put her nose to it, smelled the deep spicy scent of ginger, and she took a sip. The drink was sweet and cool. It took away her nausea; she drank until it was gone.

"Thanks," she said to the man still hovering over her. "That was good."

He smiled. "I am Miguel," he said. "You are *Señor* Aaron's wife?"

"Eliza." She smiled back at him. "My name's Eliza."

"*Señora* Wallace to me," he corrected.

"Oh." It took her aback; for a moment she didn't understand what he was saying, then she realized he was a hired man, that as Aaron's wife, he had to respect her. The notion took away her nausea and exhaustion, filled her with a strange satisfaction that made her forget that she was alone here, that Cole was gone. She was the *lady of the house.* My, what a nice sound it had.

Her smile broadened. "Well, it's nice to meet you, Miguel," she said. "I guess we'll prob'ly get along just fine."

"I am" — he looked like he was searching for the word — "I cook here. But I will be most happy to give it to you."

The thought of being in charge of that kitchen made her nervous. She didn't know the first thing about running a house, or cooking for so many people, or even using that monster of a cookstove. But she was the lady of the house now, so she lifted her chin and gave Miguel what she hoped was a regal nod.

"Maybe tomorrow, you could show me —"

He nodded fervently. "*Sí. Sí.* I will be most happy."

He left her then, mumbling something about making supper. Eliza heard him clanging away in the kitchen, and before long she smelled frying ham. It made her mouth water; she'd been craving salty meat for days now, and the jerky Cole had fed her on the trail hadn't satisfied at all.

But then she heard a slow tread on the stairs, and looked up to see Aaron — her husband.

He was halfway down when he saw her. She knew just the moment he spotted her, because he froze there on the stair, and stared at her for a moment before he seemed to catch himself. She saw the sharp rise and fall of his chest, and then he came down the rest of the way and stood stiffly in front of her.

He shook his head a little, as if he were clearing it.

"Uh . . . you're here."

His stare made her so uncomfortable she looked down at the floor. She wished he would walk away, maybe go outside, disappear. This was a farm, surely he had some work to do. God knew Daddy had always been busy. "I guess Miguel's making supper," she said.

She thought maybe he'd go then, but she heard the scraping of a chair, and his heavy sigh as he sat down. She looked up to see him sitting across from her, looking down at the hands he'd clasped on the table, his too-long hair shifting forward, hiding the edges of his face. She didn't know why, but there was something about the way he looked now that caught her attention, some quietness, a very still calm.

At least Aaron was a handsome man. Almost . . . pretty, she decided. He needed a haircut, but if she'd seen him walking through Richmond, she would have noticed him. Now, with his heavy lashes lowered, his chin tilted so the shadows accented the sharp angles of his face, he had an air of religiousness about him that Eliza had only seen once or twice before, mostly on the pastors who came and went through the Methodist church in Richmond.

Almost as she had the thought, he looked up, breaking the spell, swallowing her up with those deep-set, dark eyes as if he'd never learned not to stare at strangers. She didn't think she would ever get used to that. Eliza looked away for a long time, but when she turned back again, he was still looking at her.

"Something wrong?" she asked.

He looked surprised, and a slow flush moved over his cheeks. "N-no," he said. "I mean . . . your hat."

She'd forgotten she had it on. Eliza went hot with embarrassment. She was home now, and ladies didn't wear their hats in the house. Quickly she reached up and took it off, laying it aside. The little bird bobbed so violently at the motion she reached out to calm it.

"It's . . . uh . . . it's pretty."

"Ain't it?" she agreed. "When I saw it, I just had to have it. Will thought I was being silly, but —"

"W-Will?" He was frowning.

"A friend of mine," Eliza said quickly. "In Richmond."

He nodded jerkily. His fingers tightened so she saw his skin turn white. "I . . . uh . . . I . . . saw Cole leave."

"Yeah," she said. "Looks like we're all alone."

The color swept from his face. He nodded.

"Yeah," he said. His dark brows came together in a frown as he got to his feet. "I'll . . . uh . . . see about supper."

But before he could leave the table, Miguel came out, carrying a steaming platter of ham steaks in one hand and some plates in another.

"Ah, *Señor* Aaron," he said. "I am calling you to eat *un momento*. Good, good." He set the plates on the table, along with the ham, and gave Eliza a reassuring smile.

Carefully, looking for all the world like it was the last place he wanted to be, Aaron sat back down. Miguel brought out two more dishes: corn and some tortillas, and set them on the table with a flourish.

"Carlos and me . . . we eat in the fields tonight," he said. He winked broadly at Aaron. "The two lovebirds, they should be lonely."

He meant *alone,* Eliza knew, but the word lonely seemed so apt that she didn't say anything. And lonely was what she felt when Miguel disappeared back into the kitchen. The noises stopped, and she knew he'd gone out that back door, out to the fields to meet the other Mexican, Carlos.

It was very quiet, just the sound of crows from the open front door. The start of a headache pressed at her temples. It was so silent she heard Aaron's swallow. He held up the platter.

"Ham?" he asked.

She nodded, and he forked a piece onto her plate, and one onto his. That was the last thing he said for what seemed like a long time. He didn't look up at her for the rest of the meal, and he ate with a single-mindedness that spoke of years of eating alone. Eliza had barely taken three bites before he was finished with his ham and starting on the corn.

She wasn't hungry suddenly; her stomach tightened, her nausea came racing back. The headache began to pound. She wanted to push her plate away and leave, but then she remembered she was married to this man. *"You be* his *wife,"* Mama had said, and Eliza knew now she had no choice but to be just that. Cole had left her alone here, and he wasn't coming back, and she had nothing else, no one else. Her life here had started. It would be what she made it.

She pushed back her plate and folded her hands on the table and looked at him.

"I never saw corn so high as what you got in the field," she said, and at her first words she saw him jerk up like she'd scared the spirit from him. She forced herself to go on. "It must be growing good."

She smiled at him. He swallowed and leaned back, as if trying to put distance between them.

"D-drought," he said. He cleared his throat, and then added, unnecessarily, "No . . . rain this year."

Eliza frowned. "Oh."

He swallowed again, but he didn't move away, and she saw how he blinked, how his brow furrowed. She could almost see him searching for something to say, and that was encouraging — at least he was trying. She remembered what Cole had said, about him being shy, about not being very good with women, and so she tried to help him out.

"I guess . . . d'you think it'll rain soon?"

"Um . . . no." He closed his eyes for just a moment, and she saw the muscle of his jaw work before he opened them again and took a deep breath. "I think it's going to be a hard year."

It was an obvious effort, and Eliza smiled. "Well, I'm here to help you out now."

He glanced down, and nodded. "Yeah," he said.

She wanted a smile from him, a reassurance . . . something that made her feel welcome, something that made her believe he'd wanted to marry her, that he wanted her help. But his tone held surrender, and resignation, and she knew then that Cole had lied to her, that Aaron hadn't wanted to marry her, that he'd been forced to agree.

It took all her control to mumble "Excuse me," and rush from the table. He wasn't behind her as she stumbled to the porch, down the steps to the yard, and when she fell to her knees and threw up in the grass, he was not there, pulling her into his arms, comforting her with a clean handkerchief or a worried, "Are you all right?"

But he was her husband, so when she was done, Eliza wiped her face on her skirt and got to her feet and went back inside. He was still sitting at the table, and when he looked up at her, she wiped her watery eyes and tried not to look so bedraggled. She looked for kindness in his gaze, or sympathy, but there was none. Just a mild curiosity, that quiet stillness, and in that moment she missed Cole so much she thought she would die of it.

13

He didn't know what to say to her, how to comfort her. So Aaron just sat there and watched her come inside, wiping at her face. She went to the big bay window and stood there for a long time, hugging herself, staring out at sunset-touched leaves of the pecan tree whispering in the faint, hot breeze. Without her hat on, her hair was a true, pure gold that hung straight and thick past her shoulders. He saw her profile, the slope of her nose and the way it turned up low at the end, the faint pout of her mouth, the fine, classic height of her forehead.

She was so pretty it made him hurt, and he felt useless and stupid sitting there, unable to string two words together in front of her, unable to go to her now, when she so obviously needed . . . something. He told himself to get up, to go to her. He thought of what his brother would have done, how Cole would have taken her in his arms, how she would have buried her face in his shoulder.

The ham Aaron had eaten settled like a stone in his stomach; he sat there for so long, watching her, that the sky began to darken. For the first time in his life, he wished he had the excuse of tending to his father, but Carlos had volunteered to care for the old cripple tonight, and he'd done it with such martyred grace Aaron hadn't told him he didn't want to be alone with his wife, didn't want a honeymoon, not even a single night.

So he was stuck here, now, thinking about the night ahead and having her in bed beside him. He tried not to think of what she would expect from him or how she would compare him to Cole. He tried not to think of what he would have to do — what he yearned to do, what he couldn't do.

Ah, she was so pretty. Trust Cole to find the prettiest girl in Richmond.

He rose; at his movement she glanced over her shoulder, and he motioned weakly to the settee. "I'm . . . uh . . . I'm just . . . going to read."

Something crossed her face then, some expression he couldn't see in the growing darkness, and then she turned away, and he went over to the table by the settee, lit a lamp. It illuminated only the space around him, left the rest of the room in gloomy dimness, and he relaxed then, unable to see more than her shadow, cocooned in his favorite spot, the rest of the world in darkness.

He settled himself, angling his body into the corner, shifting until he found the spot where the patterned silk had worn to roughness and he didn't slide. He rested his head into the elbow created by carved wood and upholsterer's braid and picked up the book at the top of the pile beside the table, a collection of poems by Alexander Pope. He'd been reading *An Essay on Man*, and the pages opened easily to the blade of grama grass he'd tucked inside, but when he started to read the words swam before his eyes, dancing in the half light: "Know then thyself, presume not God to scan, / The proper study of mankind is man. . . ."

Aaron felt Eliza's presence beyond his circle of light, heard her breathing, and he was nothing but a tight knot of yearning, of fear. He heard the katydids in the fields, their nighttime song. He heard Carlos come down from upstairs, heard the slosh of water in the bowl he carried. Then he heard the farmhand go out the kitchen door, to the lean-to bedroom he shared with Miguel, and Aaron listened until the Mexican's whistle was so faint he was imagining its fading notes in his head.

They were turning in. Pa was probably

already asleep. It was time for bed; the corn would be waiting for him in the morning.

"It's getting late," she said quietly.

He looked up, trying to find her in the darkness beyond the lamp. His mouth was so dry he could barely force out the one word. "Yeah."

"I guess I'll go on up," she said. He heard her footsteps across the floor; his head pounded in time with them. He heard the squeak of those old floorboards beneath her as she went down the hallway, the creak of the bedroom door as she opened it. His room. Her room now. Their room.

He got up and blew out the lamp, leaving himself in darkness. He stood there for a moment, getting used to it, even though he didn't need to — he knew the contours of this house completely blind — and then he walked to the stairs.

He went up slowly, driven by fear and a vague, titillating excitement. She had lit the lamp in the room; though the door was half-shut, the light slanted across the floorboards of the hall. He paused at the top of the stairs, seeing her shadow beyond the crack in the door, the flash of her movement — white and skin, a chemise, an arm.

His heart moved into his throat. When he got to the door, he laid his hand flat against it, pushing it open. It creaked with the movement, and she jumped a little and turned to see him, an uncertain smile on her face. Her dress was pooled around her feet, along with a red petticoat, her boots and stockings piled neatly beside his. She was wearing nothing but a worn, thin chemise that showed the pinkness of her skin in the lamplight. He saw the taut stretch of the material across her breasts, the outline of her nipples through it.

He closed his eyes for a moment. The blood was pounding at his temples, his heart racing. *I can do this,* he thought, and he wanted to. He wanted to touch her. He wanted to kiss her. He opened his eyes again. She was looking at him nervously, expectantly, her hands compulsively smoothing the chemise at her hips.

He closed the door tightly behind him. The night was cooler now; he felt the breeze coming in through the open window, saw the soft rock of the blind against it. Still, he was sweating. He edged past her, sat on the bed, took off his boots. She came over and sat beside him — not touching, but so close he was trapped against the headboard — and he started trembling, felt the drip of sweat at his temple.

He finally got his boots off, kicked them

aside. He didn't look at her. He stared at the rocking blind and pulled his shirt from his pants. He got it partially unfastened before he was shaking so badly he couldn't finish. He felt her watching him, but she was too close — he smelled her, that faint, seductive fragrance of her skin — and he jerked away, got to his feet, went to the window. He braced his hands on the sill and leaned over, taking huge, gulping breaths of the corn-scented air.

"You all right?" she asked.

He wondered how many times she'd asked that of him. Aaron closed his eyes, took a deep breath. *Be a man. You can do this.* He nodded. "Yeah," he managed. "Yeah."

"I'm your wife now, you know," she said quietly. "You know I'll . . . I'll let you kiss me. If you want."

He would have laughed at her statement if it hadn't hit him so hard. She wanted him to kiss her, and for a moment he thought, he wondered, if he'd ever kissed a woman. Had he? Had he kissed that whore Pa brought out from White Horse so long ago?

Had he?

He couldn't remember. He tried not to remember much of that time, but the sense of fear had never left him, the vision of arms twisting and open legs and white teeth flashing, laughing, a mouth closing around him . . .

The room spun. Aaron gripped the windowsill, holding himself steady, forcing himself calm. *Don't think of it,* he told himself. Not now, not when Eliza was waiting there, waiting the way she must have waited for Cole, asking him to kiss her the way she must have asked Cole —

"What's wrong, Aaron?" she asked, and there was a fear in her voice he recognized. "Don't you . . . ain't I good enough for you?"

He heard the pain in her voice and he felt bad for her — bad that she needed reassurance and he was not the man who could give it to her. Hell, he could barely touch her. He was nothing like Cole, who could soothe her with kisses and touches, who could make her feel like she was more than good enough. . . .

"I — it's not you," he said.

He made himself let go of the window, made himself straighten. He concentrated on each tiny button of his shirt, opened the placket. The night air caressed his chest; he felt its touch like soft, warm fingers. Aaron shrugged out of the shirt, let it fall behind him. There were only his pants now, and he couldn't bring himself to take them off before he turned to look at her.

She was so pretty in the lamplight. That

gold hair falling over one shoulder, the gentle arch of her dark brow as she looked at him . . . he had a thousand words for her, each one more beautiful than the last, each one singing. Looking at her, he forgot the reasons he married her, the reason she was here. Looking at her, he felt a hunger so deep and painful it made his whole body hurt.

"So, then . . . you think you might want to kiss me?"

Yes. Yes. No. He couldn't talk around the hunger in his throat. He took the few steps toward her, and she eased over on the bed, making room for him again. He sat down beside her, and she moved over until he felt the press of her skin against his, the soft, hot, smoothness of it, backing him against the headboard. She turned a little, leaned into him. He felt the swell of her lawn-covered breast against his arm, the heat of her breath as she offered her mouth to him.

He looked at her. Her eyes were closed, her lips slightly parted, chin tilted up, expecting a kiss, waiting for it, and he felt something collapse deep inside him, a darkness falling in on itself, bending, breaking. He leaned forward. Her lips were only an inch from his, a half inch; he heard their voice, the temptation of desire. *Take me. Kiss me. Touch me.* He heard his own breath coming ragged and fast.

She turned then, twisted just a little, so her breast went into his palm, filling his hand, and with that movement, the memory slammed into his head again — twisted arms, open mouth, red lips, and laughter.

He wrenched away so hard and fast he slammed his shoulder into the headboard, knocking it hard against the wall, a *thump, thump, thump,* the sound of sex, mocking him. *Be a man. Be a man.* Those words were mocking too, stealing his fear, turning it into the hot, sickening wash of humiliation.

"Aaron . . . you all right? Aaron?"

He felt her hand on his bare shoulder. Felt her hair brushing his skin as she leaned over him.

"Aaron?"

He forced himself to look at her. She was staring at him in concern and bewilderment. His humiliation grew; he felt the heat of it in his face, felt sick to his stomach.

"I'm sorry," he managed in a thick, raw voice. He turned away. "I . . . uh . . . I'm . . . tired."

"Tired?" The disbelief in her voice made him wince. She sat back. "I . . . see."

Maybe she did. He didn't care. He did feel tired then. Washed out, hollowed, with that deep, empty hunger drawing back to where he kept it, so far down in his belly he knew he would never be able to feed it.

He got up from the bed. He turned down the covers to where she was sitting, and then he motioned to it.

She didn't say anything else. She slid inside, pulling the blankets up to her chin even though it was a hot night, scooting over to the far side. She turned to face him, and those blue eyes watched him. He felt her question deep into his heart. He turned away, blowing out the lamp, closing the room in darkness, blinding him to her body, her eyes, taking his senses.

Then he crawled into bed beside her, keeping his pants on, his one barrier. He turned his back to her, looking out into the dark, but he felt her move closer, felt the hush of her breath on his shoulder, moving his hair, and he concentrated on the sound of the blind-pull in the faint breeze, the light click against the window, until she was long gone in sleep, and he could face her.

She woke when he did; it was barely dawn. She saw the blue-edged morning, pale beyond the window, lighting the shade, felt the quickly warming air of sunrise.

He thought she was still asleep, she knew. He eased back the covers and rose almost soundlessly from the bed, carefully, so even his movement wouldn't wake her. The muscles in his back flexed and twisted as he rotated his shoulders, and then he dragged his hands through his dark hair and went to the window, barefoot, bare-chested, clad only in his pants. He didn't look at her, but she kept her eyes nearly closed, watched him through cracked lids, how he bent to the window and took a great, deep breath, how he closed his eyes, how he shuddered.

The bed was warm where he'd left it — Eliza had never known that before, not the soft warmth of a shared mattress, the sudden chill when a man left, then the easing out, stretching, the languid space. Deliberately she stretched out her foot, rolled over, angled her arm beneath his pillow. Aaron went stock-still, so still it brought back that sinking in her stomach from last night. He didn't want to talk to her, or touch her.

Last night, she'd told herself she shouldn't let it hurt, that it meant nothing. He'd said he was tired; maybe it was true. But the way he froze now . . . well, that told her better than words that he'd lied last night, and then she remembered supper, and how she'd discovered that Cole had lied too, that Aaron really hadn't wanted to marry her.

She felt the tears start and closed her eyes

for real this time so he wouldn't see.

She heard the soft *ssshush* as he pulled on his shirt, the thump of his boot, his careful footsteps. She heard the creak of the door, the sudden stop, then the slipping out. She heard his walk down the hall, down the stairs, hushed voices, the clanging of dishes. Then it was quiet, and she was alone.

She turned onto her back again, felt the twist of her chemise across her waist, the tangle of cotton about her legs. She stared up at the ceiling, at a water spot that spread brown and cracking over the foot of the bed, at the cobwebs in the corners. This was home. She tried the word out in her head, and it felt foreign and strange. Home. A home where no one wanted her. Cole had abandoned her here, and it was clear Aaron had no use for her. She'd thought last night that if he'd kissed her, if he'd loved her, well . . . that would mean he at least cared a little. But he hadn't even been able to kiss her, and she'd never met a man like that before, not ever.

Yesterday she'd decided to be his wife, and now it looked like it was going to be harder than she'd thought. If Aaron didn't like her, he might throw her out, and then where would she go, what would she do? The only person in this house who had any use for her at all was Mr. Wallace, and once he found out she couldn't read . . .

It was overwhelming, she didn't want to get out of bed. She already felt tired and sick, and the day hadn't even started. But she guessed she couldn't give them a reason to think she wasn't willing to be a wife, and she'd promised Cole's father that she would be a good one, so she pushed back the blankets and eased out of bed.

The floorboards were dry and cool beneath her feet, but there was a deep-down warmth to them that didn't feel at all like the dank chill of the hard-packed dirt of the shanty floor. Eliza lingered, pressing her feet flat, feeling the wood clear out to her toes, and suddenly the sense of it — of this room — filled her with a tingling pleasure that eased her exhaustion. She wasn't in Richmond anymore, she wasn't living in a dirty sharecropper's shanty. She was Mrs. Aaron Wallace. And this house was hers. Even if Aaron didn't care for her, she still had that. She had a bedroom with a door and a real bed, and a kitchen. She had windows that looked to the horizon as far as the eye could see and a big bay window and a pecan tree.

This house was hers. . . . The realization overcame everything else — her worry over her husband, Cole's abandonment — and

Eliza felt a soul-deep satisfaction. This house was hers, and she would do whatever she had to keep it that way. No one would find a reason to throw her out. She had always been good at keeping men happy with her. All she had to do was figure out what made Aaron happy.

She sighed and got out of bed, washing quickly at the basin on the washstand, then digging through her bag for her other dress. She slipped it on, tugging at the bodice — it was so tight now, and it looked fairly like she was going to spill right out of it. It was the only dress she had besides the one she'd worn the whole way here. She supposed she'd just have to make the best of it.

She paused at the door, listening. The hallway was dark and quiet, the door to the old man's room tightly shut. It seemed the whole house was still sleeping. But when Eliza went downstairs and saw the way the morning sun burst through the mullioned windows of the front room, she felt a surge of such pure joy it startled her. The inside of the shanty never saw the sun, and this — this was so beautiful it warmed her heart and her blood; she felt the warm tingle of it on her fingertips as she stepped into the golden squares lighting the floorboards.

Eliza stood there, drinking up the sunlight,

listening to the quiet peace of the house, loving it. She lifted her face to the sun one last time, and then she went into the kitchen.

The back door was open again, and the rapidly warming morning air rushed into a room that was already hot with the heat from the stove. There was a steaming coffeepot on top, and a bunch of biscuits lay uncovered on a plate. Eliza took one and bit into it. It was burnt on the bottom and hard as rock. She put it aside and poured some coffee, but it was black as tar and twice as thick, so she left it, too. There seemed to be nothing else to eat in the kitchen, and she wasn't that hungry anyway. Eliza went out onto the back porch — really just a stoop — and looked at the outbuildings. A privy, she knew already, and a smokehouse. Maybe a springhouse. She'd seen a couple of cows when she and Cole had come riding up yesterday, and the thought of milk sounded good. She headed to the springhouse, dodging a few weather-beaten chickens pecking at the dirt.

The door of the little house creaked when she opened it, and there was the smell of old milk, but it looked dry, and there were nothing but a few old milk pans sitting inside. Eliza backed away, disappointed. She looked around the yard. There was a barn a little ways away, but it was small, the size of a

lean-to, and she saw the cows tethered beyond it — a couple of skinny, bony animals
who didn't look like they could give milk,
even if she'd known how to get it from
them.

She was really thirsty now, thirsty enough
that even that coffee was tempting. But then
she saw the well just beyond the corner of
the house. Eliza went eagerly toward it. The
sun was bold now, and it was already hot
enough that she was starting to sweat. When
she reached the well, she was ready to dip
her whole head in. She cranked the pulley,
heard the light slosh of water as the bucket
came out, the creak of the rope. It was a
hard crank; her arm was tired by the time
she saw the top of the bucket, but finally it
was there. Eliza reached for the dipper hanging on the post beside the well, leaned over
to dip —

She heard the rattle before she was halfway
there, saw the rise of the snake from the
bucket, the beady eyes, the hiss. Eliza jerked
back, and at her movement, the snake struck
— Eliza saw the sun on its wet scales, the
extended fangs — the second she let go of
the crank. The bucket fell, the snake struck
the side of the well; she heard the clunk of
its body, the splash before the bucket hit the
bottom.

She dropped the dipper. She was shaking so hard she nearly lost her balance as she sat back hard on the dirt. Her blood tingled, her face went hot in the aftershock of fear. There had been a snake in the well. A rattlesnake in the well. She'd nearly been bitten. . . . In all her years playing along the marshes in Richmond, she'd never come so close. She'd known to look for cottonmouths and coral snakes, for canebrakes and alligators. She'd watched every step. But who would've thought to find a rattler in a well? It wasn't normal, was it?

But then again, maybe it was, she didn't know. Maybe there were all kinds of things like that in this part of Texas. She couldn't remember. The last time she'd lived out here, she'd just been a little girl. She remembered snakes, of course, but not like this. Not hiding in wells.

Her thirst was gone; she felt weak and a little sick, and the sun was burning the top of her head. Slowly, Eliza rose, dusting her hands off on her skirt. She wanted suddenly to go back to bed; the charms of the empty outbuildings and the far-reaching land faded, the farm seemed big and dusty and overwhelming. She didn't have the first idea of where to go or what to do.

It was stupid, how that snake got to her,

but it did. It brought everything she'd been feeling back in a rush, everything she'd been trying to ignore, and she longed for Cole so hard it seemed her whole body ached for him.

When she went back to the house, the kitchen seemed hotter than ever. Even the light breaking through the windows didn't cheer her now that there was nothing to do but look at it. There wasn't even anyplace to sit; books and papers were all over everything.

She went over to the settee and picked up the book Aaron had been reading last night. The cover fell open in her hands; she saw the piece of grass marking his place, and she squinted down at the words. Little black scratchings on paper so thin she could see through it. Meaningless dots. She closed the book again and set it aside, wondering what he saw in it. Whatever it was, it interested him more than she did.

Not that she cared, she supposed. It was just that —

Somewhere, a bell rang.

Eliza stopped, tilting her head, listening. It was hard and fast, a *ringringringring*, an angry sound. She thought it was coming from upstairs. Eliza went to the bottom of the steps and looked up. The sound was louder, and just as angry. Coming from Mr. Wallace's room.

She remembered yesterday, when Aaron was showing her their room, how that bell had rung. She remembered Aaron calling out that they'd be right there. Eliza hesitated, looking around, waiting for Aaron or one of the farmhands to come rushing in to care for the old man. But no one came and the bell kept ringing. Then it stopped suddenly, and she heard a *clang* against the wall, a faint tinkle as it fell.

Eliza hurried up the stairs. She knocked first, and then flushed when she remembered he couldn't answer, and pushed the door open.

"Mr. Wallace?" she asked. "Are you all right?"

He'd been frowning ferociously, but the moment he saw her, he smiled, and that smile warmed her. Even if Aaron didn't like her, his father did, and that couldn't hurt. She saw the little bell on the floor beside the door, and she picked it up and carried it over to the bedside table, laying it carefully down.

"You dropped your bell," she said.

He made a sound — she supposed it was a laugh, because he wasn't frowning.

It was sweltering. Eliza went to the window and pulled up the blind, lifted the sash.

What breeze there was came inside, pushing faintly against the heavy, hot air in the room, the smell of alcohol and unbathed skin.

She heard a sound from him, and quickly Eliza filled the space between them with talk. "There was a snake in the well," she said. "I never saw anything like that, but I guess maybe it's like that here. It like to scared me to death."

She laughed a little and turned to face him. He looked concerned, her heart dropped when he reached for that chalkboard and scrawled on it.

Eliza looked away. "It's hot, too. Hotter than I thought."

He banged on the bed. She knew he wanted her to look at that slate, and she went all tight, but still she turned, still she looked at that board like the words might suddenly take form before her, like they might suddenly mean something.

They didn't. They were just lines crossing each other. She could no more read them than fly to the moon. She looked up at the old man, who was watching her carefully, and tried not to blush. She gave him her best smile.

"Can I bring you something, Mr. Wallace?" she asked. "There's coffee, and . . . and biscuits."

He sat looking at her a moment. Then he wiped off the board and wrote something else and held it up. Her gaze dropped to the slate, then she looked back at him and tried to keep her smile bright.

"Coffee?" she asked again.

He didn't smile back. His eyes were dark and measuring, and Eliza's heart dropped, her mouth went dry.

Then, he nodded. Slowly.

"You would like some coffee, then?" she said to make sure.

He nodded.

"Biscuits?"

A quick shake of his head. Eliza could hardly breathe.

"All right then," she said, backing to the door. "I'll be right back."

He was staring at her, looking at her like he knew, like he suspected. . . . Her fear and loneliness welled up inside her; she felt the start of tears, and Eliza hurried from the room. But instead of going downstairs to the kitchen to fetch his coffee, she went to her bedroom. For just a minute. Just long enough to settle herself.

But once she got there, she sagged onto the unmade bed and stared at the books and papers surrounding it, and she knew her life here was over before it had even begun. Mr.

Wallace knew she couldn't read. He knew what she was. Just a sharecropper's daughter. A nobody. She would never be a lady, and she would never belong to this family.

Eliza buried her face in her hands, and the morning swelled over her, disappointing and too hard, and she sat there crying until the tears stopped coming, and wondered how long it would be before he told her to leave.

14

When Aaron came in for dinner, there was no sign of her. The front room was as messy as always, and it was Miguel, not Eliza, clanging pans in the kitchen. Aaron stopped just beyond the door, his chest tightening as he waited — for what? For her to come rushing out to greet him? To kiss him hello?

He sighed and raked back his hair. The truth was he didn't want to see her, and he liked the fact that everything seemed unchanged.

But he couldn't escape; evening would come, and it would be time for supper, and then bed, and eventually he would have to face her. He would have to look into her eyes and see her condemnation, her disgust, her derision. Eventually, he would have to consider what he'd done last night.

But not right now. Not at this moment. He felt a swift, cold relief that died the second he heard his father's bell. The loud, relentless ringing gave him an instant headache.

Miguel peered out the kitchen doorway. His expression cleared when he saw Aaron standing there. "Ah, you are here. You will go?"

It was the last thing Aaron wanted to do. He didn't know if he could face the old cripple this morning, if he could look in Pa's eyes and pretend he'd done his duty last night. He didn't know if he could ignore the voice that haunted him. *BE A MAN*.

Miguel was waiting. Aaron exhaled slowly and nodded. "Yeah," he said. "I'll go."

The Mexican popped back to the kitchen quickly, as if he were afraid Aaron might change his mind. Aaron glanced at the ceiling. He wondered where Eliza was. He had the sudden image of her sitting in that room with his father, waiting for him, the two of them sharpening their knives, and the thought made his heart pound as he walked slowly to the stairs.

But when he got to the old man's room, she wasn't there. Whatever relief Aaron felt was lost at the sight of his father. Pa had that shrewd look on his face, that blades-drawn viciousness in his eyes. He didn't stop shaking that damned bell until Aaron stood beside him.

Pa put the bell aside. He wrote on the chalkboard. "IS SHE YOUR WIFE?"

Aaron translated the words in his mind —
Did you sleep with her? — and looked away.
"Of course she's my wife. You married us
yourself."

Pa banged on the side of the board until
Aaron looked at him again, and then the old
man shook his head to tell him it wasn't what
he meant. Deliberately, Aaron pretended
confusion, and finally Pa erased the board
and wrote again, and this time the question
was crude and to the point, impossible to
misunderstand.

"DID YOU SCREW HER?"

For a moment Aaron felt a chill so cold it
took his words. He wondered if she'd been
in here today, if she'd talked to the old man,
if she'd told him . . .

Aaron forced himself to meet his father's
gaze. "That's none of your business, old
man."

Pa's eyes narrowed. "YOU MAKE HER
YOUR WIFE?"

Aaron turned away. He went to the window. It was open; he felt the dry, hot breeze
on his face. He looked at his father in surprise. "The window's open."

Pa motioned for Aaron to shut it, but instead Aaron stood there, looking out on the
dwindling creek, the shimmering oak. He
could barely remember what it felt like to sit

271

under that tree and write. It seemed it had been years since he'd done it.

"Why'd you call me up here?" he asked. "You want dinner?"

Pa grunted. Aaron looked over to read the board.

"SHE CAN'T READ."

Aaron stared at the words, drawing a blank. It took him a moment to think who the old man was talking about. Then he frowned. "Eliza? What makes you say that?"

"I TESTED HER."

Aaron laughed bitterly. "That figures. Well, maybe she just didn't feel like being tested."

"TOLD HER TO SHUT THE WINDOW."

Aaron shrugged. "Maybe she likes it open."

Pa grimaced. "CALLED HER A STUPID WHORE."

Aaron stared at his father in shock. "Jesus, Pa —"

"SHE SAID SHE'D BRING COFFEE."

The old man sat back on his pillows with an air of triumph, as if he'd just proven the world was round.

"That doesn't mean anything," Aaron said slowly, but he was remembering what Cole had told him about her. He remembered she was the daughter of a sharecropper, that she was poor and uneducated. Of course she couldn't read. Of course she couldn't.

"YOU ASK HER," the board read.

He didn't need to ask her. Pa was undoubtedly right. It explained yesterday, the way she'd stared at that board, her strange replies. She hadn't understood what the old man was writing.

What a blessing, Aaron thought. He turned his back to the window, leaned against the wall beside it. "So she can't read. What d'you want me to do about it?"

The old man wrote again. "I WANT TO TALK TO HER. TEACH HER."

"You teach her," Aaron said.

Pa laughed — that sound Aaron hated, that sharp, bitter hack — and shook his head. "YOU DO IT."

There was no good reason to say no. Except he didn't want to sit beside her, feeling her lean into him, smelling her hair. Being close to her, teaching her . . . It made him too hot. He wanted . . . He didn't want . . .

Aaron remembered last night, and he felt the blood rush into his face. He turned away quickly so the old man wouldn't see. But it was too late; he knew it the moment his father growled, the moment he heard the banging on the chalkboard.

Slowly, warily, Aaron looked over his shoulder.

"COWARD."

The single word stared at him. He hated it. He hated how cold and small it made him feel. He hated that his father knew to use it. But most of all, he hated that it was true.

Aaron looked away. "I never asked for this," he said quietly. "I never asked for a wife."

Bang, bang. "MAKE THE BEST OF IT."

"I'm trying."

Scratch, scratch. "YOU TEACH HER. SHE TALKS TO ME."

Even written in chalk, the words had a self-pitying tone. Aaron frowned at his father, at the old man's suddenly contrite expression, his downcast eyes, and Aaron sighed. Pa wasn't fooling him; the old man had never been contrite or humble in his life. But Aaron felt worn down, and his reasons for not wanting to teach her seemed selfish and stupid. She *could* keep Pa company — she hadn't seemed to mind the old man yesterday. And if she was busy caring for his father, that meant Aaron would have more time to himself. More time to read. More time to write. He thought of never again having to rub down those crippled legs or bear his father's silent curses as he helped him out of bed.

274

If she could do all that, it would be worth it. He could bear the torment knowing that it saved him a different kind of hell. It would just take him a few weeks to teach her, anyway. Just a few weeks for a lifetime of freedom.

It seemed an even trade. Aaron swallowed. He looked at his father. "All right," he said. "I'll teach her."

The old man smiled. He scrawled on the board. "SEDUCE HER TOO."

Aaron's stomach cramped. It was all he could do to meet the old cripple's mocking gaze. "I'll teach her to read," he said. "So you can leave me the hell alone."

His father laughed. It took everything Aaron had to keep from racing out the door.

He waited for her a long time. Dinner was on the table, grits and ham cracklings — one of Miguel's gluey, indigestible specialties — and some of the biscuits left from breakfast. The grits had a thick, cold skin on them by the time Aaron decided she wasn't going to come and eat. He sat there, tapping his fingers on the table, feeling his nervousness grow until his mouth was so dry even the bitter coffee couldn't help. He wondered if she hated him after last night, if she was laughing at him. Maybe she was already packing to leave, and he wouldn't have to teach her to read, or think about touching her —

He heard her on the stairs. He looked up; she had not seen him yet, and her head was bowed forward, her pretty hair hiding her face. She looked dejected, and he thought about asking her why, but then she looked up and caught sight of him, and he went so tongue-tied he couldn't even answer her startled, "Oh. You're here."

She looked like she wanted to back away now that she saw him, and her expression was guarded, and he thought of last night and looked down at his plate. But there was no accusation in her voice when she sat down across from him and said, "I didn't know you were waiting for me."

He glanced up slowly, waiting for a mocking smile, a sarcastic word. Her eyes were guileless; she merely looked unhappy. It took him a moment to remember why he'd been waiting for her. "Yeah," he said. He took a deep breath, mastering himself, feeling the hot flush move over his face as he spoke. "I . . . uh . . . Pa tells me you can't read."

She looked startled, and then embarrassed, and he was surprised to see the sudden shine in her eyes. Tears. How strange. Her mouth trembled as if she were trying to suppress a frown; she wasn't quite success-ful, those full lips turned down, she looked ready to sob.

"I know I ain't what you expected." She rushed through the words as if afraid he would stop her, and the tears were coming down her cheeks now, wet, glistening trails. "I know I ain't educated, or nothing like that. But I can be a good wife, I know I can. I can clean, and cook, and I'll take care of him upstairs if you want. I'll make sure you never have cause to set me out. I'll make you happy too, if you tell me how. I promise I will." She leaned forward, reached across the table, touched his hand. "Please don't send me home."

Aaron stared at her in stunned surprise. The touch of her hand burned him, the words she'd spoken knocked away his breath. *"I'll make you happy too, if you tell me how. . . ."* He froze, and everything unfolded in his mind in strangely logical precision. She wasn't upset about last night. She thought she didn't please him. She was afraid he would throw her out because she couldn't read. *"I'll make you happy too. . . ."* He squeezed his eyes shut. He wanted to take his hand away, to keep it there, to feel her warm fingers closing around his, to be free of her.

"Aaron?"

There was so much uncertainty in her voice, a trembling that took him away from himself for a moment, made him open his eyes. "Y-you want me to . . . teach you?" he asked. "How to read, I mean."

Her dark brows came together. She pulled her hand away and sat back, staring at him. "You don't want to throw me out?" she asked.

Aaron frowned. "No," he said. "We can . . . we can start after supper. If you want."

She looked torn, like a fledgling poised on the edge of a nest, wanting to fly, afraid to try it. Her hands knotted the folds of her skirt. "You don't . . . you don't think it'd be too hard to teach me?"

He felt an unexpected warmth, a sense that for once he was holding all the cards. "No," he told her. "It won't be too hard."

She smiled at him then, a big, broad smile that involved her whole face, that lit her eyes. "Then I guess . . . I'd like that," she said. "If it makes you happy."

"After supper, then," he said.

He kept her smile in his head the rest of the afternoon. He thought of how she'd touched him, and the words she'd said, and how the breath had seemed to rush out of her when he told her he didn't want to throw her out. He had expected mockery from her, or at the very least disgust, and the fact that she didn't seem to feel those things made him feel good for the first time in a long time, in control. When it was time to quit for the day and go in to supper, his fear had retreated to a small place deep inside him. He was so damn relieved she didn't find him repulsive after last night that he thought dinner must be a dream.

But it wasn't, and she was waiting for him at supper when he came in after washing up. She jumped up from the table and served up his plate, setting it in front of him, leaning over him and then backing away in a burst of Eliza-scented air. Miguel and Carlos ate with them tonight — the honeymoon was truly over — and she sat across the table from him and listened to them talk. She didn't eat much herself, only played with a tortilla, folding it into thirds and then quarters, tearing it into pieces.

When the Mexicans finished and went into the kitchen, she looked at him expectantly. "Are you still going to teach me tonight?"

He pushed away his plate and nodded. "Yeah."

Her sigh was relieved. "Good. I was afraid —"

"Some black sausage for you, *Señora* Wallace." Carlos came out of the kitchen bearing

279

a steaming plate. He set it in front of her. "It is just done, and Miguel says" — he frowned — "you do not look —"

Eliza went white. She shoved back from the table. She was out the front door so fast Aaron was still looking at the plate of sausage before he realized she was gone. He heard her on the porch, retching miserably.

Carlos looked at him. "Miguel says it is good for her."

She was choking now, coughing a little. Aaron twisted in his chair. He saw her straightening from the edge of the porch, pushing her hair back.

"Perhaps you should go to her," Carlos suggested helpfully.

Aaron swallowed. He felt helpless again. He had no idea what to do for her, what to say. But Carlos was watching him expectantly, so Aaron got to his feet and went slowly out to the porch. He paused just outside the door.

"Are . . . are you all right?"

She looked over her shoulder at him. Her face was tear-streaked, her nose red. She wiped at her face. "Yeah," she said, but her attempt at a smile was small and miserable. "I'm sorry. I didn't mean to —"

"It's . . . uh . . . it's all right," he said. He felt clumsy and ill at ease just standing there.

"It's in the evening mostly," she said, sitting back on her heels. "Mama said it'll go away soon."

He had no idea what she was talking about. He looked at her in confusion. "What will?"

Her brow furrowed when she looked at him, she laughed a little — it came out like a snort. "Why, the morning sickness," she said.

Morning sickness? He stared at her.

"You know," she said. "Because of the baby . . ."

The baby. He'd never forgotten the reason he had married her, but until now, until this minute, the baby hadn't seemed real. Just something that would happen in some vague future, something to forget, something that had nothing to do with him. She didn't even look pregnant. Except for this morning sickness, there was no sign that she was carrying a child. Cole's child.

Aaron stepped back.

"I feel better," she said. "D'you suppose I could learn to read now?"

His pleasure in it had died; now he only felt awkward, idiotic. Now all he could think about was the baby he couldn't see, couldn't touch. The baby that didn't seem quite real. Cole's baby. A hundred images came into his head then. He thought of Cole kissing her, of Eliza letting him, pressing into him, easing close —

Carlos rushed by him with a cup of water for her, and that gave Aaron an exit. He hurried inside, thought of not stopping, of going to his room, locking himself in. But it was her room too, now, and he couldn't escape her, and he remembered that smile on her face when he'd promised to teach her to read and his father's order. So he grabbed a book of poetry from the pile on the window seat and one of Pa's three spare chalkboards from where they leaned against the wall.

When he got to the porch, Carlos was gone, and Eliza was sitting on the edge, dangling her feet over. She looked wan and a little pale, but when she saw him, she smiled and patted the space next to her. He hesitated — maybe a bit too long, because her smile began to fade by the time he finally eased himself down beside her. He kept a few inches between them, but even still, his throat tightened up just sitting this close, and he stole a look at her lap, at her belly. It was flat, there was no sign of a baby, just an indented waist and covered curves that pressed taut against the fabric when she breathed. . . .

He made himself look away. He made

himself forget. He put aside the book of poetry and grabbed up the slate, drawing out the alphabet, capital letters first, next to them the lower case. When he was done, he held it out to her.

"T-this is the alphabet," he said. His voice was whispery at first, he had to clear his throat. He couldn't look at her. She wiggled closer, close enough that he felt her hip curving into his, smelled the clean scent of her hair. It was hard for him to breathe. He pointed to each letter, concentrated on telling the alphabet to her the way he'd learned it, the soft, singsongy recitation.

"I-I'll point . . . to each one," he said. "We'll say them . . . together."

"All right," she said, and then she imitated each of his sounds, exaggerated them so by the time they reached *L* she was laughing.

"I'm sorry," she said, slanting her eyes at him. "It's kind of silly, ain't it? You sure these come together to mean something?"

He stared at her, taking in those eyes, those dark brows, the laughter on her face. He thought of leaning forward, of kissing her, of touching her, and the yearning and the humiliation of it grew so hard in his throat he couldn't answer her. He stared at her so long he forgot himself, until her smile softened, and she prodded him gently with her finger.

"What d'you want me to do now?" she asked.

Aaron blinked. He jerked away, laying down the slate with a clumsy clatter. He reached for the book, something to lose himself in, to take away the temptation of her expression, the hunger growing inside him.

He opened the book; his fingers were trembling as he spun the pages. They fell open, he read without thinking, without reading first. " 'So, I shall see her in three days / And just one night, but nights are short, / Then two long hours, and that is morn. / See how I come, unchanged, unworn! / Feel, where my life broke off from shine, / How fresh the splinters keep and fine, / Only a touch and we' " — he broke off, hearing the words for the first time. The last came out in a whisper — " 'combine.' "

He felt the sense of waiting break over him, a rush of longing that made him want to slide under the porch. He was afraid to look at her, but she was so quiet that finally he did. She was staring at him.

"What was that?" she asked quietly.

"B-Browning," he got out. "Robert Browning. A . . . poem."

"I never heard anything like that," she said.

That puzzled him enough that he forgot

the poem, forgot his discomfort. He frowned. "But I thought you liked poetry."

She laughed a little. "Well, I hardly ever heard any. I ain't . . . educated . . . you know."

"But Cole said —" Aaron broke off. Cole would have said anything to make the idea of marrying Eliza more palatable to him. It wouldn't have mattered that it was a lie. And of course it was. How could she possibly like poetry? She couldn't even read. Aaron sighed. "Cole said," he murmured. He glanced up at her. "So you don't like poetry."

"Well," she said, "I guess I liked what you just read me." She smiled shyly at him. "That man who wrote it, that —"

"Browning."

"Yeah. Browning. 'Only a touch and we combine.'" She sighed. "He sure got over that shyness of his, didn't he?"

He frowned at her. "Shyness?"

"Well, Cole said poets were shy," she said. "Ain't they?"

"Not all of them."

"Oh." She colored a little, as if she'd just realized how absurd the statement was. "I guess . . . maybe he just meant you were."

The lump formed in his throat; he looked away from her, toward the oak tree and the dying creek. *Cole said.* He wondered what else Cole had told her, what his brother had said about him. What stories had Cole entertained her with?

Aaron's heart raced, he heard its beat in the rush of blood to his head, felt the flush move over his cheekbones, stain his skin. *What had Cole told her?*

With a shock, he realized she was staring at him. Slowly, reluctantly, he shifted to meet her gaze. She smiled, but he saw the strain of it in her face.

"It is . . . just shy, ain't it?" she asked. "You don't hate me?"

He felt the same he'd felt earlier today, at dinner, when she'd babbled those words and he'd realized she didn't hate him, that she thought she didn't please him. And he realized he'd never reassured her then, that he'd been so caught up in *"I'll make you happy . . . if you tell me how . . ."* he'd forgotten what she was really asking him, what she was really saying.

The heat of his face eased, his heart slowed.

"No," he said quietly. "I don't hate you."

She nodded shortly and looked away, out to the cornfields. "Cole said . . . he said you wanted to marry me. But that ain't true." She looked at him again, and her eyes were searching. "Is it?"

He didn't look away. "No, it isn't."

"That's what I thought." She nodded a little, pressed her lips together. "I guess Cole did a lot of lying, didn't he?"

Her honesty took his fear. He hadn't wanted to marry her, but now they were married, and he didn't like seeing that look on her face, that fear that he didn't want her. There was something about Eliza Beaudry he understood. Maybe it was that she knew what it felt like to want one thing and get something else instead. Maybe it was her fear. He supposed it didn't matter. He wanted to comfort her, and he didn't know how. He wasn't good with touches, and he didn't know what to say, how to soften the truth. So he just said it.

"Cole lied," he said, "but I guess we'll just have to make the best of it, won't we?"

She gave him a tiny smile. "I guess we will."

And it was hard to say why, but he felt better. As if he had helped her, somehow. As if he'd helped himself. He picked up the slate again.

"Let's start at the beginning," he said, and began reciting the letters.

15

Dallas, Texas

When Cole rode into Dallas, the dim gas
lamps lighting the main streets were just
flickering and throbbing to life. But in spite
of the eerie, false glow of evening, Dallas was
just as busy now as it was during the day.
Hogs ran wild in the streets, dogs nipped and
barked at his horse's heels as he rode past,
men and women strode laughing and talking
from one false-fronted building to another.
The only difference was that the wagons
loaded high with buffalo hides were parked
along the streets instead of blocking them,
their owners gone to get falling-down drunk
in the saloons.

Cole paused, drinking up the music of
Dallas, the fragrance of untanned hides and
dust and blood rotting in the heat. Nothing
bad had ever happened to him in this town.
He'd won more often than he'd lost, he'd
had some whores he still remembered. And,
of course, there was Jenny.

He wondered where she was now, what
dance she was attending, whether there was

even a party tonight. If there was, she would be there, he knew. Her family was one of the Dallas elite, her father a former New Yorker who came to Texas to take advantage of the Reconstruction. *Carpetbagger* was the dirty word for a man like Robert Spears, but Cole was willing to be magnanimous and forget all that. He'd never had much use for that kind of resentment anyway. Carpetbaggers were just as likely as Texans to lose at cards.

There was a hotel not far from here, one of the finer establishments in the whole of Texas. Three stories, with glass windows in the main room. Cole had never stayed there before, but he'd already decided that this visit he would. It was where the wealthier, more respected travelers stayed, and he wanted to impress the Spearses. He rode past the flea-bitten saloon he usually took a room at and hitched his horse in front of the Eagle Hotel.

It was as well kept as some of the hotels outside of Texas, with a brightly lit main room and a carpet on the floor — though it was too dusty to see the pattern on it — and a jovial, round man buzzing behind the front desk. The room smelled of cigar smoke and money. Cole made his way to the clerk. He leaned against the desk and pulled a cigar out of his vest pocket, lighting it and taking a few puffs before the man turned to him with a big smile.

"Welcome to the Eagle," he said. "How can I help you?"

Cole smiled. "I'll take a room."

The man turned the guest book to him and dipped a pen. "If you could just fill in your name."

Cole scrawled his name on the line. "Maybe you could tell me — I've got an invitation to one of those dances tonight —"

"You mean at the Fargo?" The clerk frowned.

"No, no," Cole said. "One of those society things."

"Ah. You must mean Lucia Brainierd's dance." The clerk's expression cleared. "You'll be able to find it easily. The Brainierds' house isn't far."

Cole memorized the directions and paid for his room. Then he took his saddlebags upstairs and went inside. Once a man got past the glitter of downstairs, the rooms were small and bare. There was a basin and pitcher by the door, and he washed and combed his hair. He pulled a clean shirt from his saddlebags and changed, and then he brushed the dust from his pants and his coat. He was ready for his sweet Jenny. Cole hummed as he left the room and went back into what was now full-blown night.

The Brainierds' wasn't far, and it was easy to spot because there were lamps blazing in the windows and a few dozen horses out front. The party was in full swing; he heard the music from a few fiddles and a banjo, heard the stomp of feet. He had no invitation, of course, but there was no one at the front door; it was partially ajar, and Cole pushed it open and stepped inside.

No one questioned him. He got a few curious looks from the people standing and talking in the entryway, but other than that the house was too crowded for anyone to notice one more. He pushed his hat back on his head and went to where the action was — a main room where the musicians stood at the far end. The furniture was pushed back against the walls, the carpets rolled up, and there were couples spinning and do-si-doing in the limited space. Oil lamps and candles flickered and shimmered in the breeze created by several moving bodies, and the air was close and hot, thick with perfume and cigar smoke and the heavy, leftover scent of greasy beef.

There were streamers and bright pink bunting, and a sign at one end of the room, crudely painted, that read "Happy Birthday, Lucia," with black and yellow daisies — or at least, he thought they were daisies — at each end.

Cole stood beneath the archway leading to the dance floor, wedged between a group of men arguing loudly about something and a couple oblivious to everything but themselves. He scanned the room, looking for dark brown hair and a fine figure. He didn't see her. Not on the dance floor, not over there, by a big glass punchbowl full of some sickly pink concoction. Cole moved in a little, smiling at a woman he bumped into, tipping his hat at another, until he was behind the punch table. He had a better view there, but even so, he didn't spot her. He was just feeling the sink of disappointment when she walked into the room.

She was coming through a door carrying a tray of little iced cakes, talking animatedly to the woman beside her. She was wearing a pretty pink gown with darker pink stripes and a décolletage that showed off her fine throat. Her hair was done up in flowers, with two long curls dangling over one shoulder. Her eyes were bright and smiling, and he remembered why it was he loved her. She was the most beautiful thing he'd ever seen.

He had been waiting for her a long time, and so it was easy to give her a few seconds more, to watch her hips sway and her bright laughter as she moved to the table. She set the cakes down with a little flourish, and threw a smiling comment to someone behind her, and then she straightened and started to turn back to the dance floor.

But he caught her gaze and stopped her with a smile. "Miss Jennifer Spears, I believe," he said, tipping his hat. "D'you remember me?"

She looked startled, a little confused, wary. "You look familiar to me, sir," she said. "Are you a soldier?"

He laughed and shook his head. "Cole Wallace," he said. "At your service."

She mouthed his name. "We've met before."

"We have." He came around the table. "About a year ago, I was passing through. There was a dance —"

"Cynthia Morgan's!" she said. Her wariness faded. She dimpled up at him. "I do remember you now."

"I've never forgotten you," he said. "You were the prettiest girl in the room. I see some things haven't changed."

She smiled and dipped her head, but she didn't blush. "You are a flatterer, Mr. Wallace."

"It's the gospel truth," Cole said. He had to raise his voice over the music. "There aren't many here who could hold a candle to you, Miss Spears."

"You wouldn't be trying to turn my head, now, would you, Mr. Wallace?"

He offered his arm, jerked his head toward the door. "It's loud in here. Come for a walk with me."

"Alone?" She raised a slender brow. "But I've just met you."

"You've known me for a year," he said.

"And forgotten you for most of it," she pointed out.

It was a wounding comment, but Cole ignored it. He gave her his best smile. "I've come all this way to see you," he said. "The least you could do is talk to me a while."

"We're talking just fine right here," she said. She reached for the punch and poured a cup. She handed it to him, and glanced around the room. "Do you see that man on the far wall, Mr. Wallace? The one watching me?"

He took the punch, and took a sip, looking over the rim of the cup to the heavyset, frowning gentleman she'd pointed out. "Your father, I take it," he said.

She smiled. "Why, how clever you are," she said.

"Wait until the dance starts up again," he said. "Then come with me. He'll never see you over this crowd."

She tsked, and batted at him with a gloved hand. "Now, really, Mr. Wallace. Do you think a girl would be wise to do such a thing?"

"Not wise," he said, bending until he was looking directly into her eyes. "Just a little impulsive. A bit spontaneous. A girl who wants some adventure in her life."

Her dark eyes widened. Her smile was slow and even. "You are dangerous, Mr. Wallace."

"D'you think so?" he asked, grinning. "All I want to do is take a pretty girl for a moonlit walk."

"I'm sure I'd be foolish to agree to such a thing," she said, but he saw the coquetry in her eyes, the *oh no, I couldn't unless you talk me into it,* and so he smiled and leaned close.

"Don't tell me you'd rather stay here in this hot room and drink punch," he said in a low voice. "Not when the night is so beautiful."

"Well, I —"

"Do something daring for once, Miss Spears," he urged. "Come see the stars with me."

She tilted her head up at him. Her eyes were the deepest, most glorious brown, and he saw her hesitation, the pull of the forbidden. He waited, his whole breath teetering on her answer — he let it out in a whoosh when she smiled and said, "I suppose it'd be all right — just for a few minutes."

The music started. She darted a look through the crowd at her father, and then she took Cole's arm, and the two of them hurried to the door, her skirts tangling around his legs, her fingers clutching his sleeve.

They slipped outside. The night was hot and humid, not much cooler than the day had been. He led her onto the street. The music from the party followed them, fainter now, a melody to accompany the stars that glittered in the darkness. In this part of town, there were no gaslights to obscure them. They looked pure and clear as they did on the prairie, and Cole felt their lure deep in his soul. For a moment, he could barely believe he was here, that Miss Jenny Spears was clinging to his arm, that it was her perfume he smelled wafting on the air, the heavy, hothouse gardenia. He'd dreamed of this day for so damned long.

"They are pretty, aren't they?" she asked. She sighed, and he glanced down to see her looking up at the sky. "Orion, and Ursa Major, and — oh, look, Cassiopeia — how bright she is tonight!"

He followed her gaze. He saw the Big Dipper. The rest were simply stars. "Yeah," he said. "No clouds tonight."

"There haven't been clouds in ages," she said. "And it's been damnably hot."

He grinned at her. "Why, Miss Spears. Such language."

"Well, it has been," she said defiantly. "And I don't care if it's not ladylike to say it. Sometimes I think men are lucky, only having to wear trousers instead of all these" — she flicked her skirts — "petticoats."

"Well, I, for one, appreciate the sacrifice," he said. "I don't care much for women in trousers."

"That's what my father says, too," she said. "But I still think it's not fair." She pulled away a little, swaying into him as they walked down the street. "So tell me, what brings you to Dallas, Mr. Wallace?"

"You," he said.

She dipped her head and smiled. "I mean really."

"You," he said again. "Really."

She laughed. "I suppose you flatter all the girls this way."

"Just the ones I've decided to marry."

She looked at him with raised brows. "Why, how many girls would that be?"

"Just one," he said. "Just you."

She laughed again. The curls bounced on

her bare shoulders; he caught the strong and heady whiff of gardenia. "How can you want to marry me?" she asked. "Why, we hardly know each other."

"That's why I'm here," he said. "I mean to amend that."

"You are the most audacious man," she said, but he could tell she didn't mind it, and his heart soared. "What if I don't want to marry you?"

"You will," he said, and he believed it.

"Oh my," she said. She stopped and loosed her arm from his, and stood looking up at him in the middle of the street. The moonlight fell on her face, made her bare shoulders look alabaster, unbelievably smooth. She was smiling. "You sound mighty confident, sir."

"I am confident," he said. The music from the party was fading, the dance was over. She heard it too; he saw her look toward the house, saw the catch of her breath.

"I have to get back," she said. "My father —"

Her words fell into nothingness when he touched her cheek. She looked back at him, surprise in her eyes. "Mr. Wallace —"

He ignored her protest. He took her chin in his fingers and lifted her face, and then he kissed her. A light, nothing little kiss.

Barely a touch. It inflamed him. It was all he could do to move away. She gasped a little, stepped back.

"Mr. Wallace!" she said. "Really —"

"Come with me on a picnic tomorrow," he said.

She gave him a strange look. "Why should I?"

"Because I want you to."

"Unchaperoned?"

He gave her his best smile. "Miss Spears," he chided softly. "I thought you had a more adventurous spirit than that. Afraid you won't be able to control yourself?"

"I'm not worried about myself, Mr. Wallace."

He leaned closer. She didn't move away. "I promise I'll be on my best behavior," he said.

From the Brainierd house came the sound of clapping. She looked quickly toward it, took a step. "I really must get back."

He grabbed her hand, keeping her in place. "Tell me you'll come with me tomorrow," he said. "And I'll let you go."

"You'll let me go in any case," she said, but in spite of her words, he saw that glint in her eyes again, that response to a dare, and she didn't jerk back her hand. "What time?"

"One o'clock," he said quickly, unable to stop his broad grin.

"I'll meet you at the milliner's in town," she said. "Now, please, let me go —"

He released her. "The milliner's," he said. "Don't be late."

She was halfway back to the Brainierds'. His words fell on empty air. He stood there, watching her, the bell of her skirts, the way her curls bounced as she nearly ran back to the house. He watched her climb the steps to the door. And then, just before she went in, she turned to look at him. He saw her lift her hand and give a slight wave, and then she was gone.

But the smell of her toilet water lingered in the night air, and he still felt her touch and the soft sweetness of her lips. Cole hummed as he walked slowly back to the Eagle Hotel. He felt light as he hadn't for a long time. Jenny Spears was in his sights, and she liked him already, he knew. In a few weeks, maybe less, she would be his wife.

His wife. He liked the way the words sounded on his tongue, the way they felt in his head. He thought of her standing beside him, hearing her say "I do" to the preacher, then having their picture taken afterward, with himself sitting in a chair and her hand on his shoulder as she stood behind. His wife. Yes, he liked the sound of that. He liked it very much.

White Horse, Texas

"Add the wood and put the match to it," Miguel had said, and now, looking into the hot, yawning mouth of the huge, newfangled cookstove, Eliza's heart sank. He'd shown her how to light the thing that morning, but he'd done it so fast she couldn't really remember it, and it was so different from the sheet metal stove back home that she didn't know where to start. He twisted a lever, she remembered, but when she looked for where she thought it was, there was nothing but smooth metal.

She sighed and backed away. The stove was still warm from that morning, and there were a few coals left. She threw the few sticks of wood inside, hoping the coals were hot enough to catch. But the wood just sat there. She tried blowing on it, but all she got was a face full of ash.

Eliza closed the iron door and wiped a hand across her face, feeling ash and soot grit against her skin. The morning had started out hot, and though it wasn't yet noon, she was already sweating and her head was pounding. Miguel had expected her to take over cooking today, which was why he'd shown her how to work the stove, and she knew that any minute, they would come in expecting dinner. She had nothing to give them.

It seemed overwhelming suddenly, and she sank back into one of the chairs at the worktable and put her face in her hands. She was not turning out to be as good a wife as she wanted to be. She wanted Aaron to be happy with her, she wanted him to smile at her, maybe even touch her. It had been a week now, and he hadn't even kissed her, and she was afraid he thought she was a poor wife. He hadn't seemed to mind that she couldn't read, but she wasn't sure he would be so easy about her not being able to fire up the stove. Maybe he would decide she wasn't worth the time of reading lessons.

It wasn't just Aaron, either. She got a low, hot feeling of panic whenever she thought of their neighbors showing up. They'd be here any day now to welcome her, she knew, and how was she supposed to offer them coffee if she couldn't even get the stove to work? What was she supposed to do? *"I'm sorry, Miz Winchell, I ain't got no coffee, but how about some water? It only tastes a little like snake. . . ."* Eliza winced at the thought. It seemed like every day brought another step for her to get over, another failure, and now her head was pounding and she felt hot and sick, and she couldn't get that damn stove to work —

She smelled smoke. Eliza jerked her head up. Smoke was billowing from the seams of the stove door, and she bit off a curse and ran over to it, jerking the door open with the edge of her apron. Smoke poured out; the acridness of it burned her eyes. She slammed the door closed again and went to the bucket of water by the worktable, grabbing it up, sloshing water on the floor. She wrenched open the door again and nearly threw the bucket into it. Water splashed everywhere, smoke and ash poured out, onto the floor, onto her.

Eliza kicked the door shut again and stood there, breathing hard, seeing the mess of ash and dirty black water on the floor, smelling smoke. Her eyes pricked, she felt the start of tears, and she swiped them away with the back of her hand and closed her eyes tightly. She would not cry. It seemed it was all she did lately. Her head pounded a rhythm into her blood, she felt the heavy press of it at the back of her skull, and the smell of ash burned up her nose, burned into her lungs.

Slowly, she opened her eyes again. The stove was still; only a small bit of smoke twisted from the closed door. But it was ruined now, she knew. She'd have to clean all that wet ash out before she could get a fire to start again, and the floor was a mess, and the sight of it made her so tired she could barely move.

She took a deep breath and wiped her hands on her sooty apron, and turned away, walking through the front room, onto the porch. The hot, dry air seared her burnt lungs, and she took great breaths of it until she smelled the pines and the corn. She was readying to sit on the edge of the porch when she saw Aaron.

He wasn't in the fields, where she'd expected to see him. He was under that big oak tree near the shallow creek, and he was bent over something, his whole body leaning into it, his hair masking his face. Miguel and Carlos were nowhere to be seen — they were probably still in the corn.

At first she thought she should leave him alone; there was something about him that made her think he didn't want to be bothered. But she felt lonely and her head hurt, and she yearned for company. She wanted Cole, but he wasn't here, so she stepped off the porch and wandered across the grass to the far part of the yard, to the tree.

Aaron didn't even notice her until she was right up on him. Even then, when she said,

"Hey there," he nearly jumped out of his skin.

"I'm sorry," she said, stepping away. "I didn't mean to —"

"I-it's all right," he said, talking over her, flushing. "You . . . you just startled me."

"What're you doing?" she looked over his shoulder, at the papers on his lap, at an open box packed with scrawlings. "You being a poet?"

He pushed the papers he held into that box, and his hands were shaking so he was wrinkling them, crushing them.

Eliza knelt beside him, smiling. "Wait a minute," she said. "You want these all bent up?" When he drew back, she took them out again, smoothed them, put them back inside. She looked down at one. "These're poems?"

He took a deep breath. "Yeah."

Eliza frowned and set the last one inside. "Wish I could read one," she said.

"They aren't . . . very good," he said quietly.

"Oh?" She looked at him. "Somebody tell you that?"

"No."

"Then how d'you know?"

He didn't answer her. He took the box from her hands and shut the lid firmly, and then he shoved it away, jamming it against

305

the roots of the tree.

Eliza sighed and sat back on her heels. "You ain't working today?"

"No."

She tried again. "If you weren't being a poet, what were you doing?"

He looked down. He picked up a rock beside him and rubbed it between his thumb and his fingers, worrying it, smoothing it. Then he tossed that stone so it sailed into the creek. She heard its soft plop in the shallow water.

"Looking at things," he said. "Wondering why . . . the words don't come."

He said those last words so softly she had to strain to hear him. Eliza frowned. "What d'you mean? Ain't the words just there? I mean, you know a lot of them — a lot more than me. I guess you must have plenty to choose from."

"Yeah," he said quietly. "It's not that easy."

The silence felt strained. She rushed to fill it, but she didn't talk anymore about poetry — she had the feeling he didn't want to, and she didn't want to upset him.

"You know," she said, "I was wondering . . . do the neighbors know yet about me and you getting married?"

His dark brows came together, he looked

confused. "Do the neighbors know?"

"Well, I thought maybe they'd come by, you know, to say hello or something. My daddy and I used to do that to all the new farmers in Richmond. They were always moving out, you know, coming and going. We must've had a new farmer on the old Rawlins place nearly every other season. We'd take them a pie sometimes, or Mama would send over a jar of pickles. You know, just to make them feel at home."

"Oh." That was all he said. He looked out over the land, into the distance. She had the feeling he was holding his breath, he was suddenly so quiet, and she found herself waiting for it, for the slow exhale.

It didn't come. Finally, she felt she had to say something. "You suppose . . . they don't know we got married?"

"I don't know," he said. "Maybe they don't. I don't . . . I don't have . . . much to do with my neighbors."

There was that exhalation, then — he said those last words on a rush of breath, like he couldn't get them out fast enough, and Eliza had the feeling there was something he wasn't saying, something he didn't want her to know. But she couldn't imagine what that could be.

"Maybe I should go meet them, then," she

said. "I could maybe get Miguel to —"

"I need Miguel in the fields," he said, and there was a roughness to his voice she hadn't heard before, a finality that made her feel her headache again, and the heat, and she looked down at the ground, feeling like a child.

"I'm sorry," she said. "I didn't think. Of course you need him here. I was forgetting."

He sighed. When she looked up at him, she saw the muscle in his jaw clench, she felt his tightness in the air around them — it made her shoulders hurt, looking at how tight he was.

"I'm sorry," he said quietly, and the words trailed off like he was going to say something else. She waited for his explanation, for his *"but . . ."*

There was nothing like that. There was just "I'm sorry." He got up, and she followed him through the yard, past the house to the back. They rounded the well, close to the back door, and instead of telling her anything else, he raked his hand through his hair and said, "Dinner ready?"

She remembered the stove then. She steeled herself for his anger. "I . . . uh . . . I flooded the stove. I don't think it'll fire up again for a while."

He looked at her in surprise. "You flooded it?"

"Well, I was trying to start it up, and there were some coals in there, and when I put the wood on it started to smoke so bad I thought . . . well, I poured a bucket of water on it. I'm sorry — I won't do it again. It was stupid, I know. I hope I didn't ruin it —"

He smiled — it was so tiny and so fast she wasn't sure she'd really seen it. It shocked her so she went silent.

"You didn't ruin it," he said, and then he turned to go in the kitchen door. He stopped just inside. She saw him look at the stained floor. She could still smell the smoke. Then he turned back again. "Why don't you . . . sit down?" he said. "I'll . . . uh . . . I'll go get a shovel."

She was so surprised she did sit, right there on the porch step. She didn't move when he went past her to the barn, or when he came back again, carrying a shovel and a burlap bag. He went into the kitchen, and opened up that stove door, and she watched him empty out those soggy ashes, shovelful by shovelful, unloading them onto the burlap he'd laid on the floor.

She had never seen a man do such a thing before. Her daddy never helped in the kitchen; he never helped Mama at all. She watched Aaron work, watched the flex of his muscles beneath his shirt, the way his hair fell into his face, and she felt warm inside, and strange, and fragile, like she might break if someone touched her.

She hardly knew what to say to him when he finished, when he put aside the shovel and closed the stove door and picked up the corners of that bag to hold all the ashes together. He dragged it across the floor, out to the stoop, and she moved so he could get by. When he hefted the bag into his arms and started to the barn, she said, "Thanks. I-I'll try to be a better wife."

He turned to look at her, and there was a look in his eyes, a quiet surprise. "You're just fine," he said.

She got to her feet. "I'll make dinner —"

"There're biscuits," he said. "That'll do." And then he headed toward the barn.

She watched him go until he disappeared inside. He wasn't like any man she'd ever met. She was never sure what he thought, what he wanted. One minute he was acting like he couldn't stand the sight of her, and the next he was teaching her to read, or cleaning out the stove, making her feel like . . . well, like she mattered.

But she knew she was a failure, and if he wasn't what she expected, she knew she was even more so to him. She couldn't read, she didn't know any poetry, and he didn't seem interested in the one thing she could do well.

No, she'd never met a man like him. Eliza settled back on the stoop and waited for him to come back. He'd cleaned the stove for her, so he must like her a little, she supposed. Maybe when he came back, she'd give him a kiss to show him she was grateful. Just a little one. Maybe if she did it just right, he would kiss her back. She could show him then that she wasn't completely a failure. She knew how to kiss.

So she waited for him. But he didn't come back from the barn. She didn't know where he went, except that he disappeared, and she waited a long, long time before she finally got up from the stoop and went back inside — to quiet heat and a loneliness that felt worse than it had before — before he'd cleaned that stove. Before he'd smiled at her.

16

Dallas, Texas

The next morning, Cole was up early. The sun was already beating down, hot and relentless, and in spite of the fact that he'd washed, he was sweating by the time he reached the street. He hurried from place to place, renting a wagon, ordering up a picnic from a boardinghouse matron, trying — unsuccessfully — to buy some roses. He ended up with a tiny, expensive bottle of gardenia scent, which he supposed she would like just as much. By the time twelve-thirty came, he was ready.

He drove the wagon into town — slowly, because the horse pulling the wagon was raw-mouthed from being mishandled, and had a tendency to stop in the middle of the street until he felt like going again. Finally, Cole got him moving at a decent pace. He was pulling up to the front of the milliners when he saw Jenny. She was standing in front of the store, surrounded by four or five men who looked like they were doing their damnedest to please her. She caught Cole's eye as he approached, and with a quick smile, she came straight for him.

"I'll see you boys later," she said, and they tried to outdo each other tipping their hats. Cole was down and helping her into the seat in seconds, and once she was there, she leaned over and whispered, "Quickly now, my aunt's inside."

He didn't spare a thought for the aunt, didn't give a damn if she worried over her niece's sudden disappearance. The only thing that mattered was that Jenny was doing her best to be with him. So he did as she said; he took his seat and got that horse moving fast through town, dodging dogs and the occasional hog roaming the dust-drenched streets. Jenny seemed stiff and nervous until they cleared main street and Cole turned toward the Trinity River, and then she relaxed with a gush of breath and a smile.

"I was sure Aunt Agnes was going to come racing out just as we were leaving," she said. "Thank goodness all those boys were blocking the window." She leaned close. "How nice you look in the daylight, Mr. Wallace," she said. "I declare, you are quite a handsome man."

"You look pretty fine yourself," he said, and she did. Gone was the low décolletage of last night, but her walking dress presented her figure in a most appealing light. It was pink again, just as her ball gown had been, and the color favored her. It made her brown eyes sparkle. Her dark hair was caught up under a matching pink hat decorated with daisies. She looked cool and so pretty Cole's throat clenched up just looking at her.

She tilted her head at him. "I was talking to Bill Waits about you this morning," she said.

Cole tried to remember the name. It drew a blank, which made him nervous. He tried for nonchalance. "Oh? What'd he have to say?"

"He says you're a gambler," she said. "He says you only come through town a couple times a year, and when you win yourself enough money, you just ride off again."

Bill Waits. Someone he'd beaten at poker, no doubt. Cole looked at her, trying to read the expression in her eyes, wondering if he should try to lie his way around it. In the end, he decided not to. If he was going to marry her, it would be best if she knew what he did for a living.

"Yeah," he said, looking straight ahead. "That's true enough."

Her voice was thoughtful as she said, "My,

my, a gambler. That's not a very reputable thing to be, is it?"

"Better than being an outlaw," he said, and then he turned to her with his most cajoling smile.

She smiled back, but he thought he saw a distance in her gaze, a drawing away. "I suppose so."

A fine sweat swept the back of Cole's neck, his heart grabbed a little. He was wondering how the hell to get past the fact of his profession when the wagon bounced over a pothole and she leaned into him to catch her balance. He steadied her with a hand, and she held onto his arm just a few seconds too long before she straightened and said, "You from around here, Mr. Wallace?"

She was giving him a way to redeem himself, he realized, and shamelessly, Cole took it. "My family's got a farm out near Fort Belknap," he said. "My father's an old-time farmer. Came out from England in twenty-five and bought up a section or so, and we've been there ever since."

"Really?" Her eyes seemed to light. "You ever thought of taking up farming yourself?"

He looked at her, wondering what to tell her, wondering just what kind of woman Jenny Spears was. There were women who wanted nothing more than to settle down on a farm and start raising children, and there were women who wanted something more. He'd spent his life betting on men's expressions, on the signs written in gestures or a twist of the brow, and he used that skill with Jenny now. He looked into her pretty face and he thought he saw a wariness in her eyes, a trepidation that made him glad. She was not the kind of woman who longed to be a farmer's wife.

He turned away. "I'd make a bad farmer, I'm afraid," he said. "There are too many things to see in the world."

He heard the slight catch in her breath, and when he turned to her again, she was watching him carefully, her cheeks flushed, her eyes bright. "You want to travel, then?"

"I've got some money saved up," he said.

"You ever thought about where you'd go?" There was a wistfulness in her voice that gladdened his heart. "When I was a little girl, I always thought I'd have a grand European tour when I was married."

"Well, isn't that something," he said. "I always figure that one day I'd make a trip to Europe myself. I'd like to see the place where my father was born."

A complete lie — he'd never given a damn about Europe or about the British homeland of the Wallaces — but if Europe was what made Jenny Spears smile that way, he'd take her there and stay a hundred years if she wanted.

"Oh my," she said on a rush of breath. "My mother once met the queen, you know. She said it was the kind of thing a woman never forgot."

The only queen Cole felt that way about was the queen of diamonds, and then only if she were matched up with one of her sisters. But he nodded and agreed. "There's something about royalty. Makes you almost wish we had a monarch of our own."

She laughed, and just then they reached the spot he'd chosen for their picnic. Right now, the Trinity didn't look much like a river; it was more like a gutter filled with slowly moving, brackish water. But he'd seen it rushing its banks, filled up from a sudden rainstorm, gone from this little nothing stream to a wide, wild river in little more than ten minutes. It seemed incapable of that now, as quiet and peaceful as it was, with a few live oaks shading the banks. The perfect spot to woo a society girl. He stopped the wagon and helped Jenny down, and then he unloaded the things he'd brought and laid them under one of those trees.

She walked over, slowly, swaying her hips, her whole skirt undulating with the movement. He offered her some lemonade, and though it was warm from the ride and sickly sweet, she drank it like it was ambrosia and sat down beside him. She primped until she seemed satisfied that her skirts were just so, and pushed back a loose strand of hair, and then she liked her face to look at him and he thought of what their children would look like, whether their daughters would take after her, with her striking features, her dark brows and that long, straight nose, the heavily lashed eyes.

He was afraid he would do something stupid then, like propose to her right now, too soon, so he looked into the picnic bag and drew out the lunch that Miss Lorena's Boardinghouse had packed for him. A box of fried chicken and some biscuits, a covered bowl of chow chow, which he set aside, and some sliced cake.

He kept from looking at her as he laid out the food, and carefully, pretending his heart wasn't in his throat, he asked, "So tell me, Miss Spears, am I wasting my time courting you? D'you already have a special beau?"

"Is that what you're doing, Mr. Wallace?" she asked. "Courting me?"

She was teasing, not at all taken aback, and not displeased. He smiled up at her. "Why, yes, I am."

She smiled coquettishly. "And just why should I let you? I don't think my father would take kindly to a gambler running off with his only daughter."

"Not even if that gambler has two thousand dollars saved?"

Her eyes widened; she looked genuinely surprised. "Two thousand dollars?"

"I'm looking for a woman to share it with," he said, not taking his eyes from hers. "A woman who might enjoy a long tour of Europe."

She didn't say anything for a moment. She looked back at him, and he saw how flushed her cheeks were, how her breath seemed to come a little faster, a little shallower. He saw something come into her eyes, a quick calculation, a swift reckoning, and then it was gone, and she smiled, a smile that showed her straight, perfect teeth.

"I will only marry for love, Mr. Wallace," she said, and the words had the ring of a challenge; in his mind he heard the dare, *Gentlemen, take up your weapons.*

He smiled and lifted the jar of lemonade. "Then I'll have to make you love me, won't I?" he said, and poured more into her cup.

White Horse, Texas

"Some bug got into the corn," Eliza told

Mr. Wallace as she poured rubbing alcohol on her hands. She felt its wet dryness spread over her skin, felt the sting of its scent in her nostrils before she bent over his thin, bony legs.

Mr. Wallace raised the brow on the good side of his face.

"I don't know what it is," she said, rubbing his skin with the hard massage Carlos had taught her. "But they're out there trying to get it out."

She curled her fingers around his pale legs, feeling the hardness of bone and the dry thin skin, the roughness of hair as she moved her hands over him. Carlos had explained to her how this daily massage kept his legs from wasting away, and so she wasn't lazy. "Seems like hot work. That's one thing I'm glad of — that I ain't out there in that sun with them. Sometimes I just feel like I'm drying up and blowing away."

Mr. Wallace lifted his hand. Without thinking, she reached over and handed him his water.

"They been out there every day, from the time the sun comes up to when it goes down again. I ain't even had a lesson in a week — so I'm sorry I can't read your chalkboard now, Mr. Wallace. I wish I could. Sometimes it's like all I ever hear is my own voice."

Eliza sighed. She worked Mr. Wallace's legs and smelled the hot breeze through the window. The men hadn't even come in for supper today — Miguel had just grabbed some cornbread and some bacon and taken it out to the others with a *"No time to rest, señora."*

She'd taken to spending more and more time up in this room with Mr. Wallace. He couldn't talk to her, but she liked the company of his body, and when he was around she didn't feel so lonely. It had been a week since Aaron had cleaned out the stove for her, and she'd barely seen him in all that time. She'd never gotten the chance to kiss him; she'd scarcely talked to him at all.

So she concentrated on the neighbors. She'd been watching the horizon every day, watching the road, waiting for them to come around. Distances were far in this country; maybe it was just that they hadn't heard the news yet. Maybe they were as busy as Aaron was now, trying to save the corn. She told herself it would only be another week, maybe two. Maybe even before then, because sooner or later they'd run out of supplies, and she'd have to go into White Horse to get more. She'd learned to light the stove. She waited.

In the meantime, she was learning to be a

good wife. It was hard, since she couldn't talk to Aaron enough to find out what he wanted, what he expected. He'd been too busy; he was a quiet man.

Eliza shook her head and poured more alcohol on her hands. "He ain't much of a talker, huh?" she asked. "Aaron, I mean." She didn't bother to get Mr. Wallace's answer; she looked down at his legs, she kneaded his calves. "He ain't much like Cole, you know? Cole just talked on and on. It was like he had a whole brain full of things to say, and they were almost all pretty." She paused for a moment, remembering the journey here and how he'd talked about this farm, how nice it had seemed to her before she even saw it.

She smiled bravely at Mr. Wallace, who was watching her intently. "But I guess that's all right. It's just that Aaron . . . well, he's kind of hard to know."

Mr. Wallace frowned.

"I don't mean that in a mean way," she hurried on. "I guess it's just that . . . well, I ain't much used to quiet men. All the boys in Richmond were —"

A throat cleared. At first, she thought it was Mr. Wallace, but the sound came from behind her, and Eliza turned to see Aaron standing in the doorway. He looked ill at ease. It was the first time in a week she'd seen him without a dust-grayed face; his hair was wet, his face clean.

"You . . . uh . . . you ready for a . . . lesson?" he asked.

The words sent a shiver of excitement through her. She had to make herself sit still; she had to make herself ask, "What about the corn?"

He shrugged.

She took her hands from Mr. Wallace's legs and turned to her husband. "I'd like to," she said. She leaned over and pulled the old man's nightshirt down over his legs, and then she covered him with a light blanket and smiled. "You need anything else tonight, Mr. Wallace?"

He shook his head, waved her away, but he wasn't looking at her. He was looking at Aaron with a fierce expression that made Eliza frown.

Before she could ask about it, Aaron was gone, turning from the door, and she said good night to Mr. Wallace and followed her husband.

It was still hot, though there was a softness to the evening now that the sun was setting, a kindness that relaxed her as she went onto the porch and waited while Aaron grabbed the slate and a thin little book. He sat down on the edge, and she sat down next to him, feeling him stiffen as her skirt brushed his thigh.

"I can still remember the alphabet," she said. "Want to hear it?" She didn't wait for an answer; she spun off the letters, tripping over a couple — it wasn't quite as good as she wanted it to be.

But he only nodded and wrote the letters on the slate with a quick, sure hand. Then he looked at her and said, "All right, one at a time," and pointed to the first, to the letter *A*. Dutifully, she said it. She said each letter as he pointed, she mimicked their sounds. And by the time she got to the letter *M,* she knew she didn't want to do this tonight. She thought of her mother and father, how they sat beside each other in the quiet of the shanty, Daddy cleaning his gun, Mama sewing, how he told her everything about the cotton like what she thought mattered, how she said what she thought before the night eased on and talk faded away except for the little words and pauses, the unfinished sentences only they understood, the small, easy touches.

Before the urge to leave had hit her hard, Eliza had always thought the evenings with her parents were like dreaming, quiet and peaceful, leading into night and sleep, and she wondered if there would ever come a day when she and Aaron would be like that, comfortable with each other, easy in their skins. She wondered if Aaron would ever touch her the way her daddy sometimes touched Mama — a hand on the waist as he went by, a pat on the shoulder.

She sighed. It had been a hard few days, and though she wanted to learn, what she really wanted was to talk to someone, to really talk to them. To hear a voice that wasn't hers, to have a soft, dreaming evening, to feel a man's touch.

His fingers held the chalk, he pointed to the *M*, and she thought what wonderful hands he had, how his fingers were so long, how graceful they were for a man. She turned to him so quickly he jerked back like she'd surprised him.

"Don't take this wrong," she said slowly. "Because I ain't telling you I don't want to learn my letters and such, but I . . . I don't feel much like learning tonight."

He paused. He frowned a little. "Oh," he said. He put aside the slate and made to get to his feet. "You're probably tired —"

"No." She grabbed his wrist. Her touch stopped him instantly. He went so still she dropped her hand again and finished, weakly, "I just thought maybe we could talk.

You know? I ain't had anyone to talk to."

"Oh." He looked about as uncomfortable as a body could be. "Well . . . Eliza . . . I'm . . . uh . . . I'm not much for talking."

"I know," she said. "But maybe you could just sit here with me awhile?"

He looked like it was the last thing he wanted to do, but Eliza was relieved when he sat beside her anyway. The house cast a long shadow across the yard, the trees were glazed with gold-pink light from the setting sun, and the porch was cooling. The katydids were starting to sing.

"Carlos was telling me he thinks there's going to be a drought," she said. "You think so?"

He nodded, and then he cleared his throat. "Yeah. I do."

"The corn's dying anyway, though, ain't it?"

"Not yet," he said.

It was like pulling words from an empty can — there was a hollowness in his voice that made her think there was nothing even inside him to say. It had been like this with Will Ames once, she remembered. They'd sat out back of Olsen's General Store after the sun went down and the air was all soft and cool, and this same kind of silence came between them. He'd kissed her then, she remembered. He'd put his arms around her and stuck his tongue in her mouth, and they hadn't needed words after that.

She looked over at Aaron. He was staring straight ahead, and his hands were braced on the edge of the porch, his fingers white from how tight he held on. Maybe he was like Will. Maybe he just wanted to kiss her so bad he couldn't think of anything to talk about. She hoped it was true. She wished it hard, and looked at his profile, and willed it. *Kiss me,* she thought. *Go on and kiss me. . . .*

But he only turned to look at her with a puzzled look on his face. "Something wrong?" he asked.

Eliza sighed and sat back again. "Maybe you could read me another poem," she said dully. "Something pretty."

He looked at her and there was something in his dark eyes that seemed to cut straight into her heart, and she thought for a minute that he might kiss her then, she waited for it. But all he did was lean back, and clear his throat again and look up at the sky, and say, "A story, maybe. Would you . . . like that?"

"A story," Eliza said. She nodded. "All right."

" 'In Xanadu did Kubla Khan a stately pleasure-dome decree . . .' " he began.

He'd said three lines before Eliza realized he was reciting from memory — he wasn't even reading a book. She found that so remarkable she couldn't help staring at him, and he caught her eye and flushed, but still he went on, and she wondered why a man with such pretty words would not use them to kiss her.

But he didn't. He didn't even try. He finished the poem, and told her another, and another, until the sky went black and the stars came out, and finally he stopped and in the dark silence he disappeared. He stepped off the porch with a quiet good night and he was gone. She couldn't find him. She went to bed alone then, feeling dazed and boneless, like a woman who had been kissed breathless and abandoned without a word — though it had been words that had done it, and not a kiss at all.

17

It was so hot and dry Eliza could barely move. Miguel kept cautioning her not to waste water — *"We are in drought,* señora," — and she tried not to, but she was always thirsty, and what she wanted most was lemonade. She craved it so badly that she dreamt about it at night, about its sweet-sour taste, the way it left her mouth and her throat coated and puckered up. But there were no lemons on the farm, and no lemon syrup, and no one ever went into town to buy any. She was beginning to think the town of White Horse was just something Cole and Aaron had made up in their heads, and that there were no neighbors. In the month she'd been on this farm, supplies just seemed to miraculously appear. She never saw anyone go, and she never saw anyone come back. She never got the chance to go into town. Not a single person called on her to bring a dish of potatoes or a cake or to say, *"We heard Aaron got married, and we hurried right over to see you. I'm so pleased to meet you."*

She never had to light the stove for tea.

Eliza was beginning to feel as if she were stranded in some strange world somewhere, isolated from people, cut off from civilization by a huge, invisible fence that everyone but she could see.

There were no people to change the days, so they blended seamlessly, one into the other, each the same, each nothing but hot skies and hotter winds, and red dust that blew into every crack in the house, that coated her skin and her clothes when she went outside. The creek had dwindled to almost nothing, a muddy, warm puddle where the spring let out that eased into nothing but a dry wallow. The only thing that even showed there'd once been water there was the cracked mud left behind. The well had gone so shallow the water was warm, and when the bucket came up, it came more and more often with snakes. Eliza was only drawing it once a day now, and Miguel came with her, cranking the rope with a long, forked stick, standing ready with a hoe.

The oak shading the creek, and the fig tree and pecan bordering the house were green still, but dull now, the edges of their leaves withered and drawn up like they were trying to protect themselves. And the corn in the fields was browning so fast that each day

Aaron and the Mexicans came in covered with corn dust and worry, their brows so furrowed from frowning and squinting that they had lines of red dust staining their foreheads that no little bit of wash water could get off.

She swept the floor until the constant effort of it strained her arms and the red dust made her sneeze and stuck to the sweat on her own skin. She'd mastered the stove, but it was hot work, and though her morning sickness had gone, she got these terrible headaches that forced her to sit down and sleep in the middle of the day. Sleep was the only thing that made them go away, and sometimes even that didn't help. Sometimes Mr. Wallace rang that bell in the middle of her nap, and she would go upstairs with a pounding head and try to smile and read the words he wrote on the chalkboard.

She was getting better at reading, that was true enough. She knew the sounds of the letters, and she could put them together sometimes, for simple words. Aaron had a McGuffey's reader, and she'd got through the first three lessons. *Is the cat on the mat? The cat is on the mat.*

She knew those words would always be caught up with her recollections of this heat, of Aaron's worry. She went to bed at night thinking them in her mind, closing her eyes to look at the letters written on her memory. *Is the cat on the mat? The cat is on the mat.* She would lie there, smelling the hot air and the dust, waiting for Aaron to come to bed. *Maybe tonight,* she always thought. Maybe tonight would be the night he kissed her. Maybe it would be the night he touched her.

But he never did. Mostly, she fell asleep before he even came to bed, and she never heard him climb those stairs and take off his boots. She never heard him push back the covers and get into bed, and she never felt him, because he turned his back to her and perched on the very edge of the mattress, and he barely moved a muscle all night long, and it was only morning that made her aware he was even there. Only when she heard him splashing in the basin and putting on his clothes. She would watch him between slitted eyes as he dressed, and then she would shut her eyes tight and pretend to be asleep when he turned to look at her before he went downstairs again, out to the fields. She wouldn't see him again until dinner.

She wondered once what he did after she went to bed, and so she'd sneaked down the stairs to see. He'd been in the front room, on the settee with a single light burning, reading, so quiet the turn of pages was the loudest sound in the darkness. She saw his lips move with the words, heard his sigh, and once again she felt that religiousness in him, that sense that he was beyond her, that there were things he knew that she would never begin to understand.

She'd left him like that and gone back to bed and felt small and unwanted. It wasn't that she minded so much that he didn't touch her. It was just that she had always measured a man's interest by his kisses: Will Ames had opened his mouth and tried to suck her inside him. Pete had pressed his lips so hard against hers she felt his teeth behind his skin. Cole had kissed her all around the edges. They had all liked her; she knew it because they had each wanted to kiss her.

But Aaron seemed to duck away from her touch. Sometimes, she put her hand on his arm just to test him, and whenever she did, he cringed into himself so hard it looked like it hurt.

She was so lonely for a kind word sometimes she felt like dying.

It was on a day like that Eliza sat on the back stoop, knees drawn up, staring out at the brown and burning yard. Even the chickens were lethargic in this heat; they had retreated to the tiny bit of shade cast by the abandoned springhouse, and they were mostly just walking around, looking dumb, every now and then pecking at some poor, tired old bug.

It was close on to suppertime, and Eliza had some beans simmering on the stove that were ready for her to do something with. But her skull was pounding, and her eyes burned as she stared out at the heat waves shimmering against the brown hills in the distance. She felt invisible, though her body was too heavy and aching not to be real. She didn't think anyone had said a word to her all day — even the chickens acted like they didn't see her. Aaron and the farmhands had come in for dinner and talked to each other about the corn, and then they'd gone without even telling her whether they liked the food. Mr. Wallace had been reading some book lately, and he'd been caught up in it enough that today he hadn't even called for her, and he hadn't even caught her eye when she took him his dinner, just motioned for her to set it down —

The sound of the bell carried through the house. Eliza sighed. She rose slowly, and her head pounded so hard with the movement she thought for a minute she would pass out. But then it eased to just a steady throb, and she turned and went back inside, through the boiling kitchen, up the stairs.

Mr. Wallace's room was cooler now that the sun was moving to the other side of the house, but it was still so hot in there that she went right to the window and opened it. He grunted at her and wrote something on the board.

Her head hurt so bad it was all she could do to focus on the words. She tried to sound them out. "Duh-ahh-en-ta —"

He whipped the board away from her with an audible sigh and erased it. Then he wrote again. This one was easier. *S-I-T. Ssss-eye . . . no, ssss-i-ta. Sit.* She pulled up a chair to the side of the bed and swiped back her hair.

"What can I get for you, Mr. Wallace?" she asked.

He didn't bother with the board. He mimed drinking.

"Water?" she guessed.

He nodded, and she went to the basin near the door, wondering why she hadn't thought to set it next to him when she brought his dinner. She handed him the glass and sat back in the chair, and hoped he wanted to go back to his reading. Her head felt like it weighed a hundred pounds.

But when he finished his water and she asked if he wanted to read again, he shook his head and made a sharp, cutting motion with his hand to tell her he had finished it.

"Oh," she said, and then she sat back and waited for him to write something on the board, to talk to her in his fashion.

But he didn't. He sat there, his big hands limp on the grayed sheet, watching her expectantly, and she didn't know why, but there was something in his eyes, some little sympathy, that made the words gush out of her. She nearly fell over herself to tell him how lonely she was, how much she wanted to go into town.

". . . I know . . . well, I don't want you to be mad at me or anything, Mr. Wallace, but I think . . . to be a good wife, shouldn't I . . . shouldn't I be a part of things? You know, go to a dance, or invite the ladies to tea. . . ."

She trailed off when she saw him smiling his lopsided smile, and suddenly the risk she'd taken spread over her like a quick hot flush. She ducked her head, looked at the floor, at her worn, scuffed boots, and wished she'd had the strength to keep her mouth shut. Now he would be angry —

Tap, tap.

She looked up. He was holding the chalkboard to her, and the word on it was simple enough that even she could read it. "GO."

She frowned at him. "You mean into town?"

He nodded.

"I can't just go by myself."

He pointed to the window. Then he mimed putting a ring on his finger and pointed again.

"You think . . ." She hesitated. "You mean Aaron."

He spread his hands and smiled.

"You think he'd take me?"

Mr. Wallace gave her a look that made her feel foolish for even asking the question.

Eliza got up and went to the window. She looked out, past the oak to the cornfields. She saw the men's hats dodging among the bending, burning corn. Miguel and Carlos, then past them, pausing a moment, taking his hat from his head, running his arm over his face, was Aaron.

Eliza looked back to Mr. Wallace. The old man was still smiling, and there was a gleam in his eyes, too, a look that she thought might be affection. She smiled back at him. "All right then," she said. "I'll ask him." And then, because she couldn't help the sudden, overwhelming happiness she felt, she rushed over and gave the old man a hug. He looked surprised, but he patted her back clumsily with his good hand, and Eliza whispered her

337

thanks as she pulled away and hurried out the door, her headache forgotten. She had to fix the beans; it was almost suppertime. And she wanted things to be special tonight when she asked Aaron to take her into town. She wanted him to say yes.

She made the beans with bits of ham and onion and chilies, and they were good. She was glad her nausea was gone, because there was nothing to make her sick as she fixed them, and she could stick her nose in the pot and take deep, heady breaths of the stew and think how much Aaron was going to like it. Mr. Wallace had made her happier than she'd been in weeks, just by telling her what she guessed she should have known to do by herself.

The one difference was that she'd been afraid to let Aaron know she was unhappy, and Mr. Wallace had given her permission to do just that. So when the men were inside, Eliza served up the beans with a smile and doled out cornbread, and waited while Carlos and Miguel talked their way around their worry and Aaron listened.

As happened every night, the Mexicans ate quickly and left, smiling and tipping the hats they never took off as they passed her. Silence settled around the table, there was only the sound of Aaron's fork scraping across his plate. Tonight, he ate slowly; his plate was only half-cleared while Carlos's and Miguel's were empty, and when the farmhands left the room, he seemed to sag a little, like the wind had gone out of him.

Eliza got her courage up. She took a deep breath and straightened, and then she pushed her voice out from her too-tight throat. "Aaron."

He glanced up at her, but his eyes seemed far away, his "Hmmm?" was distracted.

Determinedly, Eliza went on. "I . . . I was talking to your daddy today."

"Yeah?"

"I was telling him . . . I thought I'd like to go on into town one day."

He took another bite of beans as if he hadn't heard a single thing she'd said.

It was that, more than anything, that took her nervousness away — the way he just sat there, not even hearing her, ignoring her — and suddenly all Eliza could think was how hot and miserable she was, how Mr. Wallace had told her Aaron would take her into town, how much she wanted it. She leaned forward on the table, until her face was even with his, and he met her eyes. He stopped, his fork suspended in midair, watching her as she said firmly, "Aaron, I want you to take me on into White Horse."

His hand clenched on his fork, his face went so white his eyes looked black against his skin. Slowly, he straightened. Slowly, he lowered the fork to the table. He swallowed; she saw the thick effort of his throat.

"I . . . I . . . can't."

Eliza frowned. "You can't?"

He shifted in his chair, looked down at his plate. His hair came forward to hide his face. "No."

"But I want to go," she said. "Don't you think it's time I met some of our neighbors?"

He glanced up again. "Eliza," he said softly. "Leave it alone."

Leave it alone. She stared at him, bewildered and surprised, and her loneliness swelled up inside her like she'd swallowed something that wouldn't fit her throat. She saw Mr. Wallace again in her mind, pointing to the window, miming a ring, and she thought how unfair it was. She couldn't believe her husband was just looking at her and saying *"Leave it alone."*

Though she told herself not to get angry, she thought of spending the rest of her days on this farm, alone. She thought of how her dreams of being a grand lady were falling apart around her, and resentment went hot into her face, she found herself rising from her chair, slapping her hands palm-down on the table.

"You can't just tell me no," she said, hearing her voice steadily rising, hearing her own anger. "I ain't going to just sit around here for the rest of my life wondering if there even is a White Horse. I want you to take me into town."

Aaron's eyes fluttered shut for a moment, and then he looked at her steadily. "I . . . can't," he said calmly.

That calmness was the last straw. Something burst inside of Eliza, a whole month of disappointment, of loneliness. Her vision blurred, she jerked away from the table, unable to look into his face anymore, that horrible calm, that white-faced *no*. "This ain't what I wanted!" she shouted, and she didn't even know if he flinched, she could see nothing but his dim figure through her tears, and all she knew was that she had to get away from him, she couldn't look at him another second.

She turned on her heel, banging her hip into the corner of the table, and the pain only mixed with her disappointment as she hurried past him, out the door, down the stairs, and ran across the yard. She couldn't even see where she was going, and she tripped over hillocks of grass and stones and kept running. There was some vague thought in her head that she would keep going until she found something else, until she found Cole again, until she was safe in his arms and he was smoothing away her tears and saying, *"Eliza, darling, I'm sorry you're so unhappy. I'd do anything to take your tears away."*

But Cole was gone, and that only made her cry harder; it felt as if the misery of a whole life was swelling through her, washing out in tears. She couldn't breathe through her sobs — big, chest-wrenching gasps that made her heart hurt.

She brushed against the big oak, slid down the bank onto the dry mud of the creek, and blindly kept going. It wasn't fair. She wanted a different life. She should have a different

—

The growl blasted into her head like a shot.

Eliza's breath caught, she jerked to a stop, blinking away tears. In half a second, her eyes were clear, and her chest was tight with a scream she kept back by sheer strength of will.

In front of her, drinking at the muddy puddle of the spring, was a bobcat. It was thin, and its fur had the nappy look of an old cat, but its eyes were a pure, mean yellow.

The cat growled again. This time the sound ended on a high, threatening note. The animal stiffened, his shoulders lowered, his tail twitched in the air as he moved into a crouch.

She couldn't breathe, she couldn't scream. Slowly, Eliza took a step back.

The cat screamed. Eliza froze. Cold sweat broke out all over, her fear formed a thick lump in her throat. Her hands went numb. She felt a little jump inside her, and she brought her hands to her stomach and thought of her baby.

"Please," she murmured in a soft whisper. "Please . . ."

It was like somebody — God — heard her plea, because there was a shot in the distance, a loud report, and the bobcat loosened up and sprang away, disappearing so quickly into the grama grass that Eliza wondered if it had only been a ghost.

Her legs gave out from under her; she sank to the ground, staring at that muddy spring, murmuring a hundred thank-yous, crossing her arms against her belly, hugging herself tight.

That was where they found her. It was only a few minutes later, but it seemed like hours, that she heard the rustling snap of bootsteps through the burnt grass, the crack

343

of twigs. When she looked up, Carlos and Aaron stepped past the oak. Carlos was carrying a shotgun.

They stopped just short of the bank, and then Aaron frowned and stepped into the wallow, only a few feet from her. "Eliza," he said, and there was a strange sound in his voice, a hoarseness. "You all right?"

She burst into tears again, because that question was so kind. She was still crying when she heard Carlos say something to him in an undertone, when she felt Aaron come up to her and stop, when he offered his hand.

She took it, and when he pulled her to her feet, she collapsed against his chest, burying her face in his shoulder. She felt him stiffen, and she clung to him harder, shaking now from fear and relief, and then she felt his hand on her back, felt his clumsy, uncertain patting, as if she were a small child and he were her mother. *"It's all right, honey, you cry it on out now . . . sssh, Lizzie, you're all right."*

Gradually, her tears stopped, but he kept patting her, and she heard his voice then. "Miguel'll take you into town," he said. "You just tell him the day."

She backed away from him, smiling weakly through her tears, taking the bandanna he offered and blowing her nose on it. She wiped at her face. "All r-right . . . then," she managed. "You . . . you think we could go . . . tomorrow?"

"Whenever you want," he said. He turned and went back up the bank, back to where Carlos waited with the shotgun held at the ready. Eliza followed. But before she left, she looked out at the dry creek bed, at the muddy puddle, and she saw the shadow of the cat hovering there, a darkness in her head, saw the white teeth glowing wet and sharp, the extended claws. She thought of what would have happened if Carlos had not shot off that gun, she imagined the cat stalking her, jumping. She could have died today. The baby could have died. The truth of it sank into her and wouldn't let go.

She crossed her arms again across her belly and turned away, following Aaron and Carlos back to the house. But there was a fear within her now that stayed and stayed, and she knew that no matter how long she lived, she would be able to look back to the moment she'd seen the shadow of the cat lurking by the spring, and say it happened then. It was then that she started to be afraid.

He had thought she wouldn't want a lesson that night, and though he understood why — a near attack by a bobcat would be enough to scare anyone — selfishly he wanted to go on with the night, to have her sit beside him on the porch and listen to her recite the alphabet. He wanted to forget the way his whole body had seized up when she went running out, when he'd seen her kneeling in that wallow and thought he was too late, that the cat they'd heard had already got her. He wanted to forget how she'd fallen into his arms and he'd felt his insides giving away, falling inward. Her fear he understood. Comfort he understood. But his need to comfort her — that surprised him.

He supposed it shouldn't. He'd been growing braver day by day. Not brave enough to touch her, but he'd mastered his words, finally; he no longer stuttered like an idiot around her. Their nightly lessons had become something he looked forward to, a progress he could feel and measure. For him, as much as for her, the lessons were a slow build, like a house going up in the middle of a vast and desolate prairie. First, the foundation had to be laid, and he was building the foundation for the next forty years.

When they stumbled back to the farm, Carlos holding that shotgun as if he were expecting another cat at any moment, Aaron was not ready to let her walk away. She seemed calmer now, no longer the crying girl he'd found trembling in the creek bed, but there was something about her, something he couldn't quite put his finger on. Something different. It frightened him, and he didn't want her to walk away to let that something different grow. He wanted things to be normal, and normal was sitting on the porch, reading the letters.

"You all right now, *señora?*" Carlos asked.

Eliza nodded. She looked up at the farmhand with a tentative smile. "Thank you for scaring him away, Carlos."

Carlos nudged Aaron. "It is not just me, *señora*, eh?"

"I know," she said. "Thank you both."

Carlos shrugged. "What is *el cuguarito* to me, eh? With this gun, I am invisible."

"Invincible," Aaron corrected.

Eliza laughed a little. "Well, I'm sure glad you came along."

"It is *no problema, Señora* Wallace." Carlos made a little bow. *"Buenos noches."*

He was whistling as he walked away, and Aaron listened until that whistle was gone. He tensed up, waiting for her to say good night and go upstairs. But she only stood there uncertainly, and when she turned to him, he saw that she was still frightened, her face still pale, those blue eyes shadowed.

"You want to go inside?" he asked slowly.

She shook her head.

"We don't have to do the lesson tonight . . . if you don't want to —"

"I meant what I said, you know," she said. "Thank you for following after me. I-I'm sorry I ran like that. I'm sorry . . . for earlier." She motioned to the porch. "I'd like to . . . can we go on with learning?"

He was relieved. He hurried to get the chalkboard, the book. When he came back she was sitting on the edge of the porch, her arms crossed over her belly looking down at her feet. When he came onto the porch, she jumped. Then she looked at him with a weak smile.

"I guess I'm still a little spooked," she said.

"I guess anyone would be," he told her.

"D'you . . . d'you see lots of bobcats in these parts?"

He shook his head. "The drought's been hard on them, too. He was probably just looking for water."

She shuddered. "Cats, rattlers . . . where d'you guess the cottonmouths go when the creeks dry up?"

"I don't know," he said. "I never thought about it."

"We used to have floods every now and then back in Richmond," she said. "The waters would come up and the water mocs would come with them. They'd rush right in the doors, and when the water went down again, there they'd be, all coiled up under the bed or in the washpan, just waiting. The whole house would just stink then, like . . . like this death smell — you know that smell? My daddy always said cottonmouths had an evil smell, and I tell you, they are one mean snake." She turned to him. "You ever know anyone that got bit by one?"

"No," he said, and when she didn't take her eyes from him, when she kept looking at him so intensely, he said, "Rattlers, mostly. I know a few people who got bit by rattlers."

"I hate them, too," she said. She turned away again, looking out toward the fields, and her eyes seemed glazed over, there was an intensity of focus in her gaze, in her whole bearing, he didn't understand. "There's so much death everywhere here, ain't there? I mean, you just turn around and it's waiting for you. A bobcat, or rattlers in the well, or a moc . . ." Her arms tightened over her stomach. He saw her fingers turn white where she clutched herself.

"It's not so bad," he found himself saying. "It was worse before, when there were Comanches, too —"

She laughed shortly, but it was humorless

and bitter. "I'm scared, Aaron." It was a simple declaration, one that cut to his heart. "I never was really scared before. But today I saw that cat looking at me, and I thought: What if something happened to me? To the baby? I thought of us both dying, just like that, because if I died, the baby would die too. And he seemed real to me all at once, like he never did before."

The baby.

"I think maybe I even felt him," she said. "Flopping around like a fish inside me. I saw that cat, and I jumped, and I swear I felt the baby jump, too. He was as scared as I was."

He didn't know what to say to that. He had no idea what she wanted from him. All he could think of was a little Cole jumping deep within her belly. Cole's baby. Eliza's baby. Not his.

He felt that falling again, deep inside him, that sense that he could not measure up, and he was letting it swallow him when she touched him, when she let go of her stomach and clutched his arm so tightly he felt each of her fingers pressing into his skin.

"I'm scared, Aaron," she said. "Tell me not to be scared."

He swallowed and saw she was waiting for him, watching him with eyes that begged for reassurance, and there was nothing he could tell her. Nothing he could give her except distraction.

"You'll . . . need things for the baby . . . tomorrow," he said. "And maybe a new dress. Miguel will tell you where to go. Just run it on the account. Get whatever you want."

She blinked and looked at him blankly. "Things . . . for the baby?"

Each breath he took seemed an effort. "I don't know what you'll need," he said. "You might have to ask someone."

"Things for the baby," she said again. She looked down at her hands. She took a great, deep breath. It seemed to calm her.

"There's a cradle in the attic," he said. "It was . . . mine. Maybe . . . Cole's . . . too. I don't remember."

Her eyes lit. "Cole's cradle?"

His heart sank, just like that, so damn easy. "Yeah," he said. "But you'll need things. For when he's born."

"For when he's born," she repeated, and she looked straight at him, right into his eyes. "Of course, he'll be born. Won't he, Aaron? He'll be born."

"He'll be born, Eliza," he said quietly.

She looked at him, a long, slow look. "You'll be with me then, won't you?"

"I'll be with you."

She burst into a smile that dazzled him. Her hand eased on his arm, now it was just a gentle touch. "Why don't you come on into town with me, Aaron?" she asked. "We can pick out things together."

The peace he'd started to feel, the joy in her smile, vanished completely, and the fear she didn't understand was back again, that deep, unspeakable fear. Going into town . . . it had been years since he'd done it. Years since he'd had to bear the stares. He didn't want to pretend not to see the people hurrying to the other side of the road to avoid him and the women hiding their daughters. He didn't want to have to explain it to Eliza. He was not ready to face those people now; it made him sick to think of facing them.

"No," he said, and then swallowed at the harshness of it, at her sudden frown. "It's better if Miguel . . . takes you."

She looked confused. He turned away and pretended to ignore it.

"Oh," she said. "I see."

There was something in her voice that made him wonder just what it was she understood. What she was reading into his refusal to escort her. But he didn't ask her. Because she took her hand from his arm and it felt icy cold where it had been.

"I guess I don't feel much like learning

right now," she said, moving away from him, pushing herself off the porch so she was standing on the ground beside him. She dusted her hands on her skirt, and then she walked halfway out into the yard and stood there, staring at the cornstalks that were as crippled and dried up as that old man upstairs.

The setting sun glowed on her hair. It was pure, hot gold, touching her dress and the edge of her cheek and the grass all around her. He thought he saw the color pulsing on her, touching her and diffusing into a soft halo. Beautiful. It froze his chest to look at her, he felt a yearning that bit deep into his soul, that made him want to rush off the porch and hurry up to her, to touch her, to feel that soft gold on his skin.

The temptation of it unnerved him. The fear was familiar, but this time it was deeper, truer, sharper. Because in the last month she'd been on this farm, she had never once belittled him or asked him why he never touched her. He knew that she assumed it was her fault, and he felt guilty about that even as it raised a terrible tenderness inside him. Her insecurity was a bruise that made him feel stronger, and he was angry at himself for allowing that to happen, for wanting her, for being afraid.

BE A MAN. He thought of that old man upstairs, watching him, every day asking him, *"TODAY?"* He thought of his responsibility to make her his wife, to erase Cole from her thoughts, to make it so she never again said *"Cole's cradle?"* in that sweet and wistful voice, but instead said, *"Yours?"*

But he didn't know how. He shut his eyes, tightened his fingers on the edge of the porch. When he opened his eyes again, she was walking back. He felt her take the steps, felt her footsteps vibrate through him as she crossed the porch and disappeared into the darkness of the house.

She left her fragrance behind; he captured the lilt of her voice in words in his head. He thought of how the sun had caressed her and diffused away, thought of the magic of her movements, the music of her smile.

The words came fast and hot, crowding him. His fingers ached to say them. Aaron was off the porch and striding to the oak without thinking. He barely felt the rough bark of the tree against his back as he sat and grabbed his box, the pencil. It was hours before he looked up again to see darkness settling all around him. The words were all that mattered.

18

Dallas, Texas

"I think watermelon is my very favorite."

Jennifer Spears took an indelicate bite of a huge slice of melon. The pink juice ran over her chin, through her fingers, and she laughed as all but one of the six men surrounding her offered a handkerchief. She set the melon on a plate and took the handkerchief from Robert Martin, and then she slid a cat-eyed glance to Cole.

"What's the matter, Mr. Wallace?" she asked. "Don't you carry handkerchiefs?"

He gave her a wry smile. "I do," he said. "But it seemed superfluous to offer mine just then, don't you think?"

"Superfluous." She rolled the word around on her tongue. "My, doesn't that sound almost . . . indecent? What's it mean, Mr. Wallace?"

"Unnecessary," Robert Martin spoke up. The man blushed and stammered when Jenny favored him with a smiling glance — a glance Cole knew was deliberately meant to punish him for ignoring her.

"Why, Mr. Martin," she drawled. "You are the most intelligent man. . . ."

Cole gritted his teeth and looked away. Robert Martin was a lawyer who had just moved to Dallas, and hardly a threat to Cole's plans. But Martin annoyed Cole nonetheless, and never more than today.

It was the annual church picnic, and they were sitting in a field outside of Dallas, a field with green and yellow bunting stretched between trees for shade and streamers dripping from the edges. Chairs had been carted out for the elderly, and tables to hold the potluck spread. Cole had never seen so many casseroles of scalloped potatoes in his life.

He hated these things. He hated this one more than usual, though, because the church potluck meant that everyone in town was there, and everyone in town meant all of Jenny's many admirers, of which he was certainly one. He felt like an idiot, competing for her attention with these other fawning men, and because of that, he'd withdrawn a little. He told himself it was stupid; Jenny loved attention. But damn if he was going to fall over himself to offer her a damn handkerchief when there were five others vying to do the same.

It was not as if it were a real competition. In the three weeks he'd been here, he'd taken her on picnics, for drives, to a drama (a troupe of traveling players pounding on a narrow stage in a too-small, too-hot *Theatre*), and to one dance. She seemed to prefer him above the others — she'd turned down Robert Martin at least once just to go out with Cole. So he was satisfied, at least in part. He'd grown more and more confident that Jenny would marry him when he asked her.

But he was growing tired of the wait. She'd wanted to be wooed, and he'd wooed her. She wanted a gentle courtship, and he was doing his best to give it to her. But it was taking too long, and he was tired of holding back. Tired of kissing her cheek when he wanted her mouth. Tired of keeping her at arm's length when he wanted her pressed up against him. How long was a man expected to conduct a courtship, anyway? Two weeks? Three? She knew he wanted her, and yet she deliberately kept him at bay.

Like today, when she'd made him part of her court instead of walking alone with him along the river. He'd learned some things about her in the last weeks, one of which was that Jenny not only liked the idea of a British monarchy, she believed there should be a Dallas version — one where she was the queen. For the most part, it didn't bother him. He wanted to worship her for the rest of his life. But he hated the way she'd done it today, how she'd settled herself on a chair and smoothed her skirts and called them over one by one. *"Robert Martin, come on over here! Why, you've left me alone all day. And bring Henry Able with you. Mr. Stevens, aren't you a handsome thing! My, that watermelon looks good — Mr. Grambs, would you mind just bringing me a tiny little slice? It's just about my favorite thing. . . ."*

He'd watched with a mildly irritated amusement until her gaze landed on him, and she'd ordered him to her side with a plea for some lemonade. Once there, they were all caught in her web, like flies begging for the privilege of being eaten by the spider.

Cole sighed. Jenny had gone back to teasing Randolph Stevens about his flowered vest, and he had half a mind to ease away, see if maybe he couldn't get up a game of poker for later tonight. But the moment he took a step back, her eyes were on him, her gaze faintly accusatory.

"You aren't leaving us, are you, Mr. Wallace? Why, I don't know what I'd do without your company. I guess I'd just have to console myself with someone else."

He smiled and he stayed. He didn't want to test her threat. She was his, and before the month was up, she'd be married to him. He supposed if she wanted to flirt a bit before then, he could allow it.

But after that, he'd put his foot down. He watched the coquettish tilt of her head, heard her insincere laugh as she talked with the others, and he thought about how their marriage would be. First a tour of Europe, because he'd promised her. Maybe a month or so there — that was about all he could take of bowing to royalty — and then back to Texas. For the first few months, he'd take her with him as he worked the towns; she was a girl who fancied travel, and he didn't want to be without her so soon into their life together. After that, he'd buy a house, maybe one here in Dallas, so she'd be close to her family when they started one of their own. It would be nice to have someplace to come home to.

Home. He smiled to himself as he thought of it, of a big front room and a porch that wrapped clear around. Dormer windows and beds complete with quilts she'd made, and a big bay window overlooking an ancient pecan tree . . .

Cole stole a look at her, in her pretty pink dress with the crimped ruffles decorating the skirt. He thought of her in the kitchen, an apron around her waist as she made his morning coffee. Just as he thought it, she turned to him. "You've been awful quiet, Mr. Wallace," she said. "Don't you have anything to add to the conversation?"

He smiled. "I'm too busy looking at you, Miss Spears," he said. "You are surely the most attractive young lady at the potluck today."

She dimpled and preened, and the others fell over themselves to compliment her as well, but Jenny caught his gaze and held it, and her smile was for him alone.

White Horse, Texas

Eliza didn't know whether to be excited or nervous as she readied for the trip to town. This was her first chance to meet the people of White Horse, and she wanted so to make a good impression. She wanted them to see her as a lady, as the wife of Aaron Wallace — a woman to be respected. She dressed in the most decent dress she had. It was stained and old, the hem and sleeves frayed, the left elbow wearing through, but it had a higher neckline than the other. She combed her hair back into a long braid and brushed the dust off her hat, and then she put it on her head and went downstairs to find Miguel.

What was left of breakfast was sitting on the table, but she had no appetite for it. She put her hand to her stomach to calm herself and thought she felt the baby move again, that tadpole-like motion, the *flip flip* that she wasn't quite sure was real.

"We're going to town, baby," she whispered, and she smiled at how real it sounded when she said the words. "We're going to *town*."

She heard a noise in the kitchen. Miguel. She got all nervous again, and excited too, and she went toward the kitchen, meaning to stick her head in and tell him she was ready to go.

She'd just leaned into the doorway and got the words half out of her mouth when she realized it wasn't Miguel in the kitchen. It was Aaron.

The memory of last night came back hard and clear. The way he'd sat on the porch, the way he'd looked at her when he said, *"It's better if Miguel takes you."* She'd understood then, like she hadn't before, why he wouldn't go into town with her, why he wouldn't touch her. He was ashamed of her. Ashamed that she was his wife, and she was a nobody, just some sharecropper's daughter out of Richmond, someone he'd been forced to wed. She knew that look, and she knew that voice. It was the same look those men in Richmond had given her, the look that said she was good enough for kisses, but not for anything else.

She thought of drawing back, but then he turned to look at her, and she said weakly, "I thought you were Miguel."

"No." He held a split biscuit in his hand; it looked like he was getting ready to pour sorghum syrup over it. His eyes looked her up and down. "You look" — he swallowed — "nice."

Eliza felt herself flush. "Thank you," she said.

"Don't forget to buy yourself a new dress."

The heat of pleasure died. It was all she could do to keep from flinching. Eliza pulled at her sleeve, at the loose threads. "I'm sorry," she said. "I know — I know you're worried about me . . . shaming you. And I'd wear something else if I had it. But I don't, and . . ." She ground to a halt when she noticed he was staring at her like she'd gone crazy.

"Shaming me?" he asked. His voice was so quiet, and his eyes were so puzzled that Eliza couldn't do anything but look at him. "Did Pa tell you that?"

"Mr. Wallace?" Eliza shook her head in confusion. "Why would he say something so mean?"

Aaron looked at a loss. "Then who?"

"You told me," she said. "Yesterday."

"How could I tell you that?" he asked. "When I don't feel it?"

Relief hit her hard. "You . . . you ain't ashamed of me?"

"Why would I be?"

"Because I'm just a sharecropper's daughter," she explained. "Because my mama is —"

"You're a Wallace now, Eliza," he said. "I don't care what you were before."

Soft, soft the words, like a touch, like a kiss. She thought of yesterday, when she'd run into his arms by the creek and he'd held her so clumsily, like he was afraid of her, and the thought opened up something inside of her, took her beyond herself. Maybe it wasn't her, after all. Maybe it was him.

It was such a startling thought. She stood there in the doorway like a fly caught in honey, and he was just as still, and she knew she couldn't walk away without knowing. She looked at him straight on and said, "D'you like me, Aaron?"

It was a simple question. There was nothing to answer but yes or no. She waited. She waited while he poured syrup on his biscuit. She watched the slow way he did it, like it was the most important thing, but then she realized he wasn't really paying attention to it, because the sorghum spilled over, dripped on his hand.

As if the feel of the syrup woke him, Aaron looked up. He put aside the biscuit. He shook his hand like he could get rid of the syrup.

Then he looked at her. "Yes. I . . . do."

The words sounded like a wedding vow, the way he said them, with such solemnness, such pure feeling. Eliza didn't doubt him for a minute. It made her feel warm again, eased that tiny knot inside her.

She smiled. "Then why don't you —"

"I am here, *señora*." Miguel came rushing through the back door, breathless. "The horses are ready."

It was like there had been an open door between her and Aaron, and it suddenly slammed shut.

Aaron turned abruptly. He picked up the biscuit and went to the door, saying, "Have a good time," as he went outside. She saw him throw the biscuit to the chickens, and then he turned the corner of the house and he was gone.

And it was funny, because when he left she felt cold again, and she thought about last night, how she'd gone to bed with the memory of that cougar still tight in her mind, how she'd awakened sweaty and scared in the middle of the night. She had forgotten it with morning, but now that Aaron was gone, the shadows from her nightmare started making noise in her head again. She looked at Miguel and said, "You bringing your gun?" and when he nodded she felt relieved.

She followed Miguel to the barn. The horses were harnessed, the wagon waited, and she climbed aboard before she realized Miguel was standing there to help her. Her nervousness started again the moment the farmhand took his seat and started them off, over the bumpy, burnt-off yard to the dust-covered road just beyond.

It was an uncomfortable ride. The springs on the wagon seat were stiff and rusty, like it hadn't been used for a long time. Its *creak, creak, creak* climbed up her back and eased into her skull, a noise that didn't stop, that grew louder with every pothole and rut. The wagon swayed and jerked, and the dust rose into her nose so that she was grateful when Miguel handed her a bandanna to tie over her face. But she didn't mind any of it. She was going to meet the ladies of White Horse. This was her first day of being a lady. The idea made her so nervous and scared and excited she didn't know which one she felt more.

This was her dream; it was what she'd spent her whole life waiting for. She was Mrs. Aaron Wallace, and she told herself that, after today, she would never be lonely again.

She saw the buildings of White Horse looming up before them, wood-sided buildings rising through the dust and the sun like ghosts. She saw the people walking and the dogs fighting in the street, and she loved it. She loved the false-fronted, unpainted buildings and the smell of raw, sun-dried lumber. She loved the shallow, brackish water well in the center of the street, and the low and constant cloud of dust blanketing it, and the way the saloons sat back from the road like eyes bracketing the nose of the blacksmith's squat stone shop.

It was nothing like Richmond. Richmond was bigger, and there was the smell of swamp and rot laying over it all day long, every day, and the heat was a lazy, wet heat, and the meanness of the people was in the squinty-windowed buildings and the broken-down boardwalks. White Horse had a clean, dusty smell, a wide-open feel. In some places the buildings stood far apart enough so that the hot wind whipped through, stirring up little twisters of dust in the middle of the street. People were looking at them as they drove up, big, frank expressions of curiosity, and Eliza smiled back at them with her biggest, widest smile. "Look at how they're watching me, Miguel. Like they want to know who I am."

Miguel grunted. He shook his head slowly, and pulled up the horses in front of what Eliza took to be the general store. It had a long word painted on a wooden sign above the door. M-E-R-C-A-N-T-I-L-E. She tried to sound it out.

"Is the store, *señora*." Miguel interrupted her soundings and got down from the wagon. He came around to her side and offered his hand.

Eliza noticed the people stopped on the broad, roofless porch of the store, a few ladies and a gentleman or two. They were watching her. She laid her hand in Miguel's and lifted the skirt of her dress and came down off the wagon with as much ladylike grace as she could muster. When she was on the ground, she adjusted her hat and straightened her shoulders and lifted her chin, just like a lady would.

Miguel stood back as she made her way to the porch. Those people by the door waited for her, and she felt a shiver of excitement that went clear through her. They were waiting to meet her. It was all she could do not to call out her name right from where she stood. But a lady wouldn't do that, so Eliza went up the two broad steps. Just as she set foot on the porch, a little girl came running out of the store.

"Mama, Mama!" she said, hurrying to one of the ladies standing there. "Can I have some peppermint? Please? May I?"

The woman leaned over and shushed her, whispering something, and the little girl looked up, right into Eliza's eyes. Eliza smiled.

"Hey there," she said, bending down, waving. "You sure are a pretty little girl —"

The girl froze, her whole face went stiff. She backed so hard into her mother's skirts Eliza thought she would fall through them.

Eliza looked up into the mother's face. It was cold and shut, and Eliza frowned, thinking that this woman must've had a hard day. She smiled and offered her hand.

"Hey," she said. "I'm Eliza Wallace. Maybe you know my husband —"

The woman pressed her lips together and turned abruptly, grabbing her daughter's hand, hurrying past Eliza and down the stairs. Eliza stared after her, so surprised she didn't know what to say. She turned back to the other woman and the two men who had been by the door. "Well, what do you suppose got into her . . . ?"

They were gone, already halfway down the street. They too were hurrying down the porch stairs like the devil himself was chasing them. Eliza stared after them. Behind her, she heard Miguel's sigh.

"Let us go in, eh, *señora?*"

She felt his touch on her arm, urging her forward. Eliza just stood there. "What was that?" she asked. "Why'd they just run off like that?"

Miguel sighed again. He pressed harder, and she moved woodenly forward. When they got to the door, and the little bell clanged against the wooden frame when they went inside, Eliza made herself forget. Maybe that woman had just remembered something, and they had to go running off. Maybe that couple at the door was already leaving, and Eliza just hadn't seen it. Yes, that had to be it. It wasn't what it had looked like. Maybe she would run into that woman again, and the lady would apologize. *"I'd remembered I had a pie baking at home. I was afraid I'd burn down the whole house!"*

The thought reassured Eliza. She stepped inside the store and took a deep breath. The store smelled of crackers and dried fish, cornmeal and leather. Just like Olsen's in Richmond. It calmed her a little. She saw the clerk behind the counter at the back, stacking dry goods, and that made her feel better too, especially when he turned at the sound of the bell and smiled.

"*Hola,* Miguel," he said. "*Como estás?*"

Miguel answered with a string of Spanish she didn't understand, and Eliza moved away from him, moving down the tables and the shelves lining the walls, easing around the barrels. She'd been in the general store in Richmond a hundred times with her father, but they'd always bought the same thing, a sack of cornmeal and some beans and sometimes — on very rare occasions — a cone of sugar. The rest they grew themselves; Daddy either hunted the meat or it was given to them. She had never been in a store when there was money to spend, and the possibilities opened before her — there were a hundred things to buy. Things she'd never even heard of.

"*Señora!*" Miguel's voice came from the counter, and Eliza hurried over to him. He motioned to the clerk, who Eliza now saw looked like a mestizo, with his dark skin and hair, and said, "This is William, *Señora* Wallace. He is the store."

"Hey there," she said. She smiled at him. "I'm Eliza Wallace. I'm Aaron's wife."

He nodded. "So Miguel says." His English

was smooth, barely accented. His dark gaze flickered over her once and then went back to her face, where it stayed. "He says you want a dress?"

William was so nice to her, Eliza forgot the people on the porch. He brought down bolt after bolt of cloth while Miguel walked around the store, picking up the things they needed, and she chose heavy, soft cotton for diapers and a length of cloth for babies' aprons, and then it was time to choose for herself. William stood back while she looked at each pattern, touched every bolt. There were satins and silks and good, strong broadcloths, and though he claimed he didn't have much to choose from, there was more variety than Eliza had ever seen. She lingered over them, choosing by feel and by brightness. The more colors there were, the better she liked it. Finally, she narrowed it down to three: a pale green silk printed all over with golden clocks and dark green leaves, a violet and flower striped calico, and a broadcloth that William said was "dragon green" that had narrow stripes of checks and dots and bigger stripes of bright paisley. She'd wanted something to match her hat, but she supposed these would look good enough with it, and the pretty colors and patterns appealed to her heart.

"I can't decide," she said. "Miguel, come on over here and help me. I like this dragon color, but I ain't ever had silk before, and these flowers sure are pretty —"

The bell at the front door tinkled. Eliza turned. A woman walked in. She wore a hat with a curling black feather and a dress trimmed with black velvet. Her hair was pulled stylishly back, and her face held that same haughtiness Eliza had seen on the ladies back home, that lifted chin and pulled taut cheeks, the tight shoulders. Eliza lifted her own chin in imitation, tried for what she hoped was a ladylike look, and smiled.

"Well, hey there," she said as the woman came up to the counter.

The woman looked up, at Eliza's hat, and then down again. "Hello," she said.

"I'm Eliza Wallace," Eliza said. "I'm so glad you came in. I been trying to decide on a new dress, and I just can't —"

"Wallace?" The woman's frown grew deeper.

"I just married Aaron Wallace, 'bout a month ago," Eliza explained. "I'm new in town, and I was hoping —"

The woman turned on her heel. She was out the door of the store so fast the bell on the door shook for about a minute after the door slammed.

It was more than a snub. Like the woman and the girl on the porch, and the two men and the woman who hurried away when they saw her. A heaviness moved into Eliza's arms, a sickness that made her feet leaden, and she knew why they'd turned away from her, why they didn't want to meet her. She stared blankly at the door, feeling that same deep-in shame she'd felt in Richmond, that sense that she was no good and everyone knew it. It was like she wore some stain on her that they could see, a stain she couldn't wash off or peel away, and the knowledge of who she was and where she came from rose up on her skin like sweat. She was a nobody. She would never be good enough for them.

"Let us go," Miguel said tightly. He motioned to the bolts of cloth. "We will take all of them, *amigo.*"

Eliza heard William wrapping the cloth in tissue paper. She heard him moving boxes on the counter, the thud of flour and corn-meal and beans, the delicate crackle of paper on the sugar cone. She thought she'd done everything right. She'd smiled and she'd acted like a lady and she'd worn her most respectable dress and her beautiful hat. *"You think it's only place that makes a lady, Lizzie?"*

She swallowed her mother's words and looked at Miguel.

"What is it?" she asked dully. "Why don't they like me?"

Miguel shot a look at William, and then shook his head. "It is not you, *señora*," he said quietly.

She went to the door. The store had windows fronting it, and she edged over to one, pressed her hands against the sill, looked out. She saw people gathered here and there, across the street, by the edge of the porch, whispering, pointing. There was a group of children pushing and teasing each other by the corner of the store. She heard their voices, loud through the window.

"I dare you!"

"I dare *you!*"

"Scaredy cat! Scared of the monster's wife!"

"Am not!"

"Are too!"

A little boy pushed a girl in pigtails to the stairs. She touched them and raced back to the corner, shrieking while they all laughed.

The monster's wife. Eliza turned back to Miguel. He stood at the counter, and he and William were looking at her uncertainly, like they didn't know what to say or how to act.

"They ain't going to be inviting me to teas, huh, Miguel?"

He winced a little and shrugged.

She looked back to the window. There were two girls down there, her age, maybe a year or so younger. They were dressed in printed calico and straw poke bonnets, and they were whispering to each other. One of them looked up and saw Eliza in the window, and they whispered again and went hurrying off. They didn't even blush to be caught staring, Eliza thought. It was like she wasn't even a person to them. But of course she wasn't. She was "the monster's wife."

She thought she should feel relief over the fact that it wasn't her. They weren't snubbing her because of who she was, but because she was Aaron's wife, and Aaron was "the monster." But she didn't feel relieved. And she didn't feel scared, though she supposed she should. She barely knew her husband. Maybe he was a monster, maybe he'd done something terrible. But she didn't feel that way, either.

"What'd he do to them?" she asked softly.

"He didn't do nothing, Miz Wallace," William said. "Old rumors, that's all."

But Eliza knew better. She knew why Aaron had not come into town with them today, why he hadn't wanted her to go. They were afraid of him in this place.

Suddenly, the town she'd loved on sight dwindled before her, like an apple wrinkling in the sun, drawing in on itself, tightening, shrinking. The sun was too bright, and the rawboned buildings were graceless and ugly. The dust settled on everything, on the street and the porch, on the window ledges. She felt it against her fingers where she touched the sill. And she felt the meanness here, just like she had in Richmond; she smelled the faint smell of swampwater and cotton-mouths even though there wasn't a swamp for miles. It seemed to fill her nostrils with its rotten, nasty scent.

"Let's go," she said to Miguel, and she turned from the window and went to the door. She heard the sudden quiet of the children when she went outside, their stage whispers, the frightened, nervous laughter. She heard the steps of one daring the stairs, then the rush away. Eliza kept her eyes focused straight ahead. She went down the stairs and climbed into the wagon, and she sat there, waiting while William and Miguel loaded their supplies in the back, waiting until the seat shook when Miguel got in beside her, and the wagon jerked to a start. She blocked out the children and the sounds of the town. She blocked out the sights. She stared at the road until they were out of that one-street town, back onto the narrow, rutted road that led back to the farm.

Then, finally, she looked at Miguel. His hat was drawn low over his eyes, his mouth pressed tight. He hunched over the reins like he was trying to make himself as small as he could.

"You know," she said. "Tell me. Why're they scared of him?"

Miguel sighed. He shook his head again, the same way he had in the store. "I am just a farmer," he said. "I work for *Señor* Aaron . . . *dos años,* no more. I come from San Antonio. I know no stories."

She looked at him silently. He stared straight ahead.

"You ain't telling me the truth, Miguel," she said.

He looked at her then. His dark eyes were sad. "You ask him, *Señora* Wallace," he said. "It is for a husband to tell. Not for me."

19

But when she and Miguel got home, Aaron was nowhere to be found. Carlos was gone, too, the dying cornfields abandoned. Miguel told her they might be out hunting, but he didn't sound convinced of it himself, and Eliza wondered if Aaron was hiding from her because he'd known what town would be like, and he didn't want to answer her questions.

She looked for him for a little while, and then she gave up. She sat on the porch and fanned herself in the hot air and watched for him. She looked out over those cornfields, the way they stretched clear out to the edges of the horizon, the green of the leaves curling into brown, the drying tassels sending corn dust clouding through the fields. She lifted her braided hair from the back of her neck, but it didn't make her feel any cooler, so she let it fall again with a soft thunk against her shoulder, and thought about town, about the way that woman had come into the store and turned right around again, about the way the children ran — and the shame she'd felt before she realized it was Aaron who made them run.

She wished for Aaron to come home, but he didn't come. When suppertime came, he still wasn't home, and Eliza's questions only crowded her mind until she couldn't think and couldn't sit still. She wished Mr. Wallace could talk, or that she could read better so she could ask him. In any case, she was fretting herself to death alone, so she made a tray to take up to him, thinking his company might make her feel better.

The old man was lying in bed, staring out the window. He looked up when she came in and smiled his lopsided smile.

"Afternoon, Mr. Wallace," she said, setting the tray on an invalid's table beside the bed, pushing it up close. The room was so hot she couldn't breathe. She went over and opened the window. A rush of hot air blasted her face, and she blinked and looked out at the cornfields, looking as far as she could, searching for Aaron. "I been looking for my husband," she said. "You seen him?"

Mr. Wallace grunted. When Eliza turned, he scrawled something on the chalkboard and held it up to her with a frown. A single word. Eliza sounded it out. T-O-W-N. To-win. Toe-en. Town.

"He didn't go with me," she said. "Miguel did."

Eliza turned back to the window. She took a deep breath. "I was wondering," she said, "why they don't like him in town. The man at the store said there were . . . old rumors. About Aaron. Miguel wouldn't tell me what they were."

Mr. Wallace was so quiet that Eliza looked around at him. He was staring at her, his heavy brows meeting over his nose, his eyes fierce.

"You know what they are, don't you Mr. Wallace?" she asked quietly. "What'd he do to them?"

He snorted and waved his arm like whatever it was hadn't mattered, wasn't important.

"Why are they so scared of him?" Eliza pressed. "You know what the children called him? They said he was a monster."

The old man scrawled on the chalkboard, held it up to her. L-I-E-S. She concentrated on it, sounded it out. "Lies?" she asked finally. "You telling me they're lying about him in town?"

Mr. Wallace nodded.

Eliza frowned. "But . . . but why would they do that?"

The old man shrugged.

"Why would they lie about him?"

He gave her a look. The same kind of look she'd seen on her father's face, that *Eliza-don't-be-stupid* look. She pressed on. "Why does he let it go on?"

Mr. Wallace frowned fiercely. He wrote on the chalkboard again, and this time the words were easy. "NOT A MAN."

"You mean, he ain't a man because he lets them lie?"

The old man nodded.

"Has he ever . . . tried to stop it?"

"NO."

"Why not?" Eliza asked. "Why doesn't he stop it?"

Mr. Wallace ignored her question. He reached for the invalid's table and pulled his plate close. She heard the clank of his fork as he picked it up, heard the way it clattered on the plate. He tried to spear a piece of ham, and his old, gnarled hand was shaking; he looked like a baby learning to use a spoon for the first time, not quite in control, jabbing the air, then the plate beside the meat, then concentrating until he got it. He brought it to his mouth and jammed it in between crooked lips, and his chew was crooked too.

She turned her back to Mr. Wallace and leaned sideways against the wall, fingering the frayed curtain, staring at the pinkness of her hand through the thin cloth. "I wish I'd known," she said. "I wish someone told me before I went into town. I could've done something. I could've said something. But I didn't know. I thought . . . at first I thought it was just that they could see . . . what I was. You know, that I wasn't a lady. In Richmond, I'd come into town and they'd just ignore me and the ladies would whisper like I was trash. Like being a sharecropper's daughter with a Comanche mama made me bad somehow —"

The old man choked. Eliza looked over her shoulder. "Mr. Wallace?" she asked, and then the words left her when she saw he wasn't stopping. He was red-faced and choking so hard he couldn't breathe.

Eliza ran over to him. He flailed out, pushing the invalid's table, tipping it, sending everything crashing to the floor. Coffee splashed burning hot over Eliza's skirt, spattered the wall, spilled on the floor. She reached for the old man's hands, and he jerked away from her like she was poison, and then his whole body started bucking and the veins stood out on his forehead, in his throat. His eyes rolled back in his head.

"Oh my God." Eliza stared at him, helpless and panicked. "Mr. Wallace —"

He jackknifed on the bed, his chest rising and falling with huge, jerking gasps.

"Miguel!" she screamed. "Someone! Help me! Please help!" She tried to grab for him, to keep him still, but his hand smacked against her face so hard she fell back. She tried to gain her balance, but she slipped in the coffee on the floor and fell hard, banging her head on the wall so it brought tears to her eyes.

The old man stiffened. His back arched, and he went limp and still, and Eliza scrambled to her feet, her heart stopped beating. He was dead. Oh God, he was dead.

"What is it, *señora?*" Miguel rushed in. His glance went right to the old man, and Miguel paled. He raced to the bed and took Mr. Wallace's wrist.

"I think he's dead." Panic raced through her so hard and fast she fisted her skirt in her hands to keep from screaming. "Is he dead?"

Miguel shook his head. He listened for a moment, and then he said, stiffly, "He is alive. I hear his heart."

Relief made her cry. Miguel's face blurred before her, and she grabbed Mr. Wallace's hand where it hung limply over the side of the bed. "I don't know what happened," she said. "We were just talking, and he —"

"*Perdón, señora,*" Miguel said. "I must find *Señor* Aaron."

He hurried from the room. She heard his racing footsteps on the stairs, over the porch, and then she heard his call. "*Señor* Aaron! *Señor!* Come quick!" Loud in front of the house, softer and softer as he went far away.

She gripped the old man's hand in hers. It was a big, rough hand, callused with years of work, but now mostly bones and dry skin. She saw his chest rise, so shallow she couldn't hear the sound of his breath, so slight she thought she was only willing him alive, that she was not really seeing him breathe at all.

When she finally heard men talking in the yard, it seemed hours had passed. She was relieved and grateful when she heard the running step over the porch and through the front room, when she heard the boot-steps taking the stairs two at a time. Then Aaron was standing in the doorway, disheveled and sweating, his hair falling into his face, his eyes dark with worry, and his breathing coming hard, like he'd run the whole way back. There was a question in his eyes, and Eliza blurted out, "We were just talking, and he started . . . choking, and then . . ." She trailed off, not knowing how to tell him how sorry she was, how upset she was.

He didn't seem to notice. He felt his father's wrist the way Miguel had done, and then he put his hands on either side of his father's head and looked down like he could read the truth in Mr. Wallace's face. He peeled open one of the old man's eyes, and then the other, and then he said, "I'm sending Carlos for the doctor," and he was gone, leaving Eliza alone there, holding his father's hand.

Aaron stood back, watching while Dr. Burns checked Pa over. The room was quiet except for the doctor's wheezing, tired breath, and the clank of instruments when he pulled them from his bag. Eliza stood near the window. She was looking out, running her hand up and down the thin curtain, twisting it so he saw the bound edges, the checked blue gingham it had been before the sun bleached it to white.

She hadn't said much since Dr. Burns had arrived, but Aaron could tell she was distressed. Her eyes shone as if she were holding back tears by sheer willpower, and whenever she stole a glance at the old man, she bit her lower lip and looked quickly away.

So much emotion there, he thought, and wondered why he didn't feel the same. When Miguel had come running out to him, breathless and panicked, and told him the old man had had an attack of some kind, Aaron's first thought was *at last,* and relief had washed over him like a cool, refreshing rain. Now all he could think was that Pa's timing had always been bad. The old man wouldn't even live to see the grandchild he'd wanted so badly.

Dr. Burns sighed and put aside his stethoscope. He ran his hand through his thinning and wiry gray hair, and then he turned to Aaron. "He's had another stroke," he said slowly. "He's in a coma now. My guess is that he's not going to come out of it."

Eliza gasped. "You mean he's . . . gonna die?"

Burns didn't even look at her. He kept his gaze pinned to Aaron's. "I think this is it for him," he said.

"How long?" Aaron asked.

"Tonight, tomorrow . . . hell, could be three weeks from now." The doctor shrugged. "He'll die when God's ready to take him, son, that's all I know." He looked at Eliza then. "You know how to make a beef broth, Miz Wallace?"

She nodded. There were tears coming down her cheeks now, and she wiped them away with the back of her hand. "I can do that."

"Make up a pot of that and try to spoon it into him every couple hours. He may not wake up again, but there's no point starving him to death." Burns got up, wheezing and creaking, and stuffed his stethoscope back in his bag. He snapped it shut and straightened. "I'll be back tomorrow," he said to Aaron. "You just send someone if you need me before then."

Aaron nodded. The doctor walked stiffly across the room, pausing just before the door, speaking in a low voice meant only for Aaron. "You'd best be thinking on a funeral."

"I've been doing that for years," Aaron said.

"Yeah, well, this time I think it's for real." Burns patted Aaron's arm, and started out the door. "You got any coffee?"

"Miguel's got some going in the kitchen."

Burns nodded and left. Aaron heard his heavy tread on the stairs, and then that faded away into soft talk downstairs, faded into the nothing sound of his father's breathing and the quiet hiccup of Eliza's tears.

It seemed odd to him that she would be so upset over Pa's stroke, odd that she'd learned to care for the old man that much in such a short time. But then again, Aaron remembered his father's insistence that he teach her how to read, the self-pitying words, *"She talks to me,"* and he remembered that Pa had always been a ladies' man in his younger days. Women had always loved him.

He looked over at the quiet body on the bed, his father's closed eyes and sunken face, the gray pallor of his skin, and then he looked over at Eliza, crying silently by the window.

As if she'd felt him looking, she turned to him. "I can't believe he's going to die," she said.

"He's surprised us before," Aaron said to reassure her, though he didn't believe it, not this time. "He was supposed to die three years ago."

"But you don't think he will," she said. "I can tell. You think he's going to die now."

"I think," Aaron said, "that he'll stay alive just to prove to me he can."

She laughed a little, sniffing through her tears, and wiped again at her face. Then she sobered. "Well, I surely hope you're right," she said. "I ain't going to forgive myself if he dies."

Her words confused him. He frowned at her. "What d'you mean?"

"I . . . well, I guess it's my fault. I don't know what I said, but . . . we were talking, and then he started . . . shaking. . . ." She looked ready to cry again.

"It's not your fault," Aaron said.

She looked up and met his eyes, holding his gaze with a brave and determined expression. "I was talking about town."

He'd forgotten. In the chaos of his father's stroke, Aaron had forgotten the reason he'd stayed away from the house today, the cowardly reason he'd stayed in the far acres. Eliza had gone into town.

He looked away from her. He looked at the old man lying weak and helpless in bed, and Aaron felt his voice come out of him as if it were drawn, slow and painful. "What . . . about . . . town?"

"I told him I thought I'd go into town and all the ladies would say hey and invite me to tea," she said softly. "I thought maybe I'd make me a friend or two, maybe I'd invite them out for cake and lemonade sometime. But it wasn't like that."

"It wasn't," he said dully.

"No." She sighed. "None of the ladies would even talk to me. And the children . . . they ran away from me like they were scared. They called me the monster's wife."

He flinched. It was still so bad, then.

"Why is that?" she asked in a quiet, quiet voice. "Why am I the monster's wife?"

He kept his gaze focused on his father. He looked at those long, bony fingers and the sagging cheeks, and his own voice was just a whisper when he answered her. "Probably because you're married to the monster."

She paused only a moment. "What happened, Aaron? I asked Miguel and he wouldn't tell me, and neither would your daddy, except to tell me they were all lies —"

"Pa said that?" Aaron looked at her. "He said they were lies?"

She nodded and then she frowned. "Why? Ain't they?"

"I don't know," he said.

She was quiet. Then he heard the squeak of the floorboards beneath her step, felt the air move, and she was beside him, quiet as a whisper, her smell and her presence all around him. She touched his shoulder, and then she dropped her hand as if she were afraid of the touch. "Why don't you tell me?" she said.

Such simple words, as if the telling didn't hold all his pain, as if it were nothing more than a fairy tale, something as simple as a fight between good and evil. The lines were much more blurred than that. He had long ago lost track of whose fault it was, of where to lay blame.

And the truth was, no one had ever asked him before. The stories were all in his mind, unsorted, tangled into a knot that his clumsy fingers could not undo. He wasn't even sure he could tell her; he had never bothered to think things out before. There was *this* here, and *that* over there, and maybe *this* led to something else, and maybe it didn't. . . .

He turned to look at her. She was watching him, waiting, her pretty face composed.

"Aren't you afraid to know?" he asked hoarsely.

She shook her head. Her brows winged together. "No," she said. "Am I supposed to be?"

He didn't know if it was faith or ignorance, and he supposed he didn't care. It was enough that she wasn't frightened, that the townspeople's reactions had only made her curious. He had the brief thought that he should thank God for her, but he squelched it quickly because there was such a tentative thread holding them together still — she wasn't his, not really, not yet, and he wasn't sure himself what he wanted from her — and he didn't want to tempt fate. It had burned him too often before.

"Ain't you going to tell me, Aaron?" she whispered.

He looked down into his father's face, and then he motioned to the door. "Come on," he said, and he led her from the room and down the stairs. Dr. Burns had just left —

Aaron could see his horse down the road, and the dust its hooves had risen still floated and clouded over the yard.

He took her over to the tree, to what little shade its leaves afforded, and he shoved aside his box of papers as he sat, wedged it against the far side of the trunk, half hiding it in the roots. He leaned against the tree, and she sat on the edge of the creek bed a few feet away and looked down into the dry sand.

She drew her legs up until the red lace of her petticoat was trailing over the edge of her boots and she leaned her elbows on her knees and tilted her head at him. "Tell me," she said.

That was how the story started. She said, *"Tell me,"* and he found it gathering in his head, the little bits and pieces coming together, gathering strength and mass, laying themselves in order for him to tell. In the end, it *was* like a fairy tale, the way he told it, the way it spilled out of him. It was like a story about someone else, someone he didn't know. And it turned out that it was easy to begin after all.

"When I was born," he said, "this house was just a cabin, and this farm was nothing but miles of grass, and though we held the title, the land really belonged to the Comanches. . . ."

20

He was born the youngest of three sons. The oldest, Eli, was nearly eight years old, and Cole was two. His parents had not intended to have more children. Cole's birth had nearly killed his mother, and his father had not wanted to risk losing her. But she got pregnant again, and it was a hard confinement. She nearly miscarried three times over the first five months, and finally she was restricted to bed, where she said over and over again, to whomever would listen, that she expected this baby to die.

She was a superstitious woman, Pa had said. "If the wind blew wrong, she'd think it was a demon spirit." There were some peaceful Tonkawa Indians who lived in the nearby forts, relying on the army for protection — both from other Indians and from whites — and early in her pregnancy, when she was at Fort Belknap for supplies, an old Tonkawan woman motioned her over and patted her stomach and shook her head sadly, and Ma had believed that was a bad omen.

Truthfully, there had been nothing easy about his birth, and perhaps the old Indian woman had seen something of the future, because the night Aaron was born was clear, bright with a Comanche moon. It was also one of the bloodiest nights ever along the Texas frontier. It was the moon that did it — the moon and the tensions that two years of Indian depredations had brought to that part of Texas. They said it was vengeance — a few nights before, a farmer had killed a young Comanche woman with an ax just to see her die — but that story was forgotten later.

That night, the Comanches raided the farms all along the Brazos. Three families were completely wiped out, their children killed, their women raped and murdered. Two families had their children and wives stolen from them — one woman had a two-month-old baby, who was found later, its skull beaten in against the side of a tree.

All through the night, Eli and Cole, Pa and Ma and the doctor, huddled in the loft and listened to the screams. Pa turned out all the lights except the one by Ma's bed, which he turned down low, and pulled tight the battens. He stood ready with a rifle and an ax, and though the Comanches took their horses and their three cows, they didn't bother the house. No one knew why. The doctor, a retired Indian hunter, said there must be sign warning them away. Maybe someone had told them there was something to be afraid of in this place.

Later, when Aaron was older, Cole told him that when the doctor said that, an eerie silence fell in the room. Aaron was a long time being born. So long, the doctor had to go in finally and pull him out, and it was like they tore the heart from her, she screamed so loud.

He was born in a caul. That in itself was bad enough — the doctor was a superstitious Irishman, and he muttered and crossed himself when he saw it. It was Pa who had to tear the membrane away and wipe off his son's face, and when the baby cried and opened his eyes, the doctor saw that the right one was strange, lolling way over in the socket so you could barely see the iris. The man rushed from the house in a cloud of dust and prayer.

The rumors started that day. The towns-people said that the Wallaces had a demon baby, born in a caul with an evil eye, and the Indians knew it, and it was why they'd decided to attack the farms along the fort. They forgot the story of the slain Indian girl, and it was said the Comanches had been angry that the settlers had allowed the devil in, but they had been too afraid of the baby to attack the Wallace farm.

His mother had not died from his birth, but she had been ill and weak for a long time. Pa had gone out to find a wet nurse for him, but no one would come to the cabin, not even the Tonkawan women taking refuge at the fort. They were all afraid. Finally, Pa managed to find a cow, and they raised Aaron on cow's milk and sugar water until he was old enough for gruel.

In spite of everything — the pain and the hardship and her own suspicions — his mother kept him close. Maybe it was because she was born a Catholic, and she believed she could turn away evil with enough prayers and catechism. Maybe, after he was finally born, she decided she didn't believe in bad magic after all. Whatever it was, his mother had protected him from the town, from his father, from the world. He grew up shy and sheltered — as his father called it, "molly-coddled." By the time he was two, the "evil eye" that had sent the doctor running had straightened out. He looked like any other little boy.

But no one forgot. The story of his birth and the superstitions surrounding it took hold in a town searching for someone to blame. Aaron rarely had the chance to show them he was normal. Whenever his mother took him into town — which was seldom — he buried his head in her skirt and hid behind her. The townspeople weren't watching anyway. They turned away from him and made signs against the devil whenever he was about. Dan Wilson at the general store told his mother not to bring Aaron in any more — he scared the customers. Back then there was no preacher to tell the people to be charitable, not even a circuit rider, so the rumors continued.

Maybe they would have gone away eventually. New people come into every place, old rumors and suspicions die away. But Texas was a hard land, and the Indian raids didn't stop, and finally that fateful spring night came when his mother and brother were killed.

It was Aaron's own behavior that fed the rumors. The way he wouldn't come out from under the bed, the way he didn't speak for weeks afterward. They thought he was touched, and mothers started telling their children: "You know what happens to bad little boys and girls? Aaron gets them!" Once, he'd gone into town, and he'd heard the children singing a song to the tune of "London Bridge is Falling Down":

Aaron Wallace is in town,
is in town, is in town,
His evil eye will cut you down,
Run, run faster!

He was twenty-eight years old now, and
he hadn't been in town for more than five
years. He supposed he'd once had the power
to fight the rumors. If he'd gone into White
Horse every day, if he'd smiled and talked
to people, if he'd tried to get to know them.
Perhaps then the talk would have died away.

But by then, the effort seemed too much.

"And you're shy," Eliza said. "It would've
been hard."

He looked at her in surprise, and then he
laughed shortly, a little bitterly. "Yeah," he
said. "I'm shy."

She sighed. She looked nervous, and
Aaron supposed she had a reason to be, after
the story he'd just told her. He waited for
her to leave, to offer up some excuse about
how she had to make supper, or check on
Pa, and the heaviness of waiting for it settled
in his chest.

She tightened her arms around her knees.
She looked away, out past the creek, to that
place where the bobcat had cornered her.
"The Comanches . . ." she said. "They did
some terrible things to your family."

His heart tightened; he wasn't sure what she was getting at, what she was going to say. "Yeah," he said slowly.

"I guess you prob'ly hate them."

"I don't know," he said honestly. "I suppose I did once. I'll admit to still being afraid if I see one off the reservation. But I don't remember much about that time — I was too young. It was a war. Pa and Cole hate them much more than me."

"Oh." She still didn't look at him. Her fingers dragged at her knees, crunching up her skirt. He saw her swallow, saw her press her lips tightly together. Then, in a voice so quiet he had to strain to hear her, she said, "That's what happened, then. It was my fault."

He thought she was talking about him, about the rumors, about the Indians, and he turned to her in confusion until she said, "Your daddy, I mean. It was my fault Mr. Wallace had another stroke. I told him . . . I think I told him my mama was a Comanche."

Her words hit him in his heart. It felt as if the air went out of him. He stared at her, and her face got longer, the tears in her eyes started to catch in her eyelashes.

"Your mama's Comanche?" he managed.

"You said you didn't hate them," she

whispered. "Was that just a lie?"

Her mama was a Comanche. Aaron looked at Eliza and tried to see the Indian in her blond hair, in her blue eyes. He tried to decide how he felt about it, whether he *had* lied to her when he said he didn't hate them. Finally, it was the fear in her voice that decided him, that told him he hadn't lied, that he *didn't* care. It was the fact that she'd just been in a town where they ran at the mention of his name, and instead of running too — or showing him pity, or sadness — she'd sat there and given him a simple excuse for not trying to change things, a sentence that both absolved and redeemed him. She had not seemed the least bit disturbed, not at all afraid. But now she was trembling and anxious at the thought that he might hate her because her mother was Comanche — something she couldn't change, something she had far less control over than he did of the rumors in White Horse.

He had been attracted to her before then. He'd thought she was pretty; he'd lusted for her in his own ineffective way. But suddenly it changed. Just a twist in time, and suddenly he was looking at her and knowing it was much more than lust. It was . . . Hell, he was falling in love with her.

It shocked him as much as her news that

her mother was Comanche. It shocked him so much that when she blinked and stumbled to her feet, meaning to run from him, he reached out and caught her wrist, stopping her. She looked as surprised at the touch as he was. She stared at his hand, and then she looked at him with a frown.

"I don't hate the Comanches," he said. "I don't . . . hate you."

She relaxed, she paused. When he was sure she wasn't going to run, he let go of her wrist. Even after he released her, he felt her warmth clear into his bones.

"You can't help who your family is," he said.

She gave him a bemused look. "That's funny," she said. "That's what my mama said."

"Must be all that Indian wisdom."

She smiled weakly. "D'you think . . . you said your daddy hates them. D'you think . . . when I said it —"

"It doesn't matter what happened, what's done is done," Aaron said shortly. "Maybe the devil will pair him up with some Comanche soul, and he can spend eternity cursing him. We all get what we deserve."

"You don't like your daddy very much, do you?"

"No."

She sat down beside him. "She ain't all Comanche, you know," she said. "My mama, I mean. She's only half. It happened like it happened to your mama. Except my grandma didn't die. Comanches came to the farm and they took her captive. It took her brother two months to find her, and by then she was carrying my mama."

It was a story he'd heard far too often. "It happened a lot back then."

She pressed her hands flat over her belly, hard enough so that her dress tightened over it, so he saw a slight rounding, the very beginnings of a baby. "Cole hates Comanches," she said very, very quietly. "So I guess he must hate this baby, too, since it'll have some Comanche blood."

He felt the power of her shame like a deep, hard blow. "It's not his baby anymore, Eliza," he whispered.

She turned to him, and her face was flat and expressionless. "But that's a lie, ain't it, Aaron? It is Cole's baby. It'll always be Cole's baby, and we'll all know it forever and ever. And I . . ." she looked away, as if it hurt her to look at him. "And I'm scared of that. I'm scared that this baby'll grow up knowing that it . . . should be ashamed of its mama."

The last words trailed off, catching in the

hot wind and dashing away like the sand over the dry clay of the creek. Aaron felt them the way he felt a poem, a dry, hot emotion that filled him up, moving through his lungs, bursting his heart, an aching press behind his eyes.

"I ain't nobody, you know?" she went on. "I came here thinking I'd be a lady, but those women in town won't even look at me. I know you think it's just those old stories about you that makes them turn away — because I'm your wife — but I can't help thinking if maybe . . . if maybe there ain't this spot inside me they see that tells them what my daddy did, who my mama is. And this baby . . . this baby's inside me. Seems to me if anyone would be able to see that spot, he would."

He didn't know what to say. He'd never known she felt those things; he'd never had any idea what Eliza wanted when she married him, what she expected, what she'd dreamed about or was afraid of. He'd thought . . . well, he'd thought only that she was desperate and needing a father for her baby, and that was all, that was enough. To find it was more than that, to find she'd had ideas in her head of what this life would be for her . . . it surprised him into silence.

She went on as if she didn't expect an

answer from him. "You said it just like my mama did. You said a body can't help who their family is, and I know that's true. But I know . . . I used to be ashamed of my mama. And today I been thinking that maybe when I was inside her, she thought the things I'm thinking now, about all the things she wanted for me. Maybe she was even scared that I'd be ashamed of her, and it . . . it pains me now, to think I was. To think I still am." She paused and dropped her gaze. "I wish . . . I almost wish I could go see her. You know, so maybe I could ask her . . ."

She trailed her finger in the dust, tracing letters. *A-B-C.* Now he felt her waiting for him to talk, he felt her expectation and her fear like an invisible force. *Talk to me, Aaron. Comfort me, Aaron.* He thought about what she'd said and the shame that drove her, about her fear. He wondered what her life had been like before she came to this farm, before she joined her life with his. He wondered, when she said she was afraid Cole would hate this baby because of its Comanche blood, if his brother's abandonment hurt her, if she'd loved Cole. If her shame came from the fact that Cole didn't love her back.

He looked down at the letters she'd formed in the sand. He traced over them himself, broadening the gullies, feeling the gritty dust on his skin, adding serifs. "I know what you mean," he said.

She cocked her head. "You been ashamed of your family?"

Not of his family. Of himself. But he caught her gaze and gave her a small smile, and felt the question he wanted to ask her pull at him, burn inside him. *"Do you love Cole?"*

He didn't ask it. He was afraid of whichever answer she would give — *no,* because it meant he would have the chance to make her love him; *yes,* because he wouldn't take the chance. So he just said, "I think everyone is a little bit, don't you?"

"You think so?"

"Yeah," he said. "I think so." And then, because he couldn't stand the thought of her thinking badly about herself, because he knew she would let her fear and her shame grow inside her until she truly did telegraph it to everyone, he said, "And those ladies in town don't see anything. All they know is that you're my wife, and that's enough. And there . . . there's no reason for your baby to be ashamed of you. I'll make sure it isn't."

"But I . . . I ain't learned."

"You're reading already. By the time it's born, you'll be reciting Browning."

"I ain't a lady."

He smiled at her. "I think tea is over-rated."

"My folks —"

"They don't matter unless you want them to," he said.

She looked puzzled for a moment, and then her expression cleared, and she cocked her head so her hair fell over her shoulder, a waterfall of gold, and smiled so he saw her crooked teeth, and her blue eyes sparkled like water in the sun. "Well, then," she said, "I guess it's just like starting life over, huh?"

"Just like a newborn," he told her.

She laughed at that, and the sound squeezed his heart. Then she looked up at him with a serious look and said, "You think . . . you think maybe I ain't why Mr. Wallace had another stroke?"

"I think he's a sick old man," Aaron said, "and that's all."

She nodded shortly, and he followed her gaze back to the house, and the last hour melted away, leaving the rest of the day heavy and overwhelming before him. He looked at the top dormer window and the fig tree bracing against the hot wind, and his responsibilities weighed so heavy on him he felt like sagging. Pa was dying. There were things he had to do.

Reluctantly, he rose. He shielded his eyes

with his hand and sighed. "We'd better get back," he said.

He heard her get to her feet beside him. Then, as he stepped away, he felt her touch on his shoulder. It sent a shiver through him.

"Aaron," she said, and when he turned to look at her, she was smiling. "Thanks. You been a friend to me today, and I won't forget it. Things don't seem so bad now."

A friend. Aaron looked away. "Well, I imagine they'll get better," he said, and then, because he couldn't help it, because he wanted the reminder of who she was, of what he could never be to her — and because he hoped he was wrong — he said, "I'm going to have to send for Cole."

He heard her sharp intake of breath, and he had the answer to his question. *Do you love Cole?* He didn't look at her. She took her hand from his shoulder, and he strode away, to the house, and tormented himself wondering what her expression looked like behind him.

21

Dallas, Texas

Once again, Cole paced to the old live oak bordering the Trinity and back again. It was hot, and he was sweating and impatient. He'd been here too long, waiting for her. He'd told her three o'clock. The note had been delivered to her house that morning — he'd dropped it off himself. *Meet me at the river,* it had said. *Our picnic spot. Three o'clock sharp. Don't be late. I need to talk to you.* He'd signed it, *Your servant, Cole,* and he'd determined he would wait here by the slow trickle of the Trinity as long as it took. If he had to wait until midnight for her, he would.

But it was only six o'clock now, and he knew he wasn't going to wait for her any longer. He didn't like to force things this way; it would be better to have her support before he met her father, but in the days since he'd decided that, he hadn't had the chance to put it to her. She'd been too busy to see him — and that made him nervous and ill-tempered. When it came to women, he was not a patient man, and he was through being patient with her.

Cole damped his cigar between his teeth and glared at his horse. Well, enough was enough. It was time for him to show Miss Jenny Spears the kind of man she would be marrying.

He threw the stub of the cigar at his feet and ground it out, and then he mounted his horse and started back into town. The sky was white-hot, so hot it wasn't much different out of the shade than in it except for the glare. It was not long back into the dusty streets of Dallas, but Cole was sweating hard by the time he got there. He didn't want to look too disheveled when he met her father, but he was through with wasting time, so he went directly to Jenny's house. He dismounted and took off his hat, smoothed back his hair, straightened his vest and brushed the dust from his coat. He gathered himself and put a smile on his face, and then he stepped up to the door of the white clapboard house with its turrets and gables and rapped the ornate gold knocker — a replica of the bank Spears had started — against the heavy oak door.

He felt nervous, and he couldn't remember feeling this way for a long time. His throat was dry, and he cleared it a few times as he heard the footsteps on the other side of the door, a *rap, rap, rap* along the hallway. He prepared himself to meet Jenny, or Robert Spears. He straightened and threw out his chest and kept his smile.

But it was a tiny, withered Mexican woman who opened the door and frowned up at him. She was wearing a plain black gown. A servant. He immediately felt foolish for assuming it could be anyone else.

"I'm here to see Miss Spears," he said. "And her father."

The woman frowned. "No here, *señor*," she said. "They is expecting you?"

"No. No, they weren't."

"They is in town tonight," she said. "At the Palace."

The Palace was the best restaurant in Dallas, which wasn't saying a hell of a lot. Cole had never been there himself, but he knew it was the place where the businessmen of Dallas and Fort Worth sometimes gathered. It was not a place that catered to cowboys or buffalo hunters, so it was safe to take a wife there, or a daughter.

The woman was waiting. Cole smiled and tipped his hat. "Thank you kindly," he said. "I'll call again later." He turned to go back to his horse.

"Your card, *señor?*" she asked.

He looked back at her and shook his head.

He'd already decided to take Jenny by surprise; there was no point in giving her another opportunity to put him off. He'd always wanted to have dinner at the Palace, and what better way to surprise her? Certainly she wouldn't be expecting him. She would have no choice but to introduce him to her father.

He was smiling as he mounted back up and rode in the direction of the restaurant. Even the hogs he had to keep dodging didn't dim his mood. All his plans would come to fruition tonight — by next week, he'd be helping Jenny plan the guest list for their wedding.

From the outside, the Palace was not much different from any other building in Dallas. It was two storied, false-fronted, weathered wood. The only thing that showed its status were the big glass windows facing the street. The sun was setting, streaking red-gold across the sky, and those colors painted the windows; he saw the reflection of the sunset and the street, saw himself sitting tall on his horse.

He dismounted and tied his horse to the hitching rail out front. Then he brushed himself off and eased open the door. The sounds of talk and silverware clinking filled his ears. He breathed in clouds of smoke from cigars and cigarillos, the rich, gamy scent of buffalo steak and the woodsmoke of bacon. His mouth watered. Perhaps Jenny and her father would invite him to dinner. He smiled in anticipation of it, and searched the room for them.

The place was full. Men and women — men mostly — were at nearly every table. It reminded Cole of some of the saloons he'd visited on the coast and over in Louisiana. Big and expensive and catering to the higher class. No wonder cowboys weren't allowed inside — they would have broken everything in sight within a week.

But he fit right in. Cole reached into his vest for a cigar and settled back on his heels, smiling as he glanced over the tables, looking for a pink dress. He belonged in places like this. One day, he supposed, when he made enough money, he'd settle down here in Dallas and spend his evenings bringing Jenny here.

He liked the image, and he let it linger in his mind as he lit his cigar. Then, as he flicked the match to the floor, he saw her. She was in the middle of the room, and her back was to him, but he would know her anywhere. She was wearing pink stripes tonight, and her hair was done elaborately in braids and coils at the nape of her neck, rich and dark, shining in the candlelight.

Without thinking, Cole crossed the room, moving to her table. He was there, standing at her side, before he realized there were two other people at the table. Her father.

And Robert Martin.

"Cole?" She frowned up at him, confused, and he saw something in her eyes — distress maybe. "What are you doing here?"

"I've been looking for you." He leaned closer, said in a low voice, "Didn't you get my note this morning?"

She smiled her charming smile and reached for his hand. "Why, of course I got your note," she said in a too-loud voice. "I'm looking forward to seeing you tomorrow."

Tomorrow. She'd misunderstood then. He was amazed at how relieved he felt, so relieved he decided not to correct her.

She squeezed his hand and turned to her father. "Papa, I'd like you to meet Cole Wallace. He's just visiting Dallas for a while, isn't that right, Cole?"

He smiled at Robert Spears, who was watching him with a guarded expression. "Well, actually, sir, I'm thinking I might stay a while longer."

"Is that so?" Spears fingered his wine glass. He was a man obviously used to getting his own way, and he had that energy about him, a faint disapproval in his eyes and a slow and self-important way of talking that made Cole feel as if he should be pandering and begging before the man. "Why would that be?"

Cole squeezed Jenny's hand and gave her an affectionate look. "I have to admit I've grown quite fond of your daughter."

"That so?" Spears acted uninterested. He directed his gaze to Robert Martin, who sat placidly, smiling as if he hadn't a care in the world. "You know Robert Martin, of course?"

"We've met," Cole said. "Martin, good to see you."

"You, too, Wallace." Robert unfolded his napkin with fastidious grace and curled his lip. "Been in any saloons recently?"

"Of course he hasn't," Jenny said quickly, bristling with such indignation that Cole forgot every doubt he'd had about her. "Cole's given all that up for me, isn't that right?"

"That's right," Cole lied. He ignored Martin and gave Spears his most charming smile. "I'm doing my best to become a man of means."

"Hmmm." Spears grunted. He reached into the pocket of his finely striped waistcoat and pulled out his watch. He flipped it open and glanced at it, tucking it away again all in the space of a second. "Meeting someone here, Mr. Wallace?"

Cole felt the man's dismissal clear into his bones. There would be no invitation to supper, and though that disappointed him, he was glad for the chance to meet Jenny's father anyway. It made things easier. Jenny loosed her hand from his, though she touched his sleeve as if she were loath to let him go.

"Tomorrow, Cole?" she asked.

He smiled down at her. "Of course," he said. He looked back at Spears. "And, sir, I'd like to have the chance to speak with you later, if I might."

Spears raised his heavy brow. "Oh? That so? Well, we'll see, we'll see."

Jenny motioned for Cole to bend down. He did, and she whispered in his ear, "We'll talk about it tomorrow, darling, all right?" And then she backed away and laughed lightly, as if she'd just told him something clever.

It confused him, but he stepped back from the table and nodded his good-bye to Martin, to Spears. He gave Jenny a lingering smile, and then he left them the way a gentleman would. But once he was outside the restaurant again, he looked through the window, to their table, glowing now in the light of the candles. He saw Jenny laugh and reach for Martin's hand, and he saw Robert Martin speaking earnestly to her father. Robert Martin. Robert Spears. It occurred to him then that they had the same first name. It made him nervous that it was Martin having dinner with Jenny and her father and not him.

The rest of the evening and the night passed anxiously. He felt at loose ends, nervous and bothered, and so he mounted his horse and rode along the bank of the Trinity until morning. Jenny had said she would see him at two, and he hurried to the place he'd said he would meet her, feeling a deep-down panic as he rode.

He got there at a quarter to two. By four o'clock, she still hadn't arrived, and something ugly began to dawn on him, something he didn't want to admit or even think about. This time, he didn't wait until six. He rode straight into Dallas. He rode straight to her house. He knocked on the door without bothering to clean up.

The Mexican woman from yesterday answered.

"I'm here to see Miss Jenny," he said.

The woman shook her head and began to shut the door. "She not seeing visitors —"

He slammed his hand against the jamb, stopped the door with his foot. "I'm not leaving until I see her. You go on. You tell her that."

The woman paused, and then she nodded. She turned and hurried down the hallway, and Cole stepped inside and closed the door behind him and listened to the ticking of a great clock in the hallway.

The Spearses' house was cool and quiet, and it smelled of rich things, of leather and Brussels carpets and humidors filled with expensive cigars. It made him feel poor. It made him feel like a gambler, and suddenly he knew. He knew before he even saw her coming down the hall what she was going to tell him.

When he saw her expression, he braced himself for her words. She gave him a nervous smile. "Why, hello, Cole. What brings you here?"

He glanced at the servant hovering in the doorway and said quietly, "I'd like to talk to you, if I could."

Her hand fluttered to her skirt, and again he had the notion she was nervous. "Why, of course," she said. She swished down the hall in a wash of rustling satin and gardenia, swept into the parlor off the hall. He followed her. The Mexican housemaid was right behind, and she stopped in the doorway. Jenny didn't tell the woman to go.

She went to the empty marble fireplace and turned to face him, braced on either side with fire pokers and a huge urn. A settee loomed between them, and he made no effort to move closer.

"You said you'd meet me today," he said softly. "Last night, you said —"

"Oh, Cole," she said with a sigh. "You are the silliest man. Didn't you see me last night with Robert Martin? Now, why do you suppose he and Daddy and I were having supper together?" She raised her left hand, waved her fingers at him until he saw the ring. A large diamond that sparkled in the sun coming through the windows. "Robert and I were engaged last night. How would it look if I ran off to meet you the very next day?"

He'd known it. Deep inside, he'd known it since last night, but still her words surprised him. He was stunned to silence, to a tingling numbness.

"Why, Cole, you look so surprised," she said. "I have you to thank for it, you know. Without you, I never would've brought Robert around so fast. He was jealous, poor dear — can you believe it?"

Suddenly, all the little things came to him, all the darted looks to Robert Martin, the way she seemed more attentive to Cole when Martin was in the room. The way she'd called him "Cole" last night, when she'd never said his name before.

"You don't love me?"

"But you must have known," she said, looking puzzled. "You must have known I couldn't. Why, you're just a gambler. What do you think this town would think of me if I married someone like you?"

She'd been using him the whole time. She'd never intended to marry him. She'd wanted someone to make Robert Martin jealous enough to propose, and Cole had stepped in and played the part perfectly. He wanted to cringe at how well he'd been used, how stupid he'd been.

He gathered himself with effort. He straightened, he tipped his hat. "Well, then," he said. "Let me be the first to wish you happy."

She smiled broadly. "You are such a sweet man, Cole Wallace," she said. She came around the settee and leaned closer, pecked him on the cheek. "I do hope one day you find this kind of happiness too."

She had dismissed him. There was nothing more to say. But there was some satisfaction in turning on his heel and leaving that room the way he'd always wanted to come into it: like a gentleman. And though his dreams were scattered at his feet as he walked to the door, he was glad to see nervousness cross that Mexican woman's face. He was glad he frightened her. It seemed important that he retain what little power he had left. That he be a man instead of the fool Jenny had taken him for.

He didn't even slam the door on the way out. He closed it quietly and stood there on the stoop, breathing in the muggy, suffocating air and feeling empty. The meaninglessness of his life swept before him — suddenly, effortlessly — and he realized he'd spent the last year working for one thing, and that all the years stretching ahead had included her. Now, he didn't know what to do or where to go. He'd expected to leave this town with Jenny.

He walked slowly to his horse — he felt so tired it required all his strength to get there, to get into the saddle. He gave the mare her head, and what he saw was no longer the promise of Dallas, but only houses. Houses filled with wives and husbands and children. He wondered how long it would take him to forget this dream, to come up with another one, and if that dream would be another woman. Ah no, probably not. Not so soon. He wanted time to mourn. To get drunk over a hand of cards and wear her rejection like a badge. *"Once there was a woman I loved, but she married another. Broken hearts don't heal so quickly, eh, boys?"*

Jenny. Jenny. He could not believe his dreams had disappeared so quickly, in just a few moments. He had not expected them to be so fragile.

The horse took him back to the livery. His hotel was across the street. Cole left the mare with one of the livery boys and went across the street. The Eagle Hotel seemed like a waste of money now, luxury for appearances only, not necessary. He crossed the expensive carpet and was to the neweled banister when the clerk called to him.

"Mr. Wallace! Mr. Wallace, you've got a telegram."

A telegram. It stopped him. Cole turned with a frown. No one knew he was here. How the hell could he get a telegram? From where?

"You sure it's for me?"

The clerk nodded. He held up a piece of paper. "Says Cole Wallace, Dallas. Charles McAlester at the telegraph office got it this morning. You're listed in the paper as staying here."

Of course. Another reason not to stay at an elite hotel. The paper printed his name. Too damn easy to be found.

Sighing, Cole went over to the desk. He

took the paper from the clerk. When he saw his brother's name, he felt a small shock of recognition, of surprise, and it made him unfold the paper quickly, thinking immediately of Pa. There was no other reason for Aaron to try to reach him. None at all.

He read the words quickly: "PA BAD stop COME HOME stop AARON."

He felt the shock of them to his core. Short and sweet. But what else was there to say, after all? He knew what Aaron meant. The old man was dying — Aaron wouldn't be sending for him for anything less. Cole had no illusions. His brother wanted him on the farm about as much as Cole wanted to be there.

But Pa was dying.

He crumpled the paper in his hand and threw it to the counter. "I'm checking out," he said to the clerk.

"Oh, dear," the man said. "I hope it's not bad news."

"Some days, there's nothing but," Cole said. He spun away from the counter and took the stairs two at a time. He had to get the hell out of this town. Pa was dying. He owed it to the old man to be there. And — he admitted this through the sadness lodging tight and heavy in his chest — he owed it to himself.

22

White Horse, Texas

Cole saw the drought around the farm the way he hadn't seen it in Dallas — dried up stream beds and cracked red clay, grama burnt low and short to the ground. He saw a herd of deer gathered around the shallow, murky leavings in the bottom of a deep buffalo wallow, and the birds seemed sluggish and listless; they merely ran instead of flying when his passing flushed them from the grass.

He saw the effects of no water on the corn long before he reached the farmhouse: brown stalks, curling leaves, small, thin ears. There wouldn't be much of a yield, and what there was would be of poor quality. He wondered how much Aaron was depending on the corn these days, if the drought would mean poverty. It had been a long time since Cole had wondered such a thing, and it disturbed him a little that he didn't know, that he had no idea what kind of an inheritance would be Aaron's when their father died, if there was money left or not.

He'd long ago given up his stake in it, so

he guessed it didn't matter much, and he put the thought out of his mind and rode on. But when he reached the farmhouse, he paused. It looked run-down, dried out. There was no gurgling creek to welcome him back, no bright green leaves blowing in the breeze, no grass in the yard. Just red dust and pounded dirt and a few listing chickens. The sun seemed to burn right down onto it — for a moment Cole thought he could even see the moisture leaching away. It seemed empty, except for the chickens, lifeless, and in a way that was fitting. The lifeblood of the farm was leaving it anyway; it seemed appropriate that Pa's death should coincide with a drought.

He'd had less complimentary things to say about his father — he'd been a difficult man to live with, a difficult man to love — but Cole did love him. It was true, he loved the old man better when he was far away, and maybe his sadness would fade with distance as well, but for now, Cole looked at that farm and felt a heaviness deep in his chest and hoped he wasn't too late.

He rode into the yard. He was just dismounting when he heard the slam of some faraway door, the rush of footsteps, and he looked up just as she came running into his arms.

"Oh, Cole, you're home!" She gave him a quick hug and then she pulled away and looked up at him with a smile on her face, in her eyes. "You're home."

Eliza.

He realized with a shock that he'd forgotten all about her. It surprised him, disconcerted him enough that he had to work to smile back at her, to pretend he was happy to see her.

"Why, hey there," he said. He disentangled himself from her, looked past her to the house. "How's Pa?"

She sobered quickly. "About the same," she said.

The heaviness in his chest abated some. "So he's not dead."

"Oh no." She shook her head and sighed. "But the doctor says it could be any time."

He nodded. He took his horse's reins and began walking across the yard. She fell into step beside him — so close he felt the occasional bump of her hip against his. When he looked down at her, she smiled — she seemed so damn glad to see him, and he tried to remember why, if he'd promised her anything when he left, if she had any reason at all to want him to return.

He couldn't remember. She looked as if she were expecting him to say something, so he did. "You look good," he said.

She beamed at him. She spread her hands on her hips, pulled her skirt taunt. "I'm starting to show," she said.

It took him aback. He'd never known a woman to even talk about her pregnancy, but then again, he'd never known a woman as low-class as Eliza — at least not for longer than it took to leave her bed. He found himself glancing to her waist, saw the slight bulge of her pregnancy — proof, if he'd needed it, which he didn't. Cole glanced away. "You feeling all right?"

"Now I am," she said. "But there for a while, it was pretty bad." Her smile grew wistful. "I missed you."

He was saved from having to answer when they reached the porch, and one of the Mexicans stepped outside.

"*Señor* Wallace," he said, nodding curtly.

Cole gestured to his horse. "Can you take care of this for me?"

The man hesitated.

"Please, Carlos," Eliza said. "I'll take Cole on up to see his daddy."

"As you wish, *señora*." Carlos went past them down the stairs and grabbed the horse's reins.

"He doesn't like me very much," Cole said in a low voice.

Eliza touched his arm. "He just doesn't know you like I do," she said.

The house was dark and hot; the smell of chicken wafted through, the sharp pinch of chilies. He paused just inside — a moment to rest, to prepare himself — but Eliza turned to him and called him on with her hand, and he followed her up the stairs, down the narrow hallway. He smelled the scents of rubbing alcohol and weakened flesh before he even reached the door, and he steadied himself and stepped into his father's room.

Aaron turned from the window. His face was stiff and expressionless. "You got my telegram," he said.

"I'm here." Cole looked past his brother to the bed, to the sunken form of his father, to the slight rise and fall of his chest. "How is he?"

"He's been in a coma for a week and a half," Aaron said. "He could die any day."

Cole let his breath out in a slow stream. He felt Eliza's hand on his shoulder. She patted him as if she thought he needed a soothing touch, as if she thought she could soothe him.

Cole stepped away from her. He went to his father's bedside. He stared down at the old man — his face was gray, his lips slightly apart, his cheeks freshly shaved. Except for his skin color, he could have been sleeping.

"He looks better the last few days," Eliza said. "I been hoping . . . maybe . . ."

Cole met his brother's eyes. Aaron shook his head and looked away.

"Well," Cole said. "I guess there's no point in just standing here staring at him." Though that was just what he wanted to do. He hadn't seen his father these last years without the old man railing at him about something, and now he wanted to look on this peaceful face and memorize it. He wanted something kind to remember, though the truth was this wasn't the father he knew — there was nothing about this still, silent man that resembled Thomas Wallace.

It was almost like the old man was dead already. Cole stepped back from the bed, feeling sick. He rubbed his hand over his eyes.

"You want something to eat, Cole?" Eliza asked. "Or maybe . . . you could lie down. I got your room all ready for you."

He looked up at her. Her brows were winged over her eyes in concern, there were frown lines about her mouth. There had been something surprisingly comforting in her voice, as if she knew how he was feeling, as if she understood it. Something mother-like, though Eliza did not look anything like a mother, with those breasts straining against that dress or her full-lipped mouth or her golden hair.

"What I'd like," he said, "is a glass of tequila."

"Well, we got that," she said, smiling, and whatever it was he'd seen that moment fled. She was just Eliza again. She inclined her head toward the door, an open invitation, and he found himself moving toward her, drawn by the promise of liquor. He felt tired suddenly, and dirty, and there was a raging thirst inside him.

He thought Aaron was behind him as he followed Eliza downstairs, but when he got to the table and turned to see his brother, Aaron wasn't there. Cole didn't think on it. He sank into a chair and waited while Eliza got the bottle of tequila. She set it before him, along with a glass, and he didn't protest when she sat opposite him and leaned her elbows on the table as if she was settling in for a good listen.

He grabbed the tequila and poured a healthy measure of it, and when the first sip was down his throat he felt better. The image of his father's face receded. He downed the rest of it and poured more.

"How you been doing, Cole?" Eliza asked. She pressed forward, and her face was drawn and avid, as if she hungered for his talk. "You been gambling?"

"Some," he said. There was no point in telling her about Jenny. It was over now, and even if it weren't, he knew better than to tell a woman he'd slept with about a woman he'd been in love with, even if the former was married to his brother now. "Spent some time in Dallas."

"I never been there." She tilted her head at him, the gesture reminded him of Jenny — he wondered if all women knew the same movements, the same flirtatious glances. Was there some school somewhere that taught it to them, or was it something they had from birth?

"You'd like it," he said. "Maybe one day you can get Aaron to take you there."

Her face drew up a little, as if she didn't think that would ever happen, but she sighed and said, "Yeah. Maybe."

The tequila was warming him. He felt good. The soreness in his heart left from Jenny's rejection was easing somewhat, his grief over his father lessening in the fire of liquor. He liked the way Eliza sat there, listening to him — he'd always liked that about her, he remembered. She had a way of giving her whole attention to a man. It was something he'd never once felt Jenny do.

"Looks like the farm's been good to you, Eliza," he said. "You're blooming."

She laughed a little, those crooked teeth flashed. "You mean I'm growing out. I guess I'll prob'ly be fat before too long."

He didn't like her reminder. He didn't like thinking of the baby at all. He poured himself another drink. "You look happy."

"I guess . . . I guess I'm all right." She drew lines on the oilcloth with her fingertip. "It ain't been" — she glanced at the stairs — "easy."

He wasn't sure whether she meant his father or Aaron, so he didn't answer.

She kept drawing. "I almost got set on by a bobcat," she went on, "and there're rattlers in the well."

"Drought," he said.

"That's what Miguel says," she said. "When I first came here, I thought how nice it was that there wasn't a swamp. But I guess there's something to hate about everywhere."

He thought of Jenny. He poured another drink. "Yeah," he said. "That's true enough."

"But Aaron . . . he's been kind to me, and so has your daddy. I'm going to miss him something fierce when he's gone."

Cole lifted a brow in surprise. He'd never

known Pa to be kind to anyone. "Oh yeah? Well, go on into town, you'll find plenty of better friends to take his place."

She gave him a quick glance, and then she looked down at the table again, shook her head. "I don't think so."

"Why not?"

"I been to town already," she said softly. "They don't like me there."

There was something she wasn't saying, and Cole sipped his tequila slowly and watched her bowed head.

"They're still telling those stories, huh?" he asked.

She looked up at him. "You never told me about those, Cole," she said. There was a faint chiding in her voice, an accusation in her eyes, but Cole didn't feel the least bit guilty over it. No, he hadn't told her, but she would never have married Aaron if he had.

"You'll charm them soon enough," he said. He leaned forward, chucked her chin. "You're a pretty charming girl."

She flushed a little, ducked her head. "I don't know about all that," she said. "I ain't a lady, you know."

The tequila tasted smooth. He wondered where Aaron got it, if one of those farmhands brought it up from Mexico. It was better than most of the stuff he'd had. Cole took a long, deep sip and found himself smiling at Eliza.

"Seems to me it'd be easy enough to learn," he said. "A few dances, some small talk . . . hell, you could do it in no time."

She laughed a little. "I don't guess that's all there is to it."

"Eliza." He leaned forward. He thought of Jenny, of her pretty clothes and her smile, and that cold heart beneath. "I've been with a lot of women in my time. Once you get their clothes off, they're all the same."

"Cole!" She sounded scandalized, but she laughed, too.

"Well, it's true," he said. "Put on a different dress, shut your mouth, and learn to dance a reel, and you're no different than the rest of them."

"You really think so?" There was a hopefulness in her voice, as if this were the most important thing to her, and he thought how strange it was that it mattered so much. The only reason he could think of to be a lady was marriage — a man didn't marry a whore, and he didn't marry trash. But she was already married, so it wouldn't make a difference that way. Then he thought of her mother, of that dark Comanche hair, and he wondered if Eliza was trying to erase her heritage. God knew, if he was the child of a Comanche, he'd do his best to erase it.

He poured more tequila. "Hell, yes, I think so," he said.

"You think . . . you think you could teach me?"

He didn't have anything else to do. He was stuck here until Pa died, and if nothing else, teaching Eliza a dance or two would help pass the time. And he was getting drunk, and feeling maudlin, and her face was pretty and her smile made him feel like a man.

"Sure. Why not?"

She grinned — her whole face came alive with it. She leaned close and touched his arm, tightening her fingers on his sleeve. "I am so glad you came home, Cole."

He heard the footsteps on the stairs. He turned, just as she did, to see his brother standing there, watching. Aaron's face was tight and stiff, and in the shadows of the stairwell, his expression was unreadable. But Cole felt a chill move over him.

Eliza didn't seem to feel a thing. "Aaron," she said. "Guess what? Cole's going to teach me how to be a lady."

"Is he?" Aaron came down the stairs. Cole felt the coolness of his brother's glance before Aaron looked at Eliza. "That's nice of him."

"Ain't it?" She was beaming.

Aaron ran his hand through his hair. He looked at the open front door, and he swallowed and said, "You . . . ready? For your lesson, I mean?"

"What lesson?" Cole asked.

"Aaron's been teaching me how to read," Eliza said. She looked at Aaron. There was a slight frown between her eyes. "But Cole just got home. Don't you think it'd be nice just to visit for a while?"

Aaron paused. He looked at Cole. "Yeah," he said. "Maybe later, then."

"By all means." Cole motioned with the tequila bottle. "You go on and do what farmers do, baby brother. I'll just sit here and listen to this pretty lady."

He waited for Aaron's reaction, and got it. A split second of concern crossed his brother's eyes, his lips tightened, his jaw jumped. But he only nodded and turned away. "I'll be back in a while," he said, and then he strode out the door.

"Ten to one he goes to that damn tree," Cole said.

Eliza frowned at him. "What?"

"That tree. He spends more time at that tree than most birds. Writing poetry." He let mockery tinge his last words.

Eliza gave him a puzzled look. "But he's

435

a poet," she said. "You told me that yourself. He read something to me once. It was real pretty. 'Only a touch and we combine.' " She closed her eyes as if she were remembering the rhyme in full. When she opened them again, she was smiling. "It was as pretty as what you said to me by the lake that day. You remember?"

He didn't remember saying anything, but he smiled at her and said, "Oh, yes," because it was easier and because — he admitted this readily — he'd seen the worry in his brother's eyes and he couldn't help tweaking it some, even if Aaron wasn't here to see Cole's mild flirtation with his wife.

She sighed and brought her hands up to her face, leaning into them. "It's good to have you home, Cole," she said again — it must've been the hundredth time. "I been lonely."

Lonely. It was no wonder. Aaron had never been good with women. He'd been shy and withdrawn his whole life. Cole remembered once, when Pa brought some whore home for Aaron's twelfth birthday, and Aaron had run from her as if she had the plague. At least it hadn't been a waste of money — both Cole and Pa had taken advantage of her services before they sent her back to White Horse again — but that was the story of Aaron's involvement with women. He stayed away.

Still, Eliza was his wife. And Cole hadn't mistaken that worry in his brother's eyes. Aaron felt something for her. So why was pretty little Eliza lonely?

Cole poured another shot. He drank it down. He had the thought that he was well on his way to getting truly drunk. Every sip of tequila tore down that wall he'd put around his heart since Jenny had broken it, and he couldn't keep her words from floating around in his brain, and he wanted consolation. He wanted to flirt with a pretty girl, even if she was his brother's wife. Because she was.

"Well, I'm here now," he said, grinning. He reached out and touched her head. "So you can stop being lonely."

Aaron told himself not to care. It was just Cole, doing what Cole did best, and Eliza was carrying his baby. It was natural that she should love him. It was what Aaron had expected, after all. But he couldn't help the hard squeeze of his heart, the sickening drop he'd felt in his gut when he'd looked out the window of Pa's room and saw her run into Cole's arms as if she'd been yearning for him forever.

She'd barely taken her eyes from Cole, and when Aaron came downstairs finally, it was his brother she was touching, his brother she was smiling at.

He hated that, but mostly he hated the way he ran from it, the way he always ran. There was Cole, making love to his wife the way Aaron could not. Cole, traveling the land while Aaron minded withered, crippled cornfields. Cole, charming everyone he saw, gathering friends the way Aaron gathered words on paper.

Now, Aaron sat beneath his tree and clutched paper in hands that trembled as he tried to write the words. He pictured her staring into Cole's face, her eyes shining. He heard her laughter in his head. *"I love you, Cole. I've always loved you."*

He'd known it would be this way when Cole came back. He'd known it as he sent the telegram calling his brother to the farm. What could he do? There had been no choice. Cole was the oldest. He was the heir. Aaron had to call him home.

But now he wished he'd waited — another day, perhaps, a week. Maybe in that time he could have shown Eliza how he felt, maybe he could have won her. . . .

Ah, but that was just a silly dream. He hadn't even tried to kiss her. He'd felt safe, the way things were, the slow quiet of their relationship, the building trust. He'd thought, maybe one day —

But he was lying to himself, and he knew it. *"You been a friend to me. . . ."* A friend. That's what he and Eliza were. Not a husband and wife. Not lovers. Just friends. There was a time when that would have been enough, even more than he'd expected or wanted. It was not enough anymore.

Aaron put aside the paper, shoved his pencil into his pocket. He couldn't write. When words should have been dancing in front of him, he saw images instead. He tormented himself by thinking of Cole and Eliza together, and he knew that, as long as he stayed out here, it wouldn't stop. But he didn't want to go inside either. He didn't want the effort of being with them.

In spite of that, he got up, he went inside. He heard them talking before he even reached the door, heard Eliza's laugh and Cole's low, slurred answer. The bottle of tequila was nearly empty. Cole was drunker than Aaron had seen him in a long, long time.

He stopped in the doorway, and Cole looked up at him, squinting blearily. "Ah, there 'e is, my baby brodder," he said. "Still mad at me?"

"He ain't mad at you," Eliza said. "Why would he be mad?"

Cole lifted his glass. "Oh, I think I know why," he said. "Come on over, Aaron, share a glass with me. Talk to your wife."

He accented the word. *Wife.* There was a sneer beneath it, a mockery that made Aaron's hands clench. He shook his head and came inside. He went over to the settee, to his pile of books.

"You just going to read?" Eliza asked. "When your brother's come home?"

He didn't look at her. "Yeah," he said — even that word was hard to manage. He sat down. He picked up the first book in the pile.

"Well, hell," Cole said. "Why don't you read to us, baby brodder? Tell us some pretty poems."

Aaron ignored him. He opened the book.

"Come on, Liza," Cole said. "Tell your husband to read us somethin'. Somethin' 'bout . . . love, mebbee? You know anythin' 'bout love, Aaron?"

He could have ignored it. He could have opened that book and read himself into a stupor and tried to forget his brother. But then Cole laughed — that laugh that said he knew Aaron wouldn't try, that mocking, victor's laugh, and Aaron put aside the book.

Deliberately, he looked for the collection he'd read to Eliza all those weeks ago. Deliberately, he looked for Browning. Cole had just issued a challenge; Aaron heard the words as clearly as if they'd been said. *"Do you know anything about love, Aaron?" "Can you win her, Aaron?" "Can you love her, Aaron?"*

He picked the poem carefully; he read it to meet his brother's challenge. He read it to woo her. " 'Escape me? Never, Beloved! While I am I, and you are you, / So long as the world contains us both, / Me the loving and you the loth, / While the one eludes, must the other pursue.' "

He glanced up. Eliza listened avidly, her chin propped in her hands. Cole was leaning back, dangling a glass half-full of tequila before his mouth. His eyes were lowered, contemplative.

"Lonely, little brother?" he asked softly, all slur gone.

Aaron caught his brother's glance. Cole looked steady and sober.

"Well?" Cole asked.

Aaron closed the book. "Just a welcome-home poem for you, Cole," he said. "Think you can remember it?"

"Depends," Cole said cryptically, "on whether I get bored or not."

"We'll just have to keep you busy, then."

"Oh, I'll be busy," Cole said with a smile. "I'll be teaching Eliza here how to be a lady."

The words hit Aaron in a panic, just as Cole had meant them to. Aaron looked at Eliza. She'd been watching them with a puzzled look on her face, a frown between her eyes, but at Cole's statement, she smiled. "Ain't that a good idea, Aaron?" she asked, and she was so eager he felt himself pulling in, dissolving.

"Yeah," he said, looking away.

"Go on," Cole said. "Read some more. It was very . . . soothing."

Aaron heard the laughter in his brother's voice, the scorn, and the fight went out of him. He couldn't compete with Cole, not where women were concerned. He hadn't the slightest idea how to compete. If Cole wanted Eliza, Aaron couldn't stop him. He told himself it wasn't important enough to try.

But he knew he was lying, and he was ashamed and sick as he picked up another book on the pile. Something safe. Something to soothe his own ears because Cole couldn't appreciate poetry anyway, and Eliza . . . well, Eliza just liked the sounds.

Percy Shelley. He opened up the book and read. " 'I met a traveler from an antique land . . .' "

23

Eliza woke the next morning with a sense of purpose. It was a good feeling; during the last week, since Mr. Wallace had collapsed again, mornings had been hard. Most mornings, she lay there and thought of him in that room dying. She would wonder if today might be the day. Those thoughts would keep her in bed until the baby inside her demanded to be fed, and she couldn't deny her appetite another second.

But this morning she woke up and thought of Cole waiting for her, Cole teaching her to be a lady, and relief made her race down the stairs to find him. There were some things she couldn't fight, like the way the town thought of Aaron, but at least she could change herself so her baby wouldn't be ashamed of her. So Aaron wouldn't be ashamed of her.

He'd told her he wasn't, of course, but she didn't really believe him. His words to her had been pretty, and they had soothed her for a time, but words didn't matter in the end. It was what a person did that mattered. And in the six weeks since they married, he'd still never kissed her, never touched her. It was more than shyness, she knew — after all, he was a man, and no man stayed shy that long. It pained her heart to think it, but she couldn't help herself — she didn't know what else it could be. So when Cole told her he would teach her how to be a lady, relief had welled up in her so hard she almost cried. Besides, she had missed Cole. She'd missed his kindnesses. He didn't love her, and she knew that, but he liked her. He'd liked her once enough to kiss her — to do more than that — and she never once felt like he was ashamed of her. She never felt anything but pretty when she was in Cole's company. She never felt like there was someplace else he'd rather be.

He wasn't in the front room, or at the table, and he wasn't in the kitchen. She knew the others were out in the fields already — she hadn't managed to get up early enough to fix them breakfast in all the days she'd been here — and she wondered if maybe Cole had gone with them, but then she heard bootsteps on the stairs, and she went hurrying out of the kitchen to see him coming down. His step was heavy, his face drawn.

"You all right, Cole?" she asked.

He looked up like he was surprised to see her. "Yeah. I was just . . . just looking in on Pa."

"Ain't it terrible, though?" she asked. "It breaks my heart to see him this way."

He sighed and came to the table. He sagged into one of the chairs and pulled the coffeepot close, pouring into one of the cups left on the table. He took a sip and made a face, pushing it back again. "It's cold."

"D'you want some breakfast?" she asked. "I could make you something, if you do. Or more coffee?"

"No thanks," he said. "I'm not that hungry. Where's Aaron?"

"I don't know," she said. "I guess he's prob'ly out in the fields."

"Doing what? Watering each cornstalk by hand?"

"There ain't enough water for that, Cole," she said before she realized he was being scornful. She flushed and looked down at her hands. "I don't know what he does out there. I don't see him much until suppertime."

"That's what you said." Cole's voice was low and soft, and when she looked up at him again, he was watching her with a strange expression. "You said you were lonely."

She gave him a bright smile. "Well, not now I ain't."

"Am not," he said.

"What?"

"You said 'ain't.' You should have said, 'I am not.' " He took another sip of the cold coffee. "You said you wanted to learn to be a lady, right? Ladies don't say 'ain't.' "

She liked that he was helping her already. It made her feel warm inside. She reached for the coffeepot. "Let me make you some more —"

He put out a hand to stop her and shook his head. "I don't want any. Why don't you sit down, Eliza? I could use some company this morning."

It was what she wanted, too. It seemed lately she'd been hungering for it. She sat down at the table beside him, and leaned forward. "I know what you mean," she said, patting his hand. "It feels strange with him so quiet, doesn't it? I keep waiting for him to ring that bell."

He looked up at her blearily. "To tell the truth, Eliza, I haven't spent enough time here in years to know whether it feels strange or not."

"Oh. Well, I thought you were missing him —"

"Yeah." He exhaled heavily. He curled his

fingers around the coffee cup and smiled weakly. "Thanks."

She smiled back at him. "You know, there's days sometimes when me and your daddy just sit up there and look at each other. I mean, you know, Aaron's been teaching me how to read, but I ain't — am not — good at it yet, so I can't talk to Mr. Wallace. But I think he likes me up there anyway."

"Well, you're pretty to look at," he said.

He said it the way someone might say: *"Raining hard, ain't it?"* Like it was just a fact, like there was nothing anyone could say against it, and it lit her up inside. Eliza looked into his eyes and thought how handsome they were, all those colors of brown and green mixed up together.

"Oh, Cole," she said on a sigh. "You say such pretty things."

"What's wrong?" he asked. "My little brother doesn't keep you full up with compliments?"

"Not . . . not like that," she said. She tried to think of how to say it, how to say that Aaron was like a quilt on a cold night, while Cole was like a fire — always reaching, always sparking. "He . . . you know, he's nice to me. But he ain't —"

"Isn't."

"He *isn't* like . . ." she searched for words. Finally, she just said it. "He doesn't make me feel pretty, like you do. When you used to kiss me, it . . . it made me feel like I was the most important thing."

He lifted a brow. "And Aaron's kisses don't make you feel like that?"

"Well, I don't know," she said. She looked down at the table, unable to meet his eyes, feeling a little like a traitor as she said it but unable to help herself. It had been a long time since she'd had someone to really talk to, and things were welling up in her throat, needing to be said. "Aaron . . . he doesn't kiss me."

Cole was silent, but Eliza felt his gaze, felt the thoughtfulness of it. Slowly, she looked up to meet it. He had a funny expression on his face, something sure and a little proud — but then she thought she was wrong, it couldn't be that, because she didn't understand what that kind of a look could mean.

"Aaron doesn't kiss you?" he asked softly. "Not even when you're —"

She shook her head violently. "We never done that," she said, and she felt heat of a blush burning up her skin. She was too embarrassed to look at him.

"But you share a bed, don't you?"

Eliza got up fast; the chair scraped back

on the floor. "I shouldn't be talking to you about this," she said. "It ain't right."

"Isn't."

"You know what I mean."

"Eliza, Eliza," he said, and his voice was soft and soothing. "I'm just trying to help. We won't talk about it if you don't want to."

She looked at him. "We won't?"

"No."

She took a deep breath and sat back down. "All right then." But then he was looking at her with this . . . this caring in his eyes, and she burst out with it. "I think, you know . . . I think he's ashamed of me. 'Cause I ain't a lady. 'Cause I can't read. And I told him . . . I told him about my mama. Maybe that means —"

"Aaron's never cared about the Comanches so much," Cole said quietly.

"Not like you."

"Yeah. Not like me."

Eliza nodded. Her head felt heavy. She pressed her hands against her stomach, felt the bulge of the baby, felt its reassuring weight. "I'm sorry," she said. "I didn't mean to trouble you with this —"

"You said he told you the story," Cole said. His fingers played over the coffee cup, he didn't look at her.

"Yeah," she said. "About how he was

born, and about the Indians."

"Just that?" he asked. "Nothing else?"

She stared at him in confusion. "There's something else?"

Cole sat back in his chair. He looked at the open front door, and his lips pressed together tight; he looked like he was trying to make up his mind. "No," he murmured, but there was something about the way he said it, something that made her think he was lying. "There's nothing else."

He shook his head a little, like he was shaking away a thought, and then he pushed back his cup and got to his feet, and held out his hand. "Come on," he said.

She felt a shiver deep down inside at the way he said it. "Why?" she asked, getting to her feet. She put her hand in his. "Where're we going?"

"You said you didn't know how to dance," he said, and then with a smile he swung her into her chest, held her close. "Now's as good a time as any to learn, don't you think?"

He couldn't keep himself from playing with Eliza. She smiled too easily, and being in this house again made him feel lonely. The dream that had sustained him over the last year was gone, and Pa was dying, and he felt at loose ends. It felt like there was a hollowness inside him, and when Eliza talked, when he was busy teaching her the dance steps, he didn't feel that hollowness so much. But when she whirled away from him breathlessly, saying she had to start dinner, laughing her way into the kitchen, he was left standing there, and the thickness in his chest came back heavy against his heart. The house felt too empty. There was no Jenny. Pa was just a shell.

Cole went upstairs. He paused at the door to his father's room, took a cigar from his vest and put it in his mouth, but he didn't light it. The pleasure of smoking it was gone now that Pa couldn't berate him for it. He came into the room; it was still hot from the morning sun, the thin curtains lifeless against the open window.

With a sigh, Cole sat in the chair next to the bed. He'd already been in here early that morning, and the experience had been the same. Eerie and too silent. The energy that was Pa dissipated in the heat. It was just a room with a man in it, nothing more.

Cole sat there and watched his father breathe. He counted the breaths, waited for each rise, exhaled with each fall. He watched for some other movement, the clenching of a hand perhaps, or the flickering of an eyelid, but there was nothing. He wished for it. In all the years since he'd been gone from home, he never thought about the old man dying. In his mind, his father and this farm waited for him to visit, always the same, never changing. In his mind, they didn't really exist until he was riding onto the property. He supposed he'd assumed Pa would always be here — even after his initial stroke three years ago, Cole had ridden away believing it. Now . . . now it felt as if there was some kind of decision to be made, that the life Cole had lived up till now was over, that something had to change.

He was not sorry for the feeling, actually. He guessed he had a few more years left in him if he wanted it — a few more years before the towns blended together in his mind and the thought of moving on was too wearying to contemplate. But there was something pathetic about putting things off. He was thirty years old, and his father was dying — suddenly mortality was staring him in the face, and he wondered if that was what he wanted to be — just a footstep on a dusty street, obliterated by the wind, forgotten. *Cole Wallace was here, but then he moved on* — the story of his life. There was no one to see him go, no one to miss him. No one to mourn him.

God, such maudlin thoughts. Cole rubbed his eyes and sat back in his chair and sighed. The old man was getting to him even now, still as he was, silent as he was. Cole didn't know which was worse — Pa's tirades or this endless tranquillity.

"Any change?"

Cole looked up to see Aaron in the doorway. His brother was standing loose-armed and hesitant, dusty and tired. Cole shook his head. "No change."

Aaron hesitated a moment, and then he came into the room. He went to the other side of the bed and looked down into Pa's face.

"I've been dreaming about him," he said.

"Nightmares," Cole said.

Aaron smiled thinly. "Yeah."

"I figure he'll still be haunting me after I'm dead." Cole stuffed his cigar back into his vest pocket. "No rest for the wicked."

His words fell into clumsy silence; it had been a long time since he and Aaron talked together without the aid of tequila, longer still since they'd had anything in common. But Cole tried to fill the space between them anyway — he didn't feel like leaving this room yet, but he didn't want to be alone with their father. He didn't feel like thinking.

"What's going to happen with the corn?" he asked.

Aaron threw him a look of surprise. "D'you care?"

"No." Cole shrugged. "But when I was riding up yesterday, I thought maybe the crop was important. What with this drought and all, if you need money —"

"I don't," Aaron said quickly.

"Well, I've got it if you need it." Cole let out a short, bitter laugh. "Two thousand dollars worth."

"Two thousand dollars?" Aaron frowned. "I thought you were saving that for a wedding."

"Yeah, well, the wedding's off," Cole said. He hated to say it. He would never have admitted such a failure to his brother if not for Pa lying so still and helpless between them. Even so, the admission rankled. "She turned me down flat."

Aaron's surprise would have been laughable if Cole felt like laughing. "She turned you down?"

"Hard to believe, isn't it?" Cole exhaled slowly. "Set my sights a little high, I'm afraid."

Aaron nodded. He was quiet for a minute, and then he said, "Looking for another wife?" His tone was casual, but Cole felt the change in the room, the rise in tension. He saw it in his brother's expression, in the tightening of Aaron's jaw.

"I don't know," Cole said. Aaron had never been good at subterfuge — he spent too little time with other people for that — and Cole remembered the concern he'd seen in his brother's face yesterday, the evidence that Aaron cared for Eliza. Cole understood the question his brother wasn't asking. Now, he spoke slowly, unable to resist the tweak, the habit of the game. "Why? You know where I can find one?"

"No," Aaron said — too quickly.

"I guess I'd like someone pretty," Cole said. He leaned back in his chair, looked up at the ceiling. "Someone blond, maybe — I'm tired of brunettes — with an easy way of laughing. Someone easy to love." He glanced at his brother. "You know anyone like that?"

Aaron met his eyes steadily. He didn't mince words; Cole didn't expect him to. "She's my wife," he said.

Cole feigned surprise. "You mean Eliza? Of course she's your wife . . . isn't she?"

Aaron went still. He glanced down at Pa as if he were afraid the old man could hear — a quick, involuntary panic. Then he looked back up at Cole. "I married her," he said. "Pa did it himself."

"Then what are you worried about?" Cole asked. "If you keep her happy enough, she won't even be interested in me."

But Aaron didn't relax. There was no confidence in his bearing, no relief. He looked like he would shatter into a hundred pieces if he were touched. "Just leave her alone, Cole," he said tightly. "She's mine."

There was something about the way he said the words — that panic again, or maybe it was the lost sound of them, as if he wanted them to be true but knew they weren't. Whatever it was, Cole lost interest in teasing him. Aaron was too easy a target, and it made Cole feel bad suddenly, tormenting him this way when it wasn't serious at all, when it was just a game.

So he sighed and looked at his brother and said, "Then make her yours, Aaron. What the hell's stopping you?"

Aaron looked confused for a moment. Then wariness took its place. "What d'you mean?"

Cole didn't bother with subtlety. Wearily, he said, "Eliza told me, Aaron."

That was all, but Aaron blanched; he didn't pretend to misunderstand. He was quiet for a moment, and then he said, softly, slowly, "You don't understand. You couldn't know."

Cole looked at his brother, and in that moment he saw Aaron the way he seldom did. He saw his brother's insecurity, his fear. He saw the little brother who had cried because he couldn't protect Cole from Indians. Cole thought of Eliza downstairs, the way she'd twisted her skirt, the sadness turning down her mouth. He met Aaron's eyes.

"She thinks you're ashamed of her," he said honestly.

Aaron frowned. "That's not true."

"Well, that's what she thinks."

"But I've told her —"

"Have you *shown* her, Aaron?" Cole asked. "Damn, have you even kissed her?"

Again the quick glance to Pa. Again the tension. "It's not so easy —"

"Have you had a woman since then, Aaron?" Cole asked quietly.

He caught Aaron's glance, saw the flush move over his brother's face before Aaron looked away again, and Cole knew what his words had done, what Aaron was thinking about, the *then* he was remembering. Remembering that whore Pa'd bought him for his twelfth birthday. Cole remembered how Pa had brought the girl home, and the way Aaron had run from her. He remembered his father's words. *"Jesus Christ, boy, be a man! What the hell's wrong with you?"*

Cole had stood in the background, fourteen years old and completely different from his brother. He too had got a whore for his twelfth birthday, and he hadn't hesitated to use her. But Aaron wasn't him, and Cole remembered feeling sorry for his brother, watching their father burst into the room where Aaron's cries had brought them, seeing that whore on her knees in front of his brother, seeing Aaron's white-faced terror.

"Your brother wasn't such a damn girl! Christ, why can't you be more like him? Why can't you be a man?" Even then, there had been that competition between them, that pride that swelled Cole's chest as he stood back in the hall and heard his father yell, the knowledge that — in spite of his compassion for his brother — he'd won this contest. He was *A Man* and Aaron was not. Cole had even celebrated by taking that whore himself after Pa was done with her, and he'd forgotten all about how he'd felt watching his brother's terror. Until now, he'd forgotten feeling sorry for Aaron at all.

But the memory made him compassionate now. He looked at his brother and thought of how lucky he was to be married to Eliza. She was so damn easy. All Aaron had to do was touch her and she'd probably fall into his arms.

Aaron walked to the window. He braced his hands on the sill and leaned forward, pressing into the open air. "I haven't . . ." he swallowed as if the words were hard to say, and closed his eyes. "I can't even . . . touch her."

"Don't touch her then," Cole advised. "Just kiss her, brother. Don't think about it, just do it. Just kiss her."

Aaron threw him a look. "Easy for you to say."

"Yeah." Cole sighed. "It's always been easy for me. I'm sorry about that. But Eliza's . . . she wants you to kiss her, Aaron. She'll let you go as fast as you want. It'll be easier to go fast."

Cole threw a final look at their father and walked over to stand beside Aaron. He put a hand on his brother's shoulder, felt Aaron tense in surprise.

Cole smiled. "There are a few things I know about," he said, "and one of them is women. You're not a kid anymore, little brother. It's time you made Eliza your wife. She's a sweet girl — she'll forgive you any-thing."

"Oh?" Aaron asked quietly. He turned slowly. There was pain in his eyes. "Will she forgive me for not being you?"

24

Aaron turned away from his brother and looked for one last moment out the window. Things were drying up, dying. There was only brown out there — a hundred different shades of it, but still brown. The world was shriveling up, and it felt sometimes like it was shriveling him too, that the sun was reaching inside him and stealing everything that mattered.

He sighed and stepped away. Cole stood back. He'd taken that cigar out of his pocket again, and he was flipping it in his hands, smoothing it with his fingers. Aaron glanced down at it. "You might as well smoke it," he said. "He won't give a damn."

"Yeah." Cole nodded. Thoughtfully, he put the cigar away. "That's the point, I guess." He jerked his head to the door. "Why don't you go on? I'll stay here for a while."

Aaron left his brother. He paused outside the door, standing in the hallway smelling dinner — chicken. One of those old hens must've succumbed to the heat. He glanced back inside, saw Cole make his way to the old man's bedside, where he stood and looked down into Pa's face.

Aaron turned away. The moment seemed too private, too real. He realized suddenly that before today, before Cole's lapse into compassion, he'd never believed Cole had feelings for anyone but himself. It seemed he was wrong. It was obvious Cole mourned their father.

Aaron wondered how that felt. He hated looking down at his father. He hated knowing that the conversation he'd just had with Cole was floating in the room above Pa's ears, and even though reason told him Pa couldn't hear a thing, Aaron couldn't quite believe it. There was a part of him that believed the old man would come back with a vengeance, that the words Aaron had said today would come back to haunt him.

"Make her yours, Aaron. She wants you to kiss her, Aaron. Go fast, Aaron."

Slowly, he pulled away from the door. Slowly, he went down the hallway, down the stairs. He went to the kitchen door and paused there, watching her as she cooked.

Her back was to him; she was oblivious as she stirred something in a big bowl at the worktable. The kitchen was hot and steamy, heavy with the scent of boiling chicken. Her hair was tied back from her face. It shook as she beat whatever was in that bowl, the apron strings twitched with her hips.

He thought he was quiet, but he must have made some noise, because she glanced over her shoulder. When she saw him, her face burst into a smile.

"I thought I heard you," she said. "You're in early."

"I wanted to check on Pa," he said, "and there's not much to do out there. I don't think the corn can be saved."

She sobered, and he wished he hadn't said it. He wanted to see her smile.

"Oh," she said. "Well, I guess . . . I mean —"

"It would help to sell a crop this year," he reassured her. "But we don't need it. There's money set aside."

She let her breath out slowly, and then she turned around fully to face him, wiping her hands on her apron. "Well, that's good," she said. "You know, with the baby coming and all."

He thought he was getting used to the idea of the baby, but every time she brought it up, he realized he wasn't. He kept forgetting there was a baby on the way, in spite of the fact that her body was changing. Slowly, insidiously changing. Beneath the apron and her dress and her petticoat, she looked no different. But he'd seen her at night, clad only in her chemise. He'd seen the slight bulging of her belly.

She was watching him expectantly, so he gave her a thin smile and said, "Don't worry about that."

She smiled. She wiped her hands again and came toward him. "You know what? Cole was just teaching me to dance today. I learned pretty good, I think. Want me to show you?"

He frowned. "Why d'you need to know how to dance?" he asked before he thought. "We don't go anywhere."

Her smile faded. She stepped away, her shoulders came forward. "I guess you're right," she said. "I never thought of it that way."

He felt instantly bad. He remembered her telling him that Cole was going to teach her to be a lady. He remembered Cole saying she thought Aaron was ashamed of her, and he knew what all this was, this attempt to learn to dance, this attempt to please him.

He wanted to bite back the words, but he couldn't. So he shoved a hand through his hair and said, "I'm sorry, Eliza. I didn't mean it."

"You never say anything you don't mean,"

Eliza said. She turned away. "It's all right."

"No, it's not," he said. He came after her. She stopped at the worktable, and he stopped beside her. "What I meant to say was . . . was . . . ah, hell."

She looked up at him, waiting. Again he saw expectancy in her face.

"What I meant to say," he said slowly, "was that you should learn to dance if that's what you want. But you don't have to do it for me. I don't care."

She looked confused. "Of course you care," she said. "How can I be a lady if I can't dance?"

"It's not important to me what you are," he said, "I . . ." Her expression lightened, she was waiting. She was waiting for him to say it, and it hovered on the tip of his tongue, the admission he'd held inside him these last weeks, the admission that looking at her left him weak, that he liked her accent and her way of talking, that he wanted *ain't*s because he was tired of living in his mind and he wanted reminders of the dirt, of the body. He wanted to be a man.

Go fast, Aaron. Go fast. He reached for her. He saw her surprise when he touched her hand, when he curled his fingers around her wrist. Fine bones, such delicate bones. His mouth went dry, he felt his whole body like one muscle, one trembling nerve. He felt her expectancy like a dare, a challenge. *You can't do it, Aaron. You can't do it.*

"Be what you want," he whispered. He let go of her wrist, he backed away. "But don't become a lady for me."

She looked confused. He didn't wait for her to speak. He was out the door before she could. *Go fast, Aaron. Go fast.* He cursed the words spinning through his mind. He berated himself. He was an idiot. He was nothing. He couldn't even kiss the woman he loved.

But even as he went out the front door, even as he hurried toward his one refuge, to that tree, to words, he felt the yearning deep inside him, moving through him.

He sat down beneath the tree. He pulled his box of papers toward him, he reached for a pencil. Then he stared out at the dry creek bed and thought how her bones had felt beneath his fingers.

He had failed. But, surprisingly, there was no desperation in the admission this time, no sick sadness. Because for once he knew that, even though he hadn't been able to kiss her this time, he wanted to try again.

Eliza watched him run out, and she didn't move. It wasn't until she heard his steps fade from the porch that she wished she had called him back. Because she wanted to know what this touch had meant, what that intensity in his eyes had been for. She had the sinking feeling that she already knew, that he had tried to kiss her and couldn't. That his shame of her ran so deep even a kiss couldn't bridge it.

Her legs felt weak. She sagged against the table; her hip hit the bowl of dumpling batter and it tipped a little, rocked before it settled down. She swiped her hand across her forehead, blew away a strand of hair hanging in her face, and then she pressed her hands against the bulge of the baby.

But the touch wasn't reassuring this time. She was beginning to picture the baby in her mind, what he looked like, what he would be like. She thought of him turning somersaults inside her, felt him growing with each cramp of her muscles. She dreamt about him at night — she dreamt he could talk when he was born, that he came out of her spouting poetry, and she wondered if that could really happen, if he would be so smart. She wished she could talk to someone about it; she had the sense that Aaron would know the answer if she asked him, that maybe he'd been born like that, talking so soon after he was born. It seemed like that was how smart people came into this world, and it frightened her. Because if that baby could talk like that when he was born, then that meant he could think, too. He would know enough to be ashamed of her right off.

The way Aaron was.

There was only one thing she knew to do to change it. Despite Aaron's words, she knew it would be better to be a lady. She'd dreamed of being one her whole life; she knew how important it was. With every page she learned to read, with every dance step she practiced, she felt better, like she was being born herself. Like the old Eliza was peeling away. One day, maybe, she would peel away clear to the bone, and that stain of her birth would be gone too. That was what she hoped for, what she wished for. She had four months left to do it before the baby was born.

Eliza sighed and straightened, turning back to the dumplings. She tried not to think about Aaron as she went about finishing dinner, but she couldn't help it. The memory of his face was still there, a thickness in her throat, a weight about her heart. By the time dinner was ready, and she called them in to eat, she was so sick with it she couldn't eat herself, and she waited in the kitchen, cleaning up, listening to Miguel and Carlos talk, listening to Cole's silence. Aaron had not bothered to come in.

The men were gone when she finally decided to look for him. She went to the front window and glanced toward the tree, but he wasn't there. Instead, there was Cole, leaning against that old oak, smoking a cigar, his head angled to the sky.

He looked lonely, and she was sad, so Eliza took off her apron and draped it over the settee, and went outside. It felt hotter now than it had earlier; so hot that her hair was sticking to her neck and her nose was full of dust by the time she got to him.

He glanced up at her as she came near, drew on his cigar, exhaled a puff of smoke. "Eliza," he said. "What brings you out here?"

"I don't know," she said, and then she sat down beside him and drew up her legs. "You looked lonesome."

"Did I?" He gave her a sideways glance. "Well, don't neglect your husband for me."

"I ain't neglecting him," she said, not caring about proper grammar, feeling too low to bother correcting herself. "He doesn't want to be around me, I guess."

"Oh, I doubt that." Cole puffed on the cigar. "He's shy."

"Maybe." Eliza sighed. She scooted back

against the trunk, and her hip hit something wedged tight to the tree. She looked down. It was Aaron's box. She eased away enough to take it into her hands; papers shook inside as she went to put it aside.

Cole frowned. "What's that?"

"Aaron's box," she said. "He keeps it out here. It's got his things in it."

"His things?" Cole clamped his cigar between his teeth and took the box from her. He shook it a little, leaning close to listen, and then he set it down beside him. He took the cigar from his mouth and ground it out, and then he started to open the lid.

Eliza put out her hand to stop him. "Don't," she said. "It ain't right. It's Aaron's."

"It's just words, Eliza," Cole said. "It's his poetry. I've read it before."

"You have?" The notion seemed odd to her, faintly wrong. She couldn't imagine Aaron letting anyone read his papers, but then again, she'd never asked him to because she couldn't. Maybe he had let Cole read them before.

Instinctively, she looked around for Aaron. He was nowhere in sight. She let her hand drop, she sat back against the tree.

"What do we have here?" Cole had the box open. It was full of paper — large sheets, scraps, little bits with words scribbled on them. A lead pencil rolled around inside, marking the papers here and there with random lines and rubbings.

It made her nervous to see it — like it was some sacred box somehow. Like she was opening something she wasn't supposed to see, something to make God angry. Eliza braced her hands on the hard, prickly grass and pushed back, putting distance between them.

Cole didn't seem to notice. He was leafing through the papers, reading them with a frown, his lips moving to the words. She heard his murmur. "Trees . . . nobility and strange . . . restless . . ." It reminded her of Aaron — funny how, right now, they seemed so much the same, Cole bent over that box, his brow furrowed in concentration, murmuring half words and restless ideas. She'd seen Aaron this way a hundred times. She'd heard him sometimes, saying words beneath his breath like he was testing them out, playing with their sounds. Like Aaron, Cole seemed oblivious to her.

She felt uncomfortable. She didn't like the way he was ignoring her. She didn't like how she was a part of this and yet not. Cole had pulled one of the papers out, and he was studying it, reading it intently.

"I'm going back," she said, starting to rise. "I got things to do —"

He reached out, grabbing her wrist, keeping her from getting up. "I think you should read this," he said, then, when she sat back down again, he handed her the paper.

Eliza sighed. He was watching her like it was important, so she took the paper from him and looked down on it. The writing was cramped and small, hard to read. The words were hard, too, she found a couple she knew already: *in, I, the, and,* but other than that they were strange. The handwriting she couldn't read either — was that an *e* or an *i*? A *r* or a *u*?

She felt stupid and small. All these weeks of learning, and she couldn't read this. She couldn't do anything. She handed the paper back to Cole.

"I can't read it," she said flatly. "I ain't learned like you."

"Learned enough to captivate my brother, I'd say," Cole said with a smile.

"I told you —"

"Listen, Eliza," he said, and then he began to read in a soft, singsongy voice:

"She sings within me.
I hear her in the music of fields and grass,
The rhyme of water.

471

I hear her in the shake of cornfields in the wind
and the whispers of shadows.
In dreams she comes like a hymn,
a choir singing psalms
of places I have not been, of dreams
I once had that fade now
in Eliza's hand.
She dances; she winds and sways,
a riverbend of neck, the curve of throat
a pulsebeat like a current.
Press my lips to it and taste the poetry
of life and sweat."

He finished on a soft note, an ending sigh, and the words filled the air around her, sank into her the way sadness did, pulled at her heart, her skin, her senses. She had no words. When Cole folded the paper and put it away, she stared at his hands. She heard the light clunk of the closing lid like a far-away dream. And when Cole spoke finally, when he said, "Well," in a clear, bland voice, it seemed too loud and too destructive, like glass shattering, and she heard the sounds of the world again and realized that for a moment she'd existed in silence except for the echo of Aaron's words.

She swallowed and blinked, and realized that Cole was watching her, and there was an intensity in his face she recognized from that day at the lake.

"It's — that was about me," she said.

He smiled. "I'd say so. Still think he's ashamed of you?"

No. No, she didn't. It was strange how stupid she felt that she'd ever believed it. Just a few minutes had passed, yet the world was suddenly so different. How did that happen? How did just a few words change things so much?

"He's just shy," she said, and the sound of her own voice startled her; she was surprised she'd spoken out loud.

Cole leaned his head back on the tree. "Yeah," he said.

Eliza scrambled to her feet. She brushed off her skirt, and when Cole looked at her in question, she said, "I got to go. There's something I got to do."

She left him before he could say anything, and by the time she reached the porch she'd forgotten all about him. There was no one in the house when she went inside, and she went to the bay window, where she'd piled books and papers just that morning, and grabbed a piece of paper. It had writing on one side, but just a few scribblings, and she turned it over and went to the desk at the far side of the room. It was littered with things, with books and spilled sand, blobs of wax. She pushed them aside, cleared a small spot, and grabbed a pen and ink.

The pen felt odd in her hands; she'd never written anything except for words on a slate, and she had to concentrate hard, to remember the letters, to remember their sounds. She dipped the pen; the ink dripped and blotched, but Eliza pressed her lips together and kept on. This was the most important thing she had ever had to write. She'd been wrong before, to think that actions were the most important things. Sometimes the words *were* all that mattered.

25

The house was silent when Aaron came in from the barn; it was dark except for the moonlight slanting in through the windows, filling the room with shadows. He hoped she was already asleep. His heart pounded when he made his way up the stairs. He was sweating when he pushed open the bedroom door.

The bedroom was lit by a low, dim lamp. The bed was made; there was no one in it. The only sounds in the room were the sputtering of the flame and the light *tap tap tap* of the blind-pull in the hot night breeze. Eliza was not here.

His first thought was that she was awake and waiting for him, and that brought his nervousness into his head so his mouth went dry and his temples pounded. "Eliza?" he called softly. There was no answer.

No, she wasn't waiting for him. It was too quiet for that. His next thought was far more torturous. He'd seen her with Cole that evening, talking beneath the oak tree. He'd seen

Cole grab her wrist and pull her down when she'd risen.

Perhaps she was with Cole tonight.

The thought was like a snake, sudden and poisonous. Aaron sank onto the mattress, numb and sick. She was with Cole. Where the hell else could she be? Where else?

He hated himself then, truly hated himself. For his cowardice, for his surrender, for giving her away so easily. His hands were trembling; he swung his feet onto the bed and laid back on the pillow. He felt the crackle of paper beneath his head and impatiently he grabbed it away, meaning to crumple it, to throw it to the floor. Another useless poem. What good were words, when all he did was write them down? When he never attempted to live them?

But then he noticed the blotches, the strange writing. Frowning, Aaron sat up. He spread the paper on his thigh, smoothing it to read the words.

i ws shamd
4 i ant nobude
i m frad
mi babee ant luvin me
Yr pom sez i m rong
i m hape 4 it.
Plez ks me.

Eliza. *Eliza.* His fingers trembled, the paper blurred before his eyes. Her words cut into him, sharp and precious, even more so because he knew how long it must have taken her to write it, how hard she must have worked. He understood then just how much he must have hurt her by keeping silent, by being afraid, and his embarrassment that she had read his poem faded; he was glad she had, he was glad that it was out in the open. He was glad that she was happy.

Please kiss me.

He closed his eyes. He folded the paper carefully, by feel alone. He slipped it into his shirt pocket. He pressed it against his chest.

"Aaron?"

Her voice came in a whisper. He thought it was his imagination at first. Then he opened his eyes and saw her standing there, tentative, wary, at the door. She was clad only in her chemise, and her hair was down around her shoulders. She looked like an angel.

"Eliza," he said.

She closed the door behind her, she leaned against it. "I was waiting for you," she said. She glanced past him, to the pillow. "Did you read my poem?"

He nodded. "Yeah."

"Well, it ain't very good." She ducked her

head slightly. "I know that. It ain't near as pretty as yours. But I thought —"

"It was beautiful."

She smiled shyly. "You don't have to say that," she said. "I know I ain't learned —"

"It was beautiful," he said again.

She came over to him. She was still smiling when she sat beside him on the bed, but she didn't sit close to him. She braced one hand on the bed and leaned into it, and she looked into his eyes and her smile grew bigger; he saw those charming crooked teeth.

"You know what?" she asked. "When Cole read me that poem of yours, it was like a wind just knocked itself inside of me. I never felt so pretty in my life. I wanted to keep it in me forever, you know what I mean? Like, if I could keep it in my head, those words would belong to me until I died." She hesitated, and glanced down at the bedspread, and with her other hand she began tracing the pattern on the quilt, the entwined wedding rings. "D'you . . . d'you remember it? D'you have it in your head?"

His throat was so tight it was all he could do to say the single word. "Yeah."

" 'She sings within me,' " she quoted softly. "Ain't that how it goes?"

" 'I hear her in the music of fields and grass, the rhyme of water,' " he went on, and his voice was hoarse and raw; he heard his own effort. " 'I hear her —' "

She stopped him with a motion. She put her hands on either side of his face and held him still, and he could not help himself. It was like something in him suddenly gave way, a dam breaking within him, crumbling beneath him, and he reached for her. He lunged into her, clumsily finding her mouth, desperately kissing her, and her lips were soft and warm and he was pressing into her, wanting to draw her into him, to inhale her.

He was rushing; too roughly he pressed her back against the bed. He heard her moan as he felt the swell of her breast, the swell of her belly. Even that didn't stop him. There was only the tactile sense of her, her uneven breathing, the rise and fall of her breasts, the heat of her mouth, her tongue. The taste of coffee, the smell of sweat and the cistern-water scent of her hair. He couldn't stop kissing her, he breathed into her, he held her down, afraid she would pull away.

He felt her hands in his hair, behind his head, holding him close. She kissed him with her tongue, she pressed her breasts to his hand. When he crumpled her chemise, pulling it up her legs, over her thighs, she helped him. He shifted his hip, she shifted with him. She parted her legs when he shoved his knee between them. And then he was driven by blind instinct, by words that circled in his head, *Go fast, Aaron. Go fast,* and without thought he undid his belt, unfastened his pants. Without thought he was pushing at her, and she was hot and silky, and he could not stop, he could not slow. He pushed at her, felt her lift her hips to his. He was breathing into her mouth, he heard her moan, tasted it, heard his answer, and then his demons were pounding him, the flashing teeth, the laughter, and he was gone, he was coming, he was done before he was even inside her, and there was nothing left but the breath he couldn't catch, but sticky wetness and sweat.

He sagged against her. He tore his mouth from hers and buried his head in the crook of her neck, in her hair. His heart was racing; there was a low, steady throbbing deep in his gut, a pulsebeat, a conscience. A voice that mocked him now. *What kind of man are you? You can't even make love to a woman. . . .*

Her hand moved on him, against his back, a slow, steady stroking, a murmur in his ear. "It's all right," she whispered. "It's all right."

He wanted to cry. Her hand tangled in the hair at his neck, he heard her whisper like the sound of crickets rubbing their legs together, a *sssh, sssh, sssh.* She wrapped her legs around his, and she rocked him. He felt her kiss against his hair. And then he heard her voice like a lullaby. " 'She sings within me. I hear her in the music of fields and grass . . .' "

It was the last thing he heard until morning.

She was awake when the night eased into dawn. She'd been awake most of the night, staring into the darkness, holding him in her arms. She liked the feel of him there, the heaviness of his body on hers, his heat, the feel of his hair against her cheek, the smell of him. He slept like he was dead; still and heavy, the only thing telling her he was alive his slow, deep breathing, moist and hot against her neck.

She felt safe with him there. For the first time in weeks, she didn't lie in bed and think of horrible things, of frightening things, of rattlesnakes creeping beneath the covers or babies dying with their heads bashed against a tree. She didn't haunt herself until she was so scared the darkness smothered her.

Instead, she thought of names. She pressed her hand against his back, feeling him with every inch of her skin. She breathed deeply of his scent, and she ran just about every name she could think of through her head. She spoke them into the darkness. Aaron Junior, Jack after her father, Thomas after his. Or maybe John — she liked that name, it was good, it was solid. Matthew was another. Or Beauregard. She knew a bunch of men in Richmond called that, and she'd always thought it was pretty.

Eliza liked how thinking about names signified a future, she liked that she felt so safe in Aaron's arms that she could think of something other than fear. There had been a time late last night, when she'd wiggled a little beneath him, and in his sleep, his hand had come to rest on her hip, holding her close. It seemed so stupid now that she'd ever thought he was ashamed of her. He'd written the poem. He'd kissed her. And even if things hadn't worked out exactly right last night, the words were enough to sustain her — they rang in her head, close and loud. *She sings within me . . .*

How could a woman not live forever on those words?

She felt him stir, the shift of muscle, the flexing of his fingers against her waist. Eliza held her breath, waiting, trying not to tighten her hands on him, hoping he didn't wake just yet. But he did. He moaned a little, and twisted, and his hand came across her belly —

He started awake. She felt his sudden stillness, the shallowness of his breath, and he began to ease away. He pulled back, raised up, and then he was looking at her, and she turned her face to meet his eyes.

He winced, he looked away. "You're awake," he said dully.

"Yeah," she said. She didn't move her hand from his shoulder. "You slept good."

He laughed shortly. "Yeah."

"I been thinking," she said. "What d'you think of the name John?"

"Jesus." He put his hand to his face, and then he sat up, swiveled around so his legs were hanging off the side of the bed and her hand slid from his shoulder. "Oh, Jesus."

His shoulders hunched forward, he rested his head in his hands, and she heard the harsh shudder of his breathing. Eliza reached out. When she touched his back, he flinched. It didn't seem fair, she thought, that he should feel so bad when she felt so good. It wasn't fair. She pushed up so she was kneeling behind him, and then she rested her hands on his shoulders and leaned forward, trying to see his face.

"You know," she said, "I been scared just about every night since that bobcat. I lay here and I think about all the bad things that can happen until I get so wound up I can hardly breathe."

She paused, waiting. He didn't say anything, but she heard his hesitation, knew he was listening, and she leaned closer, wanting to soothe him.

"Last night," she went on, "I didn't feel that way. I felt safe last night, Aaron. I felt . . . well, I ain't — am not — good at saying it, I guess." She leaned forward, circling her arms around him, around his bent arms. She pressed her lips against his hair. "I'm glad I came to this farm, Aaron," she whispered. "You been good to me, and I . . . I'm glad I married you."

He didn't look up at her. She felt him tighten, then she heard his voice, low and soft. "What about Cole?"

Eliza hesitated. "Well, Cole — he doesn't need me. And I think you need me."

She thought those might be the truest words she'd ever said. She liked thinking of Cole; in her own way she still loved him. He was sweet to her, and she liked talking with him and dancing with him. She liked the feel of him in her arms and she supposed she always would. But Cole never made her feel safe the way Aaron did. And he never made her feel like she was music that spun in his head all the day, like he needed her to stay alive. Cole had never written *She sings within me.* In fact, he'd left her, not just once, but twice. She had the feeling Aaron would never do that — he'd told her he wouldn't, and she'd believed him then. She believed him now.

"Ain't it true?" she asked softly. "You do need me?"

He was quiet. Then, he raised his head from his hands and looked up at her. "Yeah," he said. "I need you."

She wondered if this was what it was like to really be a wife, if it was looking into a man's face and hearing words that seemed so real and true they just hurled themselves into the heart. If this swelling feeling was what it meant to be a woman. She'd never felt it before, and it confused her for a moment; it made her loosen her hold and sit back on her heels, it filled her with this powerful sense that she could do anything, be anyone. If there was a stain on her soul, it was washed away in that moment; she forgot what it meant to be ashamed when Aaron reached for her, when he cupped his hands to her face the way she'd done to him last night, when he pulled her close.

She smiled before he kissed her, and she kissed him back, and it was so different, so different. It wasn't hungry like last night, it wasn't smooth and practiced, like Cole's had been. Aaron's kiss wasn't like anyone else's. It was soft and it was tender. He held her like he was afraid she would break if he grabbed too hard; he kissed her like she was cherished. And when he pressed into her, she put her arms around his shoulders and held him tight, and she leaned back, pulling him with her, wanting him now that she knew what wanting was.

He was a little too fast, and his hands were shaking when he pulled up her chemise, when he cupped his palm to her breast. She opened the shirt he hadn't taken off, ran her hands over his chest, over the warm smoothness of his skin. She heard him gasp into her, felt him shudder, and she felt the press of his hips to hers, she opened her legs, she felt him against her. Then his hands were on her hips, beneath her, bringing her up to meet him, and she felt the pressure and the easing in. She gasped with him when he was inside her.

It was slow, it was easy, a tender passion that rocked with them, that swelled with every thrust and every meeting. She had her hands in his hair, and she studied his face, his closed eyes, the darkness of his lashes, and when he opened his eyes and looked into hers, the shock of it, the pure feeling of it, made her gasp out loud, and she was pressing against him, cresting, trembling, and it was . . . it was not like it had been with Cole at all. It was . . . she was dazed with it.

He shuddered against her, stiffening, collapsing, and she hugged him to her, kept him there on top of her, and felt the throbbing between her legs, the harsh rise and fall of his breath, of hers. When he drew back finally, and looked at her, she smiled at him, and he smiled back — a smile she'd rarely seen. It took her breath away, how handsome he was, how pretty, and she laughed at the thought, at the pure joy of being loved by a handsome man, and he laughed with her.

"You have the prettiest smile," she said, touching his face, smoothing back his hair. "I could just look at it all day."

"You'll get your chance," he whispered, and then he kissed her again, her lips, her jaw, the pulse in her throat. "Stay here with me, Eliza."

So she did. She stayed with him all morning and into the afternoon, until she knew the feel of her husband's body and the touch of his hands, until she knew his smile.

He was lonely. It was a feeling Cole had not often felt, and he didn't like it. He didn't like how the emptiness of the house pressed in on him, he hated the silence.

He wondered where the hell everyone was. The Mexicans he'd seen earlier in the day; Aaron's watchdogs had ignored him in their usual way and gone out to the fields. Cole had watched them go and — for a brief moment — he'd admired their loyalty to his brother. He'd even been mildly envious of it. But it had been a fleeting feeling. Now, sitting at the table, dawdling over a cup of cold coffee, Cole wanted to talk to someone bad enough that even a farmhand who didn't like him would be better than nothing. Hell, it was too damn quiet — it made him nervous.

He was just deciding whether to move out onto the porch when he heard the creak of a door upstairs. He heard a quiet step — Eliza's — and then he saw the hem of her dress as she started down the stairs, watched it grow into shirt and waist and breasts, watched her slowly appear.

She looked disheveled in a familiar way, and he stared at her, puzzled, until she looked up and saw him. She burst into a flustered smile.

"Oh, Cole," she said. She stopped on the stair. "Ummm . . . good morning."

It was then he knew. He knew where he'd seen that look before, he knew that smile. Eliza was wearing the look of a woman who'd just been made love to.

The realization hit him like a blow to the chest. It confused him, too. The memory of the day at that little oxbow lake came back, the way she'd stretched all sleepy and satisfied beneath him, and he felt the long, slow burn of jealousy. Aaron had taken his advice finally, and Cole felt unexpectedly, suddenly angry, as if his brother had stolen from him — and he felt that nasty, gut-deep fear, too, the hateful voice, *Was he as good as me?*

"It's not morning," he said roughly. "It's afternoon."

"Oh." She glanced back upstairs and then back to him. She pushed a loose strand of hair back from her face. "I . . . um . . . I guess you must be hungry, then."

He was hungry. He was suddenly, absurdly ravenous. But not for dinner. Not for food at all. He couldn't remember that Eliza had ever looked this beautiful before. Not so flushed and smiling, never so voluptuous. For the first time since he'd arrived back on the farm, he noticed things about her, subtle changes, things he hadn't seen before. Her breasts were larger; they were straining the seams of her dress. She looked vibrant and at the same time serene. She had become the kind of woman a man yearned for, the kind of woman that made him want to fill his hands with her, to fill his senses.

Cole frowned. He didn't know why he hadn't noticed that before. How had it got by him? He thought of yesterday, of how she'd danced with him. He'd liked her smile then, he remembered. But he couldn't remember what she'd felt like —

"D'you want me to make you some dinner?"

He stared up at her.

Her smile grew broader; it was as nervous as her movement when she reached up again to shove back her hair. "What're you looking at me that way for, Cole?" she asked. "What's wrong? Ain't I buttoned up?" She twisted a little to try to see behind her. She looked down at herself. Each movement shifted her breasts.

He cleared his throat. "No, Eliza. You look fine. In fact," he paused until she'd stopped moving, until she glanced at him, "you look beautiful."

"Oh." She laughed. She sat at the table beside him, he felt the brush of her skirts against his leg as she leaned close, lowering her voice as if to tell him a secret. "I feel good, Cole. You were right; he ain't ashamed of me."

"No," he said slowly. "I didn't think so."

"He kissed me last night," she said in a

rush of breath. "He even" — she looked down, she blushed again — "well, we . . ."

"You don't have to say it," he said. "I know what you did."

He had to restrain himself from asking more, from asking how well his brother had made love, if she compared them to each other.

"I got you to thank," she said, and she put her hand on his arm, squeezed it. "If you hadn't read me that poem . . ."

It made him sick. Truly sick. Especially because he'd tried to bring Aaron and Eliza together. He'd wanted her to stop looking at him with those lonely eyes. Now he realized how stupid he'd been. She was no longer looking at him as if he held her happiness in his hands. She was no longer smiling because she was with him and it was what she wanted most in the world.

She was smiling because his brother had made love to her. She was looking at him with a gratitude that turned his stomach. He found he liked her better before. He liked being the light of Eliza's world. It had made him feel generous and benevolent.

Now, he felt cramped and small, and there was burning inside of him that made him want to take her upstairs to his bedroom, to lay her back on the bed and make her forget Aaron.

He took her hand off his arm. He got to his feet. "I'm glad things are going well," he said. When she looked at him with a puzzled frown, he tried to smile. "I'm going outside."

"Don't you want some dinner?"

He shook his head. "I'm not hungry."

It was a lie, of course. Cole turned away from her and went out the front door and onto the porch. He sat down in a chair and angled it back against the wall, between the windows. He pushed back his hat and looked out on the brown land, and a completely foreign hunger rose up in him. Not just sexual hunger; though he felt that, too. Hunger for everything his brother had, for the farm, for the Mexicans who cared about him, for Eliza. It seemed a good life, suddenly, the life Cole wanted. A house and a wife. Children. A place to come home to.

Once, it had all been his. He was the oldest, the farm had been his destiny until he walked away from it at sixteen. Eliza had been his until he gave her to Aaron. The baby she was carrying *was* his, but when it was born, Aaron would step in as father.

It had all been his, and he had given it away for a life of wandering from place to place, for acquaintances instead of friends, for illusions. He had given it all away for the freedom to move on. For nothing.

Now, looking out at the seared cornfields stretching to the sky, Cole felt a yearning that pulled at his skin, that settled in his throat in a lump he couldn't swallow.

He wanted it back.

26

Aaron could not remember feeling so good, so complete. He lay in bed after Eliza left and looked up at the water-stained ceiling and thought of how things had changed. She was truly his wife now, and his demons had retreated to some far place in his mind, a memory only. They had lost their power over him. He felt like a free man.

He sat up and ran his hands through his hair, and felt the heated breeze from the window settle on his bare skin and the sheet twist over his hips. The movement brought her scent into the air; he could smell it on him, and it made him smile. *She sings within me.* How true it was, especially now. Now he could almost feel her skin beneath his hands, he could taste her. The reality of it was good, so much better than his imaginings, so much better than that hot guilt, the angry shame. He was a man. For a moment, he wished the old cripple wasn't in a coma, so he could tell him — oh, not with words; he would never come right out and say it.

But he imagined Pa knowing, Pa seeing it the second Aaron walked into the room.

He had this sense now that things would be better, that his problems were gone. Even the heat didn't bother him as he got out of bed and washed up, as he dressed. He hesitated at the door, torn between wanting to race downstairs to see her again and a strange shyness that came over him when he thought of looking in her face, remembering the intimacies they'd shared.

But he knew they would share them again, and that made it easier, it brought this loose, heady excitement into him, an anticipation that made him strong, and he went down the hall to his father's room and peeked in. Pa was still, there was no change he could see, but Aaron went inside and walked over to the side of his father's bed, and something — some deep-in spite — made him lean over and whisper in his father's ear: "She's my wife now, old man. Does that make you happy?"

He couldn't decide how he felt when he stood again, whether he felt vindicated or just stupid, but he was glad he'd done it just the same. For some reason it took away his anxiety over the other day, when he and Cole had stood here and Cole had told him to make Eliza his. Aaron had the feeling then that the old man heard every word, and now he'd finished it, he'd tossed a *"Screw you, Pa,"* in his father's face.

It was something he'd rarely done in his life, and now he felt free of Pa, too. There were no more chains except the one on his heart, the one Eliza had made. It was a chain he was happy to wear.

He went out of the room and went downstairs. Eagerly he went into the kitchen, and though there was a pot of coffee on the stove and something boiling in a big pot, there was no sign of Eliza. The house was empty. He paused, wondering where she'd gone, and then he heard talking out in the yard. Cole's voice, and then Eliza's laughter, and then the jangling of bells.

Bells. Aaron hurried to the front door and stepped out on the porch. There was a wagon in the yard, its canvas cover rolled back to show copper and iron pots and pans, fabrics and scarves, ribbons, beads and rows upon rows of shiny bells that jangled at every movement of the swaybacked horse harnessed to it. Beside the wagon, Cole and Eliza stood, talking to a short, mustached man wearing a beat-up beaver hat and a brightly colored serape. A sign hanging from the side of the wagon read: *Hamlin Eggerton, Traveling Mercantile.*

A drummer. They stopped by the farm every now and then, but he hadn't seen one for about six months, and then it had been old Pierre Burton, who knew everyone about these parts and didn't listen to rumors. This man Aaron had never seen before.

He stood there on the porch watching Eliza caress fabrics and sparkle at pretty ribbons. He listened to her laugh and watched the way Cole bent to her, showing her one pretty bauble after another. *"She likes pretty things."* He remembered his brother saying it. It seemed like forever ago, and it made Aaron uncomfortable, reminded him forcibly that he didn't know his wife very well.

"Aaron!" She hurried over and grabbed his arm, pulling him off the porch, and his heart thumped; he felt warm all over. Her excitement was palpable; it shone in her eyes, and her words were quick and bright. "There you are! I was just making dinner when he drove in. I ain't never seen such pretty things."

Aaron caught Cole's glance, the quick rise of his brother's brow, and deliberately, Aaron put his arm around Eliza's shoulder, pulled her into his side. He felt a surge of satisfaction when Eliza put her arm around his waist, when Cole looked away again — too quickly — to study a piece of ribbon.

"Mr. Eggerton, this is my husband," Eliza said with a smile.

Aaron extended his hand. "Aaron Wallace," he said, and then he felt a momentary flash of nervousness, waited for the drummer to turn away, but it was clear Eggerton didn't know the rumors, or if he did, that he didn't care. The man shook his hand and then stepped back and motioned at his goods.

"The finest luxuries in all of Texas," he said. "Take a look, Mr. Wallace. Right here's the biggest — and I mean the biggest — selection of hair ribbons available. I was in Fort Belknap three nights ago, and I don't think there was a lady there who didn't find a ribbon to match her dress."

"Is that so?" Eliza asked. She gave Aaron a smile and pulled away, going to where Cole stood, fingering ribbon. She looked at the lengths hanging there, coiled satin that shimmered in the sun, deep rich colors that seemed to shine with an inner fire, pastels that glistened. "My, ain't — aren't — they pretty, though? You say all the ladies bought some? Was there a dance?"

Aaron heard the sigh in her voice, a wistfulness that made him ache. The drummer seemed to have heard it, too, because he stepped closer to her and nodded. "There surely was. A big one, too, I reckon. The hall there was all lit up, and they had great swaths of blue bunting — which I also supplied, by the by. The ladies were jewels, ma'am, simply jewels. Some of them bought enough ribbon that it dangled over their shoulders. I myself thought it was prettiest that way."

"Of course you would," Cole said wryly. "Since you sell by the yard, I imagine."

The drummer looked slightly affronted. "There should be no price on beauty, sir."

"Well, I can just imagine it," Eliza said. She took a length of pure blue ribbon into her hands, smoothing it in her fingers. "It must have been something to see."

"I can show you the style," Eggerton offered. "The next time you go to a dance in town, you'll be the envy of everyone there."

Eliza looked down at the ribbon in her hands and then carefully, slowly, she put it back. She didn't look at Aaron when she said, "We don't get into town much, Mr. Eggerton."

Aaron saw her face, the careful way she avoided him, and it hit him hard and fast and unbearably that he'd been wrong. He wasn't free. The chains were still there; they were there in the fear he felt at the word *town*.

He caught Cole's look, saw the criticism in his brother's face. Then Cole stepped forward. He grabbed the length of ribbon that Eliza had just put aside, and he handed it to Eggerton. "I'll take some of this," he said. "How much of it do you need to do that style you were talking about?"

Eliza put out her hand. "Cole," she said in a low voice. "I don't need it —"

"But I think you do," he said. He looked over her head, to Aaron, and Aaron saw the challenge in his brother's eyes as Cole said, "After all, Eliza, who knows? Maybe a visit to town is in your future."

He reached into his pocket for some coin. Eliza glanced at Aaron, and he saw the uncertainty in her eyes, desire battling with conscience. She wanted to go to town, she'd fallen into Eggerton's story of the dance, she drank up the details. Aaron remembered how badly she'd wanted to go into White Horse, how disappointed she'd been coming back. She wanted society, she had expected it when Cole brought her here, and it was something Aaron didn't know how to give to her.

Eggerton made change and handed it back to Cole, saying, "I heard in town yesterday that the circuit preacher's coming through. They're planning a church meeting on Saturday. The ladies'll be sure to be dolled up then."

"Saturday?" Cole asked. He pocketed the change and stepped back, and Aaron felt his brother's gaze like the heat of the sun. "Over at the old meeting grounds?"

"Suppose so," the drummer said. He smiled and tipped his hat at Eliza. "Can I get you folks anything else?"

"Not me, no," Cole said. He looked down at Eliza with a smile. "What d'you think, Eliza? How does a church meeting sound?"

Aaron felt his whole gut cramp when she looked at him, when he saw the hope and confusion in her eyes.

"I-I don't know," she said softly. "Maybe."

"Everyone's looking forward to it," Eggerton said. He glanced at Aaron. "Anything for you, sir?"

Aaron stood there, feeling dumb and foolish, feeling the panic growing inside him. Numbly, he pointed to a large paisley shawl hanging off the side of the wagon, but even Eliza's pleasure didn't ease his anxiety as he paid too much for it and handed it to her. It seemed not enough, it seemed too much, too overwrought when she'd taken such pleasure in the ribbons in her hand, in what they symbolized. And when the drummer was gone finally, and his bells were jangling loud and discordant over the rutted road back to town, Aaron stood there and watched the wagon growing smaller and smaller. He heard Eliza say she was going to put her new things away, and then he felt Cole come over to stand beside him, felt his brother's presence like a long, cold wind.

"You know she wants to go," Cole said slowly.

"I know."

"I'll take her if you don't want to."

Aaron turned to look at his brother. He saw the careful unconcern in Cole's eyes, but Aaron remembered the challenge of earlier, and he knew his brother. For whatever reason, Cole wanted Eliza again.

He wanted to tell his brother to go to hell, but he couldn't get the sight of her face out of his mind, the hope in her eyes, the lonesomeness. He couldn't forget the way she'd said the words, *"We don't get into town much."* With that dull acceptance, that matter-of-fact tone that didn't quite hide her longing.

"She's going to be confined before too long," Cole pointed out. "Best to give her a chance to socialize before then."

The baby. Cole's baby. In that moment, looking into his brother's eyes, Aaron knew Eliza would never be truly happy with him unless he gave her the kind of life a woman wanted. Society. Town.

And her happiness mattered to him. He realized with a start that it mattered to him more than his own did. He wanted to give her the things she cared about. He wanted her to smile and laugh, to dress for a dance and wear ribbons in her hair. He wanted her to be happy with him, to love him.

Even if that meant he had to face town.

"Well?" Cole asked.

Aaron met his brother's gaze. "Thanks for the offer," he said, not without irony. "But I'll take her."

"You sure about that, baby brother?" Cole's unspoken challenge landed squarely between them.

"I'm sure," Aaron said, wishing he felt as sure as he sounded. "I'll take her."

Cole smiled. "You don't mind if I come along, too?"

"Do what you want." Aaron shrugged with a deliberate lack of concern. "You always do."

Cole's smile broadened. "I guess I do, don't I?" he said, and then he turned away.

Aaron heard his brother's footsteps crunching in the burnt grass as he watched him go. He watched until Cole went around the side of the house and disappeared, and then he sighed. It felt as if whatever had been holding him up simply let go; he wanted to sink onto the grass.

"Aaron, look!" Eliza called.

He turned to the porch. She was standing there, the paisley shawl wrapped around her, fringe dripping down her arms, the blue ribbons tangled in her hair.

"What d'you think?" she asked, spinning around. "Don't I look fancy?"

"Yeah," he said carefully. He went to the bottom of the porch steps and looked up at her. "How'd you like to wear that to the church meeting?"

She stopped still. Her eyes grew wide. "You mean it?" she asked carefully. "But what about —"

"You want to go, don't you?"

"Yes," she said. The single word rushed out, and then she looked like she wished she could grab it back. She played with the black fringe on the edge of the shawl. "That is, if you think you want to go."

"I do," he lied. "Let's go."

And when she said, "Oh, Aaron," in that breathless, joyful way, when she nearly fell down the stairs into his arms, Aaron forgot his brother's challenge, he forgot his fear. There was only Eliza.

Eliza tried not to get too excited about the

meeting, but she couldn't help herself. That night she made a special supper, chicken and sweet potatoes and a dried apple pie. After it was over and the dishes were washed, she sat with Cole and Aaron in the front room and pulled out the bolts of fabric she'd bought in White Horse. She'd got started on some aprons for the baby, but now she put those aside and laid down the pale green silk and the violet striped calico, the dragon green broadcloth.

"I don't know which one," she said. "Tell me which one I should make a dress from."

Cole wandered over from where he'd been standing in the doorway. He was smoking a cigar, and the smoke burnt her nose when he leaned close, made her faintly sick. "The flowers in that purple match your ribbons," he said.

She looked at it. She ran her hand down it, and the rough skin of her palm caught on the smooth fabric. "What about you, Aaron?" she asked. "Which one d'you think I should make?"

Her husband looked up from the bay window. He had a book in his hands, and when he came over he stood close, right behind her. She felt the press of him against her back, she smelled his scent.

"They're all pretty," he said. He pointed

to the dragon green. "Do this one."

"How am I s'posed to choose when you both picked different ones?" she complained, but she laughed as she said it, because she was so happy she was even having to choose. She settled on the dragon green finally, because Aaron had chosen it and he was taking her to the meeting, and she had more of it than anything else. She could make the waist big to grow with the baby.

She started to cut it out, while Cole settled in a chair by the door and Aaron took his usual place on the settee. The evening was warm, and a hot wind had come up, but Eliza didn't care about the dust blowing in the open door. Everything was so good tonight. She felt like a real wife now. Aaron had made love to her, and she was going to meet the ladies of White Horse after all.

"Who's the circuit preacher these days?" Cole asked.

Aaron looked up from the book he was leafing through. "Why?"

"Well, it'll make a difference as to how much fun the meeting is," Cole said. "That old Baptist minister never liked dancing."

"How do you know that?" Aaron asked. "You never went."

"That's what I heard." Cole took a puff on his cigar.

"You mean there is going to be dancing?" Eliza asked.

"Oh, probably, after the praying," Cole said. "You think you've had enough lessons?"

"Well, I could use one or two more, I guess," Eliza said. "If you don't mind, Cole."

"Not at all, darlin'." He smiled at her, his eyes lit up the way she liked them. "We can turn a couple steps tonight, if you want."

"She's cutting out a dress," Aaron put in.

Eliza smiled at him. "I hope I have enough time to get it done."

"You should be having someone in town do it," Cole said.

Eliza threw a quick look at Aaron, who had gone still. "It's all right," she said hurriedly. "I don't mind it, really I don't." She bent over the fabric, cutting carefully, following the muslin pattern. "You know, this'll match that shawl you just got me, Aaron. Look at all these little paisley things in there. There's even some of the same color — sort of."

Cole laughed. "Maybe the ribbons would be better."

Aaron didn't answer, but Eliza saw how he clenched his hand on the book, how he turned the pages too fast to be reading them.

"I think the shawl'll be just fine," she said soothingly.

Cole ground the cigar out into a flimsy tin ashtray and got up, stretching. Aaron had lit a lamp to read by, and the golden light shone in Cole's dark hair. He went to the door and stood there, looking out into the growing dark, and then he turned to her with a smile. "Come on, Eliza," he said. "Why don't we take a turn around the room?"

"I got to cut this out —"

Before she got out her protest, he was beside her, and Eliza found herself swept up into his arms, her face pressed against his fancy vest. She caught the smell of him, tobacco and bay rum, a heady smell that pulled her straight back into a memory. She smiled up at him and pushed away a little. "All right," she said. "But just one."

He started humming, and together they were moving around the room. She liked how strong he was, she had always liked that about him, but for some reason dancing with him was not as much fun as it had been the other day; it felt vaguely wrong. She turned her head and glanced at her husband. Aaron wasn't paying them any attention, but she saw the stiffness of his face, she saw how he sat there without moving. Cole's humming was loud in her ears.

"What are you frowning at?" he asked, looking down at her. "Did I step on your toes?"

She shook her head. "No," she said. "But I think," she spoke in a whisper, "ain't you holding me a bit too close?"

"You have to be close to dance the waltz," he said, but he loosened her anyway. Still, she felt his breath rustle her hair, felt the heat of his hands. She was glad when his song came to a close, when the dance was over. She stepped away from him quickly, smoothing her skirt, and she tried to smile when he looked at her with a faint puzzling look.

"I'm kind of tired," she said.

He glanced at Aaron. "Oh. Of course," he said, and there was this little knowingness in his voice that made her uncomfortable. She went back to the table. She bent over the broadcloth and picked up the shears. Her breath was coming fast, and her heart was pounding, and it was then she felt the baby move. Not a fish-feel this time, but a jump, a quick movement deep in her womb.

"Oh!" She dropped the scissors. Her hands went to her stomach. When both Aaron and Cole looked up at her, she said breathlessly, "He just kicked me!"

Aaron was half out of his chair, but Cole was beside her first. "Are you all right?" he asked, and at the concern on his face, she laughed.

"He moved," she said. "Oh, you should've felt him."

She was looking past him, to Aaron. But Cole took her words as permission, and she felt his hand on her stomach, warm and big, pressing against her. She felt the baby jump again, and Cole dropped his hand and staggered back, and there was a look of wonder in his eyes.

"Jesus," he murmured. "That was the baby?"

He laid his hand on her again, and she felt it and looked past him, to where Aaron sat there on the settee, watching them. She saw something in his eyes, but she didn't know what he was thinking, and she wished he would come over here. She wished he was touching her the way Cole was touching her. She wanted him to feel the baby, to know how real it was.

But when Cole bent over her, Aaron sat back down. His fingers tightened around his book, and she knew then that he wasn't coming over. He wasn't going to lay his hand on her the way Cole was doing, even though last night he'd made her his wife, even though he'd touched her then far more intimately.

It surprised her how much it hurt, how sad it made her. It surprised her how much she wanted his arms around her right then, how she wanted his smiling face and his laughter. She wanted to see his eyes light up the way Cole's were now.

"Good God," Cole said, stepping back. "He's strong, isn't he? He's a strong boy."

She heard the pride in his voice. The pride of a husband, of a father, and Eliza's joy in the day faded. She smiled weakly at him, and then she looked at Aaron.

"Maybe you could . . . maybe you could read me something, Aaron?" she asked, because he wasn't standing beside her. Because he was her husband and she wanted his arms wrapped around her and his hands pressing on her womb. If she could not have his arms, then she wanted his voice. She wanted him to be a part of this moment so badly it made her throat tight.

He met her gaze, and again she saw that look, that dark pain. But he opened the book. He chose a poem.

"This one's from *Don Juan*," he said. "Lord Byron wrote it."

She closed her eyes and let his voice come around her.

" 'I would to heaven that I were so much

clay, / As I am blood, bone, marrow, passion, feeling . . .' "

He made love to her with the words, and she waited until she felt Cole leave her, until she heard him sit with a sigh in the chair by the door, and she thought of tonight, of how she would welcome Aaron to bed, about how she would ask him to put his hands on her, and she would hope the baby moved again. She would hope for wonder to come into her husband's face.

27

The day of the church meeting dawned clear and hot, with a steady wind that came from the west, carrying the scent of burnt grass and pine. Eliza had been up late the night before, putting the finishing touches on her new dress, and it had been hard to sleep, she was so excited. The only thing that spoiled her pleasure even a little was the way Aaron looked as the day came nearer. He smiled with her, and he acted like he was happy to go, but she had learned to read her husband, and Eliza didn't miss the fine lines of tension on his face, or the worry in his eyes.

She had to admit, she was worried, too. The memory of how she'd been treated in town wouldn't go away. But she hoped it would be all right. After all, this was a real preacher they were going to see, a church meeting. Surely the townspeople would be charitable with God watching.

She didn't quite believe it, but it made Eliza feel better as she washed that morning and dressed. The red silk petticoat was too tight to wear now, but she had made the dragon green into a wrapper-style dress, with a high neck and long sleeves and a flowing body. She'd caught it in at the waist with pleats and basted them loosely so she could let them out when she got bigger. It was the finest dress she'd ever had. When she slipped it on, she felt beautiful.

Eliza braided her hair and wound it around her head the way Mr. Eggerton had told her, twisting Cole's ribbons through it. She settled her hat on her head. Then she took the paisley shawl and went downstairs.

Carlos and Miguel were staying near the house today to care for Mr. Wallace, and they were on the porch when she came out. Miguel smiled at her, and Carlos bowed and said, "You look very fine, *señora.*"

"You do indeed." Cole came around the corner of the porch. He stopped, staring at her. She felt his gaze move from the top of her hat to her shoes, and she blushed when he said, "You sure you want to wear that hat?"

She put a hand to it. "Why? Don't you think it —"

Just then, Aaron brought the wagon into the yard. It was already loaded up with blankets and a big folded square of canvas. She saw her basket inside — last night she'd filled it with a jar of coffee and an apple pie, and she'd found the biggest pot they had and filled it with beans and ham. It made her feel funny to see it in the wagon, ready to go. She felt shaky, like she hadn't quite believed until this minute that they were going, and now that they were she almost wished they were staying home instead. She said as much to Aaron when he came off the wagon and got to the porch.

"You know," she said, "we don't have to go if you don't want to. We can stay at home and I can learn my letters better —"

"You know them fine," he said, and then he smiled at her, and his eyes were so warm she felt heated clear into her blood. "You look beautiful, Eliza."

"D'you think so?" she asked. She touched her hat again, nervously. "What about the hat?"

"The hat's pretty," he said.

She smiled at him.

Cole said, "We'd better get going," and reached out his hand for her. Then, because Aaron stood back, she took Cole's hand and let him lead her to the wagon, help her up onto the seat. Just when she thought he was going to get up beside her and drive, Aaron was suddenly there, and Cole got into the back.

The wagon creaked and groaned when Aaron flicked the reins, and they started off. He didn't say much as they rode — it was hard to talk when the wagon jarred so — but he was stiff and he looked straight ahead, and Eliza saw how his hands tightened on the reins, how his fingers were white where he gripped them. More than once, she'd sent a worried look back to Cole, but he was lounging on the blankets, smoking, and all he did was give her a smile that didn't make her feel much better.

Her nervousness was a lump in her throat when she finally saw the meeting grounds ahead. The grounds were about three-quarters of the way to White Horse, in a grove of shady pecan trees just off the Clear Fork of the Brazos. The morning sermon had already started; Eliza heard the preacher's voice booming across the hills, where there were nothing but a few trees to stop it. "We'll shout old Satan's kingdom down! Hallelujah! There'll be no place for sinners here in Texas!"

The wagon stopped. Eliza glanced at her husband. Aaron was just sitting there, staring ahead. She didn't even think he was breathing. Cole leaned forward and clasped his brother's shoulder. "Come on, baby brother," he said quietly. "They're too busy being Christians to pay any attention to you."

The words seemed to rouse him. Aaron sighed and nodded to himself like he'd just decided something, and then he urged the horses on. They went the few yards to the grounds, to where all the wagons were parked, the horses grazing, and he pulled up at the far side, away from the others, like he was creating a wedge before he even went in to meet them.

But Eliza didn't say anything. She waited on the seat until Cole jumped out and helped her down, and then she straightened her skirt and her hat. Even though it was hot, she wrapped the big paisley shawl around her shoulders, and then she stood there waiting while Cole and Aaron took care of the wagon, the horses.

Cole didn't seem to be nervous at all, or if he was, he didn't show it. He pulled out the blankets and Aaron hauled that heavy basket and the pot of beans as the three of them crossed over to the meeting.

They were in the middle of a hymn now, "The Sweet By and By," and Eliza stood with Aaron and Cole and listened. "In the sweet by and by, / We will meet on the beautiful shore. . . ." It seemed so pure and sweet, all those voices lifting up to the sky, and she watched the way the women swayed on their side of the camp, the way the men held their hats so reverently, and Eliza was reassured. They were in church, and there was a holiness in the very feel of the air. Nothing bad was going to happen here today, how could it?

She was so sure of it, she squeezed Aaron's arm. He jumped at her touch, and tried to smile at her, but it was weak and strained.

The song ended, and their neighbors sat again on the makeshift benches — rough planks balanced on big rocks, one side for the women, the other side for the men. The congregation turned their faces to the preacher, a tall, skinny man dressed in buckskins. He stood without a pulpit, without anything but an open Bible in his hand marked with a ribbon that trailed almost to the ground. His hair was dark and stringy and lank, and except for that Bible, he didn't look much like the preachers she'd seen. But he had a good, strong voice, and he shouted a lot, which was what a preacher needed to do.

She was so busy watching him it took her a minute to hear the whispers. It wasn't until she felt Aaron stiffen again beside her and heard Cole's low murmur into his brother's ear that Eliza realized they were being looked at, they were being talked about. She tore her gaze from the preacher. She saw the men nudging each other, jerking their heads to where she and Cole and Aaron stood. She saw women whispering, and the sound of it became a rush in her ears, filling up her head until she couldn't hear the preacher. She saw people rising, saw them crowding together, hurrying away, out to where blankets were spread and tables set up and loaded with food, and for a minute she thought they were running away. Then she realized the preaching was done. The preaching was done, and their neighbors were hurrying away. Not a single one came over to speak to them. No one said hello.

In the field beyond she saw mothers gathering their children, and she heard the screeches of little girls and boys. She saw the nervous glances of fathers, saw them gathering into groups, whispering, talking, rubbing chins and looking worried.

"When was the last time you were in town?" Cole asked quietly.

"A long time ago." Aaron's voice was a whisper. "I don't remember."

"This is ridiculous." Cole frowned. He turned to Eliza. He reached for her. "Come on. Let me introduce you around."

Aaron stopped him with a hand. "No," he

said, and his voice was rough and hard. "Let me do it. She's my wife."

Eliza looked up at him. She looked into his dark eyes and hurt for him. He handed the pot of beans to Cole, and took her hand. She squeezed it hard and went where he led her and pressed close into his side. She followed him through the benches, out into the field. She stood beside him when he set the basket beside the table.

He looked around the crowd and set his lips. His jaw looked hard; she saw the bones in it, the hollowness of his cheeks. "Why don't you get something to eat?" he asked.

"I ain't hungry," Eliza said quietly.

He glanced down at her. "Get something to eat, Eliza."

So she did. She went up to the table and stood beside a woman in a brown calico dress. She felt Aaron just behind her, and it gave her courage, it made her brave.

She grabbed a plate out of her basket and handed one to Aaron, and then she reached for the scalloped potatoes. The woman beside her reached at the same time, and their arms crossed. The woman laughed and turned to her with a smile.

"I'm so —" She stopped short. Her eyes passed over Eliza, and then her glance went to Aaron standing behind. She jerked away, hurrying away without another word, leaving her half-filled plate setting there on the table.

Eliza pressed her lips together hard. She felt Aaron's hand on her shoulder, and she set her plate down and stepped back from the table. "I ain't hungry," she said again. "Maybe we should go."

But Aaron's jaw only clenched harder, and there was something in his eyes, some determination she'd never seen before. She knew right then that he wasn't going to back down, he wasn't going to leave, and she also knew there wasn't a soul here that would say two words to him. This was just a waste of time, and a hurtful one, too.

"Aaron," she said again. "Let's go home."

He ignored her. He was searching the crowd. "Over there," he said finally. "I remember him."

His fingers tightened around her hand. He pulled her with him over to a man standing beside his family, a short man whose stomach was bursting out above his pants. When the man saw them coming, he whispered something to his wife and she pushed her children away. They went running off, and Eliza heard their song in the wind. *"Aaron Wallace is in town. . . ."*

Aaron swallowed. When the man looked at him, he stepped closer and said, "Mr.

Abrams, I'd like you to meet —"

The man turned away. Solidly. Deliberately Eliza knew Mr. Abrams had looked into Aaron's eyes just so there wouldn't be a mistake, so Aaron would know he was being snubbed.

Aaron froze; she felt him stumble. Eliza's heart felt too big for her chest, and it was so heavy she could hardly breathe. "Aaron," she tried.

He ignored her. He pulled her over to someone else, another man who stood beside his wife and two children, waiting with a too-sharp face and eyes as cold as ice.

"Horace," Aaron said. "You were an old friend of my father's —"

"Please," the wife said, gathering her children close to her skirts. "You're frightening the children. Please go."

She heard Aaron catch his breath. Eliza held her ground when he turned away again, when he started to pull her with him. "No," she whispered. "Aaron, let's just go on home."

He didn't say anything. He just pulled, and she came after him, to the next person standing there, a thin man about Aaron's age. He was holding a baby, and he walked away before they could even get there.

Aaron didn't pause. He went to the next

blanket. A woman this time. She was old and gray-haired, the kind of person who looked wise and kind. But she too stiffened when they came over, when Aaron said, "Miz Pearson, I heard about what happened to your husband —"

"Get away from me." She practically hissed at him. "You go on. Get away."

It went on like this. One after another. A man and another woman, children who went hurrying away. Eliza heard their chants in the fields, the screeches of, "I dare you!" "I double dare you!" People turning. Every now and then they said something, and she heard their mumblings behind her back, but the cruelest were those who just looked through Aaron like they didn't see him. It was those people who brought tears to her eyes. It was those people who left her blind when she finally got Aaron to stop, when she finally tugged on his arm and waited until he turned to look at her, when she finally said, "No more. I don't want to do this no more."

He seemed to soften then. His stiffness went away, and something came into his eyes — he looked so sad it nearly broke her heart.

"I'm sorry," he said. "I know you wanted it. You wanted teas. . . . I'm sorry."

He let go of her hand then, and he stepped

away. He left her among these terrible people and strode away, and when she would have gone after him, there was Cole suddenly, beside her, taking her arm.

"Come on, Eliza," he said. "Let's go over and meet —"

"I don't care to meet anybody." She jerked away from him, suddenly so angry she was shaking. "How can they sit here at a church meeting and act so high and mighty?"

"Eliza —"

"I don't care." She spoke loudly, not caring who heard her. "Aaron's the kindest man I ever met, and these people don't even want to know him just because of what happened when he was a baby. He was just a baby. How could a baby be evil?"

"Eliza, calm down."

"I ain't learned, I know, but I don't care to understand people like that. How can they sit here and pray to God like they ain't sinners?"

"Eliza," Cole said again. He took her arm again, gently this time. She let him lead her away, to the abandoned benches. She felt him push her gently down. The bench rocked crookedly beneath her, it creaked when he sat beside her.

"I don't understand them," she said dully. "Can't they see just by looking at him that he ain't what they think?"

"It's all right," Cole said. "He's used to it."

"No he ain't," she said. "He never goes into town, Cole, how can he be used to it? How could a body ever get used to that meanness?" She met his gaze. "Why does he stay here?"

Cole looked down for a moment. His mouth tightened, and then he glanced away, stared at the trees. "Someone has to take care of Pa," he said quietly. "I think he always wanted to move on. But I was already gone by then."

Already gone. Eliza stared at Cole, at his faraway glance, the way he held his hands together in front of him, between his knees.

"You ever thought of staying?" she asked. "Of taking care of your daddy yourself?"

He looked at her, a quick look, a deep look. It made her feel suddenly uncomfortable, the way he focused in on her, the way he watched her.

"Would you like that?" he asked, and his voice was low. It sent shivers clear through her. It made her think of that day by the lake. It felt like all her senses lit up; she felt the hot wind blowing against her skin, drying her lips; she smelled the smoke from a campfire and Cole's bay rum. And she felt danger, too, a sinking inside her, a wariness, an uncertainty. He asked again, "Would you like me to stay?"

" 'Course I would," she said nervously. "If you want to."

"That's not what I asked you," he said, and he moved closer to her on the bench, until his thigh was pressing against her skirt. "I asked if you wanted me to stay."

His eyes were so intense Eliza's mouth went dry. "It's not up to me," she said carefully. "It doesn't matter what I think. I'm a married woman."

He leaned close. He took her hands. "But you're carrying my child," he said. "The things you want, Eliza, I —"

"Fire!"

The scream cut through Cole's words. In minutes it was followed by yells.

Eliza frowned and looked over her shoulder. "What was that?"

"Fire! Fire's coming!"

She thought at first they were talking about a campfire, and she didn't know why everyone was so upset. But then Cole dropped her hands and lurched to his feet. "Jesus," he said.

She followed his gaze to the horizon. She saw it — a ribbon of smoke in the distance. It was moving fast, growing bigger with every second, and she realized the smoke she'd smelled wasn't campfire smoke at all, but the smoke of a prairie fire.

People rushed by her. Men scrambled to harness horses. Women screamed and children cried. The preacher was standing on a bench, yelling, "God bless you all! Run! Hurry!" and then he was gone, too, on his horse. She heard the thundering of hooves, the creak of wagon wheels.

She didn't know what to do, where to go. Cole grabbed her hand. He dragged her through the benches, toward the wagon. They were halfway there when Aaron came running up to them.

"It's moving away from here," he said breathlessly. "The winds are taking it toward town."

Cole nodded shortly. "I'll get the horses."

He raced away to the wagon, and Eliza started after him.

Aaron grabbed her arm. He spun her around hard, and his eyes were burning. "I want you to go home," he said.

"We are going home," she said, confused. "Shouldn't we hurry?"

"Cole and I are riding into town," he said. "They'll need our help."

She wasn't sure she'd heard him right at first. She stared at him, smelling the sharp smoke, hearing people yelling to each other. But when he didn't move, when he just looked into her eyes, she knew she wasn't imagining things.

"You're going to help them?" Eliza asked slowly. "After what they did, you'd help them?"

"It's a fire, Eliza," he said, and she saw a desperation in his eyes, a fear that made her suddenly afraid too. In the distance, the sky was turning red and black.

She clutched at him. "You can't go," she said. "They don't need you."

"They do," he said.

Cole came riding up, leading the other horse from their wagon. "Come on," he yelled. "I've got Mrs. Mason waiting for you, Eliza. She'll take you back to the farm."

She glanced at the horizon. It was dense and black with smoke, and there was a strange, unholy reddish glow. She saw birds flying wildly before it, and it was then she saw the flames shooting into the black, heard the roar in the distance.

"Let's go!"

She looked beyond Cole, to the woman waiting impatiently in the wagon. Eliza looked at her husband. "Aaron," she said. "Please —"

He picked her up and set her into the back

of Mrs. Mason's wagon, and when she reached for him, he was already gone, disappearing into the mass of people racing for wagons and horses. Mrs. Mason slapped the reins and the wagon started off. Eliza searched the crowd, trying to find him. Then she saw him. He was riding beside Cole, a crowd of men surging over the prairie, toward White Horse, toward the town that had turned its back on him.

Mrs. Mason set the wagon at a fast pace, so Eliza was rattled around with the children, who watched her with round, dark eyes. Eliza watched the black smoke. She watched the red glow moving closer and closer, and she thought about her husband, who was risking his life for these people who had given him no reason to help them.

It made her sick inside, sick and scared. She was so scared that when Mrs. Mason left her at the farm, and Eliza saw Miguel and Carlos digging firebreaks around the yard in case the wind changed, she remembered all the stories she knew about prairie fires, remembered when she was just a little girl, and her father had leaned into hot air like he was listening for a fire, like he could taste it in the air, and she knew now that a person could. It was the bitter taste of fear.

28

There was no time to dig firebreaks, though some of the men set to it the moment they got to White Horse. The fire was already burning fast, fed by the wind and the dry grass. Already, the horizon was dark with black smoke, and ashes and bunches of burning grass floated in the wind, setting small fires wherever they touched down.

Aaron urged his horse to a faster speed into the streets of White Horse, streets he had not set foot on in years. They were crowded now, with people spreading clay to protect their buildings. Birds flew through in big crowds, squawking and diving, rabbits and deer raced away from the fire through the main streets.

The flames were behind them; he felt their heat bearing down, heard their roar. He glanced over at Cole, who gave him a weak smile, and together they dismounted and hurried to join the men who were preparing to fight the fire. At the head of the street were two men killing a couple of skinny cows to serve as drags. "They're almost dead from the drought anyway," one shouted as he slit the throat of a cow. He caught the blood in a bucket. "Ain't hardly any water in the well."

But what there was was drawn out in buckets, passed from women to men. The air was full of burning grass, balls of flame that spun and crackled in the sky. Already the café at the edge of town had caught. Aaron watched as another fireball settled on the livery.

"Get the horses out!" he yelled, and he and Cole raced to the building. There were others there too, and together they wrenched open the doors. The horses had smelled the fire, and they were rearing and screaming in fear. The roof caught instantly, the dried beams splintered from the heat. Aaron plunged inside, cutting ropes, getting horses out, scrambling to avoid their hooves as the animals went tearing from the livery.

It was loud, so damn loud. The last horse went out just as the roof began to fall in, and Aaron lurched into the street to find Cole working with other men to beat out the flames.

"It's not going to work!" he yelled into his brother's ear.

"They're setting backfires!" Cole yelled back, and Aaron followed his brother's gaze to where men had set the grange hall on fire. It was on the very edge of town, away from the other buildings. The air was black and thick with smoke. He couldn't breathe; it blinded and stung. The sun had turned a bright, painful red.

It went on for hours. The backfires caught, and men dragged the dead cows back and forth over the flames set by bunches of burning grass, others dragged burlap wet with blood or water from the nearly dry well. Aaron dodged jackrabbits and confused antelope, children with dirty, soot-smudged faces, screaming women beating out flames with their petticoats and their shawls, stamping it out with hot, charred shoes. He did what he could; he got people from their houses, he worked with others to beat out the flames. He was hurting and tired and black with soot himself, and his arm stung where burning grass had fallen from the sky and grazed him, leaving a blistering burn.

The mercantile caught, and there was nothing they could do. It went up in seconds, fueled by the dry goods. All they could do was keep people back as the gunpowder and bullets caught. The explosion rocked the sky, and Aaron heard a scream as a man was hit, and then the scream of his wife. The only good thing about the store catching, he thought, was that it was another backfire, and the prairie was racing on.

He lost track of Cole in the confusion. He lost track of everything but the fire, the moment-to-moment need to help someone, to do something. Tiny fires grew in the streets, and he stamped them out with his boots as he passed. He carried a length of burlap over his shoulder; it was almost dry now, the cow's blood he'd wet it with stiffening it, flaking in rusty flakes onto his shoulders. Like the others, he worked from building to building, saving one, letting another go, watching women cry as their homes disappeared around them, crashed to the ground in burnt and blistering beams, watching the flames leap to the sky before he raced on.

Then the winds changed.

Aaron was on the roof of the Lone Star Saloon when he felt it. He was beating out the flames licking the edges of the eaves — and winning — when the air felt suddenly . . . different. He looked up, and he saw the fire turn. Amazingly, quickly, as if it were a living, thinking being, the flames swept back to the west.

To the west.

Aaron froze. The farm. *Eliza.* Panic made him forget the saloon roof. He rushed so quickly to the edge he nearly fell. He jumped to the makeshift ladder of beer kegs, stumbling to the ground. His breath was a hard knot in his chest, he couldn't seem to grab enough air. His horse. He had to find his damn horse. The fire was moving west, and he wouldn't be able to beat it. He would never beat it —

"Aaron!"

It was Cole. He was racing down the street, already on horseback, and Aaron knew in that moment that Cole had seen the same thing he did.

"The fire —"

"I know." Aaron nodded breathlessly. He reached out a hand. "Help me up. Get me to my horse."

Cole reached for him.

A woman screamed.

Aaron wrenched around. The house behind him was going up in flames. He saw the woman in the upper window. Mrs. Pearson, the widow. She was clutching a book and a pair of boots and screaming, "I can't get down! Help me! Help me, please!"

He could never say afterward what made him do it. Some voice deep inside him, perhaps, or maybe it was God pushing him. But Aaron looked up at his brother and said the words he knew he was going to live to regret.

"You go," he said. "Go to the farm."

Cole frowned. "But —"

"They don't even have the wagon," Aaron said quickly. "And there's the baby. . . . Just keep Eliza alive, Cole. I'll be there as soon as I can. Just keep her alive."

He didn't wait for his brother's answer. Aaron turned and raced for Mrs. Pearson's house. He rammed his shoulder into the door, and it swung open. The house was full of smoke; he heard the flames, heard Mrs. Pearson's screams. But all he thought of was Eliza as he took the stairs to the second story.

Eliza listened for the wind and watched the black smoke boiling in the distance and prayed out loud, her lips forming the words as she grabbed pots from the kitchen and lugged them out into the yard. She heard the farmhands' shovels clanging on the hard earth, a drumbeat to her prayers, a steady, reassuring rhythm. *Please, God, don't let the wind change. Don't let it change. . . .*

Eliza went to the well and stood ready with a hoe. When the first rattler appeared in the bucket, she whacked it clean in half and tossed its body aside. Then she drew bucket after bucket of warm, brackish water. She emptied it into each of those pots and then dragged them to the edge of the yard, ready

535

to pour them on the grass if the fire came.

She was sweating and breathing hard by the time she was done, but when Miguel yelled at her to get the burlap from the barn, she ran to do it, tripping and stumbling, finding the pile of burlap feed bags in the corner and pulling them out, dislodging rats and mice who went scurrying away. Anything to keep busy, to keep from thinking about the fire, about town, about Aaron . . .

Eliza squeezed her eyes shut and dragged the burlap to where her pots stood. It was hard work. The bags were heavy, and dust from them billowed into her nostrils, making her sneeze.

She was panting and hot by the time she got them all out, and she didn't hear it at first, didn't hear anything but her own heart pounding in her ears. But then, something felt different, something felt strange, and she stood there and looked at the ballooning smoke on the horizon. Miguel shouted, and it was then Eliza realized.

The wind had changed. The fire was coming toward them.

Mr. Wallace.

Panic clutched her chest. She yelled for Miguel, for Carlos, but the wind was roaring, and they didn't hear. She saw flames shooting up into the smoke now as the fire raced closer, and she ran into the house, up the stairs. She was breathing hard by the time she got to Mr. Wallace's bed, and she went to the window and screamed again for Miguel.

"I've got to get you out of here, Mr. Wallace," she breathed, racing back to the old man, grabbing his arm. He was so thin, she thought she'd be able to move him easily, but he was a dead weight, and when she pulled his arm, he barely budged. Eliza pulled it again. She sat on the floor, trying to wrap his arm around her shoulders, to get him to lean on her, to lever him out. But he was limp and heavy. He couldn't grab, he couldn't help at all.

"Please," she said, and she grew so desperate she started shaking him, trying to wake him even though she knew he wasn't asleep. "Please, Mr. Wallace. Please."

She went to the window. The fire was so fast, too fast. Already, smoke was pouring in, she saw the flames starting into the cornfields. "Miguel!" She screamed. "Carlos!"

She hurried back to the bed. She yanked on Mr. Wallace's arm, she threw back the covers, tried to gather his legs. But she wasn't strong enough to move him, and now she felt the baby inside her, moving, kicking. Her belly cramped. Her heart thumped so hard it kept her from breathing.

"Please," she prayed again. She put Mr. Wallace's arm around her neck, held onto his hand with hers, and then she braced herself and pulled. "Please, move. Move." She got him to a sitting position, and she moved forward. Her hold on him slipped; he crashed down again to the bed.

She grabbed his hand again, she started to pull. But her legs were weak; they gave out from under her. She fell to the floor, and her stomach jerked and twisted; she felt the strain all through her body. She heard the fire outside, its roar, heard someone yell, heard the whoosh as the corn went up in flames.

She didn't want to die here, not now. She didn't want to die. She didn't want her baby to die. Eliza pulled herself up. She reached again for Mr. Wallace. "Please, Mr. Wallace. It would break Aaron's heart if you died now. It would break mine —"

She heard steps on the stairs. When Miguel burst into the room, she nearly collapsed with relief. He said nothing. He came to the bed and lifted Mr. Wallace into his arms, threw the old man over his shoulder like a sack of grain.

"Can you make it, *señora?*" he asked.

Eliza stumbled to her feet. "Yeah," she

said, and she nearly fell after Miguel down the stairs, out of the house. The fire was everywhere; she saw the flames shooting up into the clouds of smoke, reddening the sky. The far acres of corn were burning, crackling — she could smell it in the air, like burnt popcorn, fields of flame. Carlos had an old feed wagon waiting out front, with the two mules harnessed to it, and Miguel dumped the old man into it without ceremony.

"There is a backfire," he explained to her haltingly. "We must pray."

Eliza had no idea what he was talking about. She started to climb into the wagon, and it was then she saw the old oak. Aaron's box. His poems.

Eliza jumped to the ground. She heard Miguel's protest, Carlos's question as she hurried back across the yard, to the oak. She felt the heat in the air, the smoke burnt her eyes. She could barely see as she stumbled to it. A ball of burning grass fell before her, her skirt caught, and she took it into her hands and beat it out. Then she ran. She fell at the roots of the oak, she fumbled for the box. It was there, and she took it into her hands and held it close against her chest as she raced back to the wagon. Carlos grabbed her and nearly threw her in, and she sagged in the corner. The wagon jerked to a start;

the mules hurried like they'd been waiting to escape the fire. Eliza looked at the old man, still sleeping. She hugged Aaron's box tightly to her chest.

Miguel slapped the reins hard, and Carlos yelled at him, hard, short words in Spanish. Eliza heard the panic in his voice, and she glanced up to see him gesturing. She looked past him, and suddenly she knew what he was yelling about. They could not outrace it; the mules were too slow, even in their panic. They were barely out of the yard, and the flames were sweeping across the corn — it was so fast; she hadn't known it would be so fast. She knew in that moment that they would have to fight it. There was no place to go.

Carlos looked over his shoulder, his eyes wide with fear. "We cannot run."

Eliza nodded shortly. She set aside the box, tucked it under Mr. Wallace's arm. Then she took a blanket and covered him to protect him. She stood up in the wagon. "We got to fight it," she said.

Carlos hesitated, then he nodded. He and Miguel jumped off the wagon, and she did too, and then they were running to the edge of the yard. There was a fire on the other side of the dry creek; it took Eliza a minute to realize it was the backfire Miguel had set.

Flying, burning grass was everywhere, and Eliza grabbed burlap with the men and set to beating out the tiny fires starting in the grass. Soot and ash flew in the air; she trampled out fire, beat it until the burlap was burned through, and she grabbed another bag. Finally, she used her petticoat. She tore it off and beat until her arms hurt and her lungs were burning. The smoke billowed around them, the flames were coming closer — she saw them coming, shooting into the sky. She heard their roar in the wind, the crackling of grass, the whoosh of a tree.

Her shoes were burned through, but she kept going. There was nothing else to do. She didn't want to die. Not now. Please God, not now. She prayed with everything she had. Desperately, she worked in the blinding smoke. She heard Carlos and Miguel yelling, but she couldn't see them. There was only smoke and ash, only bright flames shooting up as the grass caught, only the mindless urge to get to it, to kill it. Only the prayer for the wind to die.

A ball of burning grass shot past her, landing near the wagon. Eliza yelled, her voice felt torn from her scorched lungs. She ran over. The petticoat caught, but she kept beating. Ash and dirt flew into her face, and then the flames leapt; they were all around her, a red flare, and Eliza realized her skirt was on fire. She heard Miguel scream, and then he was beside her, beating on her with his hands and his burlap sack. She threw herself down, rolling in the grass, putting out the flames. Then she laid there, panting, exhausted, burning. She wanted to cry, but she had no tears. Her eyes were burnt up.

Miguel was breathing hard over her. He looked up to the sky, and she looked up with him and saw the flames racing through the cornfields like a hungry monster, roaring, eating, and she knew they were dead. They were going to die here in this yard. She would never see Aaron again. Her baby was going to die. Eliza grasped her stomach, she bent to protect it, and she watched the flames spread to the backfire; she watched them join, held her breath, and waited.

It sounded like thunder. She felt its heat on her face; it was so close she saw the color of it reflected on Miguel's skin. She heard the mules screaming and bucking, frantic to get free. The flames leapt up, raced to the creek bed —

And stopped.

The flames didn't jump the creek. She heard their frustrated sigh, and then they turned and were off, gathering strength across the prairies.

Eliza looked up at Miguel. They were still alive. Sitting in the middle of a smoldering, blackened field with little fires cresting and dying and the house rising like a miracle beside them. Outside of the yard, there was nothing left to burn.

There were no words for the strength of her relief, there was nothing to say. Miguel took off his hat and ran his hand through his hair, and then Carlos came walking over, coming out of a cloud of smoke like a ghost, dragging a burnt-up burlap bag behind him. He was covered with soot; only the whites of his eyes shone in his face.

She felt dazed. The world spun when she got to her feet; she took Miguel's offered hand and nearly stumbled into him. None of them said a word as they looked around at the destruction. There were no more cornfields, just smoking black ashes. The roar of the fire was faint, already like faraway thunder, and she thought of how it would have been to die in it, to be eaten alive by its rage, and Eliza shuddered and hugged herself hard.

The oak was still there, but its leaves had been singed by the heat, and the trunk on one side was black. There were circles of ash all through the yard. The trees had curled in their leaves, and the windows looked wavery;

the fire had passed so close that heat waves came off them like thin smoke.

"Well," Eliza said finally. "Guess we beat it."

Carlos nodded wearily. Miguel said nothing. He sagged against the buckboard and closed his eyes.

Eliza looked down at her new skirt. The dragon green broadcloth was black and ragged, the fire had burnt holes in it so she could see her stockinged legs. Her hands were blistered and stinging. There was a burn on her thigh that hurt so bad it was hard to walk, but still she went to the wagon. She pulled the blanket away from Mr. Wallace's face and she reached for Aaron's box.

"Guess we should see what's left," she said. "I'll go —"

Thump, thump.

Eliza frowned. Miguel jerked away from the wagon.

"What was that?" she asked.

Thump, thump.

"*Dios,*" Miguel whispered. His face went white. "*Madre de Dios.*"

He was staring into the wagon bed. Eliza followed his gaze. There was nothing there, nothing unusual, just Mr. Wallace lying there, looking up at her with those rheumy eyes —

She staggered back. Mr. Wallace. The old man was awake.

"Oh my God," she said. "Mr. Wallace. Mr. Wallace."

He blinked at her and reached up. His fingers curled around the edge of the buckboard and he slowly, slowly, brought himself up. He looked around him, and she saw what he was seeing, the burnt fields and the blackened grass. She felt a sinking in her chest when she thought of what he must be feeling, what he must think. Then his eyes came around to her, and she stepped back, ready to tell him about the fire, to explain. She opened her mouth to say something.

Then he smiled at her, and took her words away.

29

Cole rode as hard as he could. He raced the flames and the smoke. He raced quail and antelope and wolves. He knew, even as he rode, that he was going to lose. He watched the fire sweeping over the plains a mile or so away. It was too fast. Unless the winds changed again, there was no way he could beat it — if the winds changed again, he might very well be caught up in it.

The smoke blinded him, he felt his horse gasping beneath him, felt his own lungs scream for relief. Soot and ash itched on his skin, mixing with his sweat. He bent low over his horse's back, closed his eyes and let them burn. "Please let her be safe. Let them be safe." He loved Eliza. He wanted his son to be born. He wanted Pa to live. He wanted the farm to stand forever.

It seemed a long time before he neared the hill sloping down toward home. He crested it and looked at the road below, and his heart sank when he saw the blackness every-where, when he saw nothing but ash and soot where cornfields had once stood. His whole body felt seared as he looked across the fields, and he expected to see the farm burnt to the ground. He expected to see nothing.

But the house rose like a ghost from the smoke, an oasis of burnt grass and seared trees in an expanse of black, windows glittering like diamonds in the sun. Cole's relief hit him so powerfully he nearly fell from his horse. The house was standing. The fire had passed it by.

He rode quickly down the hill, hope battling with wariness. He saw the barn was burnt to the ground, and there was a wagon in the middle of the yard. But nothing living. No chickens, or mules, or cows. It felt abandoned as he rode in and dismounted.

"Cole!"

The shout startled him; he looked around to see Eliza rising from the wagon. She dropped the blanket she held and jumped out. She was soot-blackened, and her skirt was in rags around her knees, her hair littered with dirt and bits of ash.

He had only a moment to take this in, because she threw herself in his arms, staggering him. She hugged him hard, but before he had a chance to wrap his arms around her, to hug her back, to thank God, she

547

pulled away. She looked beyond him to the road, and he saw the sudden fear in her eyes. A fear that made his heart sink, because he knew what she was looking for, and he knew what it meant.

"You're all right," he said.

"The fire turned," she told him. "It didn't jump the creek. Where's Aaron —"

The panic in her voice broke his heart. Cole didn't take his gaze from her face.

"He's back in White Horse," he said. "When the winds changed, only one of us could go."

"And he sent you," she said dully.

"No," he said truthfully. "No. I was already mounted. He was looking for a horse when Mrs. Pearson's house caught fire. She was upstairs, and he was . . . right there. He had to go in."

She turned to him with wide eyes. "He went in?" she asked. "He went in a burning house?"

"I'm sure he'll be all right, Eliza. He'd said he'd come as soon as he could."

She looked dazed. "He went into a burning house?"

"Well —"

"You should have stopped him." Her voice was rising, there was an intensity in her eyes that seared him. "You shouldn't have let him go in there."

"He wanted to go —"

"You shouldn't have let him," she said again. "He's your brother. How could you let him go in? How could you let him?"

She launched herself at him, pounding him with her fists, and he grabbed her arms and held her back with effort. His own hands shook with the strength of her anger and fear. Then she collapsed against him, and he held her tight, buried his face in her hair, felt her worry and her fear and understood it, because he'd felt it himself.

"He asked me to go, Eliza," he whispered to her. "He was worried about you. He wanted you to be safe."

It seemed to calm her. She pulled away from him, then, and he let her go reluctantly; his whole heart ached when she looked up at him, her eyes red and burnt, her cheeks streaked with black.

"I want him back," she said brokenly. "Tell me he's coming back."

He lied to her because he knew how badly she wanted hope. "It wasn't so bad. He'll be fine."

She didn't believe him, he knew, but she took his words at face value. She bowed her head. There was something so fragile about her just then, so beautiful. "I want him back," she said again. "He's a good man."

He heard the implicit criticism, and Cole glanced out at the blackened horizon. "I could have given you church socials," he said quietly, and then wished he'd kept the words to himself when he saw her eyes.

"I never heard an offer like that when it mattered," she said, and there was no emotion in her expression, nothing but a matter-of-fact tone that hurt more — much more — than he wanted it to. Then, as if she'd never heard his words, as if she'd never answered them, she said, "Cole. Your daddy . . . he's awake."

Those words took what was left of his strength. Cole pressed his hand to his horse to keep his balance, and he realized then that his prayers had come true, that God had answered them. Eliza was alive. Pa was alive. The house was still standing.

Cole felt the bitterness of those prayers deep into his soul. His prayers had been answered, but he'd meant so much more, he'd wanted . . . so much more. Eliza didn't love him. The farm was his brother's. And now that Pa was out of his coma, Cole would have no excuse to stay. He would have to ride on. There were towns that waited for him, men who waited to lose their money. There was the life he had chosen at sixteen.

The life he'd wanted.

He felt so tired that when Eliza held out her hand to him, he took it and let her lead him. He followed her into the house, and up to his father's room, and when he got there, when he looked inside and saw his father sitting there as if nothing had happened, Cole reached into his pocket and took out a bent and flattened cigar, and even though his throat was dry and his lungs were burning, he lit it up and took a deep, blistering breath.

"So, Pa," he said. "If you're going to drag me here all the way from Dallas for a funeral, the least you could do is have the decency to die."

White Horse was in ruins. The randomness of the destruction was heartbreaking. The Silver Dollar Saloon hadn't been touched. The mercantile and the brothel were gone. Miss Ettie's Hats was standing. The house Aaron had dashed into was already ashes. Beside it, Mrs. Pearson sat wordlessly clutching her late husband's boots — the only thing she'd managed to save. The streets were crowded with families who had no place to go, and everyone was covered with soot and rags; a few were huddled, crying, around the bodies of those who had died.

There was nothing that could stop a prairie fire; the best you could hope was to turn it, and this knowledge scared the hell out of Aaron, worked into a worry lodged so deep in his chest it wouldn't go away.

The plains were black, stubbly soot, and he saw the fire in the distance, a red-gray light against the night sky, an eerie sight. He wrapped a bandanna around the burn on his arm to protect it, and raced across the burnt prairie. He prayed he would find Eliza waiting for him. He prayed she would be alive to kiss him, to hold him, to welcome him home.

Home. He'd never thought of it that way before. It had always been a prison, and his jailer had been his own fear and a crotchety old man. But now the vision of it burned within him, and he longed for it so hard that when he crested the hill and saw it below, a shadowy house with lights burning from every window, a beacon in the night, he thought it was his own imagination, he thought it was an illusion.

Aaron stopped. He caught his breath. He stared down at it and heard the whisper of the trees in the slight breeze, he heard the music of home.

His mouth went dry. Then he nudged his horse and rode down the hill, down the road.

He crossed the soot fields and went through the creekbed, and suddenly he was on grass again.

"Aaron?"

Her question came out of the night. He jerked around to see her running from the porch. She was holding something tight in her arms, pressing it to her chest. His box, he realized. His poetry. She was holding it as if it held something infinitely precious, something she was afraid to let go of.

"Aaron."

He dismounted, and she dropped the box and flew into his arms so hard she nearly knocked him down, and he held her tight. He buried his face in her hair, he smelled her with the pores in his skin, felt her in his bones. "I love you, Eliza." He heard her breath, heard the catch. "I love you," he said again, because he couldn't help it, because he could not say the words enough.

She pulled away. When he tried to hold her, she smiled at him. She took his hand and laid it on her belly, pressing his fingers flat. He looked at her in confusion, and it was then he felt it, a rhythmic jump, a steady beat. Aaron's breath stopped. "Is that —"

She nodded. "He's got the hiccups," she said. "And I . . . I been waiting for his daddy to come home so I can introduce him."

He looked up at her. "Eliza —"

"I love you, Aaron," she said, and those words . . . they were the most beautiful poetry he'd ever heard, they nearly made him cry. She cupped his face in her hands, and she looked up at him the way she had the first night they'd made love, as if she was afraid he would break before her and disappear, and then she kissed him. Softly, lingeringly, and he felt the touch of her lips and felt the baby moving inside her and knew he had not lived before this. He had only dreamed about living.

She eased back and smiled up at him, that broad, crooked toothed smile. "You're going to be the best daddy a baby ever had."

He thought of his own father. "I don't have much of an example to live up to, you know."

"Your daddy loves you," she said. "I know it."

"What was it, a deathbed confession?"

"Oh, he ain't dying anytime soon," she said brightly. "He woke up after the fire. He's been asking for you."

He stared at her in stunned surprise. "He's awake?"

She nodded. "He said he's got some things to say to you now that you're a man." She gave him a puzzled look. "Whatever that means."

Whatever that means. Aaron threw back his head and laughed. He laughed until the sound echoed into the sky, until it seemed to catch in the lamplight, in the smoke, in the stars. And he knew then that he was alive, that he was free. That the poetry that had sustained him all these years was more than words finally; it was a feeling deep in his heart, in his soul. It was in Eliza's eyes and in the beacon of her smile, and it would be there forever, shining within him, lighting the way home.

Epilogue

Lila Margaret Wallace was six years old when she told her best friend, Virginia Dale, that she was really an Indian in disguise. Virginia didn't believe her at first, so Lila pointed out that she had long, black hair like an Indian's, and that even though folks said she looked like her daddy, she knew they were only saying it to fool her. She'd been left on the doorstep by her Indian parents, and one day she was going to see if she could find them.

When Virginia still didn't believe her, Lila did an Indian rain dance just to show her. She shook the pretty bead necklace her Grandma and Grandpa Beaudry had given her for her birthday, and hopped around the yard on one foot making Indian noises while her brother, John Thomas, and her baby sister, Genevieve, watched from the porch. Then, Lila told Virginia she was going to paint her face with blood, and Virginia ran home to tell her mother.

Lila had thought of Indians ever since her uncle Cole had visited and told her there'd been Comanches all over this land once. She should go out to the old, scarred oak tree by the creek and look at the rows of corn shivering in the wind. She would listen to its *creak, creak, sssh* and think of Indians walking through the fields. She remembered the last time her uncle was home, how — after he'd told her about the Indians — he took her out there and told her to be quiet, to listen to the corn, and he looked like he missed the sound.

She hadn't seen him for a long, long time, not since Grandpa had died just after John Thomas was born, and she wished Cole would come visit again. He'd brought candy — some lemon drops and peppermint — and when he left he took with him a picture of her sitting on Grandpa's lap. He said he would keep it in his pocket and take it out to look at when he was Faraway, and when she told him she would go along with him to keep him company, he looked real sad and told her to go get him a drink of water.

She thought of Uncle Cole whenever her daddy read to her at night. She would snuggle in Daddy's arms while he told her about places that he said were Faraway, and Lila would go to sleep thinking of Uncle Cole surrounded by coconut trees and in a big palace like Xanadu. Someday, she thought, she would go visit him there. Daddy said there were monkeys in those trees, and she wanted to see a monkey. Some days, the wanting to see them got so bad she would put her dress in her mama's old knapsack and start out across the field, looking for her Indian parents to take her to Xanadu.

But then Mama would call to her, *"Lila Margaret, you ain't going to leave me, are you?"* and Lila would turn and smile and go running into Mama's arms. She would wrap her arms tight around her mama's legs and bury her face in her apron and be very, very glad that she wasn't really an Indian child, and know that where she wanted to be was right here, with her mama's soft *ain't*s like a lullaby in her ears and Daddy smiling at her from the chair.

She would decide then that her uncle Cole would wait for her in Faraway, and maybe she could write to him there, and he would send her a coconut.

She would wait until she was seven to go see the monkeys.

The employees of Thorndike Press hope you have enjoyed this Large Print book. All our Large Print titles are designed for easy reading, and all our books are made to last. Other Thorndike Press Large Print books are available at your library, through selected bookstores, or directly from us.

For information about titles, please call:

(800) 257-5157

To share your comments, please write:

Publisher
Thorndike Press
P.O. Box 159
Thorndike, Maine 04986